# THE DOWNCAST WOLVES

## CAMERON LORIS

# DEDICATION

To everyone who has ever tried to teach me history.
Thank you. And I'm sorry.

# PROLOGUE

## Nuremberg, Germany 1938

"It was like nothing else in the world," Detlef Kühn said.

The smile he wore was a lie, but the words were true. He had never seen so many people in one place. The rally had been Mass for a million. Alabaster pillars flanked the grandstand like an overabundance of teeth. Crimson banners hung between them, so heavy they did not flutter in the wind. Two thousand girls with white arms and even whiter dresses twirled across the field in interlocking circles. Their mothers wore brown skirts and their fathers brown shirts. Their little brothers clutched flags bigger than they were and marched with arms held low. They kept their elbows locked like wooden dolls.

It was a hellish bonfire, frightening and beautiful at the same time. It scorched Detlef's eyes until they watered, and yet he hadn't been able to look away. So when the *SS-Oberschütze* caught his gaze and asked, "what did you think of yesterday?," Detlef told the truth. And he was grateful not to lie, because it had taken all his strength just to craft that forgery of a smile. Even then, he could not hold it long. The heavy briefcase in Detlef's hand weighed his face down. Every part of him drooped in its direction.

The briefcase did not look like anything special. An architectural model fit tightly within—not too different from dozens of others Detlef had made before. With luck, he would be the only one ever to see it. Even so, he had spent weeks carving and painting the diorama. It was everything he hated at 1:200 scale, but he had needed it to be perfect. Amid so many variables, the balsa wood model was the only thing he could truly control.

It was an amphitheater—all square columns and diagonal lines—a concrete jewel meant to crown Hitler's beachside Prora resort. Viewed from the side, the pillars rose and fell in the shape of an eagle taking flight. From above, they twisted into the quadruple hooks of the swastika. The hotel itself, on which construction had already begun, would stretch from the amphitheater's sides like open wings.

A dusting of faux sand and glue covered the diorama's weighted base, and it was there that the model deviated from any other that Detlef had built. It was far heavier than usual, weighed down by the three capped steel pipes within. No matter what, they would keep the structure steady, but that was not why he had put them there. It was not why Detlef had glued iron nails to their outsides nor why he had stuffed them with gunpowder as if they were sausages.

Above ground, the model was perfect and glistening; below, it was ugly, brutish, and unspeakably cruel. Detlef liked that about it. It had the same duality he saw everywhere now. Germany's streets were clean; those who had once lived on them were dead or in prison. Jobs abounded in the factories of war; those who labored there forged guns they would probably die holding. Everything sweet was poison. Germany had transformed itself into both heaven and hell.

For Detlef, the change began on May Day, 1933. Extending an olive branch to the trade unions, the Nazi party had organized a parade—a grand celebration of the German worker and his inviolable rights. Swamped with work, Detlef had stayed home. His friend Berndt, a union rep for the *Deutscher Baugewerksbund*, had not. For as long as the sun shone, the parade was a joyous affair. Union workers and brownshirts marched side by side, united in pageantry and drunkenness.

That night, before the drink had even worn off, the raid came. By morning, there were no unions in Germany. When Detlef dropped by Berndt's office the next day, it was a mausoleum. Every door, cabinet, and drawer was open. The only sound was the rustle of papers and the toothy whistle of wind through broken glass. Berndt might as well have never existed. He had been erased.

Only it was not the Nazis who erased him. They didn't have to. The brownshirts took him away, but it was Detlef who thereafter answered any question about Berndt with, "I didn't know him." It was Detlef who truly made him disappear. Everyone was complicit. Just to live in the heaven above was to stoke the fires below.

That remained true even as Detlef clung to his false smile in the lobby of *Der Wolfsgeige*. The briefcase in his hand was just another piece of the nightmare. Every time he shut his eyes, he had watch it explode, watch it strip solid steel into shrapnel that could split bone and plunge through flesh like water. The bomb in his briefcase was the kind of thing *they* would make. But *they* had not make it. Detlef had. Everything he did fed the fire. Even resistance was an atrocity.

"I'll need to check your case," the *Oberschütze* said.

Detlef blinked and chased away his thoughts. That wasn't the plan. He didn't know who was supposed to be at the checkpoint—the fewer names he had the better—but he knew there weren't supposed to be any questions. The *Oberschütze* reached out for the briefcase and Detlef pulled it back out of instinct. That was the worst thing he could have done and he immediately stopped himself.

"I'll just set it down," Detlef said. He gestured towards the long table that took up half the lobby. "My work is very fragile."

Detlef swallowed. It felt like one of his iron nails had slid down his throat. He took as much time as he reasonably could to reach the table, then set his briefcase down and clicked open the clasp. Detlef started to lift the lid, but he moved too slowly. The *Oberschütze* shoved him aside and threw it open. The whole briefcase shook as the hinge hit its limit. Detlef cringed. The *Oberschütze* jammed his fingers into the cloth siding and down under the base of the model. He lifted it, not seeming to notice the metal contact that disconnected as it pulled away.

"Careful," Detlef begged. "That's for the *Führer*."

Again, he did not have to lie.

"It's heavy," the *Oberschütze* said. "What's it made out of?"

"There's a brick in the base," Detlef supplied quickly. "For support."

It was a bad excuse. He should've drawn attention to anything but the base. The *Oberschütze* lifted the model over his head and eyed its bottom suspiciously. He turned it around. His partner by the wall narrowed his eyes. Detlef could feel his gaze tear straight through him.

"How do I open it?" the *Oberschütze* said.

Detlef fished around for any kind of answer, "It's— There's tools to do it. I can fetch them, but I wouldn't want to make the *Führer* wai—"

"Armie!" interrupted a shout from behind. "What are you still doing here?"

Two more *SS* men—one of them an officer—pushed into the lobby and brushed past Detlef. The *Oberschütze* balanced the heavy model on one hand while he used the other for a salute. Detlef jumped one step forward, reaching out. He could already picture the heavy model slipping and crashing to the floor, splintering apart. But the *Oberschütze* kept it balanced. He lowered it back into the case while the officer bounded over and shook him jovially.

"Come on! There's no such thing as a second first birthday. You should be home with your son. Beiler and I will take your shift."

Detlef tried not to let his relief show, but it poured out anyway. He masked the loud exhalation with a laugh.

The *Oberschütze* reached for Detlef's model. "*Rottenführer*, let me just—"

"No excuses," the officer barked. He just about had to drag the *Oberschütze* outside before he relented and threw up his hands.

The other newcomer, Beiler, turned to the *Oberschütze*'s partner and winked, "It's a lucky day for you too, friend. We can take it from here."

This man did not object. He saluted and then, in a blink, he was gone.

Detlef didn't move even as the officer shut the briefcase and offered it back. A moment passed before he realized that he was supposed to reach out and take it.

"Do you know where you're going?" the officer asked.

"I do, thank you, *Rottenführer*," Detlef said, tamping down a grin. "The Elephant Room."

"That's on the third floor. *Schütze* Beiler can take you. Do you need anything else?"

Now Detlef had to fight to keep himself from grinning. "No, sir."

The officer snapped out a salute then gestured onwards out of the lobby. "*Heil Hitler.*"

"*Heil Hitler*," Detlef echoed.

In a daze, he let *Schütze* Beiler lead the way into the stairwell and on up. Ordinarily, *Der Wolfsgeige* was a clubhouse, but this week it had been hastily repurposed into a forward operations center for the rally down the road. Detlef had spent endless hours scrutinizing the building's layout, but that all seemed distant now. Every step he took gave him the feeling of having woken up somewhere different than he'd gone to sleep. The only thing that connected one moment to the next was the low murmur and punctuating roars of the crowd.

The rally—now moving into its second day—was the tenth such Party Congress, but this year it was special. It was a nativity, a grand festival in honor of the birth-by-annexation of Greater Germany. It came six months late, but the people's enthusiasm for bloodless conquest had not dimmed with time. They shouted as if it had been only yesterday that Hitler's motorcade spat across the Austrian border.

Detlef only had to listen to them shout to know that it would happen again. Another line would be crossed; another rally held. On and on it would go until suddenly it could not. Until some invisible wire beneath the continent snapped and the hell below broke free. The fields that had only just regrown would again be tilled by mortar fire and watered with blood. With every roar of the crowd, the old wound in Detlef's side flared with pain. It remembered even if they had forgotten.

Detlef was far from the only one who could see war on the horizon, but few were willing to do something about it. So many self-styled conspirators had told him to wait. *Just a little longer*, they promised. *Soon Cousin Adolf will make his move for Czechoslovakia and the British will intervene. Then we will have our coup.* But Detlef had even less faith in the British than in the would-be insurgents who awaited their signal. Neither would move until their hand was forced. That task fell to Detlef and those few others who agreed to act. That was fine with him. He had no idea how to lead a coup but a pretty good sense of how to start one.

*Schütze* Beiler reached the third floor and waited for Detlef to catch up. As he took the last step onto the landing, he realized that he would never do that again. Everything he did was his last something. If he sneezed, it would be his last sneeze. If he ate the piece of chocolate in his pocket, it would become his last meal.

They left the stairwell and proceeded out onto the thin red carpet that stretched all the way down the third-floor hall. It was empty of people and would have been silent were it not for the rally in the distance. *Good,* Detlef thought—or he tried to. He couldn't shake the sense that the emptiness was decidedly *not good.* There should be more *SS* in *Der Wolfsgeige* than there were cockroaches in the walls. Had one of his anonymous friends cleared it? That seemed as unlikely as it would be unwise. Is the *Führer* ever really alone? They arrived before Detlef could think of any answers.

"The Elephant Room," *Schütze* Beiler said. He grabbed the knob and twisted.

An inordinate amount of time seemed to pass before the door moved. As he waited, Detlef stared at the set of carved tusks that were mounted on it and wished more than anything that he could see past them. He wished that the other side would not be so empty as the hall. That Hitler and Robert Ley and all their entourage had simply arrived early. That Detlef would only have to step inside, check the distance, throw out a salute, and jam his finger onto the switch. Ten seconds later it would be over. The fever gripping Germany would break. The dream and the nightmare would end at the same time.

*Schütze* Beiler pushed on the door and the room he revealed was empty. Of course it was. Detlef would have to wait. Hitler made everyone wait. *Schütze* Beiler moved to the side and stood at attention. Detlef nodded to him and stepped inside. He walked around the edge of the wide Indian table and over to the back of the room where he took a seat facing the door. The table was bare but for a carafe of coffee and six upside-down cups. It steamed gently. Slowly, Detlef set his briefcase down on its side and tried to remember to breathe. It was so quiet. He couldn't even hear the rally anymore.

The clock was behind him and Detlef promised that he wouldn't twist around to look at it more than once per minute. He tried to picture the thin, brass second hand in his head, counting each time he thought it ticked. Whenever he concluded that it had completed a revolution, he would swivel only to find it hadn't even crossed the four.

Ten minutes passed. Then twenty. Detlef ate the chocolate in his pocket and wished he had brought two. The coffee stopped steaming. He considered pouring himself a cup, but he doubted his hands would hold steady enough. After another twenty minutes, he decided to do it anyway. But as he reached for the carafe, a question struck him, somehow laughable and chilling at the same time. *Did Hitler drink coffee? And if he didn't, would they still have put it in the room?* It was a stupid question—why would that matter? —but it suddenly felt like the most important one in the world.

There were so many conflicting rumors and stories that it was hard to keep track. *The Führer never smokes. He smokes all the time but only in secret. He eats asparagus and rice for every meal. He won't permit meat to enter his body. Except sometimes he eats liver. Or is the diet for his liver? He doesn't drink. He flies into a rage at a whiff of alcohol or smoke.* Detlef sniffed. Was there smoke in the room? It was hard to tell. He wished he hadn't had a cigarette before coming in, but he couldn't blame himself. In retrospect, he should have had two.

Detlef twisted around in his seat. It had been almost an hour. He knew that was too soon to give up. He would not be the first person to be kept waiting so long. But too much else felt off. The quiet. The emptiness. Somehow that felt more threatening than if the halls had teemed with *SS*. Detlef leaned over to peer outside. He couldn't see *Schütze* Beiler, though he almost fell out of his chair for trying.

"It's over," Detlef said, out loud though he hadn't meant to.

Hitler and Ley were not coming. He didn't know how he knew that, but he did. It was time to leave while he still could. Detlef swept up his briefcase and took off into the hall as briskly as the pain in his side would let him. There was no one—not even *Schütze* Beiler. He pressed his back into the wall and listened. The tumult of the crowd had returned, but there was another sound too. A clopping. Footsteps so heavy they could have been hooves. They aligned such that he had no idea how many people there were.

It could be them. If Detlef left now, he wouldn't get a second chance. The footsteps were approaching quickly, not quite at a run, but close. That seemed wrong. Still, *it could be them*. Detlef knew he should stay and find out—consequences be damned—but already he was moving. Once dangled in front of him, the opportunity of escape was impossible to ignore.

Already he was at the stairwell. His left hand clutched the railing as he peered over the edge. Directly below would be a badminton court and an exterior door. He could be on a train to Switzerland within an hour. Detlef took the steps two at a time, but even before he hit the second-floor landing, he slowed. *It could be them*, Detlef reminded himself. *Hitler could be sitting at that Indian table right now, scowling at the cold coffee that he most certainly does drink. Easy pickings.* But there were a lot of other people that could be up there instead. People with guns. People who were already fanning out to find him.

As everything twisted back and forth inside his head, Detlef heard a voice from down the second-floor hallway and realized he was standing in the clear. He dove forward, almost tripping over his leg, and slammed into the corner of the stairwell. The impact shook off the doubts that had come over him and he suddenly wanted to scream. What had he been thinking? How could he come all this way only to choke at the last minute? He almost deserved to get caught.

But no one had seen or heard him. He waited a moment and then slowly poked his head out. There were only two people in the hall, both heading into one of the rooms. The first—a bushy-bearded man in a slate grey suit—was a civilian. The second wore a uniform, but he was holding the door and Detlef couldn't see much of him. Detlef wished they would stay in the hall longer. Once they left he would have to decide: up or down?

Just before the door shut behind him, the uniformed man turned so that Detlef could see him. His wire-thin body looked at odds with his pudgy, almost infantile face. A pair of pince-nez gripped his nose and the scratchy mustache below them fell short on one side. Detlef had to stifle a shout. He could have recognized the man even without the wreath and triple feather insignia on his collar. This was Heinrich Himmler, *Reichsführer-SS* and Chief of German Police.

Of all the disappeared people whom Detlef would now claim he had never known, only one of them, the Reverend Rupert Sachs, had ever returned. Sachs rarely spoke about what he called—with a smile that never reached the eyes—his holiday in Dachau. But Detlef had pried from him one story, which concerned a visit from Heinrich Himmler. From the moment Detlef heard it, he had known that he would one day end up here, gripping the handle of a briefcase packed with gunpowder and iron nails.

It had been mid-January and Sachs, along with every prisoner in the camp, had been lined up to greet their esteemed visitor. But the *Reichsführer* was delayed. Five hours passed in the cold. Sachs' voice shivered as he recalled it and Detlef had the impression that Sachs hadn't truly felt warm since. Even so, he'd had it easy. In the priest barracks, they got to keep their coats. Most of the other prisoners had only scraps and their own arms to get them through the winter. Those without shoes dug their toes into the ice-flecked mud for warmth.

There was a man on the far side of the yard—one of the greens, the so-called criminals—who had a terrible tremor. It would start in his leg and spasm all the way up to his shoulder. Everyone had long since gotten used to it and even the guards had given up trying to beat it out of him. But when the procession of cars finally arrived and Himmler got out, he took one look at the assembled mass of prisoners, pointed straight at the man with the tremor and loudly asked, "Why is that one moving?"

As if it were an answer, the closest guard stepped between the lines, drew his pistol, and shot the man with the tremor clean through the skull.

"All he had done was ask a question," Sachs said. "But something happened to it in the air. What reached our ears was not a question any longer. It was an order."

"But you're out now," Detlef said, foolishly. "We can change things."

At that, Sachs laughed. "There is no *out*. Not for you or for me or for anyone. There are more questions to come and not enough bullets in the world to answer them."

Detlef wished he could have forgotten the story. It would not help him now. He had only two reasonable choices: go back upstairs and risk everything on the chance that he'd been wrong or go downstairs and run. Killing Himmler would change nothing. Someone else would ask the questions instead. But by the time Detlef confirmed to himself that it was a bad plan, he was not in the stairwell anymore. He was in the room adjoining Himmler's and he had his ear pressed against the wall. The walls here were thin—too thin, if he recalled from the building's plans.

"How many?" came a muffled, nasal voice. Himmler, Detlef assumed.

Someone laughed nervously. The bearded man? "That sounds like business," he said. "I thought we might do a demonstration first. Show you what you're getting out of this."

"I've seen the boys," Himmler said. "They aren't unimpressive. But they will not quarry stone and they will not fill shells. So we'll start with business. How many?"

"Six thousand for the year," a third voice said.

"I can send half that," Himmler countered. "As things progress there may be more."

"That's not enough. The *Führer* wants twenty in this—"

"That's plenty," the bearded man interrupted. "We'll double them up."

"Good," Himmler agreed. "There will have to be a gap as well. For supply. You started with the other schools, correct? After Easter." There was a pause—a nod perhaps. "For next year you'll have to delay a while. We can make August at the earliest."

The third voice tried to speak up again, but the bearded man cut him off, "August will do. Now are you sure you wouldn't like to see our demonstration? Remember that they started in April, just as you said. Think what you'll be able to see by the end of the year."

Nothing the three were saying made sense to Detlef. They were haggling over something, but what? And why were they there at all, alone and unguarded? No answers were likely to come from the other side of the wall. The talking had died down and now there were only noises: a scratching like claws against wood then a pained, feline yowl and a thud. Laughter erupted from all three men, only now there were two other voices in the mix, both high and bright. The scratching stopped and there was a very long applause.

"Spectacular!" Himmler crowed. "Just one word of advice. Give a different demonstration for the *Führer*. He doesn't like to see animals get hurt."

"Who does?" the bearded man said.

The goodbyes started. There were other meetings to attend and, for Detlef, no more time to decide on a plan. He tried to picture the room on the other side. How many meters across? Eight? Twelve? The blast would be weak, probably not strong enough to bring down the wall or collapse the ceiling, but the shrapnel would go far and fast. It could work from here. If he hit the switch now, he could end it. He might even have time to run. It wouldn't change much, but at least Sachs' man with the tremor would have justice.

As Detlef steadied his finger over the switch, he heard another sound. It was one of the two unidentified voices that had been laughing earlier. Both of them, actually.

"It was an honor to meet you," they said almost simultaneously.

Detlef's grip loosened. The briefcase fell from his hand. He covered his mouth to avoid making a sound. They were children's voices.

Himmler, he could kill. Himmler's two associates, whoever they were, he could kill. He could kill soldiers and guards. But he could not listen to these two children's voices and then light his fuse and run. As much as he wished otherwise, that was crueler than he was capable of. *Even resistance is an atrocity,* he tried to remind himself, but it was not enough. The briefcase remained on the floor. Detlef slumped and pressed his back into the wall. His chest shuddered wetly every time he inhaled through the cracks in fingers.

Footsteps—two sets of them—came and then went. Himmler was gone, but some of the others remained. Detlef waited a long minute and then, though a part of him no longer wanted to escape, pushed himself up. He reached for his briefcase, but he could hardly lift it. The weight of a hundred mistakes tugged it down. For one irrational moment, he considered pressing the switch even now. But before the thought could take hold, the bearded man's voice interrupted. It was loud and crisp, hardly muted at all by the walls.

"You are making a lot of noise for someone who is supposed to be hiding," he said.

Detlef whipped around. There was no one in the room.

"Why don't you come over so we can talk?"

Detlef scanned for somewhere to hide, but it was too late for that. It was time to run. He snatched up his briefcase, flung the door open, and twisted into the hall. Immediately, he stopped. He hadn't chosen to do so. It had just happened. It was as though he had crashed into a great body of water. There was nothing visible in the air around him, and yet the more he thrashed against it, the more it hardened. It turned to tar and then to rock.

Before Detlef was a boy—maybe twelve years old—with puffy cheeks and a thick smile. He wore the tan shirt and shorts of the Hitler Youth.

"Get out of the way!" Detlef cried, projecting all the authority he could muster. That wasn't very much and the boy did not budge. His smile did not slip.

Detlef turned and pulled back. That came much more easily than moving forward. Whatever invisible substance he had collided with made an audible squelch as he broke free. The boy still did not move. Detlef ran, but the second boy was right behind him and he slammed into more of the same. He couldn't move.

"Join us," the bearded man said from inside the room where they had been. "The coffee is still hot. Well, it's warm."

Detlef stopped struggling. He let his shoulders drop. He knew he should be afraid, but he wasn't. There was no room for fear amid all his regret. The pain of it radiated from his chest like acid in his blood. *He should have stayed upstairs. What if Hitler had come? It could all be over. He had left for nothing.*

The boys each took a step forward and Detlef moved back. They did it again, corralling him, pushing him into the room. He let them. Even as Detlef stumbled inside, the bearded man did not get up from his chair. He lifted his cup and took a sip, then set it down and straightened the lapel of his grey suit.

"Sit," he said. "I am Hugo. Tell us your name."

Detlef, half pushed, half of his own volition, teetered over and fell into a chair across from him. The boys moved around the table and stood on either side of Hugo.

As they turned their backs to him, Detlef noticed that each had an identical tattoo on the rear of his neck—two deep black lines that looked like they should intersect, but somehow never did. On the table was a wooden figure of a cat, about the size of a loaf of bread. All around it, thin scratches and streaks of blood marred the varnish.

The way behind him was clear now and Detlef considered running, but he knew with a cold certainty that it would do him no good.

"My name is Detlef Kühn," he said. "Chief Architect at IAFB."

He took a dry swallow then looked down to where his palm gripped the handle of the briefcase. As if observing himself from afar, he understood why he had told the truth. The switch hidden inside the latch was depressed. Detlef didn't remember touching it. A part of him wanted to scream for the two children to run, but another, colder part saw their red armbands and did not care. They would grow up to be killers if they were not already. Someday, Himmler would ask a question and they would answer. Silent, Detlef let the briefcase fall and closed his eyes. He counted. Each second dragged.

"God forgive me," he whispered.

His count reached ten. Then fifteen. Nothing happened. It was like the clock upstairs. He must have counted too quickly, but then what seemed like another ten seconds passed and, still, silence. Detlef opened his eyes. Hugo and the two boys were watching him blankly.

"Are you waiting for something?" Hugo asked.

Detlef tried to breathe and he choked on his own spit. Something was wrong. The grim comfort of the bomb had been his last scrap of armor and now, finally, he was afraid. Hugo inclined his head towards the boy on the left, who beckoned with his hand. On its own, Detlef's briefcase lifted off the ground and, still floating, twisted to its side. Detlef took too long to comprehend what was happening and by the time he grabbed for it, the briefcase had already flown out of reach. It settled into place just in front of Hugo, still hovering above the table.

The clasp released itself and the briefcase lid pulled away. The model amphitheater lifted up from within. Immediately, Detlef understood why it had not gone off. The model was backwards. He had watched the *Oberschütze* downstairs turn it around and thought nothing of it until now. How had he missed it? The metal contact was disconnected. It would not detonate now or in ten seconds or in ten minutes. And, Detlef had to remind himself, the whole thing was floating in mid-air.

"Beautiful," Hugo said. "What is it for?"

Detlef surprised himself with a clear answer. "It's for Prora. On Rügen."

Hugo laughed. "You two are from Rügen, aren't you?" The boys nodded. "That hotel will be a sight once it's finished. It's unfortunate that the *Führer* will pick someone else's design instead. Tragic, really. This one would have been much better."

The wood panel at the base of the model slid back and the three steel pipes dropped out, slowing to a stop just before they hit the table. One of the boys turned his wrist and the model hurled at Detlef. He ducked and it crashed against the wall behind him, shattering in a spray of balsa fragments. Detlef tried to shout, but before he could the air rushed out of him. It was as if a pair of hands had gripped his chest. Fingers dug themselves into his lungs. He sputtered in pain. The second boy narrowed his eyes and Detlef's chair slid backwards.

"What did you do to them?" he wheezed, wasting precious breath. "They're children. Just children."

Hugo stood up. "That's rather insulting, don't you think? *Just* children."

Before Detlef could open his mouth to respond, a vicious spasm twisted through him. A terrible pressure gripped his head and he could hear the bones of his jaw creak under its weight. Detlef's teeth rattled like saucers on a train. He tried to form words or even a scream but everything died on the tip of his numbing tongue.

"Don't kill him," Hugo said, holding up a hand. "I imagine the *Reichsführer* will want a word."

Identical grins crawled across the two boys' faces. Detlef no longer felt any pain, just a dull crushing so great he thought his head might pop. His teeth groaned and bent outwards. They tore into gums until something snapped. His skull rocked one way; everything inside it went the other. Detlef blinked and his eyes did not reopen.

# CHAPTER ONE

## Messerich, Germany 1938

The restless boys squirmed and the line suffered for it. They snaked through the waiting room like an unruly vein. Erich fidgeted near the front. The angles and corners of the packed army clinic defied him. No matter where he put himself, he stood out of place.

After six months of training, these ten-year-olds did not ordinarily form such sloppy ranks. Erich and his peers had mastered marches and formations, anthems and oaths, but now their perfect discipline had evaporated in a cloud of nerves and excitement. Their time as provisional members of the *Jungvolk* were over. Only the *Mutprobe* stood in their way. Pass this test of courage and the junior branch of the Hitler Youth would welcome them as full members. The possibility that anyone might fail had not been discussed.

Erich's lungs threatened a yawn, and he sucked in a quick breath to stifle it. The previous night still hung over him, a scratchy blur of fitful sleep and rumination on the trial ahead. He didn't know what to expect, or which of the older boys' stories to believe. August said they had dunked him in a tub of ice until his heart stopped beating.

Konrad had leaned in to Erich's ear and whispered that they'd thrown him into a cage with a she-wolf and her three hungry pups. Konrad was a liar, but shivering under the blankets, Erich hadn't quite been able to dismiss the rest of them.

The exact nature of the *Mutprobe* would depend on the whims of Erich's *Fähnleinführer*, Klaus, whose imagination rarely disappointed. All week Erich had dreamed of nothing but blood and sweat, fire and vertigo. Yet nothing had prepared him for this interminable waiting, a battle against his own agitated body. Rather than administering the *Mutprobe*, Klaus had marched all sixty boys into a clinic in the garrison on the edge of town and announced a blood test.

"Blood," he had said, "separates the wolf from the lamb. Each has it in their veins, but only the wolf tastes it on his teeth."

Erich didn't entirely know what that meant. Perhaps Klaus didn't either, but it sounded impressive.

"All his children will be tested, and the *Führer* will know your mettle."

"Is this our *Mutprobe*?" one boy asked.

The *Fähnleinführer's* face split into a wide grin as he answered, "No."

There was no space in the waiting room for all of them, so the line curved out the door and through the main garrison road. Outside, Erich had let his eyes wander into the army tents for a glimpse of soldiering life, but in the clinic there was nothing to distract him from his own nerves.

Still, he was grateful to stay out of Klaus's sight. Sixteen years old, yet leader to one hundred and eighty boys, Klaus never went anywhere without a mechanic's tool belt strapped around his brown Hitler Youth uniform. It was loose and far too large, which made him look very silly, but none of them had ever dared to say that aloud. He claimed the tools were for fixing machinery on his father's farm, but Erich had only ever seen them used in the *Fähnleinführer*'s creative application of discipline.

Behind Erich, Gottlob wobbled in place. Hunched over, he contorted his long arms into one position after another, unsure where to put them. As always, Gottlob's pale skin glistened under a thin layer of sweat or grease or something else unknown. Erich and the others avoided him, content simply with his absence, but one boy, Max, saw Gottlob's fearful sweat as a kind of trophy. He delighted in extracting it. With the *Fähnleinführer* outside and the nurses nowhere to be seen, Max had the moment all to himself. He wasted no time.

"Have you ever had blood drawn before?" Max asked.

Gottlob froze in place. He curled his arms so tight against his chest that Erich thought he would hug himself to death.

"My uncle's a doctor in Cologne," Max said, slipping out of formation to look his mark in the eye. "He says cowards have too much water in their blood. They're just born like that."

Gottlob backed away. His lips turned down in a queasy grimace. Erich joined a few others in a laugh. There was no quality more deplorable than cowardice.

"Once a coward's blood starts leaking out, there's no stopping it. It'll run and run until you're dead," Max said. He leaned in close. "They'll try to make it easy. Nice and quick. The doctor will fetch your parents to say goodbye, then they'll just hang you up by the ankles and let it all drain out into a bucket."

With each word Gottlob took another step backwards, sweating in dark patches that smeared the sides of his uniform.

"She's coming, get back in line," someone hissed.

Erich had completely abandoned ranks to watch the show. He snapped back into formation just as the nurse rounded the corner.

"Erich Fiehler," she called, then pursed her lips at

Gottlob, who hadn't made it to his spot in time.

"*Heil Hitler*," Erich said as he stepped forward, extending his arm in a proud salute.

She led him down the hall to a tiny office wedged into the corner. Erich took a seat on the bed while she shut the door and busied herself at the counter. A huge, red flag covered one wall of the otherwise bare room. Across from it, a lone nail protruded from the plaster, but whatever had once hung there was gone.

"Roll up your sleeve," the nurse said without turning.

Erich eyed the three bags that dangled from the rack next to her. One hung crumpled and empty with blackening drops still splattering its insides. The other two were fat with blood. A swallow caught in Erich's throat. *Was all that from the last boy?* Max's story echoed in his ears. It wasn't so funny anymore.

After a minute, the nurse sat down on the bed and pulled the rack up to Erich's side. As the bags swung to a stop, she wiped the tip of a dagger-length needle. Erich held out his wrist and stared straight ahead, trying not to flinch or look away. But she turned, and instead of reaching for his arm, she punched the needle into a nozzle under one of the full bags.

"Shut your eyes," she ordered.

Erich obeyed, somewhat relieved not to watch. He felt a soft prick, not on his arm, but on the back of his neck. It was not at all unpleasant. A tingle played across his shoulders, then suddenly intensified. He gasped as the rush spilled through his veins, and his own blood pulsed hot under his skin. It was glorious. Like some cold-blooded creature in the sun for the first time, he basked. He didn't dare move for fear the feeling might escape him.

Blacks and colors swam behind closed eyelids. In his mind, the bare walls shifted and collapsed around him. Erich rocketed up into the air. He soared out of the clinic and rose above all of Messerich. His father's butcher shop grew small and vanished as Germany curled out before him like a map. Its rivers twisted and pulsed into pumping veins that beat time, but there was no pattern to their erratic flow, no heart for them to empty into. He flew higher and higher. There were no borders, nothing to tell him where his home ended and the rest of the world began.

Suddenly, he stopped. Erich hung there, his body swung out precariously in the sky. There was nothing to hold him; there had never been. He fell. Flailing limbs grasped for purchase on clouds that sputtered apart at the touch. He plummeted through the blinding mist. As he broke through, patchwork farmland exploded out around him, filling his vision. Erich jerked forward in his seat, and the feeling drained away instantly. He bit his lip and felt tears well up in his eyes. He had been about to break every bone in his body, but he still would have given anything to go back.

Erich didn't want to move. Heavy eyelids ached as he lifted them to see the colorless world outside. The nurse scratched notes on her clipboard, pausing periodically to chew on her pen and scowl at the page. He watched her sheepishly, certain she would be furious with him for falling asleep. But when she looked up from her papers, she just smiled and gave his wrist a gentle squeeze.

"We're all done," she said. "Go on and join the other boys outside."

Erich stumbled out of the chair, not sure his feet would hold him. The nurse followed, guiding with a hand against his back. As they rounded the corner, Erich allowed himself a half smile. He had made it. Only the *Mutprobe* remained in his way.

"Gottlob Querner, you're next," the nurse called once they were back in the waiting room.

Cascades of sweat poured from Gottlob's quivering forehead. He blinked the droplets out of his wide eyes as he inched backwards, then hesitated and took a tiny step forward. He couldn't seem to decide which terror frightened him more, Klaus or the needle. Erich stopped halfway to the front door, mesmerized by the drama. He snickered as the nurse snatched at Gottlob's arm.

"Come here boy!" she shouted.

Gottlob took one clumsy step back, just enough to slip away from her fingers. Again, she reached for him. He pranced out of her grasp and the boys erupted into raucous laughter. A loud crash echoed through the clinic. Every head turned. Klaus had slammed the outside door shut and made his presence known. The *Fähnleinführer*'s bellowing erased the din in an instant.

"You call this a formation?" he roared. "If you were this sloppy in the Wehrmacht, you'd be staring down a firing squad. What kind of line would you make then?"

The boys scurried back into their ranks and snapped to attention. Only Gottlob, dumbstruck, and Erich, still too delirious to think clearly, stood out of place.

"Gottlob Querner," Klaus said. "The *Führer* has need of your watery blood. You should be grateful he has found some use for you at all. That's more than I've ever managed."

Gottlob let out a frightened squeal but did his best to straighten up and stand tall. He knew better than to hope for escape. Klaus leaned down to look him in the eye. The clinic fell to a dead quiet.

"Are you frightened of the needle?" he asked.

With guilt welling in his eyes, Gottlob nodded. Everyone but Klaus gasped at the audacity of his cowardice. Erich shook his head in disbelief, but even that tiny motion made him dizzy.

Klaus smiled and ran a casual hand over his tool belt, as though deciding which size wrench would fit a bolt. He settled on a pair of slender pliers and caressed them.

He whipped his head high and shrieked, "For his country your father bled dry in the trenches. But you!" He stabbed an accusing finger at Gottlob. "You won't give Germany one drop."

In a single swift motion, Klaus snapped the pliers over Gottlob's ear and clamped them down tight. Reflexively, Gottlob tore away, howling in pain. A crimson spray arced out behind him. It seemed to hang in the air for too long before it splattered down across the checkered floor. Gottlob clutched at his ear. A red trickle dribbled between the cracks in his fingers to run down his flushed cheek.

Even from across the room, Erich could smell the blood. It wasn't like anything he had ever smelled before. It reeked so much more pungently than the stink that clung to his father's hands or poured out from a pig's inverted neck. It wasn't a pleasant smell, but he found himself sucking in big gulps of it anyway. Coppery fumes crammed into his lungs until they were ready to burst. With every shuddering breath, he slipped further back into his strange, soaring dream. Every vein throbbed and pressed against his skin as if trying to escape it.

On the other side of the room, Gottlob still sobbed and wailed. Klaus hadn't stopped his shouting either, but his words meandered too much in the red haze. They reached Erich garbled and muted, no longer important. Erich's breath quickened. The room swam as the blood on the floor called out for him. It sang.

Erich felt the urge to run at it, to tear off his clothes and roll around on the tile until his bare skin had soaked up every drop, but he couldn't move. He glared at his disobedient feet, and as if on ice, they slid backwards out of view. The floor pounced up to meet him.

# CHAPTER TWO

Erich woke alone, slouched against the fraying upholstery of a waiting room seat. An odd silence filled the clinic, suddenly cavernous without the crowd of fidgeting *Jungvolk*. One uneven chair leg screeched loudly against the floor as Erich pushed himself forward and onto his feet. They felt solid enough, though his vision clouded with black as he got up. He shook his head and waited for it to clear.

A cool breeze pushed in from the crack in the outside door and brushed across his face. Erich let out a deep breath and tasted something mineral on his tongue. He shuffled towards the exit, then turned around and took a few aimless steps back, unsure of where to go.

*The Mutprobe!* The thought of it slammed into his gut, and he sputtered out air. He was late. It would be a whole year before he could try again. By then he would be the oldest, an inadequate disappointment to *Führer* and fatherland. The one who was left behind.

Footsteps pattered down the hall. The nurse was returning. She would be furious, but Erich knew that her anger would be nothing compared to Klaus'. He cringed as she popped her head around the corner.

"Oh good, *kleine*, you're awake," she said, smiling gently.

Erich rubbed at his ear, confident he had misheard. This was not the tongue-lashing he had expected. Somehow that made it worse. His cheeks burned and his head dropped below his shoulders. Like a coward, he had fainted at the first sight of blood. The whole *Fähnlein* had seen him for the yellow-blooded worm that he was. He would spend years overcoming the shame of it.

"Your *Fähnleinführer* took the boys to his father's farm. You should hurry if you want to catch up," the nurse said.

Erich hesitated, not sure how to respond.

"Go on, don't you want to earn your dagger?" she prodded, still inexplicably kind. "It's at least five kilometers."

Erich nodded, gritting his teeth in determination. There was still time. The hazy lethargy slipped off his shoulders like a heavy pack. He ran.

Erich shot through the clinic door and sprinted past the rows of empty tents, still cursing himself under his breath. He didn't know what Gottlob's blood had done to him or why he had fainted at the sight of it. He didn't understand how the nurse could be so unperturbed by everything. But he could run, and the sound of his heart pounded the doubts away.

Every cold breath seared Erich's lungs, and he knew that at this pace he would burn out soon, but he didn't care. He would not be held back. Erich took every shortcut he knew, trespassing with abandon. He vaulted the Mayers' fence, sprinted through the just-tilled fields, and crashed into the woods. There was no path between the dense trees, but he charged through anyway. Scratching brambles shredded his clothes and clawed at his skin. He hurled himself through puddles of mud, knowing full well how Aunt Mila would murder him when she saw the state of his uniform. Nothing mattered but the next aching step.

Erich rocketed out onto the road. There were no more

shortcuts from here, just a long, straight strip of dirt all the way to Klaus' farm. His eyes were narrowed in so intently on the path ahead that he didn't notice the girl pull up beside him on her bicycle. She kept pace, pedaling leisurely while he panted and heaved, still shedding little burrs and branches from the forest.

Her voice startled him.

"*Heil Hitler*," she said in a bored monotone, more a mockery than a greeting. "Who are you running away from?"

Erich turned to look, but he refused to slow down.

"No one. I'm no coward," he said between gasping breaths.

She snorted out a laugh. "My father says only cowards need to say that."

Erich glared at her, but he couldn't muster the air for a rejoinder. She looked familiar.

"But he says a lot of things I don't believe," she added.

They traveled in silence for a moment, a curious couple. Erich in disarray and her profoundly composed, perched on her bicycle seat like it were a throne. Her starched blouse glowed blinding white in the midday sun.

With a false air of reluctance, Erich slowed down. She had given him an excuse to relent, which he took with a twang of guilt. He looked over, more carefully now, and finally recognized her. She was the daughter of Herr Engel, Messerich's chief of police. Her father often came to the shop, though he never seemed to want to be there. Prone to furious outbursts, Herr Engel had once demanded that Erich's father throw away an entire pig because he'd detected a sour taste in the previous night's meal. They had complied with haste, but sniggered to each other later about Frau Engel's cooking.

"If you're not running away, then where are you going?" the girl asked.

"The *Mutprobe* is today." Erich puffed out his chest. "I'm going to join the *Jungvolk* and get my dagger and take my oath and make the *Führer* proud."

"Unless you're late. Then you'll just be the sad boy who got nothing," she said, grinning a little too eagerly. This girl wanted something.

"If I'm late, it'll be because you distracted me," he said.

She stuck out her tongue. "What if I let you borrow my bike?"

Erich skidded to a stop. The fire in his limbs finally caught up to him. He bent over, clutching his knees. She kept going and arced into a graceful halt ahead of him. Erich held up one finger to beg for a moment.

"I'll take it," he said once he had recovered.

"No, no, no, that's not how it goes," she admonished. "You're supposed to ask me what I want in return."

Erich pulled himself upright and narrowed his eyes. He tried not to look desperate, but his chest still heaved with every word, "What do you want then?"

"Your dagger. If you pass the *Mutprobe*."

Erich sputtered with shock. "What would a girl do with a dagger?"

"What would a boy do with a dagger?" she spat back.

He considered the offer for a moment, then frowned. "I can't. They'll think I lost it. Klaus would kill me, and if he didn't then your father would for sure."

Erich lowered his head and kicked around the dirt at his feet.

"I'd rather be left behind," he said, but before the words had even left his mouth, he knew they weren't true. She knew it just as well. She toyed with one pedal, taunting him. Erich slowly lifted his eyes and cringed as he noticed the multicolored ribbons dangling from her handlebars.

"I'll do it," he mumbled.

He said the words so softly that he thought she might make him say it again, but she took pity and hopped off her bike. She held out her hand in expectation, "Deal?"

"Just hurry." Erich averted his eyes while he gave her hand one quick shake. He clambered onto the bike and pedaled forward a few paces, then stopped, wobbling, to look back over his shoulder. "What's your nam—"

"You do know how to ride, right?" she interrupted.

"Of course I do," he said, holding up both hands to demonstrate. It almost lost him his balance.

"It's Johanna," she said, giggling.

"Erich."

They paused for a moment, unsure what else needed to be said, what protocols they had missed in their transaction. Johanna broke the silence, "You should probably go. If you're late you owe me a dagger."

Erich shot out a salute and careened away as fast as he could push the little pedals. Johanna's ribbons streamed out behind him, twirling in ostentatious pirouettes. Erich started to rip them off, but he pictured her sliding a shiny, new dagger into his gut and reconsidered.

The bike helped, but Erich had exhausted himself far too early. Acid ate at his legs as he forced the wheels around again and again. By the time he broke across the edge of the Schuster farm, he knew that if he stopped for even a moment, there would be no getting back on. He prayed the *Mutprobe* would not be a cycling challenge.

The sun blinded Erich as he approached, but squinting past the glare, he spotted a crowd of uniformed boys arranged in a neat square. They all craned their necks up to see the top of the squat grain silo ahead of them. Two boys of Klaus' age sat on the roof with their legs dangling off the edge. Below, Klaus himself paced back and forth at the front of the formation, so lost in his oratory that he didn't notice the bicycle that torpedoed towards them.

Erich grinned. The *Mutprobe* hadn't started yet. Exultant, he threw the remaining dregs of his energy into a last, desperate push. He barreled towards the group at full speed. Before he knew what had happened, he was almost there. He threw out his legs, but he couldn't stop. The pedals spun wild with their own frenzied agenda.

Instantly, the formation scattered. Terrified boys hurled

themselves in every direction, desperate to escape the oncoming missile. The bravest stood their ground, but after a second their courage broke and they too jumped out of the way. By the time Erich came to a crashing halt, only the *Fähnleinführer* remained in place. Erich's bicycle teetered and fell forward, depositing him at Klaus' unwavering feet in a tangle of legs, gears, pedals, and ribbons.

"You've decided to join us. Are you feeling better?" Klaus sneered. "Nurse Huber, speaking from the womanly depths of her heart, has asked me to let you take part today. She says your craven little fainting spell was 'The desired reaction'. Well, it was not mine!"

The boys took advantage of Klaus' preoccupation to scurry back to their ranks. Erich could hear them laughing as he disentangled himself from Johanna's bicycle and scrambled to his feet. He did his best to stand tall, resisting the temptation to glance down at his ruined uniform.

Klaus stroked his chin melodramatically. "Fine. I'll let you prove yourself, even in this sorry state. You can go first." Klaus took a step back. "You faint at the sight of blood, but what about heights?"

He motioned up towards the silo. It didn't look so squat from up close. Erich had to tilt his head all the way back before he could see the tower's discolored bricks give way to the steep roof. Though they looked as though they might slip off at any moment, the two older boys clamored around the spire without fear. Erich wondered if he would be so effortlessly courageous when he reached Klaus' age. A thick cable ran from the silo's flagpole down to a spike in the ground. With a painful swallow, Erich realized what it was for.

Klaus stepped over to the rope ladder that hung from the edge of the roof and gave it two sharp tugs.

"Up you go," he said, then louder to the group, "Boys, it's time to show the *Führer* your bravery. Form a line behind our fainthearted brother and make Germany proud."

Klaus snatched up a piece of bent metal from the ground next to him and pressed it into Erich's chest.

"You'll need this," he said.

Erich stared at the thing in his hands and tried to identify it. It had once been a set of handlebars. An oval ring was roughly welded to the center, and from each side there hung a tiny Nazi flag. Patches of rust spotted the metal where the paint had chipped away. Flecks dug into Erich's palm as he gripped the bars.

He felt strangely calm. Almost from a distance, he observed himself: out of breath, aching, still a little dizzy from the curious blood test, but he knew what had to be done. It was simple. No more decisions, just one ladder rung and then another. He climbed slowly, the metal bar tucked under his arm. Below, Klaus led their group in an anthem. Erich ignored it. Nothing mattered but the *Mutprobe*.

He didn't even realize that he had reached the top until he felt one of the older boys grab his arm and yank him up onto the roof. He struggled to keep his feet from slipping down the slant. One of them took the handlebars and ran the zip line through them, then reattached it to the flagpole with a tricky knot. Erich lost himself momentarily in the boy's deft movements. When would he learn to tie a knot like that?

With the bars back in his hands, Erich stepped out onto the roof's lip and peered down at the hushed crowd below. Before he could even take a breath, something rammed into him from behind. His feet lost the ground. Rusty metal screamed against the line. A pincer of vertigo gripped his stomach, and he squeezed the bars so tight he thought they might snap. Then suddenly everything relaxed. The vicious tension slipped away and the world slowed around him. Erich closed his eyes. He floated down.

An impact. Legs slammed against ground. They were

running even though Erich hadn't told them to. He opened his eyes and the world blazed back at him, sharper than it had been when he shut them. He had done it. He was the first to complete the *Mutprobe*. For a moment, he forgot the shame of fainting in the clinic.

Surprising himself, Erich belted out the last line of the Hitler Youth anthem, "Our banner means more to us than death!"

When Klaus strode over, Erich did his best to restrain his excitement and snap to attention.

"Good enough, Fiehler."

It was the closest thing to praise he'd ever heard from Klaus, and Erich repeated the words again and again in his head as he marched across the grass to form a new line. He stood to the side, alone, the first in a formation for freshly christened boys. Before long, more joined him, brimming with enthusiasm as they bounded over to take a place at his side. Erich's outburst from the anthem became tradition, and everyone who followed him shouted the words as their feet touched the ground.

Even poor Gottlob, his ear wrapped in a thick bandage, made it safely down. The sweat stains now ran all the way down his thin flanks, and he squealed when they shoved him off the ledge, but there was still a place for him in the formation.

Max came next. Almost as soon as he had swung off the platform, his grasp on the right handlebar slipped. The bars flipped vertically and he clung to the bottom half with both hands. For a moment, it looked like he would make it, but the metal ran slick with sweat and his grip faltered. He fell, crumpling to the ground with one leg crushed painfully beneath him.

Klaus hit him across the head until he stopped screaming, then declared the leg broken and dispatched one of the older boys to help him. Klaus turned away, shrugged, and wiped the handlebars dry on his uniform. He winked at Gottlob. "I guess you win in the end,

Querner."

When the last boy had landed, Klaus ordered them to line up single file. This time, the procession was perfect. Erich waited without impatience, standing absolutely still until his turn arrived. He stepped forward and squared his shoulders. Klaus handed him the *Fähnlein* flag, a white sig rune on black cloth. Erich ran his hand down the pole as he extended his right arm with three fingers raised high.

"In the presence of this banner, which represents our *Führer*, I swear to devote all my energy and all my strength to the savior of our country, Adolf Hitler. I am willing and ready to give up my life for him, so help me God."

Erich relinquished the flag with a tinge of reluctance, but what Klaus handed him in return was worth it. The dagger. He hurried to the back of the line to unsheathe it. Running his finger along the cool blade, he felt each notch of the inscription. *Blood and Honor.* With a simmering smile, he returned it to the sheath and let it swing from his belt. He barred Johanna from his mind and let himself imagine that the gift was his and his alone, that the *Führer* had entrusted the weapon to him personally.

Erich closed his eyes and made a promise. *I will be worthy.*

# CHAPTER THREE

Erich found Johanna perched on a low fence at the edge of the Moritz family land. She nibbled at the remains of an apple. As soon as he was within striking distance, she tossed the core at him.

"Took you long enough," she said. "Where's my dagger?"

Johanna held out her palm, wiggling her fingers expectantly. With a grumble, Erich unlooped the dagger from his belt. The moment her eyes glimpsed it, she leapt down from the fence, clapped her hands together in anticipation, and started to bounce on one foot. Erich scowled at her, but he held out the dagger anyway. He refused to meet her eyes as his prize slid into her eager hands. It rang when she unsheathed it. Johanna turned it over a few times, felt the weight, admired the inscription, then shrugged and slipped it back into the sheath.

"Ok, it's yours," she said, tossing the dagger at him.

Erich was too stunned to catch it. It slapped him across the chest and plopped down into the dirt. He eyed her suspiciously, wondering what kind of trick she would play once he leaned down to pick it up.

"Don't you want it?" he asked.

Johanna rolled her eyes. "I just wanted to see whether you'd actually give it to me."

She bent down to retrieve the dagger and held it out for him.

"Honestly, I didn't expect you'd go through with it," she said. "My father doesn't think much of your family."

"And what do you think of us?" he asked.

Johanna smiled slyly. "I haven't decided yet."

"All right then," Erich said. "Let me show you something."

She turned her head and eyed him sideways. "What is it?"

"You'll see. It's not far."

Erich pulled himself over the fence, more clumsily than he had meant to, and held out his hand for Johanna. She ignored it and scrambled over on her own.

They left her bike leaning against the slats and ran through the fields, making airplanes with their arms. Erich bounded ahead at first, but he was so tired that she quickly passed him. When he stopped and bent over to catch his breath, Johanna threw back her head in aggravation.

"You're so slow. Do they stick bricks in the pockets of those silly uniforms?"

"No. They do not," Erich puffed. "And there's nothing silly about them. What would *you* have us wear?"

"Swastika swim trunks," she said and waltzed off into the woods in mocking goose step, shouting, "Strength through nudity!"

Erich chased after her, laughing. He stopped to listen for the gurgle of water ahead and turned to follow it. "Not far now," he said.

They trekked through the trees to a tiny creek, not much more than a trickle here, then traced its widening path upstream. Erich kept looking back to make sure she was still following him. Johanna groaned every time.

"Here we are," Erich said as they pushed through the trees into a clearing. Ahead, two enormous rocks flanked the stream. Almost twenty meters separated them, but Erich thought they must have once been a single boulder. Their smooth cores were hollow, like two halves of a scooped-out melon. He had always considered them thrones.

"You take the far one. This one's mine," he said.

When they had both curled up in their respective domes, he stared across the water at her and whispered, "Hello, Johanna."

She jumped in surprise and yelled back at him, "How did you do that?"

Her voice echoed in his ear, painfully loud. He shushed her. "Don't shout here. I can hear you at just a whisper."

"Is it magic?" she asked, glancing around in every direction at the concave stone.

"Don't be silly. It's science." Erich pumped a triumphant fist in the air.

"How does it work then?" she whispered.

He shrugged. "No idea."

They let the words hang in the air while Johanna slowly ran her hands over the surface of the rock.

"Look," she said, "there are markings on the stone."

Erich must have been here a dozen times, but he'd never noticed the writing before. Faintly etched, it traced a curve all the way around the hollow. He didn't recognize the alphabet.

"I wonder what they say," he said.

"I think it's..." she trailed off.

Erich opened his mouth to prod for more, but Johanna interrupted him with a scream. It stabbed at Erich's ears, reverberating violently through the stone. He clapped his palms tight against his ears, but her shriek pierced right through them. She pointed towards the creek and shouted again. "Wolf!"

Erich followed her finger, eyes widening as he saw the beast slink out from between the trees, branches snapping under its thick paws. Sickly, bald patches matted a smoky pelt. The wolf padded to a stop and arched down, letting its mangy underside brush against the dirt. It stared straight at Johanna, curled back its lip, and snarled, ready to pounce. She stood stock-still. Her mouth hung open.

"Run," Erich yelled. "RUN!"

She wouldn't move. He sprung out of the hollow and charged into the water, throwing his arms in the air with frantic splashes and shouts. The wolf whipped around to fix its amber eyes on Erich. They glowed in the dusky air. He turned to run, but then remembered the dagger at his belt. *I am not some frightened child. I have teeth too.* He squared off, weapon drawn.

The wolf leapt. It closed the distance in a blur of flickering limbs.

Erich slashed at the air, but his swing flew too high. Thick jaws snapped around his left arm. Teeth twisted. His lungs burned from screaming, but he couldn't hear it. The dagger slipped from his hand, forgotten.

Erich stumbled back, but his foot caught against an errant stone and he fell with a splash. The wolf was on him in an instant. It planted its heavy paws on his chest and snarled. Hot breath buffeted Erich's face. It stank of days-old kill.

He closed his eyes and waited for those huge jaws to close around him. He could imagine them tearing into his throat, his soft flesh giving way like water. But instead it was painless, just a weight against his chest and then a spreading wetness. Erich smiled. It was very warm. Blood wrapped him up like a blanket, and he couldn't feel the frigid water running down his back anymore. Erich opened his eyes, and Johanna smiled back at him, her face so close their noses almost touched. She lay on top of the wolf, bloodstained hands clutching the hilt of Erich's dagger where it protruded from between the creature's ribs.

He let the warm flow trickle over his arm, wishing he didn't have to move, but the heavy carcass pressed into his lungs, and he couldn't breathe. Johanna got to her feet as

Erich wormed his way out. She took his hand and yanked him up into a hug. Blood smeared her blouse as they touched, but she didn't seem to care.

"It really is my dagger now," she said as they separated.

Erich grinned back at her, blushing. The rush slowly trickled out of his body and a sharp pain replaced it. His dumb smile twitched into a grimace as he took back the dagger and saw the gashes that ran down his arm.

A twig snapped behind them and Erich jumped, his nerves heightened. The rustling of wind and footsteps intermingled. Orange light filtered through the trees, growing closer.

"Who's there?" Johanna shouted.

"Johanna Engel? Is that you?"

A man stepped out into the clearing. His lantern threw deep shadows across his broad, leather apron. It was Samuel Moritz, the dairy farmer who owned the land they had just crossed through. Erich often visited the Moritzes when his father came to buy spent cows, but lately, Klaus had warned him to stay away. Around Passover, Klaus said, Jews like the Moritzes prowl the night for stray German children whose blood they must bake into bread. Erich had been too nervous to ask when Passover was, but he hoped it wasn't November.

He fingered the dagger at his belt anxiously. A tiny part of him hoped Herr Moritz would prove dangerous and let him repay Johanna for saving his life. But she didn't seem to share any of Erich's reservations. She rushed into the farmer's thick arms with gratitude. Erich approached more slowly. Herr Moritz listened in silence while Johanna explained what had happened. A hint of sadness flickered across his face as he saw the wolf's carcass. Erich tightened his grip on the dagger.

"Doktor Goen isn't far," Herr Moritz said. "I'll take you both."

Suddenly, Erich realized what that would entail—who the doctor would call. As wary as he was of Herr Moritz, he feared Johanna's father even more. There was no telling what he would do if he found out Erich had put her in danger. He blurted out his objections.

"No, it's nothing. We learned how to dress a wound in the *Jungvolk*. I can take care of it on my own."

Herr Moritz frowned. "That doesn't look like nothing. It could get infected."

Erich whipped his injured arm behind his back, and Johanna's face suddenly dropped. She must have arrived at the same realization as Erich.

"We'll wash it in the creek," Johanna said.

"Yes, I can make a bandage with my uniform," Erich added. He tried not to let the pain show on his face. "It's already ruined."

"I'm not letting you out of my sight until someone's seen to that arm," Herr Moritz said.

Johanna stared up at him with pleading eyes, and after a moment, he slumped his shoulders in resignation. "Fine, we'll take care of it at the house. Nobody has to know."

She grinned and wrapped her arm around the farmer's as the two of them started back the way they had come. Erich hesitated, wondering if they were headed into some trap. He imagined himself tied up from the ceiling with a whole clan of Jews standing around him, poking him full of holes with their tiny knives. Blood poured from him like wine from a barrel, and devil-eyed children danced a ritual circle, catching what they could in bowls of flour. Erich shivered as the glow of the farmer's lantern receded into the trees.

"We aren't going," he said, not as loudly as he'd meant to. Neither Johanna nor Herr Moritz were close enough to hear. It was a token objection anyway, and the throbbing in his arm soon had him running after them.

"You're not going to carry Erich?" Johanna grinned.

"If he's well enough the shirk the doctor, he's well enough to walk," Herr Moritz grumbled.

This proved not to be true. At the edge of the woods,

Erich would have collapsed if Johanna hadn't run back and held him up. Herr Moritz shook his head and swooped Erich up into his stocky arms. Erich was too tired to be frightened or embarrassed anymore. As they crested the hill, he leaned his head back and looked up at the night sky. Matted strands of hair covered his eyes like the branches of trees, letting only a few stars flicker through. He was shivering and sweating at the same time, yet despite it all, Erich realized that he was also smiling.

# CHAPTER FOUR

The Moritz home was a flat, sparse affair, free of both clutter and decoration. A handmade table dominated the room, far too large for a family of two. The rest of the Moritzes lived in Cologne now, so only Herr Moritz and his son Arden remained.

Arden scowled at the sight of Erich's *Jungvolk* uniform, but Herr Moritz barked at him and he grudgingly pulled out a chair. Together, they lowered Erich's wounded arm onto the table. He could barely feel it anymore. His own limb surprised him when it came into view, as though it belonged to someone else. Herr Moritz ordered Arden off to fetch bandages, while he pulled jar after jar of unmarked herbs off the shelves. Erich's face burned and sweat dripped off his nose, but Johanna looked cold. She huddled by the fire, shivering.

"My mother taught me this recipe," Herr Moritz said. He planted a tower of stacked jars onto the table. "You won't enjoy it, but you'll thank me in the morning."

He measured out the herbs from memory, crushing them between his fingers and letting the pulverized pieces dribble out into a thick, stone bowl. It looked a bit like one half of the whispering rocks that Erich had shown

41

Johanna. Herr Moritz pulled a jug of milk out from the icebox, poured in a thick splash of it, then ground the mix down with a pestle. A pungent aroma soaked the air, sweet but tinged with a smell like fresh mulch.

Arden returned with a linen bolt and dumped it on the table. It kept rolling and tumbled off, trailing fabric onto the floor. Herr Moritz calmly bent down to pick it up. He tore off a few strips. Arden's glare bored into the back of Erich's head, but he refused to give the satisfaction of returning it.

"This is going to hurt," Herr Moritz said.

"A lot," Arden added. He laughed and clapped a hand across Erich's left shoulder. Pain stabbed through his arm, but he kept silent. Even so, tears leaked from his eyes.

Johanna floated over from the fire and slid into the seat next to Erich. She took his right hand in hers and the pain dulled a little.

"I'm not afraid," Erich said through gritted teeth.

"Liar," Johanna teased. She brushed a tear off his cheek and stuck out her tongue.

Herr Moritz slowly pulled back the tatters of Erich's uniform. His hands were surprisingly gentle, but the clinging rags still stung as he peeled them away. Erich's stomach churned when the last piece tore off, carrying a tendril of flesh with it. He shut his eyes, but he could still see that unsettling edge where his own ragged skin curled up into a lip.

With his fingers, Herr Moritz scooped out a clump of the earthen mixture and held it in the air. Erich clenched his teeth and promised himself he wouldn't shout or cry. Herr Moritz's hand dropped, gently pressing the strange paste into the cut. Erich cringed, anticipating the pain, but he felt nothing. He grinned. *Easy.*

"Now we wait," Herr Moritz said.

Erich stared at his arm, wondering what the medicine was doing to him. In his mind, injured flesh chewed on the green paste like cud, then spat out something fresh and healed. A second skin. Herr Moritz looked Erich in the eye and hesitated, as though trying to decide whether or not to speak.

"I was just thinking about your mother," he finally said. Arden rolled his eyes, but Herr Moritz ignored him. "Brighter than the sun, that woman. Not that you could see her through the crowd of suitors."

Johanna planted her elbows on the table and leaned in eagerly.

"And you were at the head of the pack?" she teased.

"I never stood a chance," Herr Moritz said, ruffling Johanna's hair. "A young policeman had that honor. At least until Selda ran off and married someone else."

Johanna grabbed Erich's shoulder.

His eyes opened wide. "You mean Herr Engel and my m—"

Erich's voice cracked as a shiver shot through him. Whatever the medicine was doing, it was doing it now. A thousand tickling fingers danced across his skin. Then suddenly, jarringly: fire. He could almost hear the flesh sizzle like a hot poker had been quenched in his veins. Erich forgot everything and screamed his lungs raw. He howled and cried, twisting in Herr Moritz's grip, desperate to get away. He wanted to run to the icebox and seal his arm away until the blood froze, but iron hands held him down.

When at last the lava on his skin cooled to a simmer, he blinked away tears to see two rows of stitches patterning his forearm.

"What was that?" Erich choked out.

"My mother's recipe," Herr Moritz said.

Erich smiled weakly. He realized how hard he was gripping Johanna's hand and dropped it, blushing. Arden's nasal laugh filled the room, then cut off in an instant. Herr Moritz whipped his head around at a sound that Erich hadn't even heard. He nodded towards the window, and Arden scurried over, carefully lifting up one corner of the curtain to peer outside. Erich could hear it now. The crunch of tires. An engine's low murmur.

Arden ducked down with a start. "It's her father," he hissed.

Johanna's eyes widened. There would be no explaining this to him. Erich's wound. Her soiled clothes. Simply that they were together, here of all places, would infuriate him. She dashed for the door, but Herr Moritz was quicker. He grabbed her by the shoulders and planted a finger across her lips. Already, headlights trickled through the crack below the door.

"Quickly, here," Herr Moritz said. He swept them into a cramped closet and pushed them back between aprons and winter coats. Arden scrambled around the room, cramming bandages and medicine anywhere he could hide them. He tossed a tan cloth over the table to cover the smear of Erich's blood that still stained it.

"You mustn't make a sound," Herr Moritz said, gently shutting them in. His brown eyes brimmed with fear and his hand shook while he latched the slatted doors.

Johanna held a hand over her mouth to silence her breathing. Erich followed suit. His nose pressed against her auburn hair as he peered through the cracks. Outside, Herr Moritz and Arden slowly took their seats at the table. They tried to look natural, like a family settling down for an evening coffee, but it wasn't working.

Anticipation clouded the air. Neither Moritz attempted conversation. Outside, the engine snarled to a stop. Boots crunched against rough ground. The four of them held their breath, waiting for a knock, but they all still jumped when the thumping rocked the door, impossibly loud. Herr Moritz paused at the threshold, his hand poised over the knob, as though deciding whether or not to open it. He made up his mind, pulled back the door, and Johanna's father pushed into the room in a rush of long legs and sweeping coattails.

A thick mustache squatted under Herr Engel's curled

nose, and a cap hid his bald head. Another man—Heinz Volker, his second in command—tailed behind, two heads shorter and built like an ox.

"Heil Hitler," Herr Engel said with an echo from his lieutenant. "This is an inspection. Up against the wall. Now."

Was he there for them, Erich wondered, or did he not know? Arden sprung out of his seat and stood at attention by his father, while Herr Engel strode over to the table. He twisted up his lip in disgust. Wincing, Erich followed his eyes to a spot on the tablecloth where blood had seeped through. Herr Engel threw back the cloth and let it billow to the floor. He scowled at the stain.

"Is it customary for the Jew to slaughter his pigs on the same table that he eats them?" Herr Engel asked.

Volker moved in close to the two Moritzes, daring them to step back.

"No, sir," Herr Moritz replied. "We don't eat pork."

Engel slid his finger down the table, then raised it to his nose. He recoiled from the scent.

"Filthy!" he shouted. "You sell milk from this rat hole to your neighbors?" Herr Engel pushed Volker aside and ran a bloody finger down Herr Moritz's cheek. "You sell this to my wife?" He gripped Arden by the chin. "To my daughter? Show me. Where do you keep your stock?"

Herr Engel took a step towards the closet where Erich and Johanna huddled. She squeaked softly as her father reached for the knob.

"Over here. In the icebox," Herr Moritz said, remarkably calm. "Messerich has drank our milk for two generations. I doubt you'll find anything amiss."

Herr Engel snapped his hand back with an amused snort. He threw open the icebox door, yanked out a jug, and slammed it down on the table. Unlatching the top, he sniffed the milk gingerly, then proffered it to his lieutenant.

"What do you smell, Volker?" he asked.

"Milk, sir," came the reply.

"Rat's milk!" Herr Engel corrected, planting his own nose on the lip of the bottle. He breathed in deep, then burst into a coughing fit like he had just sucked in too much from a cigarette. He hurled the jug across the room. It shattered just above the closet where Erich and Johanna hid. A spray of milk misted their faces through the slats.

Engel grabbed a second bottle while his lieutenant thrust Herr Moritz against the wall, pressing a thick elbow into his neck. Arden moved to help, but his father shook his head. The boy backed away slowly, his mouth twitching in anger.

Engel advanced, expressionless. He held one hand under Arden's chin and pushed the jug up to his nose.

"Can you smell it, little rat?"

Arden shook his head. His whole body quivered— whether out of fury or fear, Erich couldn't tell.

Engel turned to Volker. "He can't smell it. He's lived in this filthy burrow so long he's mistaken it for a home."

He rammed two fingers against Arden's nostrils, pinning them up into a snout.

"Do you know why the Jew has such a large and twisted nose?" he asked.

"Because they can smell gold?" Volker said, erupting in a spray of spit and laughter.

"Because otherwise they couldn't smell anything at all past their own stench!"

Herr Engel upturned the jug over Arden's head. Milk rivered through the boy's hair and sputtered over his lip.

"Do you smell it now?" he shrieked. "Can you smell it?"

Tossing the bottle aside, he pulled Arden's sopping head back by the hair and drew his truncheon. Herr Moritz begged him to stop, but Volker clamped a rough hand across the farmer's mouth.

The baton whipped down. It cracked against Arden's jaw, and he fell to his knees, skidding on the wet floor.

Blood and milk drooled from his mouth. Johanna buried her eyes in one of the hanging coats, but Erich couldn't look away. It was that smell again. The same coppery tinge as in clinic. It saturated the air in an instant. Each breath Erich took in was strangely intoxicating. Why did it suddenly affect him like this?

Slumped against the back of the closet, he lost count of the blows and shouts. Even with his eyes shut, he could feel everything that happened outside. A crack. A burst of scent. Every ruptured capillary added its own taste to the air. Erich's lungs drank in too much. His stomach churned and a rotten metallic taste burst up from the back of throat. He tumbled forward, clutching his mouth to hold it in. Johanna caught him before he could crash through the closet doors. She pushed him down against the back wall.

"Quiet," she whispered. Pale green eyes stared straight into his.

Erich relaxed. His arms slumped against the hanging coats. He listened. Boots shuffled across the floor. The engine sputtered out a belch. Erich and Johanna watched each other in the dark. Minutes passed, but neither of them dared bring their eyes up to the slats.

Finally, Johanna gave the door a push. The hinge creaked painfully loud. Erich wondered if the whole world had heard it. Herr Moritz sprawled out on the floor, holding his son's head in his lap. His fingers curled through Arden's soiled hair. Erich could barely make out a face amongst the boy's bruises. One arm bent where an arm should not and the other lay limp in a mingling pool of milk and blood.

Johanna tugged on Erich's hand and took one step out of their hiding place. She met Herr Moritz's anguished eyes and opened her mouth to say something, but only a tremble of air came out.

"Just go," he mumbled.

Johanna shook her head.

"GO!"

He turned away from them, rocking Arden in his arms. Tears glistened on Johanna's cheeks, but she still didn't move.

Erich wrapped his good arm around her shoulder and pulled her outside. They fell to their knees and gulped in breath after breath of freezing air. Not sure what could be said, they kept their silence. There was something comforting about the darkness. Out here, it didn't matter whether their eyes were opened or closed. Smoke curled on the horizon. Far away, the night rang with shouts and the shrieking of glass, but here they clung to one another and heard nothing.

# CHAPTER FIVE

A hand shook Erich awake. It smelled of blood. He kneaded blurry eyes with his palms, and by the time they cleared, his father was gone. Erich sat up and bunched the covers under his chin. Memories of the night before crept over him like a chill.

He had parted ways with Johanna at the edge of town and walked home through changed streets. On his corner, glass and moldering vegetables splayed across the cobblestones. The grocer's ruptured storefront gaped like a mouth, baring crystal teeth. *Jude*, Erich read in a dozen places. It stretched across the awning and clung to lingering blades of glass. Crude sketches blocked out the labels on ransacked crates.

Erich picked his way through the debris as quickly as he could. His father's store was untouched, but across the street what was left of the Weissblum's watch shop glowered at him. He tried not to look at it as he crept up the back steps to their apartment and into his room. Just before he fell asleep, Erich promised himself everything would make sense in the morning. Now light filtered through the curtains, but it was all just as confusing.

Erich peeled the bandages off his arm and wiped away

the pale ooze that still clung to his stitches. The wound didn't look so bad in the morning light. The blood was long gone, and his skin was already closing around the neat threads. There might not even be a scar. A little disappointed, Erich threw off the blankets and slipped into a fresh uniform. He crept down the hall, following the smell of coffee from the kitchen.

Aunt Mila hovered over the stove, smiling when she saw him. Erich sat down and perked up his head like a dog waiting for scraps. Aunt Mila rolled her eyes and pushed a plate across the tabletop, then slid into the chair next to him.

"What happened last night?" Erich asked.

"Men happened," she sighed. "They live for excuses to break things."

"Which men?"

"All of them, *kleine*."

She flattened his morning hair with her fingers.

"Was father there?" Erich asked.

Aunt Mila tipped a splash of milk into her coffee and waited for it to swirl to the bottom before she answered.

"I didn't see. Eat."

Erich scraped some cheese over his bread and didn't press any further. Something hung in the air, thicker than grease. When he finished, Aunt Mila pulled him into a hug and sent him out the door.

**\*\*\***

At school, Herr Baumeister paced back and forth at the front of the class. His heels squeaked against the floorboards each time he turned around.

"I've warned you before about the terrible desire that the Jew carries in his blood. He fights this temptation hour by hour, year by year, but blood always wins out in the end.

"You must have heard how two days ago a seventeen-year-old boy surrendered to that murderous compulsion. It was so strong that it dragged him through the door of the German embassy in Paris and bade him to shoot one of our own, Counsel Ernst vom Rath. Yesterday, despite the efforts of the *Führer's* own doctor, the Counsel succumbed to his wounds."

Herr Baumeister chalked the names large across the blackboard. Vom Rath on one side and Hermann Grünspan on the other. One by one, he called the boys up to the front and yelled out a word for them to write. *Patriot,* Gottlob dutifully scratched under vom Rath's name. *Jew,* Max wrote below Grünspan's.

"Bolshevik!" Baumeister shouted on Erich's turn. Erich added it to Grünspan's column.

August stepped up to the board next. *Homosexual,* he wrote for vom Rath, but the moment he set down the chalk, Herr Baumeister's rod whipped across the back of his neck. He yelped and transferred the word to the Jew's side, erasing the mistake with his sleeve.

*Assassin. Coward. Conspirator. Murderer.* Grünspan's list snaked around the edges of the blackboard, gobbling up all available space.

"Do you know what makes a forest grow?" Herr Baumeister asked.

"Seeds?" one boy answered.

"Rainwater?" said another.

"Fire," Herr Baumeister corrected. "Fire cleanses. It clears the ground of useless growth until only the strongest trees remain.

"Last night, I watched our forest grow. I saw the start of a new Germany." He looked Erich straight in the eye. "Since the beginning of time the Jews have tried to stifle us. But for nothing! Adolf Hitler has burned away the traitors and criminals like weeds in the underbrush. And all this he has done for *you.*"

He jabbed a finger at Gottlob, who shot up straight in his seat.

Herr Baumeister spoke for two hours, then they stopped for lunch. The boys filtered outside in eager clumps, but Erich drifted away from the others and climbed onto a mossy rock in the yard. It was his favorite spot. He frowned at the smashed out jeweler's across the street. Herr Baumeister would probably prove right in the end, but for now Erich switched to the other side of the rock so he didn't have to look at it.

Gottlob sat on an empty bench across the yard, crammed into the corner as though he expected six or seven others to squeeze in next to him. He peeled the lid off his lunch pail and squeaked as a rush of water dumped out from it onto his lap. His lip quivering, Gottlob pulled a soggy roll of bread out of the pail. It fell to mush in his hands and slopped to the ground. Even hobbled with a broken leg, Max had found his revenge.

After lunch, Herr Baumeister turned to less exciting subjects. Erich fidgeted with his pen, struggling to follow the arithmetic that scurried across the blackboard.

A German worker puts away 5 marks per week towards a Volkswagen that costs 990 marks. How long will it take him to own it? *3 years 10 months*. It costs 2 million marks to build an asylum for lunatics and the retarded. How many Volkswagens could be purchased for the same amount? *2,020*. The Treaty of Versailles demands Germany pay 132 billion marks in reparations; a German worker earns 40 marks per week. How long would it take him to pay the total cost? *63 million years*.

The problems blurred into each other until Erich lost track of the numbers and his eyes drifted to the window. Outside, a girl crossed the grass and took a seat on Erich's rock. It was Johanna. She stared straight at him, unblinking and unashamed. Erich blushed and tried to focus back on Herr Baumeister's problem. The average German woman has 3 children—Erich snuck a furtive glance in Johanna's direction—if an Aryan woman marries a Jew, how many mixed-blooded children will there be after 5 generations? She still hadn't dropped her eyes—243. He counted down the minutes.

When the day was almost over, the door snapped open, interrupting Herr Baumeister mid-calculation. A man stepped into the classroom. He leaned against a polished black cane, though he barely looked over forty. An *SS-Scharführer's* insignia adorned his upturned collar and a dappled, gray dachshund scurried behind him. Herr Baumeister's upper lip twinged when its paws crossed the threshold.

"My apologies, students," the *Scharführer* said. "Your class will be cut short today."

The little dog licked at the hem of Herr Baumeister's trousers. He stiffened, but the *Scharführer* whispered something in his ear and he dismissed the class with a curt wave.

Erich was the first out of his seat. He glanced at Johanna out the window, then bounced a few eager steps towards the door, but Herr Baumeister pointed a finger right at him.

"Not you, Fiehler."

Erich twisted to a stop. He crept back to the bench, his face burning. Too nervous to laugh, the other boys exchanged cautious glances. After a moment, they reached a collective decision and all twenty of his classmates rushed out of the room in unison.

Feet stampeded through the hall and out onto the grass. Erich watched wistfully through the window as boy after boy passed Johanna's perch. Quiet settled over the room, and the stranger flashed Erich's teacher an expectant look. He bristled with indignation, then huffed out the door, muttering something under his breath.

The *Scharführer* brushed away a stack of papers and sat down on top of Herr Baumeister's desk. He swept his little dog up onto his lap and beckoned Erich to the front with a curl of his finger.

"I'm Doktor Ernst Kammer," he said. Erich shook his hand cautiously. He had a soft grip and tender skin. He was not from Messerich.

"And this is Mateusz," Kammer said, pointing to the dachshund in his lap.

"Erich Fiehler, sir."

"Yes," he said, his piercing eyes narrowing. A drop of sweat fell down Erich's back. Kammer erupted into a high-pitched laugh.

"You look terrified," he grinned. "I'm here with good news, boy."

Kammer jammed a finger into Erich's chest.

"There's something special about you and the *Führer* can see right through to it."

"All we need is a few answers to make sure you're the one. How's that sound?" he asked, still beaming.

"Yes, *Scharführer* Kammer. Or- I mean good. It sounds good."

"Excellent. And, please, it's Doktor to you," he said. He clapped his hands together so loud that Mateusz jumped out of his lap and scuttered across the desk, kicking up loose papers with his paws. Hesitantly, Erich met Kammer's gleaming eyes.

"Let's talk about your family."

He pulled out a notepad and hovered his pen over the page like a sprinter on the starting block.

"I want to know absolutely everything. You can start with your father."

They proceeded through Erich's ancestry in meticulous detail. His birth, his mother's death, the family butcher shop, his uncle and older brother in the city. The *Scharführer* hung onto every word. If Erich paused even for a moment, he would pounce in with a barrage of new questions.

"Is there anyone in your life who lacks conviction to the party?" Kammer asked.

Erich thought of Aunt Mila's distant mood at breakfast, Johanna's prancing goosestep, her swastika swim trunks.

"No," he replied. "Nobody."

"You're a better party man than I," Kammer chuckled, but for once he didn't probe any further. "What do you want to do when you're older?"

Erich thought about it for two seconds, then surprising himself, blurted out, "I'm going to be a doctor."

"Good. We need those. More than soldiers, I'd wager."

Kammer grabbed his cane and pulled himself up from the desk.

"Let me have a look at you," he said.

Erich craned himself up as tall as he could stand without his heels leaving the ground. Kammer circled around him, taking down angles and measurements with a folding ruler. The curve of his nose. The slant of his shoulders. The distance between his eyes.

"Look at the floor," he said.

Kammer pushed Erich's head down until his chin touched his chest, then kneaded his thumb against the back of Erich's neck, feeling for something. Whatever he found seemed to satisfy him and he put away the notepad.

Erich reached around to the spot Kammer had touched. A mound of rough skin bubbled up on his neck like a callous. When he held his finger to it, it pulsed with his heartbeat.

"Don't touch that," Kammer said. "It's just a birthmark."

Erich shivered. He didn't think it had been there before he'd went to the clinic, but how could he know for certain? It was probably only a mole or a pimple. Still, his imagination kept conjuring up horrifying new possibilities. Was something incubating there? A third arm? An eye? A massive insect that would one day shuck him like a chrysalis?

"You see a lot of blood at your father's shop, I

suppose," Kammer said.

Erich nodded.

"That's a messy business. No good for a boy like you. You'll stay away from all that."

"Yes, sir," Erich agreed, knowing it would be impossible.

"Just let everyone think you're squeamish," Kammer grinned.

Erich hung his head. "I'm pretty sure they already do. What's all this about, sir? Are we going to war?"

"Probably," Kammer laughed. "But war isn't for children. War is for furious things. Men and guns and bombs. You children are for after. For the future. The *Endsieg*. The *Führer* is considering you for something very special. Your blood results were extraordinary."

"But that was only yesterday," Erich interrupted.

"Yes," Kammer said. "It's not a sure thing. Not at all. Germany has a lot of boys like you. But if you are selected, I'll see you here again in one year's time. If not, this will be goodbye. In the meantime, I recommend you assume nothing. Work on your grades. You won't be much of a doctor if you end up in trade school. You'll need to get into a good Gymnasium. Entrance exams are coming up in August."

"I don't think we can afford it," Erich mumbled.

"It's already paid for. Look for me next year."

He tucked Mateusz under the crook of his arm, patted Erich on the shoulder, and disappeared out the door. In stunned silence, Erich stared at the scattered papers that littered the floor, the only evidence that the *Scharführer* had been there at all. He wandered outside, squinting into the sun, too dazed to really think about what had happened. He half expected Johanna to still be there, poised and silent on his rock, but she was gone.

# CHAPTER SIX

The day before, Erich had raced down the road out of town as fast as his legs could carry him. Now, he took it in tiny steps as though his ankles were chained together. He wanted to run home and tell Aunt Mila everything Doktor Kammer had said, but he needed to see the Moritz farm first. They weren't like other Jews. They didn't deserve what had happened to them.

He wondered what would be left of the house. Rubble and scorched grass? Or would the hill be empty, as though the Moritzes had never existed? This he feared more than anything. Not that something terrible had happened, but that it might already have been forgotten.

Dread snarled Erich's stomach into knots. The trees were thinning on the side of the road. Another moment and he would see it. His feet couldn't move any slower. He closed his eyes and counted the steps. At ten, he opened them. The house looked exactly the same. An off-center chimney still stuck out on the flat roof. The same plain windows flanked the open door, drapes pulled closed. Erich stopped at the foot of the hill, unable to cross some invisible line.

A curtain pulled back and Johanna's face pushed

through the window. She wormed half her body out so that her waist rested on the frame.

"Are you coming in or not?" she shouted.

Erich glanced over his shoulder, then broke across the line and scurried inside. The house was empty, but he still scanned the corners as though the Moritzes might be hiding in them.

"I needed to see it too," Johanna said. "They're gone."

"Where?"

"Not here. Cologne maybe." She cleared her throat and spat out a crass glob that lodged itself in a crack between the floorboards. "My father's a pig."

Erich stepped back in surprise. "You heard what that Grünspan boy did. Maybe it's a go—"

Johanna shot him an icy glare and the words caught in his throat. He looked away.

"Wherever they went, I hope things are better for them there," she said.

Johanna dropped down crosslegged on the floor, ignoring the half-dozen empty chairs.

"Me too," Erich said, joining her. "That's all I meant."

He stared at his ankles in silence. One at a time, he flattened the creases on his trousers. Every time he smoothed one out, another would ripple up to replace it.

"I'm leaving tomorrow," Johanna said. "He's sending me to ballet school in Frankfurt."

"Your father?" Erich asked.

"Who else?" Johanna said. She bit her lip. "If I write you a letter, will you send me one back?"

"Every time," he agreed.

"Then I want to show you something." She dug a crumpled paper out of her pocket and flattened it against the floor. With a pen, she divided the page into quadrants. A capital A went in the first corner, then she struck a vertical line down its center. "This means add one letter. A becomes B. B is C."

She filled in the other sections, explaining the meaning

of each mark.

"We'll be the only ones who can read it," Erich said.

"Exactly."

Johanna's eyes widened. She jammed the paper into Erich's front pocket, her gaze fixed on something over his shoulder. Erich whipped his head around and sprung to his feet. Herr Engel loomed in the doorway, his shadow stretching out to meet them. Stilt-like legs swept across the threshold.

"Fiehler, isn't it? I'm not surprised to find the likes of you here, but what in the blazes are you doing with my daughter?"

Erich tried and failed to croak out a response. Johanna leapt up and pushed ahead of him. She held her arms out like a shield.

"Papa—"

"Don't interrupt," he snapped.

Herr Engel shoved Johanna out of the way. She fell back against the wall, her defiant eyes quenched in an instant.

"The Fiehler boy and I were having a con-ver-sation."

Herr Engel grabbed Erich by the shoulders. Bony fingers dug in painfully.

"I knew your mother, you know." He leaned in close, eyes wide and unblinking. "Remind me, boy. What happened to her?"

"She died," Erich whispered.

Engel's grip tightened until Erich thought the stitches on his arm would burst.

"When I was born," he yelped. "She died when I was born."

Something cracked against Erich's skull. His vision flickered black.

"Ingrate, she died *because* you were born." Herr Engel shoved down on Erich's shoulders until his knees gave out. "I've seen firsthand what your brutish family can do to a gentle girl. If I find you with my daughter again, it will

CAMERON LORIS

be the end of you."

He snatched Johanna by the arm and dragged her out the door. She didn't make a sound.

Erich no longer bothered to withhold tears. He clung to his shoulders while the aching impressions left by Engel's claws faded. When his cheeks were dry, he pulled Johanna's paper out of his pocket and held it in a crumpled ball, afraid a sudden wind might gust through and carry the page away.

Erich counted the stitches on his arm until his heart stopped racing. In the corner of the room, a milky outline stained the floorboards. The house had a scar of the night before. Just like Erich. He sat down where the puddle had been, flattened the page against the floor, and began to practice Johanna's code.

# CHAPTER SEVEN

Johanna's letters arrived every Tuesday at the tailor's shop where Aunt Mila worked. Each came addressed to a different name, crass puns that Erich could never manage not to smile at. He would wait by the door for Aunt Mila to come home, then stay up the rest of the night writing. Their cipher gave him trouble at first, but he reread her letters so many times that soon he didn't even notice they were in code.

In their correspondences, Erich obsessed over his interview with the *Scharführer*, while Johanna seemed more fascinated by his sudden admission that he wanted to be a doctor. She constantly pushed him on it, encouraging and taunting in equal measure. All her letters began with "Dear Doktor", which she probably meant as a joke. But when Erich felt most desperate and the piles of notes threatened to smother him, he would take out one of her letters and repeat the salutation to himself again and again.

Johanna's other fixation was how much time Erich spent with the *Jungvolk*, which she endlessly disapproved of. Though he tried not to talk about it, she always seemed to know what he was up to. Erich suspected she had a correspondence going with Aunt Mila, the only person who thought less of the Hitler Youth than Johanna. But as much as they tried, neither of them could do anything to deter him from participating, no matter how little time it left for his studies. It was too important. The *Führer* needed Erich in a way neither girls nor adults could ever understand.

Klaus pushed his charges hard, but even as Erich froze and sweated under the young *Fähnleinführer's* command, there was nowhere else he would rather be. Everything they did made him palpably stronger. After the lake south of town froze over, Klaus would send them crawling on their bellies from one shore to the other until their uniforms were soaked with melt. Once their cheeks had turned blue, he would march them around the edge of the lake, every boy shivering in lockstep and belting out anthems.

After one such practice, Klaus pulled Erich aside, which was never a good sign. Erich eyed the *Fähnleinführer's* tool belt, shaking with cold and fright. His mind raced to work out what he had done wrong and how terrible his punishment would be. But instead of reaching for one of his instruments, Klaus flashed a rare smile and pressed a wooden box into Erich's numb hands. The initials E.S. were engraved on its bronze clasp.

"It was my uncle's," Klaus said. "He died in the war. I imagine he didn't need this much in the trenches."

Erich lifted the lid gently and peered inside. A stethoscope nestled against the faded purple lining. The weave around its long cords was unraveling and dozens of scratches marred the brass chestpiece. Erich didn't care. It was battle-scarred. He pulled off one glove and ran his fingers along the freezing tongs.

"Thank you," he whispered.

"I figure you might find a use for it when you're older," Klaus said. He smothered his smile. "But if you lose it, I'll skin you alive and wear your hide for a winter coat."

Erich nodded, not really listening. He wanted to jam

the prongs into his ears right away, but he was afraid to do anything disrespectful in front of Klaus.

"I'll take good care of it. It might even see a second war," he said.

Klaus laughed. "If there's going to be a war, we'll win long before you're ready to use that."

\*\*\*

After practice, Erich nestled into a nook in the trunk of an old tree where he could croon over his prize without interference from the other boys. Everyone else had hurried off towards shelter and warmth in town, but a glow of excitement shielded Erich from the chill.

Before he could settle in between the roots, someone called Erich's name from behind him. He jumped up in surprise and whipped the box around his back. A second later, he recognized the speaker and slumped down with relief. Johanna danced around the tree trunk, laughter steaming off her in clouds.

"You said you were staying in Frankfurt for Christmas," Erich said, feigning indignance.

Johanna shrugged.

"I saw you out there on the lake," she said. "You're all pretty good at crawling on your knees. I'm sure your father's very proud."

She stuck a finger-cum-mustache under her nose to make clear just which father she was referring to and then plopped down beside Erich.

"You shouldn't talk like that," Erich snapped. "It's not right. You could get in trouble."

Johanna ignored him.

"What's that?" she asked, reaching for the box. Erich yanked it away.

She rolled her eyes. "They're not going to send an

eleven-year-old girl to the *KZ*. Come on, what's in the box?"

Erich sighed, but he pulled the lid back anyway, too excited about his prize to be upset with her for long. Johanna's eyes gleamed and she whistled in amazement.

"Where'd you get that?"

"Klaus gave it to me."

"Klaus?" she snorted. "I thought he hated you."

"It's not like that. He just always expects better from us. The only thing he wants is to make the *Führer* proud."

"How can someone who doesn't even know you be proud?" Johanna asked.

Erich fingered his stethoscope, considering it.

"I know him," he said. "That's all that matters to me."

"Fine," she sighed. A grin slowly spread across her face. "Doktor Fiehler!"

Giggling madly, she scooped up a clump of snow and dropped it onto Erich's head. He shook his hair like a wet dog, spraying icy chunks in every direction.

"Laugh all you want," he said, then popped the prongs of the stethoscope into his ears. "I'm never taking these off."

They sat together in giddy silence until Johanna whipped a crisp ten mark note from her pocket and waved it in his face.

"Do you want to go see a movie?"

"Where did you get that?" Erich gasped.

"Selling cigarettes at school."

"You're lying," he said. "Your father gave it to you for Christmas."

"Christmas isn't for another week, idiot." Johanna smacked the back of his head. "So, do you want to go?"

"Okay!" Erich rocketed to his feet. Then he realized how eager he sounded and added, "I mean, at least it'll be warm there."

They trudged off, stopping only to peg each other with snowballs, but Erich's heart wasn't in it. There was something off-putting about what she had said. It gnawed at him whenever they fell silent. Johanna had always had a dissident streak, but in their coded letters it felt more like a game. Now this long-distance rebel had come home, and he wondered if she knew what she was getting herself into. She didn't mean the things she said, but the wrong word to the wrong person could go very badly for her. He promised himself they would have another talk later.

After they crossed back into town, Erich kept glancing over his shoulder for any sign of Herr Engel, but they didn't have far to walk. *Der Atlas* was the only theater in fifty kilometers and a point of pride for most of Messerich. No matter how many times he stepped under them, the sunburst marquee and frescoed map always made Erich brim with anticipation for the film.

Gottlob stood alone outside the theater, hands punched deep into his pockets. He stamped his feet in the cold and stared longingly up at the marquee. In towering typeface it read: OLYMPIA.

"Are you coming in?" Johanna asked Gottlob as they passed.

He looked down, blushing. Erich didn't need to wait for an answer.

"Max took his money," he said.

Gottlob nodded glumly.

"That prick," Johanna spat. Gottlob gaped at her.

"You can come with us," she said, dancing circles around the lanky boy. "Come on!"

She grabbed Gottlob's hand, yanked him over to the box office, and slapped her money down on the counter. With a yawn, the attendant doled out three tickets.

Johanna picked seats for them in the front row, insisting that she sit in the middle between the two boys. Erich was relieved not to be next to Gottlob, but Johanna didn't seem at all bothered by his greasy skin or odd pallor. She chatted idly with him before the movie started, asking about his family and telling him her plans for the holiday.

When she joked about Klaus' misfitting tool belt, Gottlob cackled and broke into a grin. Erich realized that he had never seen him smile before.

The lights dimmed and Johanna shushed Gottlob mid-sentence. Blaring trumpets welled up around them as the camera slid past ancient columns and lingered on marble faces. Johanna sniggered at the naked discus-thrower and shook Erich in excitement when they took off from the ground to see the continent from the sky. It stretched out ahead of them, the names of countries flashing bright across the screen.

*Bulgarien. Sofia.*
*Jugoslavien. Belgrad.*
*Ungarn. Budapest.*
*Österreich. Wien.*
*Tschechoslowakei. Prag.*

The audience held their breath until finally *Deutschland* soared in. They answered with furious applause. The camera burrowed down through the clouds to see the land stretch out below. It looked exactly as it had been in Erich's blood hazed dream, but where before the fatherland's veins and arteries had flowed aimless and random, now a great stadium marked their focal point, reverberating with the roars of the crowd.

Ten-thousand outstretched arms saluted the *Führer* as he declared the Olympic games begun. An awed silence fell across the theater. Every mouth in the audience was fixed agape at the slow-motion feats. Erich swelled as each anthem played, though none rang more proudly than Germany's.

Midway through, Johanna reached over and took the stethoscope's horn that dangled from Erich's neck. She pressed it against her chest until he could hear her heart beat time with the music. Erich held one finger against the strange bump on the back of his neck and let his own heart echo hers. His eyes unfocused and the hurling bodies on the screen blurred into one.

They stayed in their seats long after the music ended and the lights came on. No one could let go. For a brief moment, they had been somewhere else, somewhere warmer in both weather and spirit. Erich remembered that he was supposed to confront Johanna, but it didn't seem so important anymore. He was full up with pride, and she beamed right back at him. Whether that was patriotism or simple joy didn't seem important anymore.

Even Gottlob looked happy. An impish twinkle lit up his eyes as he whispered something in Johanna's ear. Erich had a hunch this was the story of his ribboned crash landing on her bicycle, and he glowered while she bellowed with raucous laughter.

**\*\*\***

He didn't see Johanna much after that. Erich started to wonder if Herr Engel had locked her up in a cage for the rest of the holidays. His own father spent all day and night in the shop under the pressure of the seasonal rush, and his older brother announced in a terse letter that he would be staying in Cologne. This left Erich and Aunt Mila to themselves, but he didn't mind.

Erich loved the nights they spent huddled around the stove while the radio crackled with music and grand speeches. He would hold his breath when the familiar fanfare signaled the beginning of a news broadcast. *Is it time? Has the war begun?* The answer came back the same every night. Aunt Mila would loosen her grip on his hand and nod gratefully while Erich sighed with disappointment. Not today.

He didn't even realize Johanna had gone back to school until she sent her first letter, but they soon returned to a rhythm of coded gossip. It hurt Erich how often she wrote that she dreaded coming home, but he knew it was probably just her father she was avoiding.

Every week Johanna cooked up a new harebrained plan for escape. If she set the headmistress's bed on fire, would they ship her off to an asylum? What if she made a rope out of leotards, climbed out her window, and ran away to join a convent? Erich did his best to talk her out of these ideas—Johanna would make a terrible nun—but she kept sending them anyway.

Shortly after Easter, her letters changed. Dozens of overlapping ink stamps now covered their envelopes. Her address switched every two weeks. Erich could never predict where she would go next, and he was certain that some of his responses were slipping through the cracks. She told him that all her mail was being read, and they couldn't write in code anymore. Sometimes a word or even a whole sentence would be blacked out.

Without the freedom of secrecy, a stiff formality suffocated her wry humor. Though they had usually made him uncomfortable, Erich missed her stupid jokes more than he would have expected. Before the change, he had never left the house without her latest letter in his pocket. Now, he stashed them under his bed and never read them again.

From what pieces he could put together, one of Johanna's schemes had finally come to fruition. She had maneuvered herself into some special assignment in the BDM, the League of German Girls, which she had never expressed any interest in before. She was at a school, she said, working not studying. The censor blotted out any mention of where it was located, but a bit of her old gleefulness seeped through when she told him about her father's many failed attempts to bring her back. *When I was in Messerich,* she wrote, *all he wanted was to send me away to Frankfurt. Now that I'm at* ███████ *, he wants me in Messerich. He doesn't care where I am so long as he's the one who controls it.*

But letter by letter, Johanna leaked out of the page.

Soon even these rare flickers of personality were gone. She no longer addressed him with "Dear Doktor", even once he hintingly started to sign his own letters with that moniker. Erich wondered if she even received them anymore.

As he skimmed her latest work, bored eyes glazing over, Erich noticed something. The e at the beginning of an *einen* was crossed out like a mistake. He took in a sharp breath. A diagonal slash. Two letters forward. E becomes G. He crawled under his bed and scrambled together her last few notes. Fanning them out across the floor, he scanned each for a coded letter. He marked them on a fresh page: *Rouhhenberg*.

The word meant nothing to him. It didn't even seem like German. Perhaps it was a place, but no one he asked recognized it and no matter how many maps he scoured, he found no mention of it. Still, the strange word gnawed at him for days. His dreams brimmed with endlessly rearranging letters. Always the strange word hovered at the edge of meaning, dancing on the tip of his tongue.

The entrance exams for Gymnasium came and went. Erich had no idea if had passed or failed. For all he could remember, he might have just written Rouhhenberg as the answer to every question.

It took three weeks for Johanna's next letter to finally arrive. Erich snatched it out of Aunt Mila's hand before she could even shut the door. He dashed upstairs and hungrily scanned it for cross marks, but there were none. Johanna had changed again. Her handwriting looked different, and this time she called him Doktor Fiehler. A second later, Erich squeaked in surprise as the actual contents sunk in.

A soft knock on the door interrupted him and Aunt Mila slid into Erich's room. Smiling, she set a second envelope down on his lap, ruffled his hair, and left without a word. Thick and sealed with wax, the new letter came on official stationery from the Leibniz Gymnasium. Judging from its heft, it was an acceptance, but Erich didn't even open it. He brushed it aside. Only Johanna's letter mattered and he read it over and over. There was no code to be deciphered. It said exactly what it meant.

She was coming home.

# CHAPTER EIGHT

Erich hovered outside his new Gymnasium, circling the statue of Leibniz in the courtyard until his head spun. The rest of his classmates were already inside. They had probably arrived a half hour ago. After working so hard to get in, who would want to be late on the first day? Yet Erich hung back.

He had sent off one final letter to Johanna and asked her to meet him here. She never replied, but he waited anyway. He was beyond late and he knew the longer he stayed outside, the worse his punishment would be. One more minute and they might send him back to Herr Baumeister at the *Volksschule*. But what if one more minute was all Johanna needed? Every time he started up the steps, his feet changed course before they reached the top.

"Doktor Fiehler," a voice called out.

Erich whipped around. Surprise became excitement, then curdled into terror when he saw who it was.

"I should have known her little pen pal would be you," Herr Engel snarled.

Erich cringed. The change in handwriting. Johanna returning home without complaint. Herr Engel wasn't the only one who should have known. Erich bolted for the schoolhouse steps, but Herr Engel's spindly legs got there first. He snatched Erich's collar in both hands and yanked him up until his toes barely touched the ground.

"I- I- I'm late for class," Erich squeaked.

"Not anymore," Herr Engel said. "Imagine my surprise when the postman dropped the first of your insipid love notes at my door."

Engel pressed one of Erich's letters into his face. *Last known address* had been inked across the top. He dragged Erich up the steps by the collar, shouting as they went. "You think you can steal my daughter from me? I'll not be made a fool of again. Not by that dirty butcher and not by his litter!"

They crashed through the double doors and swept down the hall. Erich's feet skidded against the polished floor, but he didn't dare pull away. Outside the headmaster's door, Herr Engel stopped and pulled Erich up so their faces almost touched.

"I didn't do anything, sir," Erich pleaded. "I don't even know where she is!"

"I had a chance to deal with your father once before, but I let him go. Now Selda is dead," Herr Engel said. "I won't make the same mistake again. Your headmaster and I are about to have a talk about your future."

Erich's stomach slid to the floor and a cold panic set in. He'd spent so much time fixated on Johanna and her secrets that he'd let everything else go. Now this school, which had accepted him despite everything, which had been paid for despite everything, was about to be torn away.

Herr Engel let go of Erich's shirt and pushed into the office. Inside, the headmaster jumped up from his desk and pointed angrily at the door. Another man sat across from him. Black coattails dripped over the edge of his seat. The man twisted around to face Herr Engel with a wide-mouthed grin. Window light glinted off the *SS-Scharführer's* insignia on his collar. It was Doktor Kammer. Herr Engel took a stumbling step back.

"Apologies," he stammered.

"No, I was just on my way out," Kammer said. He beamed at Erich. "You brought exactly the one I came to see!"

With a wink, Doktor Kammer dragged himself to his feet, Mateusz the dachshund cradled under one arm and his cane in the other. He pushed past the slack-jawed police chief and gently shut the door behind him. Alone with Erich, Doktor Kammer leaned over and let Mateusz scurry out of his arms.

"I think you've grown," he said. "Go on, let's have a look. Give us a good spin!"

Erich shuffled around in an awkward circle, not quite sure what he was supposed to be showing off. For a moment after he faced forward again, a frown hung on Doktor Kammer's lips.

"Wonderful!" he said and swept Erich into one of the chairs lining the wall. Kammer lowered himself into the seat beside him, wiggling until he was situated.

"Would you like to hear what they're saying in there?" he asked.

Erich nodded hesitantly.

"Me too," Doktor Kammer said, eyes agleam. He held one finger to his lips. "You must be absolutely silent. If we want to hear them, then they must be able to hear us. Do you understand?"

"Yes," Erich lied.

"Good," Kammer whispered. "We'll both be quiet little mice."

He licked his index finger and held it out, curling it through the air as though he were feeling for the direction of the wind. Like a conductor's baton, it arced wider and wider, inciting a silent orchestra to crescendo.

Voices fizzled in and out of Erich's hearing. They crackled like a poorly tuned radio, but amidst the noise Herr Engel's sneering drawl was unmistakable. Erich stifled a shout of amazement as the buzzing bent into a pristine stream of sound. The voices inside the office reached his ears as clearly as Johanna's whispers at the rocks. His lungs burned for lack of air, but he was too afraid to take a breath. Would even that tiny sound ring loud in Herr Engel's ears?

"Quite interesting reading material you have here," Engel said.

Two fingers hissed as they slid over dusty wood. A tired binding cracked open, and pages fluttered like windblown leaves.

"Communist literature?"

"That's Clausewitz," the headmaster huffed.

Engel slammed the book against the table. The whole room hummed in its aftershock.

"It is whatever I say it is," he said through gritted teeth.

A nervous gulp slid down the headmaster's throat.

"Fine," he squeaked. "You don't want the Fiehler boy at my school either? Then he's out."

Erich flashed Kammer a pleading look, but he was too busy conducting to notice.

"Between the two of you, I can't tell if the boy's a disgrace to his country or Adolf Hitler's favorite son, but obviously he's more trouble than he's worth. I've already signed the papers." The headmaster's dry lips pressed together for a long pause, then he rushed out the rest. "Where he goes next will be up to the *Scharführer*, who if I'm not mistaken, is right outside."

After a moment, the door creaked open and Doktor Kammer's conducting hand whipped to his side. He looked up at Herr Engel as though he were his favorite person in the world. Erich started to get up, but Kammer pushed him back down into his chair.

"I can't seem to figure you out, sir," Herr Engel said, pausing between each word. "Should I be thanking you or do we have a problem? Where are you taking the boy?"

"I'm afraid I can't say," Kammer said brightly. "But

rest assured that Erich Fiehler is going to a school far, far better than this one."

"Not on my watch," Herr Engel shouted.

Doktor Kammer rose slowly, ignoring his cane propped against the wall. The air crackled and the hairs on Erich's neck pricked up. Had he always been taller than Engel?

"I am taking the boy," Kammer said, his voice suddenly deep. It rumbled like an oncoming storm. "And the only thing you are going to do is watch."

Engel quivered with rage and his mouth flapped open and closed, but he stepped aside when Doktor Kammer grabbed Erich's hand and pulled him down the hall.

"He's bad blood. He'll bring you nothing but pain," Engel huffed after them as they reached the corner.

Kammer didn't stop until they were on the steps. Erich let go of his hand and bounded down to the statue in the courtyard, but he slowed once he saw how Doktor Kammer clung to the railing.

"I seem to have left my walking stick inside," he smiled weakly. "But I think it would be better if I didn't go back."

Erich held Kammer's arm as they walked towards the street.

"Am I going to learn how to do... whatever that was?" Erich asked, holding up his index finger like a baton.

Kammer laughed. "That took me ten years to master."

Erich's shoulders slumped—*of course it wasn't going to be that easy.*

Kammer lifted Erich's chin up with one finger and looked him in the eye. "When you're ready, you'll learn that and more in an hour."

A black car bumped up onto the sidewalk and stopped harshly in front of them.

"You won't be able to say goodbye," Doktor Kammer said, ushering Erich into the back seat. "Your train is already waiting."

"But, my Aunt—"

"Your family's been informed. You can write home once you're there, though the censors are prickly bastards."

He slammed the door shut. Erich cranked down the window frantically and leaned out to see Kammer waving goodbye as the car slid away.

"Once I'm where?" he called back.

"Rouhhenberg, Erich. You're going to Rouhhenberg!"

# CHAPTER NINE

The driver said nothing as they wove through town, muscling aside pedestrians, cars, and horses alike. Every blast of his horn drowned out one of Erich's questions. *Where are we going? How long will I be gone? Can we please stop so I can say goodbye?* Erich gave up on asking long before they turned off onto the dirt road to the train station. The car rocked with each crack and crevice, but the driver refused to slow down. As they passed into the woods, he careened around a bend and slammed to a stop in the middle of the road. Ahead, a broken-down buggy blocked the path. Erich broke into a wide smile.

Hans Martin, Aunt Mila's boyfriend of several years, crouched by one of the wheels, wrench in hand. The driver squeezed his horn over and over, as if it might somehow speed up the repairs, until finally he gave up, scowled, and cut off the engine.

"Don't move," he said, twisting around in his seat.

He climbed out of the car and spat on the ground. The moment he was gone, a voice hissed from behind, "Erich!"

Erich jumped at the sound. He pushed the rear door open and peered around the back. Aunt Mila crouched next to the wheel with a finger over her lips.

"Did you think you could get away without saying goodbye?" she whispered.

"No," Erich grinned.

She had something behind her back and she pulled it out with a wink. It was the old box with the stethoscope that Klaus had given him.

"There's a few of her letters in the bottom," Aunt Mila said.

"Thank you," Erich mouthed.

He set the box down on the on the back seat. Aunt Mila grabbed his hand as he turned around.

"You have to make one promise before you go," she said, trembling.

"What is it?"

"You've said you want to be a doctor, right?"

Erich nodded.

"Promise you still will be."

"I don't know if I can keep that," he said.

"You must."

Erich nodded. "Then I promise."

Aunt Mila squeezed his hand. She forced a smile and stood up.

"Don't go yet," Erich hissed, but she shook her head, blew him a kiss, and disappeared between the trees.

As soon as she was gone, Herr Martin discovered that there was nothing wrong with his wheels after all. He clattered off towards town in his buggy, calling out his apologies as he passed. The driver chased after him with a flurry of curses before storming back to the car. He slammed the door and stayed silent all the way to the station.

Erich had assumed that Doktor Kammer was exaggerating when he said that the train was already waiting, but when they pulled up, there it sat, rumbling impatiently and coughing up smoke. A sign on the vacant ticket counter read *Closed for Special Departure*, and there was no one on the platform but a portly conductor with a clipboard.

"Fiehler?" he asked as they approached.

"Fiehler," the driver repeated.

The conductor perked up with sudden excitement. "Welcome, welcome! Right this way."

Erich said an unreciprocated goodbye to the driver, then followed the conductor up onto the gangway. He looked back at the road into town and wondered if he would ever see it again. Before Erich could take two steps, the train lurched into motion. The conductor slid open the door to one of the cars and beckoned Erich inside.

"Watch your step," he shouted over the clattering wheels. "Take any bunk you can find. We'll arrive in the morning."

With a salute, he scurried off towards the front of the train. Erich hesitated just inside the door, one muddy boot hovering over the lush red and gold carpet that flooded the hall. With a sigh, he took off his shoes and strung them around his neck by the laces. Even so, he felt out of place and every padded step seemed like a transgression. Erich clutched the stethoscope box tight to his chest and tried to act like he belonged.

"New boy! Over here," a voice called out from a compartment down the hall.

Erich cringed. He had hoped to find some quiet spot where he could hide for a while and figure things out, but it was too late to get away now. He sucked in a deep breath and hurried over.

Inside, two *Jungvolk* boys sat across from one another on benches that overflowed with upholstery. A bunk hung over their heads, held up by eagle-crested columns.

"I'm Fritz von Keppler," one of them said. He didn't offer a hand.

The other boy squinted at Erich, his forehead scrunched into knots.

"And that's Anton," Fritz said as if it wasn't very

important.

Though he was not a large boy, Fritz had splayed himself out so he took up an entire side of the compartment. Erich slid in next to Anton where there was more space.

"Pleased to meet you both," he said. "I'm—"

"What's that?" Fritz interrupted pointing at the stethoscope box.

Erich blushed and covered it with his hands. He imagined the two of them rooting through it, cackling as they read Johanna's letters aloud.

"It's…" Erich scrambled for an explanation. "Medicine."

Anton's eyes widened and he threw himself into the corner of the bench as if whatever illness Erich had might be catching. Fritz didn't move.

"Huh," he said. "Out of all the boys in Germany, they pick some sickly kid for this? Now I'm curious. Give it over."

Anton interpreted this as an order, and he lunged for the box with both hands. Erich yanked away, but the other boy already had his fingers curled around the edge. Fritz giggled and reclined against the cushions while they tugged back and forth.

A loud knock against the wall startled Anton and his fingers slipped. Erich recoiled across the bench, hugging the box to his chest. All three of them stared up at the figure in the doorway, a heavyset boy with a gigantic smile.

"You made it!" he said, yanking Erich out of his seat and into a smothering embrace. Erich wobbled awkwardly, arms pinned to his sides.

"Pardon us, gentlemen," the stranger said. "My friend and I haven't seen each other since the '38 rally."

He threw one arm around Erich's shoulder and swept him out the door. Only once they were safe in another compartment, did he let go and hold out his hand.

"I'm sorry about all that, but you looked like you

needed rescuing," he said. "My name's Karl."

"Thanks, I guess," Erich said. He shook Karl's hand cautiously.

"If you want, you can stay here," Karl said. "I don't have a bunkmate yet."

Erich slid the door shut. "I'd like that."

He sat on the puffy bench and set his box out in front of him on the table. Karl hauled himself up onto the opposite bunk then let his legs dangle over the edge.

"Do you know where we're going?" Erich asked, craning his neck.

"Rouhhenberg they said." Karl shrugged. "Not that I have any idea what that means."

Erich relaxed. "I thought I might be the only one who didn't."

"I guarantee those two don't know a thing," Karl said, pointing back towards Anton and Fritz's compartment.

Erich wasn't sure what else he could say and for a long moment nothing passed between the two of them. Then to break the silence, Karl reached over on his bunk and tossed down a little cloth satchel. "Take a look at these."

Erich pulled on the drawstrings and turned the bag over. Three painted miniatures tumbled out onto the table. Their faces were smudged and blocky, yet unmistakable. Hitler. Göring. Goebbels.

"I'm jealous," Erich said. "I wanted these for Christmas so badly a couple years ago."

"What'd you get instead?" Karl asked.

Erich grimaced. "A birdwatching book."

"*Mutti* wouldn't buy them for me either," Karl laughed. "I guess having to say goodbye made her change her mind. Still, I wish she'd done it earlier. We're getting a little old for toys I think."

"True," Erich said. The words rang a little hollow given that he had already lain them out in a line and tilted their articulated right arms up into the Hitler salute.

The compartment door slid open. A girl in a blue and

white BDM uniform hovered outside. She looked twelve or thirteen, a year or two older than Erich and Karl.

"*Heil Hitler.* My name is Sabine," she said, then glanced down at Erich. "Playing with dolls are we?"

Erich blushed and hurriedly swept the miniature Nazis back into their satchel. Behind Sabine, another girl scrambled down the hall towards them. Her thick blonde pigtails flopped back and forth over her shoulders as she tried to catch up while pushing a cart stacked high with covered plates.

"This is Mathilde," Sabine said.

She snapped her fingers and Mathilde slid two plates across the table.

"Do you know where we're going?" Karl asked from above.

"Of course," Sabine said. "We're headed home."

She laughed and waved goodbye before skipping down the hall to the next compartment. Mathilde had to dig her heels into the ground to get the heavy cart to move on her own.

Karl dropped down from his bunk and shared a bemused look with Erich before sliding the door shut again. In between hurried mouthfuls, Erich told him the story of how Doktor Kammer had bent the air outside the headmaster's office and stood down Herr Engel.

Karl whistled in admiration. "I wish it had been like that with Herr Larat. All he did was drop off a letter."

"At least you got to say goodbye," Erich said.

He looked down and toyed with the latch on his box.

"So what *is* in there?" Karl asked, then quickly corrected himself, "I'm sorry, you don't have to tell me."

"It's all right," Erich said.

He opened the box in his lap so Karl couldn't see the letters and handed over the stethoscope.

"I'm going to be a doctor. Or at least I was."

"I think you still can be," Karl said.

"I hope so," Erich nodded, not entirely convinced.

**\*\*\***

Long after the lights went out, Erich lay awake, peering out the window over the top of his pillow. Dark trees blurred by while the stars stayed fixed in place. He missed the uneven mattress of his own bed, its familiar knots and fraying edges. Even over the clattering wheels, he could hear Karl's snoring. Erich didn't understand how he could sleep at a time like this.

Once the sunrise finally poked out through the trees, the terrain grew more rugged and the track pitched uphill. They rushed through tunnels, screeched around winding bends, spanned chasms, and crossed rivers on trestles of wood. Always they pushed higher.

A few hours after dawn, Sabine and Mathilde came back around with coffee, a crust of bread, and some fruit. The smell woke Karl and the two of them sat together in silence, elbows on the table and eyes fixed out the window.

With his nose pressed against the glass, Karl noticed it first. A great cloud of smoke billowed up from a mountain on the horizon. Erich thought it was a forest fire, but then the train turned and he could see the smoke's source.

A castle wrapped the mountain's backside like a cloak. Its walls dripped down the slopes as though they had been poured out from liquid stone. Ramparts and barracks wedged themselves between the trees at odd angles, propped against the incline by a jumble of stilts and buttresses. Rickety iron smokestacks sprouted from the central tower like a fungus, coughing up endless plumes of black.

It was the ugliest castle Erich had ever seen, but there was something enrapturing in its sprawl. His eyes flitted from lopsided turret to winding battlement, never quite able to connect one piece to the next.

The train sputtered to a stop at the base of the mountain. Outside the window, a green and gold sign read

*Station One.* Even as large as the castle was, Erich wondered how they could possibly need more than one train station.

"Do you think we're going to live there?" Erich asked.

"If not, then I'm going home," Karl laughed, already halfway out the door.

They joined a trickle of others headed outside, but there was no one there on the platform to greet them. Twenty or so boys Erich's age milled around in awkward pairs, looking in every direction for some indication of what to do. Every one of them had the same lumpy callous on the back of his neck.

"I think we should get back on the train," one agitated boy whispered. "What if it leaves without us."

"Look," his bunkmate shouted, pointing up at the road that lead down from the mountain.

Every head followed his finger to where a procession of black cars curved around the bend. One by one, they drifted to a stop. The gaggle of boys below snapped into ranks, reacting instinctively to even the suggestion of authority. Erich peered through the windows, expecting to see an adult, Doktor Kammer or perhaps Karl's Herr Larat. But when the doors opened all at once, eight boys, each barely older than Erich, stepped out.

"*Sieg Heil,*" the younger boys shouted in unison.

The eight walked side by side down the steps.

"Welcome to Rouhhenberg, *Nassfüchsen,*" one said.

"Your future home," another continued. "It's a bit misshapen, but you'll get used to it."

They split into groups of three. Erich and Karl packed into the backseat of a car next to a boy named Walther Tuerk. He wore thick-rimmed glasses and a waist-pouch. One of the older boys got in the front. He turned around in his seat to face them as the car kicked off down the road.

"I'm Uwe," he said. "Uwe Dodd. I'll be your *Jungenschaftsführer.* I'm sure you're still a little overwhelmed.

I know I was the first time I went up the mountain. But back then we were the only ones. Things will be better for your class."

Uwe turned away as though the conversation were over. Erich brimmed with questions that he was too timid to ask.

"*Jungenschaftsführer,* if I may, I don't think overwhelmed is accurate," Walther said. "Primarily, we're confused."

Uwe laughed. "Confused is all right."

They threaded up the mountain in tight switchbacks. If Erich stuck his forehead against the window, he could see where the side of the road dropped off. Pebbles kicked up by their tires plummeted over the edge. Erich's stomach clenched at each bend, but he couldn't look away. He soon wished he'd picked the middle seat.

After a while, the road flattened and they passed under the castle's outer gate. A flaking layer of rust coated the iron lattice, and Erich doubted it could ever be lowered again. They pulled to a stop in the inner courtyard and squeezed out of the car.

Though the whole castle grounds had seemed at a distance to be on a steep grade, it was remarkably flat here. The smokestack encrusted tower—Uwe called it the bathhouse—loomed on the other end of the grass, taller than anything else in sight. From its sides, the castle's two largest wings spilled like outstretched arms.

"We take our evening meals in the chapel," Uwe said, pointing to one of the wings. "Strangely enough, it's bigger on the inside than the great hall."

It seemed more a cathedral than a chapel. Countless spires jutted from its roof, and a gilded eagle perched on the highest steeple where there might once have been a cross. Walther giggled and brought his hands together in a mock prayer. Karl grimaced.

"*Mutti* always wanted me to be a priest," he whispered in Erich's ear. "I should probably tell her to give up."

A second car pulled up behind them and one of the

older boys got out. He strode over to Uwe and clasped him on the shoulder.

"This is Otto," Uwe said. "We'll be paired up with his *Jungenschaft* for now."

Erich peered through the car's rear windows and cringed to see Fritz and Anton in the back seat. The door popped open and Fritz gave Anton a shove out onto the grass. Fritz stumbled out a second later, bent over, and clutched at his knees, breathing heavily.

"Are you alright there?" Uwe asked.

"Get away, I'm fine," Fritz snapped.

Taken aback, Erich stared at Uwe and waited for him to respond. This was the kind of impudence that Klaus would punish immediately with a vicious implement from his toolbelt, but Uwe merely shrugged and turned to beckon the boys up the chapel steps.

Otto, however, looked as upset as Erich. He took three big strides over to Fritz, grabbed him by the neck, and lifted him clear off the ground. The two boys were almost the same size, and yet Otto's arm didn't waver at all as he held Fritz up.

"Say that again, *Nassfuchs!*" Otto bellowed, impossibly loud.

The sound of it buffeted Erich and he could almost feel his heels scrape back against the dirt. Fritz could manage no more than a gargle in response. Spittle dribbled down his chin and onto Otto's hand. Erich had to resist the urge to snicker at what seemed like justice for how Fritz had treated him on the train.

"Give him a rest," Uwe called down from the steps. "He's just sick from the ride."

Otto scowled, then relented and let Fritz drop. As Fritz lay on his crumpled knees and struggled for air, Otto wiped his hand on his trousers and then kicked a big spray of dirt into his face.

"Get up, *Nassfuchs,*" he commanded. "Your *Jungenschaftsführer* is a merciful fellow who just wants to give you a tour."

Fritz wiped the dirt from his eyes and rose, quivering with fury.

"Yes, *Jungenschaftsführer*," he hissed through clenched teeth.

Ignoring him, Otto gathered up a few more boys and then joined Uwe at the top of the steps. The two looked tiny against the chapel's massive double doors, but they pushed them open as though they weighed nothing at all.

Inside, three tables made from tree trunks lay out perpendicular to where the pews would have been. The one in the middle sat on ground level, while the two surrounding it were raised up on high platforms draped with long swastika banners. The altar had been removed and above its place was a balcony with a podium and no railing.

"The high tables are for the upperclassmen corps. The *Wehrbären* and *Schützenadler*," Uwe said, pointing to them in turn.

Otto gestured toward the low table between the platforms. "You *Nassfüchsen* will eat down there."

"We'll be like fish in a bowl," Karl muttered.

Erich craned his neck up to the vaulted ceiling where the morning light still trickled in. The stained glass cast everything in red and amber.

"There are worse things to be," he whispered back.

Walther clearly had some burning question, but Otto and Uwe were already beckoning them through one of the side doors and they had to run to catch up.

The *Jungenschaftsführer* drew the boys through Rouhhenberg's labyrinthine passages at a blistering pace. They threaded in and out and back through barracks, courtyards, tunnels, and towers, all connected at odd angles by twisting bridges and wooden walkways. Height lost any meaning. They would come in on one floor and leave on another without seeing a single flight of stairs. Every hallway sloped and undulated along the curves of the mountain below.

Each part of the castle had its own style, but everywhere strange iron statues littered the halls. They came in all different poses, but always their mouths were open. Erich couldn't tell if they were shouting with joy or screaming in pain. It was unsettling to look at them for long, but Otto and Uwe moved so quickly that Erich rarely had to.

It struck him how few people they saw. Occasionally they would pass a group of BDM girls or another set of touring *Nassfüchsen*, but most of the time they traveled the castle alone.

"Where is everyone?" Erich asked when they finally stopped in one of the gardens.

"It's going to be a seven year academy," Uwe said. "But you're just the second class. We have the privilege of watching it fill up."

Otto pointed over at a narrow path heading up the mountain.

"The *Siegfeld* is that way. Make sure you remember this spot. You'll be back in the afternoon."

Erich had no idea what Otto meant by the *Siegfeld*, but Uwe whisked them off to see the exercise rooms before he could ask. Half of the time when they paused, it was for Otto and Uwe to show them some corridor or doorway that was off-limits to the *Nassfüchsen*, but Erich couldn't imagine how he was supposed to follow the rules if never knew where he was. By the time the two *Jungenschaftsführer* dropped them off at their dormitory, Erich didn't feel any more capable of finding his way around than he had at the start.

"We'll have our eyes on you up there," Otto said, shaking each of their hands. Erich wasn't certain if he should take that as encouragement or a threat.

Once the *Jungenschaftsführer* were gone, Karl, Erich, and Walther wandered the dormitory looking for their bunks. The *Nassfuchs* wing had none of the extravagance of the train or the other parts of the castle they had seen. Every wall was bare stone and the rooms were furnished like prison cells. Erich found a bed with his name on it and collapsed on the thin mattress. In a way, he preferred it here. For the first time since he got in the car in Messerich, he didn't feel out of place.

A schedule lay on Erich's pillow. He read it eagerly, but his classes didn't sound any different from the ones he might have taken at the Leibniz Gymnasium: History, Racial Studies, Physics. On Friday, September 1st, he paused. Someone had scribbled an unintelligible note at ten o'clock. It took him a moment to recognize Johanna's code:

*Bittrich Hall, 2nd floor.*

# CHAPTER TEN

After a simple lunch in the *Nassfuchs* lounge—really just a large empty room—Karl, Walter, and Erich set out for the *Siegfeld*. A half hour of fruitless searching later, they gave up on trying to find it themselves and let a group of BDM girls point them in the right direction. They had to ask for help three more times before they finally found the right combination of stairs, walkways, and ramps to lead them to the mountain path. Each time, Erich scanned the girls' faces, hoping to spot Johanna, but she was never there.

Halfway up, they joined another group of *Nassfüchsen*. Erich wanted to ask where the other boys were from, but he had a curious feeling that it no longer mattered and might somehow be inappropriate to ask. Though he had only just left, Messerich already seemed enormously distant, a childhood home filled with vague, warm memories.

At the top, the path flattened out before a thin, rusty gate. Most of the other *Nassfüchsen* had already arrived and were milling about impatiently like they had been waiting a long time. An *SS* officer approached from the other side of the gate. He was the first adult Erich had seen since coming to Rouhhenberg. Ivory hair cascaded over his shoulders and a saber swung from his belt. Erich gaped at the officer's insignia on his collar—two feathers for *Oberführer*. He recognized it from a chart in one of his schoolbooks, but had never seen someone so high-ranking in the flesh. This man should have been out there commanding swaths of the men, but instead he was here, about to speak to them.

"That's *Oberführer* Ehrenzweig, the one who interviewed me," Walther whispered to Erich. "He reports directly to the *Führer*."

No matter what Walther was saying, he always took on the tone of an adult trying to explain something complicated to a child.

Ehrenzweig unlocked the gate and examined their group, his arms crossed behind his back and a sour look on his face.

"*Nassfüchsen*," he shouted. "Onto the field, now!"

They scurried into a hasty formation and did their best to march through in unison. Erich's foot kept catching against another boy's boot, but he was relieved to see that Karl also struggled to find the cadence of the unfamiliar ranks.

Past the gate, the trees cleared into a wide field that ended in a cliff's edge. The whole area was so flat and precise it could have been carved from the peak with a chisel. A clean cut trench ran through middle of the grass, spanning all the way from a little shed on the cliff side of the field to a massive hangar on the other end. There were rail lines on the trench floor and a chain hung above them, each link a quarter of a meter thick.

Wooden seats ran along the sides of the field, empty but for a small clump of onlookers. As soon as the boys stepped out onto the grass, the tiny crowd burst into shouts and jeers, disproportionately loud for its size.

"Go home, *Nassfüchsen*."

"The train station is the other way!"

A rain of pebbles and sticks sailed out from the stands, but no one seemed to actually be throwing them. The procession of boys halted at the lip of the trench and Erich did his best not to flinch from the peppering projectiles. *Oberführer* Ehrenzweig stood in front of the group and waited patiently for the noise to simmer down.

"The *Führer* has made a promise," he said. He unlooped the saber from his belt and stalked down the row of boys. "He has promised that every boy of your generation will be trimmed of fat."

Ehrenzweig lashed Karl across the shoulder with the sheath of his saber. Karl bit down hard to stifle a pained shout. He held his ground. Ehrenzweig continued down the row and every boy held their breath until he passed them.

"You will be swift as a greyhound," Ehrenzweig said.

He struck at Fritz, who twisted himself to the side. The sheathe tore past him. Ehrenzweig gave a mirthful shake of his head and then smacked his elbow into Fritz's face. As Fritz howled and clutched at his bleeding nose, Ehrenzweig moved on without so much as look back. Laughter rained down from the stands.

"You will be tough as leather and hard as Krupp steel," he said. One of the boys flinched as the saber whipped down again, but Ehrenzweig stopped just before it reached his shoulder. He stepped back and returned the sword to his belt.

"When Adolf Hitler makes such a promise, it becomes the job of every German to fulfill it. Thus falls to me the unenviable task of turning you cowards into the men their *Führer* deserves." Ehrenzweig pointed with his arm at the trench to the boy's rear. "This field will be the forge for that transformation. Back home, your *Fähnleinführer* may have settled for wrestling or football or boxing, but here we have more to sharpen than just your bodies. In Rouhhenberg, we make *Siegvorbereitung*."

"What is that," Erich whispered.

Karl shrugged. "A game?"

As Ehrenzweig was speaking, two figures emerged from the hangar at the far end of the field and headed towards the boys. As they grew closer, Erich smiled to see that one of them was Doktor Kammer, Mateusz the dachshund at his side. The second man wore a long flowing scarf and introduced himself as Herr Larat. Together they handed out team ribbons. Erich and Karl both ended up on Kammer's red team, while Walther went to Larat's greens with Fritz and Anton.

"For today, the upperclassmen will captain for you. That way your shrunken minds won't have to do any real thinking." Ehrenzweig pointed up at the group of boys in the stands and shouted, "*Jungenschaftsführer* Puhl will take the greens and *Jungenschaftsführer* Dodd the reds."

This seemed to be the first that the two had heard of it. After an exchange of surprised glances, Otto and Uwe popped up from where they sat and strolled down the steps arm-over-shoulder to shouts and applause from their classmates.

Erich kept his eyes fixed forward while Uwe passed through the ranks of their team, peering at each boy intently. When he finished his survey, Uwe laughed and threw his hands up in the air.

"You all look the same to me," he said. He pointed at two boys Erich hadn't met. "Why not? You and you on first and second lane."

The chosen two rushed up to the front, while Uwe stroked his chin theatrically.

"*Ene, mene, miste,*" he counted, twirling his finger in a circle. It landed on Erich. "You can play third."

Erich didn't fully realize what had happened until Karl gave him a push on the shoulder. He swallowed his surprise and stepped up next to the other two, whose names were Richard and Felix. Uwe waved the three of them closer.

"*SV* is simple. The other captain will pick a course for

our team, that's three rows. If you make it to the flag at the end of your lane before time runs out, you'll score a point. If all three of you make it, it's an extra two points for five total."

"*Jungenschaftsführer*, what's in between us and the flag?" Erich asked.

"Oh, all kinds of things," Uwe said. "It's better if you don't think about it too hard. Now come on, you have to wait in there while Otto sets up."

He ushered them into the wooden shack, which he called the starting box. Inside, it was divided into three sections, one for each boy with only a tiny window between them. Erich felt like a racehorse at the gate.

"Whatever you do, don't leave your lane," Uwe said, closing each door. He held up five fingers. "I want to see points, okay?"

It was so dark inside that even when Erich stuck his head through the window, he couldn't see Felix in the stall next to him.

"Are you ready?" Richard asked.

"No," Felix squeaked.

Erich shook his head. He realized a moment later that they wouldn't have been able to see that, but stayed quiet anyway.

After a long wait, the ground shook. A grinding metal sound mingled with a rising cheer from the onlookers. The chain in the trench was moving. It churned and creaked until some gear far away staggered to a stop and the doors of the starting box popped open. Sunlight flooded in. Erich could feel his heart slam against his ribs with every beat. He wished he could sneak back into the one corner of the box that was still dark, but Felix and Richard were already on the move.

Squinting, Erich took a few slow steps outside. The rest of the red team tried to cheer them on, but the taunts and boos from the upperclassmen and the greens mostly drowned them out. Erich glanced over at Karl on the grassy sidelines and got a reassuring smile.

While they waited, the chain had dragged over a wooden platform to fill in the trench. Like everything else, it was divided into three lanes, all identical. On each, a short staircase led up to a hanging metal pan. It looked like a giant scale. A few meters further down, a solid wooden gate, braced in iron, blocked each lane.

A pistol shot startled Erich and his two teammates rushed forward onto their lanes. It was time to go. Determined not to be left behind, he scurried after them and up the stairs. At the top, he paused, then took one tentative step out onto the pan. It wobbled in place, but was stable enough to stand on. Even after he walked all the way out to the center, it barely dipped under his weight. Erich thought he saw the gate move a little as he did so, but it was slight enough that he could have just imagined it. He jumped up and down like it were a trampoline. There was no response.

Erich jumped and jumped until he ran out of breath, then gave up and stopped to look over at the other boys. Felix was much bigger than he. Whenever he landed on the scale, the gate in his row would lift up a crack. Much to the amusement of the upperclassmen, every time Felix tried to get off the scale and scurry under it, the gate would slam back down just before he reached it.

Erich gave up on jumping and hopped down. Ignoring the jeers, he got on his knees and dug his fingers into the lip where the gate met the floorboards. He heaved with everything he could muster, but it was far too heavy for him. Erich's sweaty fingers slipped off the iron and he fell back on his rear, thudding painfully into the floorboards. Even his own teammates were laughing now. Tears welled in Erich's eyes. He wondered if this whole game existed just to make fools of them.

In the next lane, Felix rammed his shoulder into the gate again and again, as though he thought he might eventually batter through. Richard was still jumping up and down on his scale, which was equally pointless.

"One minute!" Otto shouted.

Erich wiped his eyes dry with the back of his sleeve. How could he let the *Führer* send him here only to discover him so useless that he couldn't even manage to play a game? He lifted his body up, squeezed the dagger at his waist, and reminded himself that it had seen blood.

Erich slowly walked over to the bottom of the stairs and dug his feet into the floor. After closing his eyes for a moment, he lunged. He took the steps two at a time and crashed out on the scale without slowing. At its edge, Erich leapt.

The onlookers fell to a hush as he hurtled across the gap. Erich's chest slammed into the wood with a crack that emptied his lungs, but his arms had already wrapped themselves around the top. His feet fought for purchase against the braces.

"Thirty seconds!"

Over and over, Erich tried to haul himself up, but every time he fell back, his arms burning and barely holding on. Sucking in a shaky breath, he promised that if failed now, he would just let himself fall. In a last scramble of feet and struggling arms, his chest cleared the top. He tumbled over to the other side and landed on his flank with a loud smack that he was too numb to feel.

Erich rose slowly, a smile spreading over his face. Uwe had said there would be a flag, but where was it? He looked out at the lane ahead, past a spiky column and a set of swinging bars. From far away, the flag stared back at him. He remembered the rest of what Uwe had said and his shoulders slumped. He had only cleared the first of three rows.

On the sidelines, Otto stuck two fingers in his mouth and blew a shrill whistle that hailed the end of the round. Caws of laughter rained down from the stands as Erich sulked off the platform, his face afire. Richard and Felix were already waiting for him with the rest of the red team.

He wondered if they had just given up early.

Karl rested a hand on Erich's shoulder. "It wasn't...
too bad."

"Thanks, I guess," Erich mumbled.

He shut his eyes and wiped a sloppy mess of sweat
from his forehead. When he opened them, Fritz was there,
a green ribbon wrapped in his fist. Dried blood was still
caked onto his smugly grinning lips. Anton hovered
behind him.

"Pathetic," he said. "Like watching three pigs in a pen."

"And you'll do better?" Karl spat.

"I will," Fritz said. "Make sure Fiehler pays attention.
There's a lesson for him in it."

He strutted off towards the starting box with Anton in
his shadow. Karl rolled his eyes as they left, but Erich
couldn't help but feel that Fritz was right.

"We really were awful," he moaned. "They'll probably
ship us home on the next train."

"I doubt that," came a voice from behind them. Erich
turned around and shot to attention when he saw that it
was Otto.

"In our year, nobody made it past the first row," Otto
said.

At that, Erich cheered up considerably. To his surprise,
the *Jungenschaftführer* lingered with them on the grass while
they watched the preparation for the next round. The
grinding sound filled the air again as the chain slowly
pulled the three rows back through the hangar door. Uwe
followed them in. After a while, he came out and the
whole system churned back into motion.

Uwe's rows slid into place one at a time. The first was
simple and undaunting, nothing but a tall staircase divided
between the three lanes. At the top, it met with the floor
of the second row. There each path was blocked by a door
with an unusually large knob. Further still, a tall tank of
water filled the last row.

Every one of the obstacles seemed trivial compared to

what Erich had dealt with. He didn't know what to expect from the door, but the staircase looked like just a staircase, and even a boy who barely knew how to swim could paddle his way across the small stretch of water. Barring that, he could jump the gap.

Karl puffed with indignation. "That looks..."

"Easy?" Otto said. "I wouldn't worry about it. The high rows are the hardest ones."

"Why's that, sir?" Karl said.

Erich smiled. "Maybe because you have to put the stairs first."

"Exactly," Otto said. "The captain has to waste a row to use them. Your friend won't get far if that's what you're worried about."

Karl cocked an eyebrow. "Isn't Fritz on your team?"

"My team is the *Schützenadler*," Otto laughed. "You lot are just for the week."

At the crack of the starting pistol, Fritz hurled himself up the stairs in the middle lane. Perhaps expecting some trap to spring out and toss him down, his two teammates hung back. But as Otto had said there was nothing, and they soon followed him. The greens roared in approval as their whole team crossed into the second row. The upperclassmen in the stands remained silent.

Fritz stopped at the door and leaned in to inspect its knob. It had a hole at its center and he reached in with one hand. Erich covered his mouth as Fritz fished around inside. After a moment, Fritz stared back over his shoulder at the assembled boys, grinned, then pushed the door open as though there were nothing to it.

"No!" Karl shouted.

On the way out of the hollow knob, Fritz's hand caught against something. He scowled and pushed with one foot against the door until it wrested free. The knob snapped off and clunked to the floor, trailing a long chain that ran up to a shackle around Fritz's wrist.

A howling laughter broke out from the stands. Karl

shook Erich by the shoulders in delight. Fritz shot the upperclassmen a defiant glare and staggered ahead, ball and chain dragging behind him. He looked out at the next row and growled in frustration. The only thing standing between Fritz and the flag was a tiny stretch of water that he would never be able to cross.

The boy to Fritz's left had copied him and his hand was already caught in the knob, but the third one was smarter and had hung back to watch. He ignored the trap and kicked at the door. The wood was thin, but was still far too strong for him to break through.

Over in the left lane, the other enshackled boy trudged through and tried to throw himself across the water. Weighed down as he was, he barely had enough momentum to make it half way. He smacked into the pool with a tremendous splash and flailed helplessly as the iron knob dragged him down to the bottom of the tank.

Uwe shook his head in disbelief. He turned a crank on the side of the boy's tank and the water flooded out through a sluice, soaking the grass. When it had all drained away, the boy fell to his knees, coughing up the contents of his lungs and sucking at air.

Expressionless, Fritz surveyed his teammate from above. As two upperclassman came down and carried the sopping boy away, he smiled at something. Fritz dragged himself back through the door and carefully shut it. With a grunt, he grabbed the chain around his wrist with both hands and rolled it around in a slow circle. Little by little, it picked up speed until soon it spun so fast that the knob lifted off the ground.

A high pitched whistle shrieked out from the hollow center as it circled. For a moment, it looked as though Fritz might hit himself or simply twirl off the edge, but he found his balance and kept spinning until his arms were held out straight. With a shout, he took a step forward and brought the full weight of the knob crashing down on the edge of the door. The thin wood splintered and sprayed out as it twisted off its frame, held up by a single fragile hinge.

Erich looked back at Otto, hoping to still see his confident smile, but it had vanished. Fritz twirled the knob back around in a second arc. More practiced this time, he barely faltered as he took aim at the remaining hinge. With a shuddering snap, the knob cleaved into the frame and the door teetered. It hung for a moment, then smacked down across the gap.

One step at at time, Fritz pulled himself across the makeshift gangplank. His manacled arm hung lifeless behind him but he didn't seem at all concerned as Uwe counted down to the end of the round. With only a few seconds to spare, he wrapped his left hand around the flag.

The *Nassfüchsen*, red and green alike, broke out into a cheer, finally loud enough to overwhelm the upperclassmen's disapproval. In a way, it was their whole class that had won. It was a victory for youth—though they were really only a year younger than the upperclassmen. Even Karl joined in, but Erich found it hard to be very happy for Fritz. Otto rushed over and tried to console Uwe with a hand on his shoulder, but Uwe pushed him away, turning pink.

Fritz strutted down off the platform, acting as though nothing really important had happened. A crowd gathered to shake his hand, but Anton stepped in and repelled them all.

Evidently, *Oberführer* Ehrenzweig hadn't prepared for the possibility that a team might score. He scurried over to remind them this was a practice match.

"There's another match tomorrow. I expect better from you reds then," the *Oberführer* said. But even he sounded impressed.

# CHAPTER ELEVEN

After *SV*, the *Nassfüchsen* headed down to the soaring bathhouse tower for something listed on their schedule as "Hygiene". It was the only place in the castle that was easy to find. An iron smokestack wound its way around the spire from bottom to top, held in place by a rickety jumble of bolts and scaffolds that looked ready to collapse at any moment.

Erich had assumed they would go up to the top, but at the door a grey-shirted *SS* man pointed them down a spiraling set of stone steps. They wrapped so many times around that Erich wondered if the whole tower mirrored itself underground. A stale, mineral smell hung in the air, thickening as they descended. The hairs on the back of Erich's neck bristled and hummed.

Doktor Kammer waited for them in an antechamber at the bottom. In the corner, a stranger in a grey suit and tie leaned against the wall. His crisp attire clashed with his wild hair and coarse, black beard. Doktor Kammer paced back and forth, rapping his cane against the tile floor, an unlit cigarette jittering between his fingers. When the last boy had filtered into the room, he tucked it into his shirt pocket.

"Welcome, children, welcome! I trust your first day here has been eventful," he said, unable to keep his hands still. "Some of you I knew before, Martin, yes, Fiehler, von Keppler, yes. Others of you I've just met today. I'm sure you're all very overwhelmed, so let me introduce myself again. My name is Doktor Ernst Kammer and I will be— I mean I will have the privilege of teaching you all history."

Doktor Kammer had always been energetic, but today he positively vibrated. His words tumbled over each other and he punctuated every sentence with a flickering smile.

"But we'll get to history next week. What we undertake tonight and the three hundred and sixty-four nights thereafter is the most important thing you'll do as a *Nassfuchs*. You might even say it's the entire point."

Doktor Kammer took his cigarette back out from his pocket and started to twirl it between his fingers as he shuffled back and forth. Erich didn't see Mateusz anywhere. He wondered if that was why Kammer was so agitated.

"You are going to take a bath, though not quite an ordinary bath." Doktor Kammer sucked in a long breath. "It won't be so much water as… as pig's blood."

Anxious whispers broke out amongst the boys.

"Pig's blood?" Karl hissed.

Erich attempted a brave shrug, reassuring himself that it wasn't all that different from working with his father in the butcher shop. Inside, he shuddered.

"It's really not so strange as it sounds," Doktor Kammer said. He seemed a little calmer now that he had spat it out. "This sort of thing goes back a long time."

He prodded the boys into a line and then called over two of the *SS* men. Kammer handed one a clipboard and the other a small porous stone.

"There's one more thing we have to do first. Tilt your heads down and stand still," he said.

Erich stole a glance at the stranger in the corner. He hadn't moved since they came in. He met Erich's gaze and

Erich quickly dropped his head. From the corner of one eye, Erich watched the *SS* man's boots slowly move down the line. Some of the boys yelped when their turn came, but Erich couldn't see what had happened to them.

When finally the boots clipped to a stop next to Erich, he shut his eyes and scrunched up his face in anticipation. A firm hand gripped Erich's chin and something hard scraped against the back of his neck. He stifled a cry as it tore back skin. The *SS* man scratched furiously for a moment, then yanked Erich's head up while the other scribbled something down on his clipboard.

Erich wiped the tears from his eyes before anyone could see them. His neck burned and he could feel something dripping down his back, whether blood or sweat he wasn't sure. Once the pain slowed, he opened his eyes and peered out with curiosity at the other boys. The odd calluses they'd worn before had been ground down to a stretch of raw skin. Beneath was a tattoo of sorts, inescapably dark. It was as if an endless hole were carved into the back of every neck.

There were a dozen different designs. A spiral with no beginning or end. A notched cross that looked upside down no matter how Erich turned his head. Two slanted lines that should have intersected, but never did.

Doktor Kammer moved down the line, pairing up the boys who shared the same mark.

"What's mine?" Erich whispered.

"It's like a half-circle, but wider," Karl said, drawing the shape with his finger.

Erich cringed and pointed at Fritz. "Like his?"

"You're meant for one another," Karl giggled.

Doktor Kammer squeaked excitedly when he saw that Erich and Fritz matched. He pulled the two of them over to a spot on the side, then hobbled off to find more.

"I can't believe they would make an invalid our teacher," Fritz whispered. "I thought this school would be better."

"They let you in," Erich grumbled under his breath.

Chatter danced around the room. Everyone had a different theory on what the marks meant, but their voices fell away as the stranger in the grey suit got up from the corner and spoke.

"They are names," he said, his voice hushed. "Almost like a signature. And with that signature comes an oath."

He drifted through the assemblage of boys, running his cold fingers along each of their necks. Erich shivered as he passed.

"Don't be afraid. This is an oath that you have already sworn. You need do nothing to fulfill it."

Having apparently said everything he intended to say, the man resumed his post in the corner, while the *SS* men ushered each pair of boys out of the antechamber and down the hall. When Erich and Fritz's turn came around, Doktor Kammer gave them a gentle pat on the back to send them off.

Door after door lined the hallway, each designated with one of the symbols. An *SS* man drew them into a little square room marked by Erich and Fritz's half-ellipse. Two spigots and a pull chain hung from the ceiling like a chandelier. The floor sloped down to a drain at the center.

"Take off your clothes," the man ordered as he shut the door. He wrinkled his nose at them.

They stripped out of their uniforms and hung them on a rack in the corner. The *SS* man grabbed Fritz by the shoulders and shoved him into position under one of the spigots. Erich scurried over unbidden to the opposite side.

"Don't move," the man said, then gave two quick tugs on the ceiling chain.

A dull, mechanical rumbling echoed down from above. Erich shivered as he stared up at the spigot and waited.

"Scared, Fiehler?" Fritz sneered. "Surely a little blood won't frighten you."

"My father is a butcher. I'm not scared," Erich said, belied by his shaking fingertips and the tangled snarl in his stomach.

"Quiet!" the *SS* man hissed.

He jammed both their heads down until their chins touched their chests. Erich stared at his toes while the distant rumbling grew closer. There was clink from above, then another and another. The sound came faster until it burst into a pounding clatter like a torrent of rain against a metal roof. Already, Erich could smell it. He sucked in a breath and held it in his lungs.

Even without seeing it, he could feel the exact moment the blood tipped over the lip of the spigot. It seemed to fall forever without reaching him. In that instant, he realized it wasn't the fear of the bath that gripped his insides. He wasn't quivering out of some childish repulsion at the ick or the stink of it. Rather, it was the sense that at any moment the blood would crack across his neck and it would find him unworthy. It would demonstrate to the whole world that he didn't belong.

The impact wiped all those doubts away. Whatever tension he had felt vanished and he knew unequivocally that his fears had been unfounded. Warm, oozing blood wrapped him like a cocoon. This was the only place he could ever possibly belong. He could hear the drumbeat of a thousand marching boots against stone. Trumpets blared in his ears. Blood fell off his shoulders and danced down his back. Erich shuddered and gasped and cried. It dribbled down his arms and welled up in the cracks between his toes. Though it filled his mouth with an iron taste, he threw back his head and sang.

*The rotten bones are trembling,*
*Of the world before the war.*

The *SS* man rushed over from the door and slammed his neck down, but Erich wouldn't stop belting out his garbled verse. Even Fritz moaned along to the refrain.

*We march unending onwards,*
*Though all may sink and drown.*
*For today Germany hears us,*
*And tomorrow the world around.*

The song and the last few drops from the spigot sputtered out together. Erich fell to his knees and tried desperately to slop up what remained. It slipped through his fingers. So much had already drained away. His head lolled drunkenly as he stared up at the spigot and begged for more. At last, the grinding of gears came again, but when Erich jumped up to meet the flow, only water crashed across his face. He shrieked and it washed him clean.

Pressing his back into the wall, Erich whimpered as the last precious thread slid down the drain. Fritz stood locked in place, slack-jawed and oblivious to the water that poured over him. The *SS* man had to grab his arm and pull him away.

They dressed in stunned silence and then wandered back up the endless spiral steps. Outside, a dozen other boys milled about the courtyard in a dazed reverie. The bathhouse tower spat out a thick cough of smoke. It drifted up and thinned into the last of the summer air.

# CHAPTER TWELVE

Every morning at dawn, Otto, Uwe, and the other *Jungenschaftsführer* crashed into the *Nassfuchs* dormitory, shouting into their bullhorns, and marched the boys back up to the *Siegfeld* for *SV*. Though Fritz never stopped boasting that he would score, neither team ever managed to do so again. As the sun set, they would trudge down to the bathhouse and drown their disappointment in blood and song. Each night before bed, Erich ticked off the days until Friday when he would see Johanna. He slept as deeply as he ever had.

On Thursday, they ate in the chapel for the first time. The *Nassfüchsen* sat at the lowest of the three tree trunk tables. It felt like a sapling compared to the colossal timbers that loomed above them on both sides, each mostly empty but for a small pocket of upperclassmen. Everything was made to accommodate many more students than there actually were. At the far end of the hall, the adults dined on the balcony. Erich recognized *Oberführer* Ehrenzweig and Doktor Kammer. The man in the grey suit was there was well, sitting by an empty chair. Karl whispered that this was Hugo, the headmaster.

Tempting smells drifted down from above, nothing like

the dry potatoes and cabbage the *Nassfüchsen* ate, but Erich didn't mind. They could have been served sand and he would have fought for a seat at the table.

The red and green team sat at opposite ends, leaving a healthy buffer of seats between them. Erich and Karl cleaned the last of their plates and watched Walther laugh on the other end with Fritz and Anton.

As the meal wound down, Hugo stepped up to the podium at the edge of the balcony.

"Good evening, friends," he said. His voice came at a soft drawl, but carried to Erich as easily as if he were sitting next to him.

"Today we officially welcome our second class. You may be wondering why they've joined us in the chapel a few days ahead of schedule, but all will be clear before the night is done."

A sudden warmth spread across his face and he smiled.

"*Oberführer* Ehrenzweig tells me that this year's *Nassfüchsen* have already scored a point in their *Siegvorbereitung*. I'm sure our engineer, Herr Jensson, is already hard at work to correct this oversight before next year's boys arrive."

Erich glowered at Fritz as the rest of the *Nassfüchsen* started up a raucous cheer. Hugo waited for the room to quiet.

"On Monday, they will start their lessons. They will open their eyes and join the future we are building here."

He paused for a moment and frowned, as though he were weighing whether or not to say something.

"There is one final thing before we all bid one another goodnight. *Oberführer* Ehrenzweig has an announcement to make."

Hugo lingered at the podium a long time before he finally stepped away and let the other man take his place. Ehrenzweig pulled back his silver hair and looked out on the students with eager eyes.

"There are vultures in the skies tonight," he said. "They

are there every night, these greedy men with greedy minds. To them, you and I are nothing but carrion. If you should ever find yourself at Germany's border, throw a stone and you will strike one. That is how thickly we are encircled. And if you should ever find yourself in the East, just look up. You won't even see the sun.

"Fellows, we live in terrible and wonderful times. Everywhere the German race is under siege. And nowhere is this more evident than in Danzig. This is a German city, separated from us by land that is German by right, and yet to be German there is to be persecuted for every breath. We have lodged complaint after complaint with Poland, all of which have fallen cold, deaf ears.

"Thank God for the *Führer*. Could anyone else tolerate this treatment with such level-mindedness? Could anyone else stand amidst this shrieking, vulturous horde of diplomats and still demand negotiation? Who else could endure these endless indignities and every time respond, 'No, dear neighbors, no. There is another way. There must never again be war in Europe."

He gripped the lectern with bony fingers and leaned out over the edge.

"But there are some things that even he cannot abide."

Boos and hisses filled the room and the upperclassmen began to slowly beat their fists against the table. Erich had had his hopes for war raised and dashed so many times that he was afraid to believe, but Karl met his eyes and together they joined the growing drumbeat. The room vibrated with pounding wood and clattering plates, yet still the *Oberführer's* voice carried over it all.

"I have received two reports tonight. The first is that only hours ago Polish soldiers opened fire across the border. German blood has been spilt on German soil." Ehrenzweig breathed in deep. "The second report contains the *Führer's* response."

The pounding stopped and every rattling dish fell still.

"Blood will be met with blood!" he cried.

Thundering shouts erupted from every corner of the chapel. Their voices echoed from the stone floors to the arched ceilings. Windows shook with the stomping of feet.

*Blut für Blut! Blut für Blut! Blut für Blut!*

***

That night, Erich and Karl huddled around the radio in the lounge with the other *Nassfüchsen*, eager for news of the counterattack in Poland. Every face in the room sank with disappointment when Dr. Goebbels instead introduced a two-hour music program. Nervous whispers drowned out the opening trumpets. No one wanted to believe that *Oberführer* Ehrenzweig had been wrong. Walter jumped up and switched off the radio.

"Don't you see?" he said. "Look how deeply the *Führer* trusts us. Our parents and our friends back home sleep in ignorance tonight, but we know the truth. And tomorrow... tomorrow the world around!"

The mood brightened in an instant. That had to be it. How long would the war last, they whispered to one another. A week? A month? A year? Felix sighed and pointed out that it didn't matter. However long the it ran, the fighting would be over well before any of them had the chance to join in.

Long after the lights went out, Erich lay in his new bed, unable to shake a tickling unease that kept him awake. He should be happy. Moments ago he was. He tried to recall the rapture that had ran over him in the bathhouse or the thunderous unity of the chapel, but all he could bring to mind was the look Aunt Mila had given him just before she disappeared. The calm, even breathing of the other boys grated against his ears. While he stewed in bed missing home, they were all already dreaming of war and glory.

In the predawn hours, Karl shook Erich awake and together they stumbled back over to the radio, but there was still no news.

"We should be patient and trusting," Walther said as they scaled the rocky path up to the *Siegfeld*. "We'll know more when it's time to know more."

It was Walther's turn to play that day and Erich hoped he might score. Walther was on the green team, but it was clear by now that they were not really competing against each other. They were competing against the impossible game itself and a point for either team was a point for the *Nassfüchsen*. Sadly, Walther proved to be a terrible player. Only seconds into the round, he ran headlong into a swinging pole that knocked him off the lane.

Erich's team did no better. After Fritz's victory, Otto and Uwe no longer took chances. Every round came with some insurmountable obstacle. A gate too heavy to lift. A space too small to squeeze through. A gap too wide to jump across. The whole game seemed like it had been invented for a different species with three arms and two-meter legs.

In the afternoon, the boys once again hung their heads and trekked down the mountain, but their wounded spirits were lifted when the radio in the common room crackled on. It was time. *Oberführer* Ehrenzweig had been right. Germany would answer bombs with bombs, Hitler vowed, and poison gas would be met in kind. Walther radiated vindication. He circled the lounge shaking every hand.

### ✳✳✳

After the excitement died down and all the *Nassfüchsen* went to bed, Erich lay awake and waited. Tonight, he would finally see Johanna. Just before ten o'clock—an hour after their curfew—he slipped out from under the covers and made his way towards Bittrich Hall. Even though he had scouted out the spot the day before, it still took three wrong turns to get there.

When he arrived, the corridor was empty. Erich paced back and forth anxiously. Almost a week had passed since Johanna left her message. It would be just like her not to show up. He covered the length of the hall ten times before he finally heard a whisper from behind.

"Over here."

Erich spun in place. He couldn't work out where it had come from and he kept turning, scanning every room, until eventually Johanna popped her head out from a closet door in the opposite direction.

"I'm in here, idiot," she hissed.

He scurried over and she yanked the door shut as soon as he was inside. They stood in total darkness, pressed up against a jumble of brooms and aprons. Erich could hear her fishing around for the light chain. It switched on with a clink.

At first glance Johanna looked just like all the other BDM girls in her climbing jacket and midnight blue skirt. But there was something in the way it hung on her that was uniquely hers. She wore the uniform as though it belonged to someone else.

"I didn't believe it when I saw your name on the rolls," she said. "Did you really give up on everything just to come to this stupid place?"

"It's not stupid," he snapped. "And I didn't give up. I'll still be a doctor. I promised Aunt Mila."

Johanna laughed. "How does it go then? You do your seven years here, then they send you back to Messerich to hand out pills to old *hausfrauen*?"

"It won't be like that," he said. "But I think I'll be able to help people."

"That's not always a good thing, Erich."

"Then why are you here? You never liked the BDM."

Johanna shrugged. "I didn't want to go back to

112

Messerich. I didn't want to do land service. So I came here."

Erich stared at her for a moment, waiting to hear the rest of the story, but she didn't offer it up.

"Your father almost killed me," he mumbled.

"Well he can't reach us now." Johanna bit her lip and quickly changed the subject. "Do you even know what this school is for?"

Erich thought knew the answer—he had that M word on the tip of his tongue—but he couldn't quite bring himself to let it leave his lips. Instead, he shook his head.

Johanna scowled at him. "It's magic, dummy." Relief flooded over Erich. She had said it first.

"Come on, I'll show you something you're not supposed to see," she said.

The feeling turned cold. This kind of thing with Johanna was exactly how the whole mess had started in Messerich. If all this was real that meant it could be taken away.

"It's my first week," Erich mumbled. "I don't want to get in trouble."

"You won't," Johanna said, grabbing him by the arm.

Erich continued to protest, but she ignored him and dragged him out down the hall. After a few more token groans, he relented. He did want to see whatever it was she had to show him.

As they snuck around, Erich realized that his strategy for navigating the castle—to always anchor himself at ground level—was hopelessly lacking. Johanna moved in a completely different way. She had mastered the jumble of wooden skybridges that connected every keep and tower. She jumped from one building to another, never once stopping to get her bearings. Every so often she would push him up against the wall and wait for someone to pass by.

"How long have you been here?" Erich asked.

"I don't know, months," she said. "It's easier to get

around than it looks."

"I never see you in the halls."

Johanna grinned. "I work in the kitchen. I'm not supposed to be in the halls."

That had clearly never stopped her. Out the back of one of the old barracks, she paused and pointed at a thin overgrown path that ran uphill.

"Where's it lead?" he asked.

"It's the back way up the mountain."

"You mean to the *Siegfeld*?"

"Exactly," Johanna said. She rubbed her hands together eagerly. "The second years have a game tonight."

Johanna held Erich's hand while they picked their way up the narrow path. She had a flashlight, but kept it low to the ground in case somebody saw. Scattered shouts from the game reached them as they grew closer to the top. At the edge of the tree cover, Johanna switched off her flashlight and pushed Erich to the ground. They crawled up as close as they could get without being spotted.

An array of huge lights beamed down on the platforms, illuminating the field as brightly as in the middle of the afternoon. Erich had expected more of a crowd—the sound they made was loud enough to be hundreds—but there were really only twenty or thirty boys to fill the stands.

The doors to the starting box flung open and the players strode out. Erich recognized Otto and Uwe, but he had never seen the third boy before.

"He was the captain before." Johanna pointed at Uwe. "I don't know why he's playing now."

"I think I do," Erich said, remembering Uwe on the verge of tears as Fritz reached for the flag. It must have been a terrible embarrassment to lose to a *Nassfuchs*.

Otto and Uwe gave each other a quick nod and then stepped up to the edge of the first row. In each lane, two thick wooden beams—one high and one low—jutted off from a spinning pole.

At the crack of the starting pistol, the players bolted forward in unison. All three ducked under the high beam, but the bottom plank knocked the third boy off his feet and he tumbled out across the edge of his lane. Otto and Uwe leapt into the next row without looking back.

They skidded to a stop before a set of gates that looked not unlike the one Erich had tried to hurl himself over in the first game. Otto rolled up his sleeves and held his arms outstretched, while Uwe dropped down onto his belly and crawled towards the gate in his lane. Otto closed his eyes and drew his hands up into the air, achingly slow. With a groan, the gate began to lift. All on its own.

"Look!" Erich yelped. "Lo—"

Johanna clapped a hand over his mouth, but his garbled exclamations still leaked through her fingers, only stopping once Uwe had scurried through to the other side. Otto dropped his arms to his sides and the gate crashed to the floor.

Johanna hesitantly lifted her hand off of Erich's mouth and he promised to stay quiet. He watched, enraptured, as they repeated the maneuver for Otto's gate. Uwe had a much harder time lifting it and the heavy gate slipped a moment while Otto crawled through. Johanna grabbed Erich's arm and didn't let go until Otto was safely on the other side.

There was only one row left and just a minute on the big clock. On each lane, a snarling rottweiler, chained to a post, guarded the path. Otto wasted no time. He charged, one hand raised up as he ran, then slammed it down. The hound yelped as its legs gave out under a sudden vertical force. It scrabbled and barked, but Otto kept it pinned flat long enough to dash to the other side and grab the flag. He let go of his hold on the dog and it leapt after him. Its chain leash snapped taut mid-pounce, sending it tumbling to the ground in a mess of flailing legs and paws.

Uwe had barely moved. He crouched down like a sprinter ready to dash, eyes closed and one hand held out just beyond the rottweiler's reach. A folded paper bird sat cupped on his palm. Uwe opened his eyes and the bird twitched. Erich shook Johanna with excitement.

"You saw that, didn't you?"

She shushed him, but he could tell she was as thrilled as he was.

The paper bird spasmed once more and then shot out from the boy's hand, suddenly feathered and flapping. Uwe bolted for the flag. Distracted, the dog jumped up and snapped its jaws around the fleeing bird, then tumbled to the floor, clamping its prey between both paws. Teeth tore into flesh and pulled back only shredded paper.

Uwe gripped the flagpole and the two friends raised each other's arms up in triumph. Johanna had to gag Erich again to stop him from cheering.

"Let's go," she hissed. "It'll be over soon. We need to get back before the game ends."

On the way down, Erich kept glancing up towards the field, but Johanna never once let go of his wrist.

"Have you played yet?" she asked. "They don't let me go to your games."

"I've played," he said. "I didn't make it past the second row."

"Next time, then."

Erich didn't reply, but all the way back to the castle he kept replaying the round in his head. He saw himself in the third lane, running with Otto and Uwe, raising the hulking gates for the three of them with a casual flick of his wrist.

As they parted ways, Johanna promised to mark another time for them to meet on his schedule. Erich nodded, barely listening, and let his feet carry him back to the *Nassfuchs* dormitory. He fell asleep to the roar of the crowd in his head.

# CHAPTER THIRTEEN

When Erich and Karl woke for their first ever class on Monday, the dormitory was empty. In a groggy panic, they threw on their uniforms and stumbled out into the lounge. Walther sat on the floor in the middle of the empty room, smiling and nodding his head to the Mozart that poured softly from the radio.

"Where is everyone?" Karl asked, his voice hoarse.

"I don't know," Walther said. He switched off the radio and pointed to the schedule in his lap. "I don't have class for another hour. Physics with Herr Larat."

"Me too," Erich said.

"If I had to guess, I would say they picked the three of us for a special class. Everyone else is probably in remedials," Walther said. "I for one am very glad they're taking physics seriously here. The whole field has become totally Jewified."

"I don't know anything about physics," Karl said.

Erich didn't either. "Are you sure it's not just a mistake?"

"That's an interesting idea," Walther said. "In that case we would all be very late."

He thought for a moment, then popped to his feet.

"Yes, I think that's it," he said, rushing out the door.

Erich and Karl exchanged a puzzled glance before hurrying after him. For once, they didn't have any trouble finding the room, a basement lecture hall underneath the *Nassfuchs* wing. They burst through the doors and came to an abrupt stop, almost slamming into one another. The rest of their classmates were already there, standing at attention between rows of long black desks. Strangely, everyone was turned around so as to stare at the back wall of the classroom. They didn't look away even as the three newcomers barged in.

Herr Larat sat at the front, his feet propped on his desk and his nose buried in a book. Erich had been certain they would catch a beating for being late on the first day, but he didn't acknowledge them at all. Grateful, Erich hurried over to a spot in the corner and turned to match the other boys. He eyed the back wall for some hint of what they were staring at and found nothing. It was completely bare. Karl did the same, but Walther ignored everyone and faced towards the front.

Erich itched to turn his head around and peek at their teacher, but he didn't want to draw any further attention. A few minutes passed, then he heard Herr Larat slam his book shut.

"Herr Teurk, is it?" Larat said.

"Yes, sir," Walther replied.

"What does a physicist study?"

"The laws of forces and matter, sir," Walther said.

"In a sense," Herr Larat tutted. "But there's no way to study the laws themselves. The universe does not deliver its commandments from on high. Newton did not discover his principles engraved on some stone tablet." Larat's voice grew closer with every word. "Everything a physicist knows, he learns by observation, and what is it that he observes?"

There was a crack and a yelp as Walther took too long to answer.

"Obedience, boy, he observes obedience. He learns the laws by seeing how they are obeyed."

It was a long moment before Walther understood. Erich heard a hard swallow and the shuffling of feet as Walther slowly turned around to face the back of the classroom like everyone else.

"Good," Herr Larat said. "As any physicist should, you've inferred the rules. But in my class, we will go a step further. First we will learn the laws, and then I will teach you to break them."

There was long pause as the students waited for him to continue.

"That means face this way," Herr Larat snapped.

All at once, the boys whipped around towards the front. Herr Larat stomped through the rows, handing a deflated red balloon to each student and instructing them to fill it up. The room swelled with blubbery rasping sounds. This should have broken the tense mood, but somehow it only made it worse. When they were done, Herr Larat grabbed Fritz's balloon from the front row and kicked it up into the air. Slowly, it settled to the floor.

"See how it drifts downward," he said. "The whole system is barely denser than the air around it, and for that, gravity demands it fall. But as Herr Teurk kindly demonstrated this morning, laws are flimsy things. They are enforced by suggestion alone."

Herr Larat crooked a finger at Fritz's balloon on the floor. Erich stared at it, but it did nothing. A moment later, Walther let out a squeal of delight.

"It's moving!"

"I don't see it," Erich whispered.

"It's just slow. Look!"

Walther was right. The balloon was already a few centimeters off the floor. It seemed static when he stared at it, but if he shut his eyes for a moment, it would be higher than it was before. After a few minutes, it settled at waist level and the boys burst into applause. Herr Larat took a long theatrical bow. Erich just smiled. He had watched Otto and Uwe raise wood and iron as though they were paper. This was nothing.

Larat sat back at his desk and picked up his book. "Before the day ends, I expect every one of you to lift your balloon to the ceiling."

He put his feet up and didn't seem willing to give any further explanation. The students exchanged sidelong glances and nervous chuckles with their neighbors.

Erich glared at his balloon, hoping that alone would somehow be enough. He scrunched up his eyes and tried to imagine it lifting into the air. Minute after minute passed, but nothing moved. His head throbbed. In the front row, Anton stamped and grunted like a bull. He snatched his balloon and hurled it up into the air. It bounced against the ceiling. Fritz scowled and thwacked the back of his head.

Herr Larat poked his eyes over the top of his book. "We all know you can lift it with your hands, idiot boy."

After an hour, Erich gave up on trying and watched the others. None of them had managed to coax any more life into their balloons than he had. Karl's forehead was coiled into knots and his long hair was drenched. Fritz paced back and forth in the front row, while Anton slumped at his desk, looking almost ready to fall asleep. The only boy who remained immune to the restlessness was Walther. He stood calmly with arms crossed and his head cocked to one side, his expression peaceful and inquisitive.

Erich had watched for a while before he even realized that Walther's balloon wasn't touching the desk. It hovered ever so slightly above the surface, but it was moving. It rose, faster and faster as more heads turned to watch.

"There we are," Herr Larat sang, jumping up out of his seat. "Herr Teurk has it."

Even Walther looked astounded.

"Is it… magic?" he asked.

"What I did was magic," Herr Larat said. "What you did, that's patronage."

"Patronage," Walther repeated. "Whose patronage?"

Erich mouthed along with him, testing the unfamiliar word on his tongue. Patronage. What did that mean? Herr Larat didn't answer the question. Instead, he cracked his book over Felix's head. "What are you all staring at? There's work to do!"

Reluctantly, Erich returned his attention to his own balloon. He had no better idea where to begin, but something in the air had changed. One by one, the other boys figured it out. Before long, a swarm of balloons crowded the ceiling, jostling for space. Fritz already looked bored. He tossed his balloon back and forth between his hands, never letting it touch either.

Erich's still hadn't budged. He wondered if there was something wrong with him. The confidence he had felt his first night in the bathhouse had abandoned him. Perhaps they had mixed up his blood test with someone else's. There had to be a million boys in Germany of purer breeding than him. He could already see the smirk Herr Engel would wear when Erich had to beg to be let back into the Gymnasium.

"Please," Erich whispered to Walther. "How did you do it?"

"It's no different from lifting with your hands. Trying pinning them down so you can't use them."

Erich nodded and crossed his arms into a tight knot. He squinted his eyes and tensed against his own restraints. After a few minutes, he felt something on his fingertips. There was a friction there, rubber against skin, and the tighter he twisted his arms, the more he could feel it. The balloon hummed with static as his mind circled the surface. He had imagined that it would be smooth, but in reality it was covered with ridges and crevices. He gave a push and the air above the balloon parted as it slowly rose. It was easy, really.

Walther beamed with delight as their two balloons danced with one another just below the ceiling. Erich dropped his arms to his sides. He didn't need to restrain them anymore.

After another hour of practice, Karl was the only one left who hadn't figured it out. Sweat cascaded off his drooping chin and his arms were gripped so tight against his chest that Erich wondered how he could still breathe. The balloon ignored Karl's efforts, mocking him with its stillness. It was infuriating, like watching someone failing over and over again to thread a needle. Karl didn't look up even as Herr Larat loomed over him and dug in.

"Such a pity," Larat said. "The *Führer* went to so much trouble to haul your sagging backside to Rouhhenberg. And now what? We find you're little more than a wasted mouth. And a hungry one at that. Tell me, students, how much do you think it cost to bring him here? Did they have to load this whale onto his own carriage?"

Herr Larat snapped his fingers and pointed straight at Erich.

"You, boy, give me a guess, was his mother a gypsy or a Jew?"

Erich blushed and flapped his jaw helplessly as he struggled to answer. Snickers filled the room.

"He's trying," Walther said. "Please give him—"

Larat slammed his palm down on Walther's desk. "One success and now you intend to teach my lessons for me?"

Herr Larat spewed invective in every direction. It was no longer clear whether he was shouting at Karl or Walther or both. Erich couldn't watch any longer. He jammed both hands in his pockets and gave Karl's balloon a nudge, careful not to make it look too easy. Karl gasped then a grin flickered across his lips. Erich smiled at him and nodded his head, encouraging. He gave another push, harder this time. The balloon bounced up and Karl's face fell with the realization that it wasn't his efforts that were propelling it.

"Just go with it," Erich whispered.

"Stop," Karl said. He flashed Erich a pleading look.

"Look, sir!" someone shouted and Herr Larat snapped out of his tirade.

Karl glared at Erich. His cheeks ran bright red, but it was too late for him to do anything other than follow the charade. He reached his arms out and mimed lifting the balloon to the ceiling.

"Very well, boys," Herr Larat said. He dusted off his hands, suddenly calm. "Not everyone gets it right away."

He strode over to his desk like the outburst had never happened and gave them have the last half hour to practice on their own. Erich toyed with his balloon but it gave him little joy. The angry looks Karl kept shooting him soured his mood. Walther moved over closer to Karl and tried to help, but Karl shook him away. He stood silent at his desk for the rest of the class, shoulders slumped and hands limp at his sides. He no longer even cared to try.

# CHAPTER FOURTEEN

As Erich settled into a seat at the back of Doktor Kammer's class, Karl and Walther pushed past him and headed for the front row. They plopped down and leaned in towards each other, whispering. Erich was certain they were talking about him. He wished he could bend the air like Doktor Kammer had in Messerich and listen in, but he didn't even know where to start. Doktor Kammer rapped his cane against the floor and the chattering duo reluctantly separated.

"Hello, hello, hello," Kammer said. "I know history can't compete with the excitement of Herr Larat's class, but please do give it a chance."

Erich hoped that "history" would prove to be as much of a misnomer as "physics" had been, but those prospects dwindled as Doktor Kammer dove into a lecture about Otto the Great and the First Reich. He paced back and forth as fast as his legs could carry him, Mateusz trotting happily at his side.

Whenever Doktor Kammer turned his back, Fritz would hunch his shoulders and pantomime their teacher's gait. The boys could barely restrain their snickering, Anton least of all. As Fritz clutched at an imaginary cane, Anton reached his breaking point and let loose a loud, slobbering laugh. Doktor Kammer jerked around. The students snapped back up in their seats. He eyed them for a moment, then turned around to the chalkboard and continued his lecture.

Names and dates flowed through Erich's ears like water. His eyes kept flitting to the front row where Karl and Walther were sitting. Looking around, he realized that besides them the only person he really knew was Fritz. The emptiness of the school hit Erich all at once. Everything was so big and bare, like it was intended for a hundred times more students. A kind of loneliness hung in the air and he sunk down under its weight. As much as he had been afraid of being sent home before, there was a part of him that wished it would happen. Closing his eyes he could picture himself in the comforting darkness of *Der Atlas* or cozied up to the radio with Aunt Mila.

There was a loud crash from the front row and Erich jumped up in his seat. Doktor Kammer lay sprawled out on the floor next to Fritz's desk. Mateusz scurried up and licked at his cheek, but nobody moved. Erich considered running over to help, but was afraid that would only make things worse, and he stayed back. Trying to help had already burned him once today. The threat of laughter agitated the room like a sneeze that never came.

Doktor Kammer clutched the edge of Fritz's desk and dragged himself to his feet, then bent over to pick up his cane. Fritz didn't even react, the smug half smile plastered over his mouth was the same one he'd been wearing since Erich had first stumbled into his train compartment.

Doktor Kammer scowled at the class. His eyes crinkled down into an expression harsher than his face was meant for. Erich waited for him to cast away his cane and bear down on Fritz with the same fury he'd shown Herr Engel, but he did nothing. After a moment, Doktor Kammer took a step back, pointed to a spot on the map and carried on with his lesson.

*Oberführer* Ehrenzweig came next. His classroom was dark and the boys didn't even dare whisper to each other as they fumbled to their seats. This time, Erich deliberately took a spot right next to Karl and Walther, but neither of them would look at him. At least they were no longer chattering with each other. Even they didn't dare whisper in Ehrenzweig's presence.

The only light came from a chunky black slide projector at the front of the room. A bright bulb blared within its cage, casting an empty, white square on the wall. The *Oberführer*'s shadow cut across the screen.

"Let me tell you a story about two towns," he said as he walked over and pressed a heavy slide down into the slot of the projector. "Muckerau and Kalisch."

A map appeared on the screen and a murmur of excitement rolled across the room. It was Poland. Erich leaned forward, grateful that Karl and Walther had incited him into sitting in the front row. For the past two days, the radio had given them nothing but news of the war, but Erich was still hungry for word of more victories.

"These two were among the first to fall along the border, but their natures—and the nature of their defeat—could not be more different. Muckerau might better be called a village. They don't even have it on the map." With a rod, Ehrenzweig pointed to where the town would have been. "It is small and agrarian, a place of working peoples."

He moved the rod to the other. "Kalisch is entirely different. It is urbanized and intellectualized. It is a place of unrest and revolt. It has all the ingredients that let communist thinking take root. Thus, it should be no surprise to any of you that Kalisch is a city of Jews.

"Now I can already hear you thinking, '*Herr Oberführer*, why should I care? What's the difference between a Pole and Jew? I wouldn't let my sister marry either of them.' And of course you would be right. To let the influence of either degrade our blood would be catastrophic.

"But neither will it do to lump all such subhumans into a single bucket. These races are different. We are powerless against them unless we understand what separates us from them. We must understand where they come from, what they want, and by what insidious means they will try to get it. That, my friends, is why we study the racial sciences. And it is why we must look closer at our examples of Kalisch and Muckerau."

With a loud clunk, Ehrenzweig replaced the slide and the whole class took in a sharp breath at the image that dropped down the screen. It was a war photograph, the first Erich had seen. It must have been sent straight to Rouhhenberg from the front. All across a field of cratered earth lay the bodies of men and horses. This was the vengeance of the German panzer. Alas, the photograph was of such poor quality that Erich could hardly make out the details. He wished he could see it up close.

"This was taken two days ago on the outskirts of Muckerau," Ehrenzweig said. "The Poles lack the bravery or the wits of we Germans, but they were nonetheless able to mount a defense of sorts. They gathered their cavalry and charged a Wehrmacht armored division. To no avail, I needn't add. Can any of you tell me why they might have done so?"

Immediately, Walther's finger shot into the air.

"Yes, Tuerk?"

"They thought the tanks were fake," Walther answered breathlessly. "The Treaty of Versailles doesn't permit Germany to build any, so they must have figured ours were practice dummies."

"Just so," Ehrenzweig said. "They assumed we would follow rules written down by traitors *because that is what they would have done.* Their muddled, slavish minds can't understand that we do not submit to any authority but our own.

"Now, let us compare that to the situation in the city." He changed the slide. In the new photograph, a

Wehrmacht battalion marched down an empty city street. There were no craters or shattered walls and the sidewalks were bare of bodies. All the windows were shuttered. "Here you can see the great battle of Kalisch!"

All the boys began to applaud and Erich broke into a laugh. He glanced over to Karl, who was laughing too, but as soon as their eyes met, Karl sobered and stowed his hands on his lap.

"Where are the defenders?" Ehrenzweig mocked. "The Jews have fled like rats to their warrens. This has always been their nature. They scurry from place to place because, like a parasite, they cannot survive on their own. They have no more interest in self-defense than they do in honest labor. All their wealth comes from usury and their power from conspiracy.

"In our sessions to come, we will learn why. We will explore the Jew, the Slav and the Pole, the Gypsy and the Negroid. We will document all the calamitous ways they intertwine with each other. And most importantly, we will begin to grasp why the Aryan stands so tall above the rest."

Ehrenzweig yanked the slide out from the projector. He sat down at his desk and then, when he saw that none of the rapt boys had moved, made a shooing gesture.

"Go on," he snapped. "That's all for today."

✳✳✳

After class, Erich ran after Karl and Walther to ask where they were going. Walther seemed hesitant to answer, but Karl gave him a nod of acquiescence and told him they were headed to the exercise room to practice. Neither of them spoke to him as he followed them through the halls. No matter where he stood, he felt as though he were being butted up against the wall. Erich fell back to the rear.

Their destination was in the same basement floor as Doktor Kammer's classroom, but somehow they still had go through the *Nassfuchs* lounge and climb up three flights of stairs before plunging back underground. Inside, punching bags and weights crowded up against intricate apparatuses that Erich didn't recognize. He wanted to find out what everything did, but Walther led them straight past it all and to the back of the room. He pulled a balloon out of the pouch at his waist, inflated it, and passed it off to Karl.

Karl grappled for two hours. They tied his wrists together and filled the balloon half with helium from a cannister in the corner, yet no matter how much he grunted and squealed, it never even twitched. Erich paced endlessly, tearing circles into the floor. It was too painful to watch.

Erich had so much pent up energy from sitting through history and racial studies that he wanted to hit something. He eyed the bags hanging from the ceiling and wondered if he and Walther combined could coax one into swinging, but he knew it was the wrong time to ask.

"Maybe you should try again with your wrists untied," Erich said. He held out one hand and demonstrated by sending Karl's balloon up to the ceiling. "Now that I've got it figured out, it's actually easier to use—"

Karl whipped around. "That's enough!"

Erich recoiled as Karl's hair hurled out a spray of sweat.

"I'm just trying to help," Erich snapped. "It's not my fault you can't manage it."

Walther jumped between them. "Come on. Don't make it any worse."

Erich opened his mouth to explain how unfair they were being, but he stumbled over the words. What came out sounded incoherent even to him. Walther put a hand on his shoulder and guided him towards the door. Erich shook it off. He stomped out on his own accord, cheeks burning, and ran all the way back to the dormitory.

Erich fished around under his bunk, pulled out Klaus' box, and wrapped his stethoscope around his neck. He lay on his bed and stared at the ceiling for an hour, endlessly circling over the incident in physics class. The longer he thought about, the more certain he was that he'd done the right thing. Karl should have been grateful for his help. Without Erich, he would probably already be on the train home. Instead, he was here with time to practice on his own terms.

At dinner, Erich searched around for someone to sit with and settled on Felix, who he at least vaguely knew. They exchanged a few terse pleasantries, but Erich had no stomach for conversation. All his attention went to Karl and Walther in the middle of the table. They sat side by side in the normally empty zone between the green and red teams. Neither of them ever looked back at him.

Erich could hear the clatter of forks and smell the food from above, but after almost an hour the *Nassfüchsen* still hadn't been served. They grumbled quietly to each other, but no one was brave enough to take their complaint any further.

Eventually, a tall, round-faced woman stepped up to the edge of the staff balcony. She was very thin, but she wore a broad, black jacket and white scarf that accentuated her shoulders. This was Frau Murr, the head of the BDM girls and consequently everything else in the castle. Even indoors, Erich had never seen her take off the leather gloves that now rested on the balcony podium.

"*Heil Hitler*," she said. "An egregious incident has taken place tonight."

Erich froze, certain this was somehow about him. He had only been at Rouhhenberg for a week, but had already accumulated a growing list of misdeeds. Sneaking off with Johanna. Cheating for Karl.

Frau Murr cleared her throat. "*Scharführer* Kammer's dog has gone missing."

Erich instantly relaxed. The boys chortled and even some of the teachers had smirks on their faces.

As Frau Murr spoke, three BDM girls stepped into the hall, each wheeling a cart stacked high with covered plates. Every hungry *Nassfuchs* eye turned to watch them approach. A few curious upperclassmen peered down over the railings of their high tables.

"I am holding the *Nassfüchsen* accountable," Frau Murr said.

One of the girls set a plate down in front of Anton and lifted off its cover. Underneath was a shining, silver dog bowl, heaped high with mush. She grinned at Anton and jammed a spoon into the brown slop. Fritz broke into an uproarious laugh but he cut off abruptly when the BDM girl slammed an identical bowl down in front of him.

"Hush, children," Frau Murr said, as the remainder of the dog bowls were delivered. One of the two high tables refused to quiet and she jabbed her finger at them. "That means you too, *Wehrbären*. To any *Nassfüchsen* who wish to eat with the rest of us in the future, I recommend you form a search party tonight. If you come across anything suspicious, report to me immediately."

"That's ridiculous," Felix whispered. "We didn't do anything."

"I wouldn't be so sure," Erich said, his eyes on Fritz.

Erich eyed the bowl in front of him and his stomach let out a low whine. It was the shade of mulch and chunks of it stuck to Erich's spoon when he lifted it up out. The ooze hung off the spoon for a long while, stretching, before it finally broke and slopped back down into bowl.

On the green side, Fritz leaned over to whisper something in Anton's ear. He glanced up at the balcony with a defiant smirk, dug his spoon into the sludge, and choked down a mouthful of it. A few others joined him— Anton even seemed to like the stuff—but most of the boys just picked at their meals in disgust. Erich shoved a spoonful between his lips, but as hungry as he was, he could barely stop himself from spitting it out. For a long time after he swallowed, the sour taste clung to the corners of his mouth and his tongue kept dredging up pieces of grit.

"It can't actually be dog food," Erich said. "Right?"

Felix shrugged and pushed his bowl away.

Over in the neutral zone, Walther pulled out a shaker of salt from his pouch and dumped a generous helping over his bowl before handing it off to Karl. Erich gave up on eating and spent the rest of the meal glowering at Karl and Walther while they laughed like old friends and traded off the shaker between bites.

# CHAPTER FIFTEEN

That night, the *Nassfüchsen* split up to search for the elusive dachshund. They stalked the castle with flashlights and lanterns and grumbling stomachs, cautiously tiptoeing around the ghastly iron statues that guarded the halls. Erich didn't understand how they could be expected to succeed with so much of the castle off limits, but perhaps, as in *SV*, that was the point.

When Erich finally returned to the dormitory after hours of fruitless searching, a crust of bread was tucked under his pillow. He ducked below the covers and devoured it in two big swallows. As he picked at the crumbs nestled in the bedsheets, Erich reminded himself to thank Johanna when he saw her next.

Most of the boys blamed Fritz for their predicament, but no one had managed to turn up any real evidence that he had done something to Mateusz. After a few more days of dogfood, Fritz sported a black eye and a limp of his own. Well deserved in Erich's opinion. But something in all this had turned Fritz into Herr Larat's favorite student. He would constantly bring him to the front to demonstrate one technique or another in Physics.

Karl, at least, seemed relieved by this. He was no longer

the center of attention and Walther's lessons soon paid off. Once, Herr Larat—no doubt fishing for an opportunity to humiliate—called on Karl to stop a falling pen before it hit the floor. Karl waited until the last moment and then brought it to a dead stop without even moving his hands. There were no more jokes about his impotence after that.

With every passing day came word of fresh victories in Poland. Bombs fell like rain over Warsaw and the Wehrmacht rolled unstoppable through Łódź and Kraków. Teachers and students alike walked the halls with brimming smiles and gleefully exchanged the news even though they had all already heard it.

Only Doktor Kammer was immune to the infectious mood. He suffered without his companion. Some days, he would slump over his cane and lecture too softly to hear. On others he would spark up with elation and tumble through his lesson in an anachronistic babble. After a week of this, he cornered Erich in the hall, a wild look in his eyes.

"I'm picking you to captain the red team on Friday."

"What? Why?" Erich blurted out. "I mean— Thank you. Thank you, sir."

"You can thank me by winning. I hear Vinzent is already grooming that von Keppler boy."

"I'll try, sir," Erich mumbled.

Kammer leaned in close to his ear.

"I'll send your *Jungenschaftführer* to help you pick out your rows in the morning," he whispered.

"Is that allowed?" Erich hissed back.

Doktor Kammer winked like his old self and strolled off, whistling a tune.

**\*\*\***

The match was their first since beginning their physics

lessons and their first without Otto and Uwe to captain. On the morning of, Doktor Kammer met Erich where a car waited for them by the main gate. He couldn't make the trek up the mountain on foot, so they had to drive down to the base and then come back up around the supply road on the other side. Sitting with him in the back seat, Erich tried to gauge which of his teacher's many personalities he was in the presence of. Doktor Kammer was silent, but eventually Erich worked up the courage to speak.

"Sir, why do you teach history and not..." Erich trailed off, uncertain whether he was supposed to say magic or patronage.

"'Physics'?" Doktor Kammer smiled weakly. "What would be the point? You children don't need us. I could blabber about science like Herr Larat, but all the while you'd just be teaching yourselves. Spare me that humiliation."

"But in Messerich, I remember—"

"You don't understand," Doktor Kammer cut him off. He sounded almost angry. "Listen. Do you hear the engine?"

"Yes, sir," Erich said.

"I want you to silence it."

Erich laughed nervously. He licked his finger and raised it in the air as if it were a baton. "You mean like this?"

"I told you already, you're not like us," Doktor Kammer said. He reached down into his sleeve and pulled out a wire with a tiny bulb on the end. A radio speaker. "This is all I did in Messerich. It's just a trick. We're magicians. We deceive. Vinzent gets applause every year for lifting that balloon up a few centimeters off the floor. Nobody notices the fan under the floorboards.

"You boys are different." Doktor Kammer grabbed Erich's baton-finger and jammed it into his chest. "You don't need tricks. What you've got, this patronage, it's real. It's innate. Remember what Hugo said: you need do nothing. You don't need to know how a sound works to cut it off. Just do it. Silence it."

Erich gave a confused look and let his arms drop. He closed his eyes and focused on the engine's rattle, how it seeped through the cracks in metal and upholstery. His seat shook with the sound and he followed it back to where a jungle of iron sputtered and spat under the hood. Erich tried to picture what Herr Larat would tell him to do. If noise travels through air then—

"Stop." Doktor Kammer snapped his finger next to Erich's ear. "You're still thinking about it too much."

"Alright," Erich said. He tried to forget about the engine itself and just focus on what he was hearing. It rasped like a cat with something stuck in its throat. But if Doktor Kammer was right, it didn't matter what it sounded like. The sound was just a thing he had in his hands. If Erich wanted to, he could tie it into a knot.

The engine's rumble winked out and the cabin fell almost to silence. The only sound was the crunch of rocks beneath their tires. The driver looked back nervously, but Doktor Kammer flashed him a reassuring smile.

"I... I did it," Erich marveled. "That was me."

"Of course it was," Doktor Kammer whispered.

The whole rest of the trip, Erich couldn't stop toying with the world around him. He tuned in one at a time to the thousand different sounds that surrounded him, though it was difficult to reach very far. He didn't notice that they had pulled up to the gate at the peak until the driver stepped around and opened the door. Doktor Kammer shook Erich gently and they got out of the car.

"You haven't forgotten why you're here, have you?" he said. "You have a game to win."

The elation Erich had felt on the way up vanished, replaced by an anxious fluttering in his stomach.

"Run along then," Doktor Kammer said. "Uwe's waiting in the hangar."

Crossing the field, Erich could hear his teammates

whispering to one another, confused and disconcerted. They didn't understand why he'd been chosen, and being honest, neither did Erich. He slipped into the hangar under a crack in the massive doors. Just inside, he stopped dead, gaping at the mechanical cacophony that surrounded him.

Aisles and aisles stretched out ahead, filled up with a hundred different combinations of staircases, gates, labyrinths, mirrors, lightbulbs, switches, tripwires, locks and doors, all mirrored into identical sets of three. Erich picked his way towards the back where Uwe was speaking with a tall man in worn overalls. Their conversation halted abruptly as he approached. The stranger turned to look at Erich. Thick glasses magnified his eyes, which were the same dark brown as his skin.

"*Heil Hitler*," Uwe said. "Have you met Herr Jensson?"

Erich shook his head and hesitantly extended a hand. He had never seen an African outside of drawings. This man had neither the ballooned lips nor the hyena smile of those, but Herr Jensson was unmistakably the sort of person that *Oberführer* Ehrenzweig was always warning them about in class.

"Are you... a teacher?" Erich said.

"No, no, nothing like that," Herr Jensson said. His grip left a trail of engine grease on Erich's palm.

"This is all Herr Jensson's work," Uwe said, gesturing at the countless obstacles that surrounded them. "He's made a whole new set for this year. Somehow."

Herr Jensson shrugged. "You'd figure them all out otherwise."

Erich glanced around at the countless obstacles and realized he would have to make a choice. He put on a helpless face. "Will you tell me what to pick?"

Uwe winked at Herr Jensson. "I told you, didn't I? Doktor Kammer wants me to cheat for him."

"And are you going to?" Jensson asked.

"Would you tell anyone if I did?"

Herr Jensson shook his head.

"Good man," Uwe said. "But I think he'll do fine on his own."

Erich gave a look that indicated he disagreed, but Uwe would have none of it. He yanked Erich over to a hydraulic lift in the middle of the hangar. Hissing, it carried them up to a get a better view. Surrounded by so many choices, Erich wondered if anyone would notice if he just picked at random.

"You have to remember that it's not just about one match," Uwe said. "What matters is your score at the end of the season. You can't use a row more than once, so if you blow all the tough rows in the first few games, you won't have any surprises left for later."

"What if I can't tell which ones are which?" Erich asked.

"Then you're already winning. It's very hard to resist the easy points when your team is begging for them. But you aren't here to make friends."

"There's no danger of that," Erich mumbled.

Uwe raised an eyebrow and Erich hurried to change the subject.

"*Jungenschaftsführer*, if I can ask, what went wrong in our first match?" he said. "With Fritz and the door."

Erich immediately regretted it. He expected the *Jungenschaftsführer* to flash with rage at the mention of that failure, but he looked more sad than angry.

"It's hard to say. I think you don't always need it to be a puzzle. With *Nassfüchsen* at least, a brick wall will do just as well. Otto would have known that." Uwe stared out over the railing for a long while before continuing, "Anyway, it doesn't matter anymore. There's a new captain now."

"Just because you lost one match?" Erich asked. "I won't last long if that's how it works."

"It's not that I lost," Uwe sighed. "It's who I lost to."

Erich tried repeatedly to solicit Uwe's opinions as he

picked over the rows, but the *Jungenschaftsführer* never let anything slip. He would just nod his head and give some vague encouragement. Eventually, Erich gave up on getting hints and pondered in silence.

He didn't understand how most of the obstacles worked, but he made his best guesses and before long he'd settled on a rough set of three. Uwe betrayed no judgement as Erich shouted his choices down to Herr Jensson. Only after it was too late to change them did he speak.

"Why that one there?" Uwe asked, pointing to Erich's third row. It was completely empty, just a polished hardwood floor that stretched across all three lanes.

Erich shrugged. "I guess I just want to see what it does."

"Me too," Uwe grinned.

Herr Jensson left for a moment and then returned with a few *SS* men who wheeled the rows out to the front of the hangar where they could be slotted into the trench. Erich squinted at the man who seemed to be in charge. He had one sleeve rolled up and his arm was thicker than Erich's head. An emerald, tattooed snake curled from his shoulder to where it bared fangs on the back of his hand.

"Who is that?" Erich asked.

"That's *Rottenführer* Wolff," Uwe said. "I think he loves that tattoo more than his own children. I've never seen him cover it. I hear sometimes he talks to it."

Uwe started to explain some convoluted theory he and Otto had about Wolff's snake, but Erich was too nervous to really listen, and before long the grinding of the great chain drowned him out. Everything was out of Erich's hands now. He had hoped that would make him feel better, but the knot in his stomach only snarled tighter. The boys had patronage now and he could already picture the green team tearing through his obstacles like paper. When it came time to go outside, he had to force himself to take every step.

Doing his best to ignore the taunts from the crowd, Erich followed his rows as the chain dragged them through the trench. He wished each of the platforms luck in turn. Once they were locked in place, Erich climbed up to what Uwe called the captain's perch, a high chair with a ladder carved into the side. It was supposed to afford him a better view of the match, but mostly it gave everyone else a better view of him.

Erich watched his teammates whispering to each other below and wondered what they were saying. He considered listening in with Doktor Kammer's trick, but decided it might be better not to know. Across the field, Fritz settled into the opposite perch with an easy confidence. Erich squirmed in the hard seat and wished he could look that relaxed.

The gates to the starting box flung open and the players stepped forward, shielding their eyes from the midday sun. In the first two lanes came Fritz's usual entourage—Anton, of course, and Matthias Fisser, a soft-spoken boy who since their first *SV* match had followed Fritz around as faithfully as Doktor Kammer's dachshund. The last player, Viktor Schrader, was the only unexpected choice. He'd never shown any special talent in Physics class, nor was he a close friend of Fritz's. Still, Erich reasoned, if it was unwise for Erich to expend all his toughest rows in the first match, then it wouldn't make sense for Fritz to send out his best players either.

With the crack of *Rottenführer* Wolff's starting pistol, the three boys dashed out onto the first row. A thicket of pipes awaited them, belching steam in intermittent bursts. Matthias and Viktor slowed before they reached it, but Anton didn't stop. He pulled his hands up into the sleeves of his uniform and charged through, howling as the steam buffeted him. Despite his brute approach, he moved with a surprising nimbleness, ducking below the overhanging pipes and vaulting with covered hands over any that blocked his path.

Viktor traversed the thicket more slowly, but Erich could tell he had the pattern figured out. He would bob his head as he counted down and then dart forward just as a jet of steam hissed out behind him. Matthias hadn't even started in yet and his wide eyes betrayed an escalating panic. Erich's teammates hurled taunts at him, while his own shouted for him to move.

When he couldn't take it any longer, Matthias rushed in and immediately cracked his head against one of the pipes. He yelped and then tumbled out of bounds in what looked like a very deliberate capitulation. As the red team broke into a gleeful anthem, Karl grabbed Felix by the shoulders and shook him in excitement. He glanced back, saw that Erich was watching, and immediately tempered his enthusiasm.

Erich had hoped that the steam would send Fritz's players in a frantic charge into his second row, where a web of barely visible tripwires waited for them, but even Anton didn't fall for it. He skidded to a halt the moment he left the pipes, wincing as he examined his reddened hands. He paced back and forth while Viktor caught up.

Viktor sized up the obstacle for a moment, then reached out a careful finger, gave one of the wires a pluck and jumped back before anything terrible could happen. Erich had hoped for a dramatic consequence, a burst of electricity or a jet of flames, but there was only a loud click.

Past the wires, one of the floorboards in Viktor's lane slid back and a row of iron bars poked up like nascent teeth. They were still so low that they could be stepped over, but it served as a warning. With every wire Anton and Viktor touched, the bars rose a little higher.

They inched forward through the web, contorting their bodies into odd shapes. When the clock reached the last thirty seconds, Anton's patience snapped. He bellowed and slashed at the air in an outburst of frustration and patronage. A wire snapped in two. Viktor froze and whipped around as the field fell silent for three long seconds. There was no click. The bars didn't move.

Fritz cracked a smile and Anton roared at the top of his lungs. This was exactly the sort of thing he had been waiting for—something he could break. He thrashed and clawed, arms of patronage cleaving through distant wires like a machete in the brush. Realizing it was too late, Viktor abandoned his own lane and joined in from a distance to clear the path for Anton. When the last wire fell limp to the floor, Anton vaulted over his half-raised gate and rushed out into the empty final row, abandoning all caution.

Erich held his breath and willed whatever contraption waited under the bare floor to leap out. Nothing came. Anton crossed it in a few quick strides. There was no hidden door, no sudden barrier or invisible trigger. The row was as empty as it looked.

Somehow, out of the endless obstacles in the hangar, Erich had chosen the worst possible one. The trap was not for the player but for the captain. He shrunk down in humiliation as Anton snatched the flag and *Rottenführer* Wolff's whistle rang out, just a moment too late.

### ✳✳✳

No one spoke as Erich rejoined his teammates, head held low, but their sour looks were clear enough.

"So," Karl said flatly. "Who's playing in the second half?"

Erich winced. He had completely forgotten that he would have to choose. He tried to laugh off his surprise, but no one laughed with him.

"I-I'm still deciding."

Everyone was staring at him. He scanned his teammates faces and tried to remember Uwe's advice—

*you're not here to make friends*—but he had trouble taking it to heart. In the end, he cared much more about winning their esteem than the match. Would they be bitter if they weren't chosen, or could it be the opposite? What if some of them didn't want to play?

Erich took a long breath and considered his options one at a time. Richard and Felix were safe choices. He had played with them before, but then again, neither had scored a point. Hampe and Ivo were promising, but they both spent far too much time with Fritz and the rest of the green team. Bardulf and his brother Eugen had to have very special breeding to *both* be chosen for the school, but Erich couldn't decide if it would be better to split them up or play them together. No matter who he picked, he wasn't sure anyone on his team could match what Anton and Viktor had done in the first round.

When *Oberführer* Ehrenzweig came over to ask him for his choices, Erich listed them out with as much certainty as he could muster. "Bardulf, Felix, and... Karl."

Karl's eyes bulged as he heard his name. He grabbed Erich by the arm and yanked him away from the group.

"What are you doing?" he hissed.

"I-I thought..." Erich said. "I thought after everything you'd want to do this on your own."

"Of course I do," Karl moaned. "But you don't understand. I can't do it. I'm not like everyone else." He was almost crying. "I go down to the bathhouse every night, same as you, and then every day in class Walther has to lift my balloon for me."

Erich grasped for words.

"I need more time," Karl begged. "Please. They'll find out. They'll send me home. I c-can't go back. You have to pick someone else."

"What are you girls chattering about?" Ehrenzweig shouted. "Auch, in the starting box, now!"

"Wait, sir!" Erich said, waving his hands. "I want to change. Eugen will play instead of Karl."

"Too late," Ehrenzweig barked. "Did Frederick the Great change his mind after invading Saxony? No! You don't get second chances in war."

Erich tried to object, but Karl cut him off. He gave a strained smile and then plodded towards the starting box, staring at his feet like a man on the way to the gallows.

As he settled back into the captain's perch, Erich caught Walther's eye. He stood apart from the rest of the green team. Walther had been cheating for Karl for a whole week and he looked almost relieved to see that he could end the lies soon.

After an interminable wait, Fritz's rows crawled out from the hangar. Erich craned his neck to get a look. The first row was hollowed out into a pit with a thin plank bridge running across it. A wall blocked the second, dotted with climbing handles. On the other side, a ramp sloped down to the final row, which was almost as empty as Erich's had been. In its center, a pole shot up a few meters from the floor and then bent out into a box. A pull chain dangled invitingly from it. Nothing on the field looked like it would require any show of patronage, but Erich couldn't be sure.

Karl had gone into the starting box with his shoulders slumped in defeat, but he emerged resolute, his eyes locked on the path ahead. Bardulf and Felix looked terrified in comparison.

This time, there was no mad rush with the crack of the starting pistol. The boys stepped gingerly out onto their narrow planks, arms outstretched for balance. Felix had the steadiest footing of the three, though Karl didn't fall far behind. Bardulf turned out to be terribly clumsy and he only made it a few paces before he slipped and thudded into the pit below. The green team howled with delight as he climbed up only to trip and fall again moments later.

Karl stepped off the other end of the plank just after Felix. He glanced up at Erich with a thin smile that was snuffed out immediately when a loud churning rose up from inside the wall ahead. As the sound dwindled away, some mechanism sprang into motion and half of the climbing grips were sucked back in.

Karl swore and charged at the wall. He hurled himself up to catch the first handhold. Felix hesitated a moment, looked back at Bardulf, who still struggled to find his balance, then began to climb. Even with many of the handles missing, there were still enough to make steady progress.

Karl's face ran red as he heaved his thick body from perch to perch, but he never slowed. The afternoon sun bore down on them and sweat pooled on the floor below. As Karl passed the halfway point, the churning sound kicked back up. When he reached out, the handles reconfigured themselves. He grasped at nothing and fell back on one arm, all his bulk wrenching into his shoulder as he swung out.

The wall inhaled both of Felix's handles and he tumbled back. He threw out his hands to break his fall, yelping in pain as they smacked against the mat below. Cradling his wrists, he crawled back up to his feet and started again from the bottom.

Above, Karl had managed to throw his dangling arm up to a second grip. He hauled himself from one handle to another, faster than Erich thought him capable of. Just as the sound resumed, he clapped both arms over the wall's top lip and dragged his body over onto the ramp on the other side.

The onlooking boys, red and green alike, broke into laughter as Karl rolled limply onto his back, choking on long sputtering breaths. Below, the handgrips rearranged themselves again, sending Felix back to the bottom as the clock passed into the final minute.

Still wheezing, Karl dragged himself to his feet and charged for the flag. As he reached the pole that hung over the lane, Karl cracked into a barrier he couldn't see. He fell back, clutching his forehead. The spot he had struck thrummed. He reached out a hand and pressed it flat against the air ahead of him. A pane of glass, almost invisible, separated him from the flag. Erich groaned as he looked over at the pull chain dangling on the other side. It was obvious what had to be done. Anyone else in their class could have done without blinking.

Karl dropped to his knees and dug his fingers into the floorboards. Confused whispers scurried amongst the *Nassfüchsen*. *What is he waiting for?* A few boys on the red team shouted for Felix to help, but he had fallen again and couldn't see above the wall. He threw the onlookers a confused look. Karl's arms flopped at his sides. He wasn't even trying.

"What's wrong with you?" someone shouted from the red team. "*Arschloch*, get up!"

Another boy scooped up a handful of dirt and hurled it Karl's direction. The others copied him with twigs and pebbles, none of which flew very far. Fritz cackled from his perch as the green team joined in. They hovered their tiny projectiles in the air and then sent them sailing towards the rows. A stone cracked Karl across the forehead. He hardly seemed to notice. Blood trickled over his nose. Erich jumped down from the perch and rushed at the green team, but Walther intercepted him.

"Look!"

Walther twisted Erich's head towards Bardulf, who wobbled halfway across the plank bridge on the first row. He had his arm outstretched and with casual motion, he did what Karl could not.

The chain jerked down and everyone froze. A tense silence descended on the field. The green team's suspended missiles clattered to the ground, forgotten. The box at the top of the pole cracked open and a rope swung down, an iron ball at its end. It swept out and crashed through the glass. Shards sprayed in every direction. Karl shrieked and threw his arms up to cover his face. Hurtling glass rained over him, but it did not strike him. Just before it could, it froze.

Karl blinked in surprise and a deafening roar welled up from the red team. A hundred slivers hung motionless in the air around him. Grunting, Karl dragged himself to his feet and gaped, unwilling to believe that this was his doing. He looked down at his arms as though they were not his own and then with a wave, he swept the glass away.

Erich laughed and threw his arm over Walther's shoulder, not caring that he was on the other team. Walther grinned back in tangible relief. But Karl wasn't finished. He pulled the chain in Felix's lane, and then turned back, not even bothering to watch the glass shatter. He held his palm out flat and shoved it through the air. Inside the wall, gears shrieked in protest as they were forced the wrong way by a week of pent-up patronage. The sunken handgrips shot out.

Slivers of glass slid out of Karl's path as he walked over and put his hand on the flag. The resulting uproar shook Felix into action and he jumped up onto the cleared wall. With so many handles exposed, the climb was easy. With a few seconds left, he sprinted at the flag, almost yanking his arm out as he grabbed it and kept going.

Erich had been so focused on Karl that he had forgotten about the game itself. It took him a moment to take in what had happened. They had scored twice in one round, pulling them a point ahead of the greens. Erich was too stunned to do more than limply shake hands as his teammates crowded around, cheering and singing. Even Bardulf received a few consolatory pats on the back while everyone waited for the day's real victors to join them.

Karl elbowed his way through the crowd of boys and hurled himself at Erich, almost lifting him up. He shook with a long laugh and belted out *Vorwärts, Vorwärts* louder than anyone else as they marched all the way down to the bathhouse.

# CHAPTER SIXTEEN

Erich loved and dreaded the baths in equal measure. It was not the blood that bothered him. There was nothing in the world like that instant sense of belonging that overtook him when that bubbling spigot opened. But he hated to see Fritz, who always looked at him like a cockroach that had just scurried into the shower. But today it was Erich's turn to gloat. He couldn't wait to watch the smugness evaporate from Fritz's face.

Yet when he finally stepped through the door, Erich hardly recognized him. Fritz's proud shoulders were slumped and the purple swelling over his eye had grown to consume half his face. He didn't utter a word as he stepped into position and unbuttoned his shirt, revealing a mess of bruises down his side. Between suspicions over the dogfood and anger at losing the match, Fritz had not fared well by his teammates.

Erich didn't know what to say. Agape, he stared at Fritz until the *SS* man at the door yelled at him to hurry up. As Erich hastily peeled off his uniform, his knees shook and he almost fell. After everything that had happened, he was exhausted and hungry, but he knew the bath would invigorate him.

Erich stared at the floor and waited, eager to see his troubles slither down the drain. The rain clatter sounded from above and he held his breath in anticipation. The flow tipped over the spigot's edge. A moment later, something cold splattered against his skin. It had always been warm before. This was wrong. It was all wrong. Erich jerked his head up and icy blood sprayed into his eyes, stinging. He howled, but as soon as he opened his mouth it began to pour in and he retched on the putrid taste.

Erich wanted to sing like he had before. Surely that would make it better, but he couldn't find the tune. A terrible, dissonant ringing shrieked in his ears. He gargled and spat and choked until a firm hand thrust his neck down and his eyes filled with black.

As at last the flow dribbled out, Erich lifted up his head and wiped the congealing blood from his eyes. It was caked into his hair and he wondered how he had never noticed that happen before. Fritz wore the same expression of wide-eyed shock. Beneath the drying blood, he was utterly pale. When the water finally poured down, they stayed under the spigot until they turned blue and the guard had to drag them away.

Erich and Fritz stumbled upstairs and out into the courtyard, shivering even in the summer air. Erich felt an odd compulsion to go off in the other direction. There was somewhere he needed to be, but he couldn't quite place it.

The rest of their classmates had already headed to the chapel for dinner. Reluctantly, Erich pushed open the heavy doors and joined them. Karl had saved a spot for him at the table in the center of the red team's side. The horrible bath had made Erich almost forget about their win on *Siegfeld*. He glanced over to where Walther sat with the greens and felt a twinge of satisfaction at his jealous expression.

"You look terrible," Bardulf said.

"Not as bad as Fritz does," Karl laughed.

"Was there a fight?" Felix's eyes lit up. "Did you win?"

"It was nothing like that," Erich mumbled.

"Right," Karl drawled, holding a finger over his lips.

Everyone else was so drunk on victory that they didn't even seem bothered by the dog's slop, but Erich felt too sick to eat. Amidst all this joy, he still felt cold and alone. He picked a few pale globules of meat from the mush and forced them down, then pushed his silver bowl away.

It was a relief when Hugo finally climbed up to the podium to wish them goodnight, but something was different. A man Erich had never seen before stumbled behind him, struggling to catch up in short staccato steps. He wore the same grey suit as Hugo and they looked so much alike that they could have been twins. Yet something terrible had happened to the twin's face. Fire and worse. Sallow skin hung limp off his cheeks in melted folds. One ear had been torn off and his jaw dangled, half-detached.

"Who is that?" Erich whispered.

Karl raised an eyebrow. "Hugo?"

"No, the man behind him, with his face all... burned. You don't see him?"

"See who?"

"Nevermind," Erich mumbled.

Karl shrugged and returned his attention to the podium. Erich glanced around but no one else seemed at all put off by the stranger who hovered over Hugo's shoulder. As the headmaster spoke, the twin made every effort to copy him. His broken mouth flapped open and closed soundlessly as he mimicked Hugo's gestures with limbs that bent in the wrong places. The sight was so disturbing that Erich could hardly pay attention to the words.

When Hugo was done and he returned to his seat, his twin hobbled after him to collapse in the empty chair at the headmaster's side. Had this creature always haunted Hugo? Why was he only seeing it now? Erich shivered and tried to push the images out of his mind.

As the other *Nassfüchsen* organized themselves to search

for Mateusz, Erich retreated to the comfort of his room. He burrowed under the covers and closed his eyes, but the headmaster's twin seemed to lurk in every shadowed corner. Erich couldn't shake the feeling that blood still clung to his skin and matted his hair. It was hours before he could fall asleep.

***

In the morning, the bedroom was empty. A wrenching ache twisted at Erich's stomach as he hauled himself out of his bunk. The memory of the bath gone wrong hung over him and he wondered if it was making him sick. To his surprise, Karl and Walther were still waiting for him in the lounge, though it was immediately clear that Walther had wanted to leave him behind.

"Come on, we're late," Karl said.

Ignoring the pain in his gut, Erich threw on his uniform and the three of them dashed off to Physics. Karl was so eager to show off his newfound talents that he demanded they sit in the front row. The balloons were gone, replaced by a candle at each desk.

Fortunately for them, Herr Larat was late as well. Walther scribbled in his journal while they waited for the teacher to arrive.

"What are you writing?" Erich asked.

Karl sighed. "He thinks he can catch the dognapper."

"I write down everything the other students are doing," Walther explained. "That way I'll notice if the pattern changes."

"And that'll tell you who it is?" Erich asked.

"I hope so," Walther said. "It's not as if I've done this before."

"Wait... does that mean you have a page on us?"

Erich grabbed for the notebook, but Walther yanked it

away.

"Of course I do," Walther said. He set it down on his desk and covered it with both hands. "I have to be rigorous."

Before Erich could press any further, Herr Larat swept into the room and the boys snapped to attention.

"I saw a few lackluster performances on the field yesterday." He cracked his hand on Matthias' desk as he passed. "But I also watched a few surpass the mediocre standard of your peers."

Karl shot up straight in his seat, beaming with pride. Erich glanced over at Fritz and felt vindicated to see a queasy look pass over his face.

"However, I will not permit a few simpletons to hold back my class," Herr Larat said. "Ready or not, we start something new today."

He passed his hand over the candle on Karl's desk and it flared up. When he closed his fingers into a fist, the flame flickered out. As the boys broke into applause, Erich peered around for signs of illusion—like the fan that had apparently pushed Larat's balloon aloft—but he could see no indication of how the trick had been done.

"Oxygen, fuel, heat," Larat said. "Two of these we have in abundance. Your job today is to find the third."

By now the *Nassfüchsen* had grown accustomed to Herr Larat's minimalist explanations and they all began frantically waving their hands over the candles. It didn't work for anyone, but they kept trying with increasingly exaggerated gestures until Felix threw his arms out with such gusto that he knocked his candle over.

"Slower, children. It's not about how you waggle your hands. Think!" Herr Larat said. "What makes heat? Force against friction. Electricity against resistance. It's energy and inhibition."

Erich shuttled patronage back and forth over the wick as though rubbing his hands together in winter, but it was too imprecise and all he managed to do was make the candle wobble. As he watched it spin, a nauseous surge roiled up from his stomach. The stink of blood filled his nose and he tasted bile in his mouth. Erich leaned on the desk and swallowed it down.

As he sucked on short breaths, there came a crack like thunder and a blinding flash of light. Erich blinked and tried to clear his eyes. A plume of smoke billowed from the top of Karl's desk. Erich coughed as he breathed in, but he was grateful for anything that would expunge the bloody updraft from his stomach. The tips of Karl's blond bangs were singed black and sooty streaks scorched his desk, but the candle burned with a steady flame. Erich flashed him a smile and then took an uneasy swallow.

"Not terrible, Auch," Larat said. "Let's see if you can put it out now. A little more carefully this time."

Determined not to be left behind, Erich reached out his hand for another attempt. A sour taste rushed into his mouth. He gulped it down and tried to remember what Doktor Kammer had said in the car. But he kept returning to Herr Larat's words instead. Maybe they were both right. *Energy and inhibition.* In a way, inhibition was easy. The balloon shouldn't float. The candle shouldn't wobble. There was a kind of friction there, a tension between what was real and unreal. Perhaps if he pushed, the world would simply push back. At the collision of what ought to be and what was, he made fire.

There wasn't even an explosion like Karl's. The flame shot up, smooth and gentle. Grinning, Erich leaned back and watched it bend and flicker. Suddenly, his shoulders tensed and he spasmed forward. His insides wrenched against themselves. That coppery taste welled up in the back of his throat and spewed out, bilious and acrid. Day-old dog's slop saturated his mouth until it burned his nostrils and sprayed from his nose. Vomit snuffed out his candle and dribbled from the desk.

Erich shuddered. His limbs weakened. He couldn't hold himself up and his cheek slammed down into the rancid puddle. From the corner of his eye, he watched disgust overwhelm Herr Larat's face. Erich let out a wet chuckle. *Had anyone even seen his flame?*

*** 

In the infirmary, Erich slipped in and out of a foul sleep all day. At nightfall, *Rottenführer* Wolff and a few others carried him on a stretcher to the bathhouse. The steps were so steep and narrow that they had to tie him down to keep him from slipping off as they bumped and angled around the curves. The urge to get away overtook him. He could already smell the blood from below. He wouldn't be able to handle another cold bath.

"Let me go," Erich wheezed. "I want to go outside."

He thrashed against the restraints, but a tattooed arm pinned him down with suffocating force. At least if he couldn't breathe there would be no smell. When they got to the room, Fritz was already waiting. He looked terribly ill, barely able to stand, and he didn't even jeer when Wolff tipped over the stretcher and dumped Erich onto the floor.

They stripped away his hospital gown and left him sprawled out on the stone. No one held him down, but it didn't matter. He had no strength left to move. The gurgling kicked up from the spigot above and the blood poured down to splash against back of his neck. He shuddered as it struck. It was warm again. A pleasured sigh escaped his chest. Things were right again. The blood smelled like his father's hands after a long day at the shop. Erich let the blood wrap him in a blanket and fell asleep on the hard floor.

When he woke, he was back in the infirmary. Karl and Walther loomed over him, pitying smiles on their faces. Karl tried to reassure him that nobody thought any less of him now, but Erich knew that was a lie. At least Erich hadn't been the only one. Apparently a moment after he collapsed, Fritz had blanched and ran out of the classroom with one hand clapped over his mouth.

"They won't even be thinking about you tomorrow," Karl said. "Everyone still blames Fritz for the dog food. They'll go after him instead."

"And what about you?" Erich asked. "Do you think he took Doktor Kammer's dog?"

Karl paused. "No. I don't think so."

"Oh!" Walther blurted out. "I forgot to tell you the good news. I talked to Doktor Kammer about this idea Karl and I had. We're starting a historical society."

Karl's expression made clear that it hadn't been his idea at all.

"He's thrilled," Walther continued. "He says even the upperclassmen don't have one. We can have our first meeting tomorrow night."

"So soon," Karl coughed. "Don't you want to give everyone time to... prepare."

"No need," Walther said. "I put up a notice in the lounge this afternoon. You're coming, right Erich?"

Erich scrambled for an excuse. "I— I'm not sure. I might not be feeling—"

"Great, I'll see you tomorrow," Walther said. "Karl and I had better get going. it's almost nine."

In fact, the clock on the far wall read just after eight, but Erich was too tired to argue.

"Get better," Karl said, gripping his arm.

Erich nodded, already half asleep. He dreamed that he stood in the middle of the chapel. It was dark and the high tables had been cleared away. Tiny bones were strewn out all around him. They cracked under his feet like twigs on the forest floor.

A boy, skeletal and much younger than Erich, stood underneath the balcony where the teachers usually sat. He wore a grey *SS* shirt that was so big on him it looked like a dress. Ignoring Erich, he grinned and toyed with an osseous dollhouse. There were even bones caked into his hair.

The boy opened his mouth so wide that the sides of his cheeks split open, but where they ripped there was no blood. The boy let loose an agonizing shriek. Erich threw his hands over his ears, but the sound pierced through the cracks in his fingers. Without warning, the boy hurtled up into the air. His tiny body cracked against the underside of the balcony and his shrill voice cut off. As he lay spread-eagled against the ceiling, Erich slowly walked up under him. He tilted his neck back, looked up into the boy's eyes, and, back in the infirmary, opened his own.

A strange calm filled Erich. It was just a nightmare. Maybe all the previous day's curious and sickening events had been. Good blood had washed them away.

Erich lay in the dim ward, impatiently waiting for the first rays of sunlight to trickle in under the drapes. As he looked around the room, everything peered back at him with an odd sense of translucence. The curtains that ran around one side of his bed were pure white, but they were layered with a blurry sense of the floral wallpaper behind them. Under the clock on the far wall, a portrait of the *Führer* bled through so much that his brown jacket was sprinkled with roses.

After a long time, the nurse came in to take Erich's temperature. He told her he felt fine, leaving out any mention of his jumbled vision. She put down a few notes, and then, to his relief, discharged him in time for class.

All day, Erich itched with pent-up energy. In Physics, he almost set his desk on fire. At least that gave him something to do. Doktor Kammer's class was pure torture. He could barely keep his eyes open as all the shapes and colors of the classroom blurred into one jumbled, unoccluded mass.

When the lectures were finally done, a note from Johanna waited for him in the dormitory. The coded letters kept mingling with the object behind the page and Erich had to hold it up to the wall to see them clearly.

*Bittrich Hall. Midnight. Bring your friends.*

## ***

Erich didn't know what exactly a historical society was supposed to do at its meetings, but he was certain it would be dull. Besides Karl, Walther, Doktor Kammer, and himself, the only other person in attendance was a quiet boy named Tommi, who seemed to have convinced himself there would be food. He was crestfallen when he found out otherwise, but by then he was trapped and had to stay.

"Is there a history to the statues in the halls?" Walther asked.

"Of course," Doktor Kammer said. "It's more of a legend, really. The Count of Four Alchemies. If you'd asked me five years ago, I'd have told you that Hugo had made it up. Now, though, it's hard to say."

"How does it go?" Walther said eagerly.

"It would really be better to let Hugo tell it," Doktor Kammer said. "It's a dreary story, but he does it so well I wouldn't want to ruin anything."

Now that it was off-limits, Erich and the others were interested. They looked intently at Kammer with pleading faces.

"Well, alright," Doktor Kammer said. "Since you all gave up your time to come, I don't see why not. Just don't spread it around or Hugo will get upset with me."

"We're sworn to secrecy," Walther said, echoed by enthusiastic nods from the other three.

"Did you know that this castle is built below an old iron mine?" Doktor Kammer said.

The boys shook their heads.

"Well, it is. And according to the story, many, many years ago that mine had just about run dry. The people were desperate. Iron was their livelihood and without it there was no money or food. They flocked to the great hall and begged the count of Rouhhenberg for help. So their lord turned to God. For two days he prayed without eating or sleeping. On the third day, the miners struck a vein, richer than any before it.

"Industry flourished in Rouhhenberg and with it rose the wealth and standing of the count. But the more riches he amassed, the more he wanted. Iron would no longer be enough. He needed gold. So again, the count turned to God. He fasted for a week, but there was no reply. No gold.

"This did not deter him. 'If God will not help,' the count said, 'then I will find someone else who will.' He called on every chemist and mineralogist in Europe, and when they failed to find gold, he replaced them with thaumaturges who promised to transmute what he already had. They all failed. And when they did, he cast their bodies them into iron statues to line his halls."

"That's horrible," Tommi muttered.

Doktor Kammer shrugged.

"The count was at his lowest moment. Prayer, his first alchemy, had failed him. Science, the second, had failed him. Magic, the third, had failed him too. But in the deepest parts of the mine, he found something. A fourth alchemy, he called it. Something far more ancient than the other three. Or maybe he just went insane, I don't know. They say he drank a thimbleful of mercury with every meal. Either way, he believed in what he'd found."

"Did he manage to make gold then?" Walther asked.

"He certainly intended to," Doktor Kammer said. "He penned a blasphemous gospel in the name of what he had found below and took on seven orphans as disciples."

"What stopped him?"

Doktor Kammer smiled. "The church. The count's

heresies caught up with him and the local bishop incited a rival to deal with him. They stormed Rouhhenberg and the count was burned at the stake along with every one of his adherents."

"Is that all really true?" Walther asked.

"All of it?" Doktor Kammer said. "Of course not. Hugo is a magician. Half-truths are his stock and trade. There are parts of the story that I know are true, others that I know are false. But the really interesting bits of any legend are the pieces that fall between.

"Take the statues you asked about. Were there ever real statues in these halls? Maybe, maybe not. But the ones you see out there now, they're fake. Hugo commissioned them from some sculptor in Vienna. Do you see what I mean?"

Erich nodded. "So then... does this all mean that the *Führer* sent us here to turn iron into gold?"

"No," Doktor Kammer frowned. "I think he has plenty of that. It's no different than we've always told you. You're here because you're the future. The *Führer* and Hugo may not always be... aligned, but on that one thing they are in absolute agreement. There's nothing either of them cares about more."

# CHAPTER SEVENTEEN

After the meeting, Erich considered inviting Walther to meet Johanna—the historical society had been a lot more interesting than he'd expected—but he was fairly certain that nothing on earth could persuade Walther to break curfew. He might even rat them out. Karl, though, was easy to win over.

"You aren't the dognapper, are you?" Karl asked as they snuck out from the dormitory. He only sounded half-joking.

"No." Erich chuckled. "Come on, she'll meet us in Bittrich."

Karl raised an eyebrow. "She?"

Erich scurried ahead and peered around the corner, then gestured for Karl to follow. The halls that once had seemed untamable were familiar now, but at night they took on new and twisted forms, made all the more frightening by the condition of Erich's eyes.

The iron statues lunged out from corners, their agonized faces melting into the dimly lit walls. He knew they were fake and the more he thought about it, the less sense the whole idea made, but he couldn't help imagining what it might have felt like to be cast into iron. Would he feel the liquid metal filling his mouth, or would it be painless, all sensation cauterized in an instant?

Mercifully, the second floor hallway in Bittrich was free of the statues. They found Johanna in one of the classrooms, curled up in a window alcove. She shone her flashlight in their eyes as they came in.

"Meet Johanna Engel," Erich said, feeling as though he were introducing a stage act.

Karl stammered out a greeting, still blinded by the light. There was a long silence as she sized him up.

"What do you want to do?" Erich asked.

Johanna hopped down from the window. "We're going to break into the kitchen."

"For what?" Karl asked.

"Well," she said. "Today we served welf pudding and strawberry cake."

Erich and Karl broke into the same expression of shock.

"The upperclassmen get cake?" Erich moaned.

Johanna brushed past them on the way to the door. "Now you will too."

Right away, she proved that Erich's knowledge of the castle was still primitive. Within three turns, they were creeping down a passage he didn't recognize. They hurried out onto a long covered bridge that curved on itself twice before depositing them somewhere that should have been right by where they had started but wasn't.

"Where is this?" Karl asked.

"The *Schützenadler* wing," Johanna said. "Haven't you ever been?"

"We're not allowed," Erich said.

"Neither am I," she said, peeking around a corner.

A few times as they passed a certain door or staircase, Erich felt a compulsion to veer off in search of something he couldn't put a finger on. He would hover for a moment, and then shake it off and run after Johanna and Karl.

Everything seemed larger in the *Schützenadler* wing. The iron statues loomed a little taller. The ceilings were raised higher. Elaborate lamps stuck out from the walls at every corner, their sheen reflected in the mahogany floors. With so much more to look at, the problem with Erich's eyes was worse here. A dozen colors bled together in kaleidoscopic patterns and he had to strain to focus on any one thing.

After enduring a minute or two of the boys' nervous gaping, Johanna grabbed Karl's hand and pulled him off down a winding stairwell. They corkscrewed around and around. It went almost as far down as the bathhouse. There were no landings, but eventually the stairs spat them out into a carved rock tunnel with a dirt floor. It was utterly dark.

"Frau Murr says they built this to sneak in supplies during a siege," Johanna said, switching on her flashlight. "She thinks locking us down here is a punishment, but it's actually pretty fun."

She skipped down the hallway, forcing them to run to keep up. Neither of the boys had any source of light, and Erich was afraid that if he lost sight of her, he would never find his way out. Evidently, this punishment was one Johanna had been subjected to many times before. She never stopped for more than a second when they reached a fork and she didn't let them wander too far. Once, the gnawing sensation Erich kept feeling drew him down the wrong way and Johanna ran back to yank him onto the right path.

"Not there," she said.

Eventually, they came to a thick wooden door with a barred window. Johanna stepped aside and gestured towards it.

"Your turn now," she said.

Karl tested the handle. "It's locked."

"Obviously," Johanna said. "Why do you think I brought you?"

He stared at her in surprise. "You want us to break it down?"

"That would certainly work," Johanna mused.

"Okay, I can try." Karl raised his arms. "Stand back."

"Wait, she's kidding," Erich said, throwing himself between Karl and the door. He gave Johanna a sidelong glance. "You are kidding, right?"

Johanna battled a smile. "Frau Murr leaves the key in the lock."

"Oh." Karl blushed. He jumped up on his toes and peered through the bars, but the top of his head barely crested the window. "I don't see it."

Erich blinked. The wood of the door seeped into the dark room behind. It should have been opaque, and yet above the handle, he could make out the faint gray shape of the key on the other side.

"Let me try something," he said.

Erich squinted and strained his eyes, letting his vision push forward through space. It was almost like extending a telescope. The key shimmered and warped as it drew into view. He stuck his hand into his pocket and turned it.

At the clunk of the bolt, Johanna gave a whoop and jumped for the handle. The door opened freely.

"Very good," she said, grinning back at Karl.

"Wasn't me," he shrugged, turning to Erich. "How did you do that?"

Erich made his best attempt at a mysterious smile and gave no answer. Johanna scowled at him. They tiptoed into the kitchen, trying not to knock anything over as they navigated the network of countertops and cabinets. Beside an array of ovens was their prize. Rack upon rack of treats, cooling on thin sheets of paper.

"Oooh, they've got some for tomorrow too," Johanna cooed, whipping a cloth bag out of from her jacket pocket. She started to snatch pastries off the shelf as though she were picking berries.

"Look, *Schneebälle*," Erich whimpered, reaching for one.

"Better," Karl said. "Chocolate *Schneebälle!*"

Karl lunged for the tray, stuffed a *Schneeball* right into his mouth, and then proceeded to fill his pockets, all the while letting out a gnashing, unintelligible mumble. While they scavenged, Johanna went off to another part of the kitchen and came back with her bag considerably more full.

"That's enough," she said, then slapped Erich's hand away and threw her laden bag over one shoulder.

"What did you get?" he asked.

"Nothing," Johanna said. "Let's go."

They rushed back through the supply tunnels in a frenzy of sugar and success. At the top of the stairs, they ran out into one of the many garden courtyards that dotted the castle. Throwing her arms over both their shoulders, Johanna piloted them over to a low stone wall where they could sit and divide the spoils. It was cold outside, but Erich could barely feel it.

He bit into a *Schneeball*, laughing as a puff of sugar dusted his face. Karl smiled then floated one of the pastries in the air over his hand. He concentrated for a moment and it burst into flames. Johanna cackled as a sweet smoky smell filled the garden. It didn't give off much heat, but they huddled around it anyway, giggling with mouths full.

"Who's there?" came a shout from afar.

Erich whipped around and Karl dropped the burning pastry in surprise. Johanna bolted off without looking back. They chased after her, not bothering to check the hallway before they burst out of the courtyard and around the corner. The three of them turned sharply into a stairwell, rushed outside, and clattered across the covered bridge that led back into Bittrich Hall. Still hearing shouts from behind, they ran past the classrooms and jammed into the broom closet where Erich and Johanna had first met. They barely fit.

The sound of their own labored breathing faded away.

Footsteps pattered down the hall and then came a slam from one of the classroom doors.

"Come out, you filthy beasts," an astringent voice—Frau Murr's—called out. "You can't run forever."

The three of them crammed backwards against each other, as though they would be safe if they could just get far enough away from the door. Johanna's breathing came in panicked gasps. Squinting, Erich pushed his eyes past the edge of the closet door. He could faintly make out two figures, Frau Murr and someone larger. They were close. The big one, *Rottenführer* Wolff he guessed, kicked open the classroom doors one at a time, while Frau Murr kept watch on the hallway.

"They're coming," Erich hissed.

He scanned for any possible escape. There were classrooms on either side of the closet—if he pushed his vision he could see them through the walls—but there was no way to get there without going out where Frau Murr would spot them. Erich glanced back and cringed. There was fear in Karl's eyes and it was Erich's fault. If it weren't for him, Karl would sleeping soundly right now. There had to be a way out.

Though Karl was smooshed all the way up against the closet's back wall, there was still something behind him. Erich strained his eyes and it came into focus. Another hallway, it looked like, thin and unadorned, though that didn't make much sense. They should have been up against the building's outer wall, and he remembered clearly the window alcoves of the classroom where they had met Johanna.

Erich squeezed past Karl and ran his fingers along the wood paneling of the back wall, not caring what he knocked over or how much noise he made. Johanna shushed him, but he ignored her and dug his fingers into the gap at the edge of the wall. He pulled with all the combined strength and patronage he could muster and the panel slid back a few centimeters. Dust and stale air puffed out from the other side. Through the wall, Erich could see Wolff stomp into the adjacent classroom.

"Hurry," he whispered.

Johanna and Karl caught on and crouched down to push with him. They dragged the hidden door halfway open.

"That's enough for me," Karl said.

As they squeezed through, Wolff stepped back into the hall and slammed the classroom door shut behind him. They heaved the panel closed and just as it shut, he crashed into the closet. Wolff glanced around and then kept going. Collapsed on the floor of the passage, they panted and grinned at one another with relief.

"Where are we?" Karl whispered.

"I don't know," Erich said.

The hallway was too narrow to stand two abreast. It sloped down from where they sat. The only illumination was a few dim rays of moonlight that shone in through embrasures on one side. A thick layer of dust coated the warped, stone floor and Erich wondered how long it had been since anyone had been here. Through the closet's false panel, he could see Frau Murr and Wolff in the midst of a heated argument.

Johanna held her ear to the wall, listening. She waved Erich over, but he shook his head and beckoned the sound closer.

"I'm tired of looking," Wolff said. "What was the point of taking that stupid dog if we still have to do all the searching ourselves?"

"How could I have known the *Nassfüchsen* would be as useless as you are?" Frau Murr snapped.

"Everything went fine with the first substitute," Wolff whined. "Why not let them run away and starve in the woods."

Frau Murr slapped him like a child. "Fine? Did those two look fine when you carried them down on a stretcher? And just wait until the end of the year. What do you think

*Oberführer* Ehrenzweig will write in his reports when three of them don't come back?"

"Ehrenzweig knows nothing," Wolff said. "You should be writing the reports."

"Keep your voice *down*," Frau Murr commanded. "You're worse than Hugo. Neither of you get it. Underneath the *Führer* it's a den of vipers. We are one mistake away from losing everything."

She grabbed him by the collar and pulled him down the hall, their angry voices growing faint. Johanna stepped back from the wall, wide eyed.

Karl whistled in disbelief. "Why would Frau Murr take Mateusz? Just so she could punish us for it?"

"All that dog food..." Erich groaned.

"I told you she's crazy," Johanna said. She peered down the passageway. "Do you want to see where it goes?"

"It's late," Erich said. "We need to get back."

"You're joking," Karl said, all traces of panic gone. "Look what we've found and you want to go home?"

Outnumbered, Erich relented and let the two of them lead the way. Though they had been as terrified as Erich in the moment, the close call had invigorated Karl and Johanna. The two of them skipped and chattered like old friends as they explored. Erich stayed in the rear. He kept glancing over his shoulder, half expecting to see *Rottenführer* Wolff's snake-wrapped arm reaching out from the dark.

As the corridor twisted around the castle's periphery, Erich focused on what he could glimpse on the other side of the stone walls. Some parts were unfamiliar, but elsewhere he recognized a painting or a distinctive statue. There didn't seem to be any end to the narrow corridors. Every time they reached a fork, Johanna would pause to ponder for a moment before setting off decisively in one direction or another. After a while, Erich concluded that she was choosing entirely at random.

"We should turn left," he said at the next fork. "We're under Rathe Hall right now."

"You couldn't possibly know that," Johanna scolded, but she took his advice anyway.

As they passed the exercise room in the *Nassfuchs* wing, Erich stopped and pointed to a wooden panel in the wall like the one they entered through.

"We're close. Poke your head out through there," he said.

Johanna hauled it back and peeked through the opening. She yanked her head out in surprise.

"For once you're right," Johanna said, then begrudgingly handed him the flashlight.

With Erich in the lead, they made better progress. At an opening outside the BDM dormitory, Johanna gave them each a kiss on the cheek before taking her flashlight and climbing through. Grinning in the dark, Erich and Karl groped their way back around to the *Nassfuchs* wing. They climbed out through the false back of a wardrobe, shared a salute, and slipped off to their bunks.

# CHAPTER EIGHTEEN

Every night, Erich slipped out through the wardrobe and made his way into the castle's hidden arteries. Sometimes Karl and Johanna joined him, but he liked it most when he went alone. There was a kind of freedom in the silence and the dark. He could see everyone and be seen by no one.

He dreamed of the narrow corridors as well. Every night it was the same—like the nightmare he'd had in the infirmary, but worse. He snaked through the passages in a sequence of turns that never changed. Left, right, right, left, right, left, left, left. At a dead end, he would wait for what seemed like hours, knowing that if he only looked up to the ceiling he would wake. But he didn't want to. That was where the bone boy lived. The screams haunted Erich well into the daylight.

As the weeks passed, Erich's eyes grew more penetrating and his vision less muddled, but even in the hidden corridors he never saw a trace of Doktor Kammer's dog. Perhaps Frau Murr still had him. Maybe he was lost in the woods or dead. Either way, after another week of dogfood, a train arrived with a gift from the dachshund club of Vienna. Doktor Kammer dubbed his new companion Mateusz II and Frau Murr finally ended their punishment.

Even after a month of exploration, Karl and Johanna still struggled to find their way in the indistinct stone corridors. Frustrated, Johanna taught Karl her code, and the three of them set to drawing a map. They jokingly called themselves the Cartography Club and mounted a scouting expedition twice a week.

Erich looked forward to these meetings more than anything else, more than the impossible things that they learned from Herr Larat, more than the ups and downs of the *Siegfeld*, and certainly more than the doldrums of Walther's historical society, which never again reached the peak of its first meeting.

Every time Erich thought their map complete, some new offshoot would present itself. By the time the first snows coated the castle, Erich had given up on ever calling it finished. In a way, he never wanted it to be.

There was only one place Erich was determined not to explore: the dead end hallway from his dream. He blocked it off on their map so Johanna and Karl wouldn't find it. Whenever he neared that part of the castle, he felt a disturbing urge to take those three left turns, like the temptation to jump off when standing at the edge of a cliff. But always he resisted, certain that whatever lay at their end was not something he wanted to find.

With the winter solstice around the corner, Hugo announced that *Reichsjugendführer* Baldur von Schirach, the head of the Hitler Youth, would be joining them for the feast. Karl and Walther had both seen him speak at the 1938 Party Congress in Nuremberg, but neither had come away impressed.

"It was very flowery," Karl said. "More like a poem than a speech."

Walther nodded. "It was really just a footnote to the *Führer's.*"

Regardless, Erich was eager for the arrival of their

visitor. A rumor spread that the *Reichsjugendführer* would be in attendance at the *Siegfeld* on the day of, and both teams were determined to impress. Unfortunately, they had only three boys apiece who had not yet played in the season. This made Erich's decision of who to field easier, but he had used up his best players, and the dregs would need a lot of practice if they were going to succeed.

Erich hurled himself into training. He forwent everything, even his excursions into the corridors, in favor of more time for practice. Eugen, who he had deliberately saved for this moment, was the most promising of the three. Erich was counting on him to deliver a point, but their team was down by two for the season. To even the odds he would need to score with Gisil or Humbryct, both of whom were constantly one step behind everyone else in Physics.

They spent hours going back over their lessons, levitating weights, working up electricity, fire, light, heat, sound. By the day of the match, Erich was confident that his three players could least give the red team a fighting chance.

A fog hung over the mountain as they trekked their way up the icy steps to the peak. From the captain's perch, Erich's peered through the hazy air to where the *Reichsjugendführer* sat. He was deep in conversation with *Oberführer* Ehrenzweig, and the fog was so thick that Erich wondered if their visitor would be able to see the game at all.

This turned out to be something of a blessing. Eugen and Humbryct fell out of bounds on the first row, knocked over by a spring-loaded contraption that neither of them was strong enough to stop. To Erich's surprise, Gisil deftly sidestepped it and charged into the next row. Without even stopping, he snuffed out an intimidating wall of fire and then came to an abrupt halt at the edge of the last row. A wind kicked up from the east and just as the red team was beginning to impress, the fog thinned. Erich looked down at the sidelines and wondered if one his teammates was responsible.

Gisil inched forward towards a large open pipe, its nozzle aimed at him like the barrel of a gun. He took a step forward and a torrent of water sprayed out. It cracked across his chest and hurled him to the floor. As it petered out, Gisil dragged himself up. He shook his long hair like a dog.

A smile crept across his face. He knelt down and raised one finger, then gently tapped the spot where he had stepped before. Gisil threw his arms out as the water rushed up. A layer of frost crept up the sides of the pipe. He shook with exertion. Thickening water gushed into the opening and froze solid. Iron screamed as the ice expanded and the nozzle split open, spraying everywhere, gentle as a fountain. Gisil sprinted through the rain and took the flag.

It hadn't been the sweeping play Erich had hoped for, but at least they had scored, and in the end, the greens did no better. They finished the match with the same two point spread they had begun with, the red team behind, but not by much. At the feast, Gisil's surprising performance was on everyone's lips. Even von Schirach seemed impressed.

"Do you remember the day you heard the *Führer* speak for the first time?" he asked. "I do. The sun was behind him and he stood at the pulpit in shadow. From his first word I knew this was a man like no other, someone who obeyed no law but his own."

The *Reichsjugendführer* hardly moved as he spoke, but his voice pitched up and down wildly.

"This morning I looked out from the peak of your mountain, and do you know what I saw? I saw a boy face down hellfire. I saw him cast aside all of nature's stricture and step forward as a man like no other."

As the speech ran on and on, Erich began to agree with Karl and Walther's assessment of the *Reichsjugendführer*. He couldn't pay attention and soon slipped off into a daydream. Perhaps next year it would be Hitler overlooking them from the balcony. The *Führer* would point to the high table where Erich sat and call him by name. He would dive into a long paean for the *SV* captain from Messerich as every arm in the room thrust out in salute.

As the *Reichsjugendführer* finally neared the end of his speech, his voice went quiet and he promised them a gift. He came down from the balcony and all hundred-odd students lined up to shake his hand.

"You will go far, my friend. I trust in you absolutely," he said as Erich came to the front. He pinned a medal on the breast of Erich's uniform then handed him a silver dagger. "Go on, take a look."

This was no dull castoff like the one Klaus had given him. Its pristine edge glinted when it caught the light and it let out a seductive hiss as Erich unsheathed it. One side carried the familiar inscription, *Blood and Honor,* and the year, 1939. On the reverse was the same half-ellipse that was marked on the back of Erich and Fritz's neck. Erich thanked the *Reichsjugendführer* too many times, and then stepped back, still unable to take his eyes off the blade.

That night, as he stowed his old dagger in Klaus' box, he stumbled on the stethoscope. Running his fingers over the worn metal, he couldn't remember the last time he'd thought of it. Erich stuck the prongs in his ears and slipped out into the hidden corridors.

# CHAPTER NINETEEN

By the end of January, Walther had finally given up on the historical society due to lack of attendance. He still met with Doktor Kammer twice a week to discuss whatever it was they discussed, but he no longer dragged anyone else along. Karl kept hinting that they should invite him to the Cartography Club, but Erich staunchly refused.

With or without Walther, their forbidden nighttime expeditions stagnated. The pace of discovery had slowed and the corridors no longer held the same excitement for Karl and Johanna. According to her, the upperclassmen and the older BDM girls were allowed to meet for social hours, and she and Karl began to speak longingly about a time when they might all three cavort outside of the cramped corridors. That kind of talk infuriated Erich. He didn't understand how they could so easily throw away this thing that was uniquely theirs.

By spring, a new obsession overtook the *Nassfüchsen*: the corps into which they would be drafted for the rest of their time at Rouhhenberg. With barely anything to go on, an endless debate raged on the nature of the two groups of upperclassmen who sat on opposing high tables in the chapel. The *Wehrbären* were clearly the more militarily focused of the two, but the role of the *Schützenadler* was less obvious. Karl thought this was the track for future party leadership and he was eager to join. That worked fine for Erich. He could still remember the way Otto and Uwe had danced down the *Siegfeld*. If those two were *Schützenadler*, then that was what Erich wanted to be.

Even the process of selection for the corps was kept a secret, and Erich had heard a thousand different rumors of what their final exam would entail. Stopping a bullet. Lifting a train car. Richard leaned over the dinner table and suggested that they would have to defeat a dragon at the top of the mountain. Everyone laughed, but Erich had to admit it was barely more preposterous than the other theories.

Curious, Erich even asked Otto and Uwe after one of their marching practices, but they were as tight lipped as everyone else. Even Johanna had nothing to say, though he suspected that she knew more than she let on. The only times she ever followed the rules were when he didn't want her to.

The red team ended the *SV* season sadly but respectably one point behind, 15-14. It was not what Erich had hoped for, but he was proud enough and no one seemed to blame him for the loss. He wondered what the game would be like as an upperclassmen. For the first time in the school's brief history, there would be two years of students in the same *SV* league. He presumed he would not be captaining, but the dream of holding that position in the future wasn't entirely farfetched.

The night after their final match (and Erich's twelfth birthday), the *Nassfüchsen* returned from the bathhouse high on blood and competition. As they crowded around the radio, the divisions between red and green seemed suddenly juvenile. Soon Erich and his friends would sit at their own high table and look down on new *Nassfüchsen*. They would smile and nod their heads knowingly on the night of the first bath and laugh as the new boys struggled with Physics and *SV*.

Erich closed his eyes for the opening trumpets of the news broadcast. He imagined that somewhere Aunt Mila was listening to the same crackling notes, nursing a coffee at the kitchen table or curled up in her big chair. The door to the lounge cracked open and Walther stumbled in, looking terribly pale. He had been absent at dinner. He scurried across the room and slammed his bedroom door. Karl hurried after him. Just as Erich got up to follow, the announcements began and he froze in place.

*Unprecedented offensive in the West!*

A collective hoot of excitement burst out and then immediately dropped into silence as the *Nassfüchsen* leaned in to hear more. This was the moment they had all been waiting for and it did not disappoint. The *Führer* was making his moves.

They laughed and held their breath as the announcer carried them from one daring operation to another. Swarms of panzers crashed through the Ardennes, a thousand of *Luftwaffe* bombers descended on the airfields of France, and in the crowning moment, a tiny band of patriots led a glider assault to cripple the impregnable Belgian fortress Eben-Emael.

Erich, like every boy in the room, could name a dozen naysayers from his hometown, the adults who stopped short of treason, but had scowled at their anthems or smirked from the sidewalks when they paraded past. In one glorious day, Hitler had proven them all wrong. He had taken on every enemy at once and he was winning.

With everyone else in bed, Erich snuck out into the corridors and pretended he were a paratrooper, swooping in to infiltrate the legendary fort from the skies. He crept around in the dark, letting his penetrating eyes lead the way to the enemy command. When victorious, he slipped back into the dormitory and fell asleep in an instant. For the first time in a long while there was no trace of the bone boy in his dreams. It was a night for fire and fanfare.

As he got ready for class in the morning, Erich didn't see Walther at all. Guilty to have forgotten about him the night before, he went to see if he was all right. Walther still lay in bed. He groaned and clung to his stomach as Erich sat down on the opposite bunk.

"It was cold," Walther whispered. "The bath was cold."

Erich cringed. "That happened to me too."

Almost a year had passed since the incident, but Erich could still feel the chill shock against his back, the putrid smell, and the roiling in his stomach. But as bad as it had been for him, Walther looked even worse. His cheeks were gaunt and his lavender skin was sticky with sweat.

"Do you think we're not... the right ones?" Walther asked. "What if somebody else is supposed to be here instead of us?"

"If getting sick means you and I aren't supposed to be here, then Fritz isn't either," Erich said. "And I can live with that."

Walther managed a faint smile.

"The bath will be better tonight," Erich said. "At least it was for me."

The bedroom door opened suddenly and Frau Murr stepped through. *Rottenführer* Wolff followed at her tail, dragging a chair behind him. It screeched against the bare floor. With a hint of fear in his eyes, Walther pushed himself halfway upright. He was always so calm and impassive, but today that was gone, flushed away with the sour blood. He shivered beneath the blankets.

Frau Murr glared at Erich, "Don't you have somewhere to be?"

"Yes, madam," Erich said.

He jumped to his feet and scurried out the door, but couldn't help doubling back to eavesdrop. Wolff pulled the chair over to Walther's bedside and Frau Murr slowly took a seat.

"Are you unwell, dear?" she asked.

Walther nodded.

"I see," she said. "And will you make it to class today?"

Walther struggled to swallow before he spoke. "I don't think so."

"I'm sorry to hear that," Frau Murr said. She didn't sound sorry at all. Without even removing her glove, she set her palm on his brow. A moment later, she yanked it away in disgust and wiped her hand on the bedsheets. "Do you remember last fall when two of your classmates fell ill? Von Keppler and Fiehler, I think."

Walther nodded slowly.

"I have to warn you how much concern it caused at the time. The blood test is supposed to catch these sort of things before you get here, but... it doesn't always work. The two of them were nearly dismissed."

Walther shot up straight. Erich's heart thrummed against his chest. He had had no idea how close he had come to being sent home.

"Oh, I'm sorry, dear, I didn't mean to frighten you. It's just everyone worries. Ever since..." she trailed off and glanced over shoulder. "Wolff, you remember Jens and Evert."

Wolff nodded solemnly.

"What happened?" Walther whispered.

"Nothing for your ears," Frau Murr said. "But if I were you, I'd be sure I made it to class before word of this reaches anyone else. The *Oberführer* in particular."

"I will," Walther croaked.

With hands that were bigger than the Walther's head, Wolff hauled him up out of bed and set him down on his feet. Erich wanted to stay and see more, but Frau Murr was already standing up and he had to rush out to avoid being spotted.

That Frau Murr was responsible for their failed baths, Erich was certain, but how and why he couldn't figure. She and Wolff always seemed to be working to cover something up. Erich tried to remember the argument he'd overhead on the night they first found the corridors, but he was late for class and couldn't linger on it for long.

He suffered a beating from *Oberführer* Ehrenzweig for it, but to his relief their teacher took mercy on Walther when he stumbled in a few minutes later.

"Have a seat, Tuerk. Tardiness doesn't become you," Ehrenzweig snapped. "Now, as I was saying. We have talked at length this year about the danger posed by the Jews who live among us. Here in Germany, they have shaved their beards and donned suits, but there exists no disguise that could ever hide the telltale physiognomy of the Jew.

"We have tried for a long time to make them to leave on their own. The *Führer* has put a stop to their predatory mercantilism. He has ejected them from our schools. He has confiscated their ill-gotten spoils. The German people have lit a match and year after year we have waited for the leeches to loosen their jaws. And yet Germany is still not free of them. So many remain within our borders. They persist."

Walther began to slump down onto his desk and Erich had to reach over and shake him until he got back up. Luckily, Ehrenzweig was too engrossed in his lecture to notice.

"So what are we to do?" he said. "Some have suggested that we send them off to a home of their own. To Palestine from whence they came. To some far off enclave in Africa where the world can be free of them. But what would be the point? Jews cannot survive on their own any more than a tapeworm can live outside the body. Why should hardworking Germans expend effort on futile thing like that?

"No. Instead, the *Führer* has decided that the only justice is for the Jews to be put to work. Over the coming months and years they will be deported to the Government General in Poland. It will be the first time in most of their lives that they ever experience honest labor. I doubt it will do anything to change their nature, but if they

179

till the land long enough perhaps it will begin to repay the colossal sum they have stolen from the *Volk*."

All throughout the rest of Ehrenzweig's lecture, Walther would begin to sag down and then tear himself back up, clutching at his mouth and swallowing bile. Erich felt terribly sorry for him. Later in Physics, he and Karl cheated for Walther during the physics exercises. It seemed better than letting him try to use his patronage and vomit everywhere as Erich had.

History and their other classes were easier, but it still took everything they had just to keep him upright for the remainder of the day. At sunset, they slung Walther's arms over their shoulders and walked him down the bathhouse steps to the door marked by the spiral as on the back of Walther's neck. He was one of the only boys who didn't have a partner.

As the trickle of Erich's bath ran down his neck, he stared at his feet and let his thoughts go. He tried to sort out the meaning of Frau Murr's visit, but the euphoric blood pushed it out of mind. At dinner, Walther looked so refreshed that it was easier to talk of other things: finals, next year's corps, and hopes for a swift victory in France.

That victory came faster than any of them dared imagine. After less than a month, German forces corralled the terrified British and French at Dunkirk before forcing them into a hasty retreat across the channel. A week later, panzer treads were churning up the streets of Paris.

When they heard the news, the boys—*Nassfüchsen* and upperclassmen alike—took to the *Siegfeld* for a victory march. For hours, they circled from the cliff's edge to the hangar and back, singing until their voices ran hoarse. The stands were fuller than Erich had ever seen them, and even Johanna was there, unable to resist the mood. She didn't scream like everyone else, but still she sat back and wore a smile. Her windblown hair streamed in front of her face.

That night the upperclassmen came down to the low table. All the students together crowded around a massive roast and passed tankards down the rows. *Oberführer* Ehrenzweig, ordinarily as stiff and austere as his starched uniforms, stumbled in amongst the students, flask in one hand, saber in the other. He swung it about wildly—"This is for 1918, French devils!"—until Wolff gently pried the sword from his hand and withdrew him from the chapel.

Though the glow of victory lingered throughout the summer, it was tempered by a growing agitation. The final exam approached and they still had no idea what it would entail. Erich, Karl, and Walther counted down the days until the end of August, practicing everything they had learned a thousand times over. When the test day came, they clamored up the narrow path to the *Siegfeld*, yawning from a sleepless night.

"Do you think it'll be a match?" Karl asked.

Erich shook his head. "It'll be whatever we haven't thought of."

They crested the top and looked out onto the field. There were no lanes slotted into place and the big trench and chain lay exposed. Herr Larat, *Oberführer* Ehrenzweig, and Doktor Kammer stood by the cliffside, waiting patiently while the *Nassfüchsen* gathered at the precipice.

"Is everyone ready?" Kammer asked, rubbing his hands together in unrestrained glee.

Erich doubted anyone felt ready, but they all gave a big, shouting salute nonetheless.

"As some of you may know, our Rouhhenberg sits below the mouth of an old iron mine," Kammer said, he pointed out over the cliff's edge. "The ore has long since been exhausted, but the tunnels are still there. That's where you're going."

"How will we get down?" Karl whispered. "Do you think the exam is just them pushing us over the ledge?"

Erich grinned. "There's a ladder over there."

He could see through the rock to the iron rungs that ran down to a rickety platform on the side of the cliff. A iron cage hung through its center. Karl peered out over the brink and then took a few nervous steps back.

"You'll take the test in pairs," Doktor Kammer announced. "Find your bathing partner if you have one."

"Otherwise, you go down on your own," Larat said.

Erich cringed. The last thing he wanted was to be stuck in a mine shaft with Fritz. Still, it still seemed preferable to being alone. If that aloneness bothered Walter, he didn't show it. He rushed over to the front of the line while everyone else was still looking for their partner.

"He's never met an exam he didn't like," Karl whispered.

Erich grinned and wished him good luck.

"What's down there?" Fritz asked.

Doktor Kammer gave a knowing wink in Erich's direction.

"Isn't it obvious?" Herr Larat said. "You're going to meet your patrons."

# CHAPTER TWENTY

At the cliff's edge, Erich looked back and exchanged a nervous glance with Karl. Walther had climbed down on his own, eager and fearless, but it took everything Erich had just to keep himself from shaking.

"*Schützenadler,*" Karl whispered.

"*Schützenadler,*" Erich agreed.

Fritz smirked at the two of them, turned around, and clambered backwards down the ladder.

"You're up, Fiehler," Herr Larat shouted.

He gave Erich a push on the shoulder that sent him stumbling closer to the verge than he would have liked. Erich swallowed, steadied his legs for a moment, then turned around and slowly lowered himself over the lip. He gripped the sides of the ladder with flushed knuckles. When he reached the platform, Erich squeezed into the hanging cage beside Fritz and latched the gate shut.

It swung dizzyingly under the added weight. Erich's stomach clenched as he waited to feel the first drop, but it still startled him when it came. The rusty chain spasmed as it unspooled, sending them down in lurches and jerks. Even Fritz seemed nervous. He was uncharacteristically silent as they plunged down through a gaping hole in the

183

mountainside. As the light faded away, Erich pushed his arm through the bars and let his fingers brush against the rock.

Meter after meter passed, but the shaft showed no sign of ending. It made no sense. When Walther had stepped into the cage, it returned empty only a minute later, but it seemed like more than an hour before Erich and Fritz reached the bottom.

They clattered to a stop. The crunch of iron against rock echoed up and down the shaft. Erich expected Fritz to swagger out first, but he didn't move. When at last it became clear that he wouldn't, Erich shoved open the gate and stepped outside himself. He drew up a little ball of light—what Herr Larat insisted on calling a scintillation—and let it hover over his hand, illuminating the tunnel ahead.

Erich looked back, "Shall we go?"

Fritz gave a grim nod and conjured up his own faint light. It flickered precariously above his shaking palm.

"You're afraid," Erich said, awestruck.

"I'm not." Fritz had to push the words out through gritted teeth. "It's all just... so close. I'm an eagle, not some rat in the walls like you."

Erich held back a laugh. "Come on then, eagle. We'll make it."

The air smelled stale and every step kicked up a spray of black dust. Erich untied his red armband and wrapped it around his mouth like a kerchief before pressing on. Though the tunnel forked in places, no matter which way he chose, their direction stayed the same. Always down.

Fritz lagged behind, but he seemed more frightened of being left alone than of pressing forward, so he never let himself fall out of sight. Their path would widen into a broad cavern and then suddenly constrict so tightly that they could barely squeeze by single file, sending Fritz into a wheezing panic. In the deeper parts, a glowing moss clung to the walls. It cast the tunnels in a pale blue light.

"Do you hear that?" Fritz hissed. He tugged on Erich's shoulder. "There's water!"

Erich stopped and he could hear it too. They chased the faint sound down to a stream. It ran silver and viscous over the rocks.

"That's not water."

"It's mercury," Fritz gaped.

"Let's see where it heads."

They followed the molten stream out into a dark, mossless passage. It was unnatural. The further they descended, the wider the stream grew, as though it were fed by the rocks themselves. At last, it flowed out into a cave so vast that Erich's tiny light could find no walls or ceiling. They stood on a rocky lip and watched the mercury tip over the edge.

Now that the space was wide open, Fritz relaxed a little. He pointed over to a craggy path that wound its way down around the edge of the cavern and they followed it to the bottom, where a shore gave way to black in all directions. Erich knelt down and gently touched the surface. This time it really was water, though it left an oily residue on his fingertips.

"Look," Fritz said, pointing out across the lake.

A rowboat floated not far away. They waded out and hauled it to shore. It had no oars, but it was light enough to propel with their patronage. They glided across the still water, hugging the cave's edge. A few times they came across another quicksilver waterfall that dripped down into the lake, sourced from all over the mines.

After a full circle, Erich and Fritz decided to push out towards the center of the water, only stopping when they could no longer see the shore or the walls of the cavern. Erich's little light seemed useless against so much empty space. He extinguished it and let the dark flood in.

But it was not all dark. A light flickered in the distance, there one moment, gone the next. It came again, closer now, an amber glow that twisted and refracted through the murk. It flashed once more just below them. Fritz squealed. The lights weren't flickering. They were blinking. More and more opened all around them, eyes that glinted green and gold and orange with pupils slit like a snake's. There were hundreds of them, each bigger than Erich's head. They fluttered as if in a deep sleep.

In the eyes' yellow glow, he could finally see the cavern from end to end, though the rock dome above was so far away that the light barely reached it. Erich got to his feet, feeling very small.

"Hello?" he said. "*Heil Hitler?*"

The boat rocked and Fritz crawled into the prow with a whimper. A pale hand shot out from the water and Erich jumped so high he almost fell in. The hand gripped the lip of the boat and Erich staggered back, but there was nowhere else to go. He stood paralyzed as a man, naked and swollen, pulled himself up. He had his neck turned down and long black hair dripped over his face. Slowly, the man raised his head and opened his mouth wide. Erich's knees buckled.

The man's jaw hung limp and his lips were stretched taut. From the bottom of his throat eight crustacean legs ran up to pierce out through punctures in his cheeks. He let out a gurgle and the legs twitched, yanking his mouth open and closed like a marionette.

"It's him," he croaked, thrusting a bony finger at Erich.

A second creature burst from the water and hauled herself onto the boat.

"There are two of them," she squealed. "Debtors and thieves the both!"

She grabbed Fritz and dragged him to his feet. As she leaned in, her mouth-legs clamored over his face with excitement.

"It was brave of you to come," a third voice rumbled from the water. "With vows broken and scattered at your feet."

The last man to pull himself aboard was taller than the

others and his hair fell in braids over wiry shoulders. He clapped soggy hands around Erich's ears and pressed his face in close. The legs of his mouth tore Erich's armband away. His breath stank of rot and brine.

"Did you imagine that she of so many eyes would be blind to your tricks?" he growled. "Did you suppose that one offering could simply be exchanged for another, that you could come before a god only to haggle like a beggar at market?"

Erich tried to squeak out a denial, but the tall man clamped a bloated hand over his mouth. The woman crept up behind Erich and gripped his throat, caressing.

"Such fresh mouths they have," she moaned. "Let them work away the debt in the choir."

"Lazy fool," the first creature spat. "Old mouths sing just as loudly as young. We should send them to the surface. Let them hunt the squanderer of the gospel. Let them bring her to us in chains."

"We have another for that," the tall man said. He locked eyes with Erich. "Tell me, tiny thing, how do you intend to pay your debt? Will you sing your patron's waking song?"

He lifted his hand off Erich's mouth with a wet suctioning sound, then crouched down and thrust it into the water.

"Anything," Erich wheezed. "We'll—"

The tall man's hand twitched, grasping at something. There was no air in Erich's lungs. With a shudder of his mouth-legs, the man withdrew his arm, fingers wrapped around the shell of a long-legged crab.

"Oooo," the woman squealed. "How sweet they will sound in the choir."

She grabbed Erich's head from behind. He clamped his teeth shut, but her salty fingers jammed into his mouth and pried it open. The tall man tapped the crab and its legs sucked up into its shell. Howling, the woman yanked Erich's head back so that all he could see was the endless black of the cavern's sky. The tall man gripped the crab between two fingers and lowered it down over Erich's mouth.

"Wait!" the first man hissed. He had his face pressed so close to Fritz's that they almost touched. "Look at their eyes."

"What do you mean?" The tall man said. He yanked Erich's head back down and drew in. He lifted Erich's lid with a thumb, peered into his eye for a long moment, and then broke into a throaty laugh.

"She wouldn't give them eyes like that to sing, would she?" he said. "I think somewhere up there a heart still beats. I think she wants a hunt."

"No!" the woman shouted. Her voice cracked. "The song hurts. Our throats are raw. Let them take our places, please!"

The tall man silenced her with a glare and she let go of Erich. He crumpled, clutching his mouth and sucking in long rasping breaths. The tall man knelt down at his side and lifted up his chin.

"I wouldn't delay if I were you," he said. "Our god is very, very old, but that does not mean she is patient. What you have will not last long unpaid."

His mouth legs lifted the corners of his lips into an imitation of a smile as he ran his fingers through Erich's hair. They twisted into a grip and he slammed Erich's face down into the icy water. Erich thrashed and clawed, but it was useless. He tried to shout. Water flooded his mouth, brackish and coppery. He opened his lungs and it burned them away.

***

Erich woke under sunlight and trees. Rustling leaves cast patterned shadows across his chest. He lay in the rowboat, beached amongst the rocks of a creekbed. The boat's ribs were broken and water trickled through them. It drenched Erich's shoulder. Here, the events in the mines seemed dreamlike and distant.

He stood up and woke Fritz, who was curled into a tight ball on the other side of the boat. On the horizon, Erich could see the ever-present plume of smoke that drifted up from the far side of the mountain. They couldn't think of anything to say, so they just let the stained skies carry them back to Rouhhenberg.

It was dark by the time they made it past the outer gate. Doktor Kammer and Frau Murr stood in the courtyard. Kammer waved them closer with his clipboard. Mateusz II ran up to sniff at Erich's trousers while he checked their names off his list.

Frau Murr looked shocked to see them. "Fiehler, von Keppler, I-I- congratulations, congratulations to you both."

The only thing Erich could think about was how desperate he was to wash away everything that had happened. "Did we miss the baths?"

"No," Doktor Kammer said. "There are no more baths. You passed! You're not a *Nassfuchs* anymore."

"Oh. Right," Erich said. He felt a little betrayed. It was as though someone he loved had left without saying goodbye.

"Don't worry," Fritz called back as he loped off towards the chapel. "Getting held back a year shouldn't be difficult for you."

Erich frowned at Fritz's return to form. He stayed a while with Doktor Kammer, watching the road for stragglers. When it seemed like there would be no one else, he said his goodbyes and headed in. The rest of the *Nassfüchsen* turned to stare as Erich pushed open the chapel doors. Almost everyone was done eating. He found Karl sitting by himself, toying with a few ruined potatoes on his plate. He lit up when he saw Erich.

"I was worried you got lost. Have you seen Walther?"

"No," Erich said. "He's not here?"

Karl shook his head. "Everyone else is back now. You don't think he... failed, do you?"

"Walther?" Erich said with an unconvincing laugh. "He's probably just looking for extra credit."

Karl attempted a smile. After a long day without eating, Erich had thought he would be hungry, but when one of the girls brought over a plate, he barely recognized it as food. He speared a sausage with his fork. From the taste, it might as well have been filled with dirt. Erich swallowed a few bites mechanically, then pushed the plate away.

Walther still hadn't returned when Doktor Kammer stepped up to the balcony podium. He coughed and waited for the room to fall to a hush. No one paid him any mind. Doktor Kammer cleared his throat again, and when no one responded *Oberführer* Ehrenzweig slammed his palm down on the table with a thundering crack. The echoes faded away into complete silence.

"Thank you, *meine Herren*," Kammer squeaked, more excited than angry. He waved a piece of paper in the air. "I have your corps assignments."

Rubbing his hands together, he read off the names. Karl came early and to his delight went to the *Schützenadler*. Felix, Richard, and Viktor followed him. Even Bardulf, who on size alone seemed an obvious choice for the warrior-like *Wehrbären*, joined Karl. Every time another *Schützenadler* name was called, Erich felt more and more upset, as though each spot had been stolen from him.

Watching the students at the high tables, Erich barely recognized any of the *Wehrbären*. They sat all straight and dour. Erich imagined them eating in silence every day, communicating only in brutish grunts. The *Schützenadler* had a sense of warmth. They sat close together and their faces glowed as whispers traveled the table. Otto and Uwe had their heads turned in towards each other, almost touching as they watched Kammer read the names.

"Fritz von Keppler. *Wehrbären.*"

Erich closed his eyes. He was next. *Schützenadler. Schützenadler. Schützenadler.*

"Erich Fiehler," Doktor Kammer read. "*Wehrbären.*"

Karl turned immediately and stuck out a pitying lip. Fury roiled in Erich's chest, but he was too tired to hold on to it for long. He slumped down in his seat.

"That's all," Doktor Kammer said, clicking his paper against the podium. "Now, Hugo has a few words before you go off to meet your new brothers."

Walther's name hadn't been read at all. Karl looked around frantically, waving his hand and pointing to the empty seat next to him, but the teachers ignored him. Erich thought he saw Kammer's head shake slightly as he took his seat.

Erich looked up at the *Wehrbären* and felt unbearably alone. The enthusiasm that filled the hall smothered him, and he wanted to run into some hidden corner of the castle and cry.

Hugo stepped right up to the ledge and leaned out, ignoring the podium. The mutilated twin who continued to haunt his shoulder copied him. He held it back with one hand so it wouldn't fall off.

"Seven years ago, I was nothing at all. A charlatan. I wandered the streets and peddled my tricks to any fool who would believe them. But then, I met someone who changed me forever, who made all my dreams possible."

"*Heil Hitler!*" came a shout from the *Wehrbären* table.

Hugo smiled gently in its direction. "My whole life I have only ever had one aim. To bring wonder back to the world. To bring magic to our drab lives. Today that has come alive before me. You are *Nassfüchsen* no longer."

Erich knew this was supposed to inspire him, but he felt hollowed out, a bottomless vessel that no amount of zeal could fill. Hugo's voice crescendoed, but Erich was no longer listening. His eyes were shut and in his mind he was home.

# CHAPTER TWENTY-ONE

Walther did not return the next day, nor the day after that. Talk of his disappearance became a taboo among the former *Nassfüchsen*. Karl was always met with glares and silence when he brought it up. Nonetheless, he did so often and loudly. All month, he dragged Erich with him to wheedle their teachers for information.

"This sort of thing can happen, I'm afraid," Doktor Kammer said. "But you never know. He might turn up."

Herr Larat answered even more cryptically. "He returns or he does not. It's no more or less than any of us deserve."

When they sought out Hugo, he sounded apologetic. "Do you remember what I said on your first night here? When I showed you the names of your patrons? I told you that you'd sworn an oath and that you need do nothing to fulfill it. I thought I could keep that promise, but I was wrong and your friend paid the price. If you need someone to blame, blame me."

Before Karl could press any further, the headmaster drifted away. His macabre twin shambled after him.

*Oberführer* Ehrenzweig was the only one who spoke directly. "I will be honest. I don't think he will coming back. But there's no sense in mourning. Be proud. If he has died, then he has died for the fatherland. It's a lucky man who gets to do that."

"Are you saying it would be a good thing for him never to come back?" Karl said.

"No, no," Ehrenzweig said. "Look. When you're older, the end won't as far away as it does now. One day, it'll occur to you that you're likely going to die in a bed, frail and smothered under a mountain of blankets. It'll be cold and it'll be senseless. And on that day, you'll realize that you envy Walther. He died for a cause whereas you will die for no reason whatsoever." He bent down to look Karl in the eye. "That's all life is, really. It's an allotment of time to figure out why your death should matter."

There was, however, one person who Karl neglected to question and Erich was certain that she held all the answers. Frau Murr. Whatever was going on with him and Walther, she had been determined to cover it up. She had taken Doktor Kammer's dog just to send the *Nassfüchsen* out to search the castle. Then she'd showed up at Walther's sickbed to threaten him if he didn't stay silent about the cold bath and his illness. But as certain as Erich was that she had done something wrong, he had no idea what that something could be. He doubted she would be forthcoming if they asked.

It took months for Karl to slow his relentless search for Walther, but Erich found himself distracted almost immediately. He was a member of the *Wehrbären* now, and evidently that was not something to which a person could devote only a little of himself.

The *Wehrbären* existed in a state of near-constant training, most of which consisted of hurling each other around with unrestrained patronage. This was ostensibly for *SV*, but Erich didn't understand how the violent sparring was supposed to help them out on the field. Alas, when he tried to ask the older boys, he discovered that questions were the only thing the *Wehrbären* hated more than their rival *Schützenadler.*

This and many other incidents in his first week left their mark in bruises and burns. But by the time he attended his first dueling class with *Oberführer* Ehrenzweig, Erich thought he had a handle on the basics. Immediately, Ehrenzweig disproved him by matching Erich up with an older boy who sent him soaring backwards onto the mat in the first two seconds of their bout.

Displays of patronage that might have passed muster in practice were deemed sloppy at best by Ehrenzweig. He demanded precision over power and all throughout class, he strutted around the gym, thwacking underperforming boys on the back of the neck with the hilt of his saber. The only time Erich earned even a word of praise was when they sparred while blindfolded, a challenge for which his piercing eyes were uniquely suited. Sadly, Erich's ill-gotten winning streak lasted only until he faced off with Fritz, who immediately swept him off his feet and usurped the *Oberführer's* favor.

Every night when the boys returned to their dormitory, two of their new *Jungenschaftführer*, Eckhard and Fester, would block the doorway and demand a toll. Before any of the recruits could enter, they had to take a knuckled blow to the gut. Any boy who could stay upright would be allowed in, but if he keeled over or even flinched, he would be sent away to sleep in the hall or come back when he was ready to pay again.

Fritz was the only one exempt from the toll. He had become a hero of sorts among the *Wehrbären* when he had scored a humiliating point against Uwe on his very first day in Rouhhenberg. From the very start, the upperclassmen treated him as one of their own.

Fritz's best friend Anton was not so lucky. On their first night as *Wehrbären*, he stepped up before anyone else. But when Eckhard threw his punch, Anton countered with his patronage and the older boy's fist froze mid-swing.

For a long moment no one moved, then Fester took

one step forward and launched Anton back against the wall. Anton thrashed against the invisible restraints that held him up, roaring furiously until Eckhard squeezed his mouth shut. His teeth ground against each other like millstones. Grunting through sealed lips, he slid up the wall until his back was crammed into the corner where it met the ceiling.

Like one of Herr Larat's balloons, Anton hung there, his right arm dangling out below him. Eckhard made a motion in the air as though turning a knob and Anton's drooping arm began to bend backwards. Tears dribbled onto the varnished floor. Only when Anton's forearm tensed against its limit was he finally permitted to open his mouth and loose a terrified squeal. His arm snapped and he fell.

After that, no one ever again tried to shirk the toll. For four nights, Erich slept on the hard stone of the hidden corridors, adrift in his endlessly repeating nightmare about the filthy boy on the ceiling and his pile of bones. There was something unsettling about lying so close to the three dreaded left turns, as though he might accidentally walk the distance in his sleep. Spurred on, Erich learned fast to pay the toll without flinching.

There were benefits, however, to the harsh life of the *Wehrbären*. Though he could not banish his recurring dreams from the nighttime, they no longer tormented him during the day because he simply didn't have time to think about them anymore. No so for the *Schützenadler*.

From what Erich could tell, they had it easy. They reported to Doktor Kammer instead of *Oberführer* Ehrenzweig, and while they still marched, trained, and practiced *SV*, the rest of their time was filled with softer subjects. While Erich learned dueling, tactics, and battle formations, they studied transformations and the healing arts.

Whenever Erich managed to get away to see Karl or Otto and Uwe, he felt like he were traveling to another world entirely, full of unfamiliar words and jokes that were only funny if you'd been there. He wondered how long the smiles that always adorned his friend's faces would last in the *Wehrbär* wing.

Away from the upperclassmen, Rouhhenberg's halls filled up with new *Nassfüchsen*. It was fun for a while to look down at them from the high tables or jeer at their *SV* trainwrecks, but these perks were soon dwarfed by a new one. Starting in the spring, they were permitted to attend a weekly social hour with the BDM girls in Rathe Hall.

At Erich's first session, the older *Wehrbären* and *Schützenadler* immediately broke off from the group and strode in with confidence, waving at their acquaintances on the other side. In contrast, Erich's group clumped together, stealing nervous glances across the room. He expected that Otto and Uwe would strike off with the others their age, but instead they stayed behind with Erich and Karl, who were searching for Johanna.

When they finally spotted her, she ran over to give everyone a hug. A girl tagged behind her sheepishly. Johanna tossed a glare back in the girl's direction, but before she could scare her off Karl swooped in to introduce himself and usher her into their group.

"This is Mathilde," Johanna said through gritted teeth. "She's very... persistent."

The boys started giving their names, but Mathilde interrupted and finished for them.

"I've seen you all on the *Siegfeld*," she laughed.

There were ample tables in the hall, but Johanna instead pulled the group over to an empty section and plopped down on the floor. They joined her in a circle and Karl started a tiny hovering fire at its center. It delighted Mathilde, but let off too much smoke. As soon as Doktor Kammer saw it, he made a cutthroat gesture and pointed his cane to where Frau Murr prowled on the other side of the room. Disappointed, Karl let the fire fizzle out.

Erich felt a kick to his back and he and twisted around

to see Fritz looming over him.

"Met any pretty *Schützenadler* girls yet, Fiehler? You'd better be quick." Fritz waved at Otto and Uwe. "I think those two are already spoken for."

Otto tossed him a rude gesture, but Fritz had already darted away, butting aside another crowd of *Schützenadler* to introduce himself to the group of girls they had been talking to.

"I hate it here in the mountains," Uwe said without warning. "There's no water. I can't remember the last time we heard the ocean."

"We'll be home eventually," Otto said, throwing him a soft punch on the shoulder.

"Where's home?" Johanna asked.

"Rügen."

"Oh," Erich said. "My aunt used to collect those *KdF* brochures about the resort they're building."

"That's the place," Otto said.

"I've never seen the ocean. I'd like to, though," Johanna said. "Who knows, maybe someday there'll be a rainstorm or a flood or something. The ocean can come to us."

Uwe cracked a tentative smile. "That doesn't sound likely."

"I think we should start working on the ark just to be safe," Otto said.

"We don't have the right number of boys and girls," Mathilde chided. "Someone would have to be left behind."

"I nominate Fritz!" Johanna cackled loudly.

Their laughter must have alerted Frau Murr. Immediately upon seeing them sitting on the floor, she charged over.

"Disgusting!" she shrieked. She grabbed Johanna and Mathilde by each arm and yanked them up. "How do you expect men to tell you apart from a Jewess if you spend all your time rooting around in the dirt like swine?"

Mathilde blushed and looked down, but Johanna

caught Frau Murr's gaze without blinking. Incensed, Frau Murr dropped Mathilde's arm, clapped her gloved hand around Johanna's ear, and gave it a vicious twist. Everyone in the hall turned to watch as she dragged Johanna out the door.

"She always has to do that," Mathilde sobbed. She buried her face in Karl's arm and barely looked up again.

When the hour was over, Erich slipped away from the rest of the group to find his way into the corridors and look for Johanna. He knew there was a closet on the third floor of Rathe that he could enter through, but as he stepped inside and started to pull the outer door shut, it jammed against something. He yanked again with both hands but it wouldn't move. Then the knob tore out of his grip and the door swung open, smacking against the wall.

"Fiehler!" Fritz's voice called out from down the hall. "Do I even want to know what you're planning on doing in there?"

Erich grimaced and slowly emerged from the closet. He glanced to his right and saw Anton blocking one end of the hall. Fritz barred the other, grinning with one arm held out. A wallop of patronage slammed into Erich's chest and he slid backwards without falling. He dug his feet in, but the pressure from the two of them together was too strong. His boots screeched as they tore against the floorboards.

Anton stepped aside to let Fritz push Erich past him. He fell in like a hound on a leash. After rounding the corner, Fritz dropped his hand and slammed Erich to his knees. Erich gritted his teeth and stifled a shout.

Fritz stepped closer and crouched down to whisper in his ear, "Are you a *Schützenadler*?"

"No," Erich said. "I'm not."

A sharp crack hit him from the left. For a second, Erich's vision flooded black. Another from the right. Stumbling to all fours, he lashed out, wild and flailing, but Anton and Fritz bore down from every direction. They smothered his patronage. Erich felt himself lift up and his back crashed into the wall. There was something soft behind him—a tapestry. It flooded his periphery with scarlet and gold, but did nothing to dull the impact.

"Are you a *Schützenadler?*" Fritz asked again.

Erich tried to respond, but he couldn't move his jaw. Fritz spread Erich's arms wide then stepped back. He gave a look as though admiring a painting he had just hung. Anton reached for Erich's arm and for a moment he thought he was about to drive a nail into his wrist, but then he pulled out a length of rope. He tied Erich's arms to the tapestry's crossbar and withdrew behind his master.

Fritz opened his mouth as though he were about to speak, then changed his mind, spat, and turned away. Before slinking into Fritz's shadow, Anton pulled one arm back and Erich felt his head draw forward. Anton's hand hung in the air for a moment, then shot out. The rear of Erich's head slammed against the wall and everything flickered away.

✳✳✳

They said it was Doktor Kammer who finally took him down, but the only thing Erich could remember was the glance he got at the tapestry as *Rottenführer* Wolff carried him away. It was a gold eagle, the *Adler*, its wings spread wide against a blood red sky.

Herr Larat came by once to visit Erich in the infirmary and asked him to name names. But he knew that he should not and that Larat didn't really want him to. When Erich said nothing, the formality had been taken care of, and he left satisfied.

Erich's friends visited as well, but he didn't let them stay for too long. He knew that a gaggle of *Schützenadler* around his bed wouldn't help the situation once he left the infirmary. In reality, it didn't seem to have made a difference either way. Any damage they could have done to his reputation had already been done. The speed with which the *Wehrbären* turned against him was staggering.

Egged on by Fritz, Eckhard and Fester steepened Erich's dormitory toll every night. Within a week, a sea of bruises covered his stomach and his arms filled up with the cuts that he somehow received more than anyone else in dueling class. They healed and were replaced until they no longer mattered, until they were just his skin.

Johanna was no help. She delighted in his countercultural status. In her spare time, she embroidered an eagle crest that she wanted him to pin to his shirt pocket.

"Forget Fritz and the rest," she said. "Be as much of a *Schützenadler* as you want."

Erich thanked her and then immediately hid the crest away somewhere he hoped no one would ever find it.

By the start of summer, he had given up entirely on making any allies amongst the *Wehrbären*, who had collectively come to regard him as little more than a punching bag. Even the meekest *Wehrbär* was no longer willing to be seen with him. Any time he wanted to spend practicing had to be alone. He could have just trained with his *Schützenadler* friends, since things could no longer get much worse, but Erich didn't want to drag them into the mess. They all seemed happier when he avoided talking about his troubles.

Instead, Erich would throw his frustration at mannequins and swinging bags until invariably, Fritz and company would come to interrupt. Then he would turn his blows on them. Every once in a while, he even managed to fend them off.

It did not come as a surprise to Erich that he was not picked in *SV* until the very end of the season when the *Wehrbär* captain had no other choice. The two corps were tied and, as it had the year before, the final game fell on

May 11th, Erich's thirteenth birthday.

As he and his supposed teammates crossed into the final row, a hulking cathedral bell blocked each lane. The two other *Wehrbären* teamed up to swing theirs aside, but as soon as they reached the flag, they turned their backs to Erich as though the round were already over.

By then, Erich had grown used to unfair odds. He was so often beset by two, three, or four boys that even if he could not yet overcome their patronage, he had at least learned to occasionally match it. He threw all his weight against the bell and, creaking and clanging, it gave way. Erich crossed the platform and let it fall, grateful for the resounding peals that filled the silence where his team's cheers would ordinarily have been.

That night, as he climbed the steps to the high tree trunk table, the other *Wehrbären* stopped speaking all at once. They stared at him expectantly. Exhausted and hungry from the match, Erich had no patience for their vicious games. He took a seat away from the others and looked out longingly at the roast and garnished hog in the center of the table. Closing his eyes for a moment, Erich let the smell of pork and spices substitute for companionship.

"Fiehler," Fritz taunted. Erich cringed and opened his eyes. "You're at the wrong table."

Slow, predatory smiles overtook every *Wehrbär* face. They leaned in towards him. Their eyes longed for rarer meat than the hog. Fritz's hand flicked below the table and Erich's chair shot out from under him. Erich slipped and tumbled to the floor, his jaw smacking painfully against the table as he fell. He reached for his chair to pull himself up, but it danced away.

Erich was so tired he almost wished he could lie down where he was and accept defeat. When he finally dragged himself up, all the *Wehrbären* were standing. They pointed silently towards the high table on the other side of the chapel.

Erich peered over at the *Schützenadler* table. They were all watching the commotion, but Uwe was the only one out of his seat. He stood with his hands wrapped tight around the railing of the high platform. Erich tried to catch Uwe's eye and convince him that whatever he was planning to do, it wasn't worth it, but Uwe wasn't looking at him at all. Defeated, Erich took the first step down off the high platform. He stopped. A sound had come from behind him, a loud snort.

One by one, the *Wehrbären's* pointing fingers fell. No one was even looking at Erich anymore. All their eyes were fixed on the center of the table. The sound came again and right away, Erich could see what Uwe had done; it had come from the roast that was supposed to be their meal. The hog shuddered and the apple rolled out from its mouth. Burnt eyelids peeled back and the pig's tongue broke free with a squeal. As it stood up, hooves tore apart the surrounding greens and its body burst out from its own crisped skin like a moth from a chrysalis.

The *Wehrbären* knocked over chairs as they scrabbled back from their seats, swearing and shouting. Peals of laughter from the other two tables drowned out the orders barked down by the adults on the balcony.

With a guttural slurping, the hog tried to gobble up the bed of garnishing at its feet, but its jaw was broken and it couldn't shut its mouth. As remarkable as Uwe's transformation was, the pig's wounds were not healed. Blood spilled out from its throat where the spit had once been rammed from one end to the other. Erich covered his nose and took a step back as he processed what was happening.

The beast let out a pleasured grunt. Its backside shuddered and the ragged wound at its rear spread open. Reanimated bowels loosed a torrent of feces and viscera that clinked and splattered off the hog's platter. It oozed around the plate settings like rocks in a river, then spread out to the table's edge and dribbled off, leaving solid, fleshy chunks stranded at the rim.

The *Wehrbären* had watched the whole proceeding in stupefied horror, but the moment the first sordid drops hit the platform floor, they broke out of their disgust and, howling with rage, struck back. Gore-soaked silverware and scraps of food lifted up from the table and fired themselves towards the *Schützenadler*, who immediately responded with a barrage of their own.

Caught in the middle, the *Nassfüchsen* shrieked and ran for cover while the two high tables clashed above them like warships in a broadside. Erich ducked down and threw his arms over his head, unsure whose side to take.

With an electric crackle, the lights on the ceiling sparked and suddenly went out. The chapel's massive doors flew open and let in a fearsome gust of wind. As it thrust through the hall, it sucked away all the ruckus, leaving the boys breathless and silent. Silverware clattered to the floor mid-arc. Blinding light flooded the room and a thunderous explosion roared out from the middle of the room.

When Erich's eyes cleared, he crawled up against the railing. Below, the *Nassfuchs* table lay in two broken pieces. Rent down the middle, its sides were a mess of jagged chunks and singed wood. The boys who had been closest were all strewn out across the floor, lying amongst the splinters. The upperclassmen stopped their squabbling to gape.

Hugo and his twin stood at the edge of the balcony, four arms held high. Erich's ears rang and his head swam as he tried to work out whether Hugo's display had been patronage or an elaborate trickery. Could he be so crazy as to have put a bomb inside their dinner tables?

"*Nassfüchsen*, you will conclude your meal in the lounge. The rest of you will return to your rooms at once," the headmaster shouted. He grabbed his twin by the arm and turned towards the door, but as he swept out of the room he had one last thing to say. "Fiehler. My office. Now."

# CHAPTER TWENTY-TWO

Erich had never been inside Hugo's office before, but it was not difficult to find. Amidst all the curves and undulations of Rouhhenberg, the sharp edges of the hexagonal tower on the north grounds were a rarity. Sometimes the more adventurous of the boys would dare each other to climb the wooden stairs that wrapped its exterior, but Erich had never seen anyone make it more than halfway up. He himself had always been desperately curious to find out what was in there, but had only ever braved a few steps. Now that he was about to see it up close, it was the last place he wanted to be.

The night wind whistled around the tower and each step groaned as it took his weight. At the top, the door was open, letting in the chill. Inside, the hardwood floor gleamed as though it had just been polished. There was no sign of Hugo. At each of the six walls was a single meticulously placed item and nothing else: a thin bed, a bare desk, three identical gray jackets on a coat hanger, a long red flag draped vertically, a dark oak wardrobe, and the doorway in which Erich stood. At the center, a ladder ran up to a trapdoor in the ceiling.

Erich paused at the threshold and glanced at his boots,

afraid he would track something in. He jumped at the sound of Hugo's voice from above.

"Up here. There's no need to be frightened."

"Ye-yes, sir," Erich said.

He scurried past the threshold and climbed the ladder up to the roof. Hugo stood at the parapet's edge, looking out over the castle with his back turned. His twin kept his side, barely staying upright on bent legs. Erich realized that he had still had scraps of potato slopped in his hair and hastily ran his fingers through it. Without turning around, Hugo waved him over. Erich kept his distance from the twin as he approached.

"I'm told the students are partial to the view from Rathe Hall," he said. "Is that true?"

"I think so," Erich said. "I mean, yes, we are."

Otto and Uwe had taken them there once. In one of Erich's rare free hours, they had carried chairs up to the roof and savored Johanna's pilfered sweets while watching the sun set over the forest.

"Well?" Hugo prodded. "What do you think? Is the view better from here?"

"It, uh… yes, yes it is," Erich said.

He took another step towards the edge. Past the battlement, the castle sprawled out down the mountain, illuminated by the amber glow of windows and embrasures. In the distance, the walls blended into the dense treeline so that it was hard to tell where structure ended and forest began. By now, he knew every corner and crevice of Rouhhenberg by heart, but he rarely saw it all at once. Taken together, its writhing asymmetry was just as confounding and beautiful as it had been when he first glimpsed it from the train.

"Am I in trouble?" Erich asked.

"That depends," Hugo said. "*Oberführer* Ehrenzweig thinks you and Uwe should both be expelled."

"But I- I- didn't do anything," Erich pleaded. "The pig, the whole thing, it was Uwe. It wasn't me!"

"You're right," Hugo said, his expression suddenly harsh. A horrible grimace tore open his twin's melted face. "As it happens, the *Oberführer* and I disagree on the subject of Uwe Puhl. I think what he did was disruptive, but it was nonetheless impressive. I wish all of our students had that kind of talent. You, on the other hand, did exactly as you say. Nothing at all. The only talent I've seen from you is for troublemaking and this once I'm inclined to let Ehrenzweig have his way. Do you disagree?"

"Well, I-" Erich stopped himself. He tried to think of something to say, but no excuses sprang to mind. When he really thought about it—apart from all the things that were against the rules—he couldn't think of anything that would count as an accomplishment.

While Erich fished for words, Hugo leaned against the battlement and crossed his arms. His silent twin did the same, but his back was at a crenel and there was nothing to support him. The twin lurched away and tripped over the low wall. Erich gasped and threw his arms out to catch him, but the headmaster was already there, one hand wrapped around his twin's wrist. He eyed Erich with suspicion in his eyes.

"You can see him," Hugo said.

Erich couldn't decide if honesty would help or hurt, but he nodded anyway.

"Now there's a reason," Hugo said. He wagged his finger. "You should have said something earlier."

"I'm sorry, sir," Erich mumbled. "If you don't mind me asking, wh- who is he?"

"It's better not to think of it as a he," Hugo said. "*It* is a doppelgänger. A gift from an old friend of mine. One I'm sure she regrets giving. Come downstairs and I'll show you."

Hugo grabbed the doppelgänger by the wrist and shoved it straight down through the trapdoor. Erich cringed as he heard it land with a crunching sound, but Hugo didn't seem at all concerned. He lowered himself down the ladder and then called back after Erich to follow.

Inside his office, Hugo waved Erich over to his desk. It was completely cleared but for a framed photograph and an old hide-bound book.

"The *Reichsjugendführer* gave you a dagger last winter, did he not?"

Erich nodded and unsheathed it.

"That's the one. Have you kept it sharp?"

"Yes, sir," Erich said.

Hugo held out his palm. The doppelgänger mimicked him, but Hugo smacked its hand down. "Cut me," he said.

Erich stared at him incredulously.

"Oh, don't be a coward," Hugo said. "Long before any of this, they used to saw me in half for an audience of hundreds. You can make one tiny cut."

"I- I'll try, sir," Erich stammered. Shaking, he held the dagger out over Hugo's palm, but he hesitated too long. Did the headmaster really mean for Erich to cut him or was it all some kind of trick?

"Fine, I'll do it," Hugo snapped.

He grabbed the sharp end of the blade and squeezed it tight, sliding his hand down the edge until blood welled up between his fingers. His doppelgänger let loose a pitiful moan and clutched at its wrist. Blood dribbled off its mangled fingertips, but the drops vanished before they reached the floor. Hugo pulled out his handkerchief, then opened his own palm and wiped it clean. Beneath, the skin was perfectly smooth.

"Good as new," he said.

Erich probed his tender belly and felt the familiar dull pain of his bruises. He imagined laughing while Eckhard and Fester winded themselves trying to leave a mark. "Can I learn to do that?"

"I hope you will someday. If I knew how I would teach you." Hugo picked up the photograph from his desk. "Alas, it was a gift, like I said."

"From her?" Erich asked.

"Yes," Hugo said, handing him the frame. "Isabel Colmán. Born right here in Rouhhenberg. Four hundred years ago if you believe her story. In a way, this school is as much hers as it is mine."

In the picture, Hugo stood before the bright lights of a theater marquee. He had his arm held out for a dark brown-skinned woman who was stepping down from the backseat of a taxi. She wore a lush fur and three strings of pearls that ran all the way down to her knees. Her face was broad and carried a look of quiet displeasure, but the poor contrast of the photo made it hard to see her features. In the corner, someone had scribbled something in English. The only part Erich could understand was the year, 1933.

"She doesn't *look* like she was born in Rouhhenberg," Erich said.

"I said more or less the same thing when I met her," Hugo replied. "But it's true. Her mother left her at the foundling wheel of our very own chapel. I expect her father was a Moorish trader."

"Where is she now?"

"Far away from here if we're lucky," Hugo said.

There was a long silence and when it grew unbearable, Erich finally asked the question he had been grateful to forestall. "Am I going to be expelled, sir?"

"No, I think not," Hugo said. "You're a mystery, Erich Fiehler. I collect mysteries. Even so, something has to be done about the situation. The *Oberführer* will throw if a fit if there's any more chaos like that. I'm moving you to the *Schützenadler*."

"Oh," Erich said. A part of him wanted to spring up and scream from the top of the tower with his hands in the air, but there was another part that harbored a kind of pride in his time in the *Wehrbären*. His teachers and peers treated him like the dirt on their boots, but faced suddenly with the possibility of turning coat, he began to wonder if that was how the world was meant to be. Maybe that kind of suffering was how a boy became a man. Klaus would have said so.

While the *Wehrbären* trained for war, the *Schützenadler* were being groomed to become party bigwigs. He could already imagine Karl and the others sitting in lavish rooms all day signing papers. Was that what Erich wanted? It sounded exactly like the work of the "golden pheasants", the fat party functionaries that Klaus had always promised his *Fähnlein* they would one day make redundant.

When he'd been a *Nassfuchs*, Erich had had spent all his time obsessing over which of the two corps his friends would join. That was where he'd wanted to be. But he'd never considered the obvious question: If the *Führer* had come to Rouhhenberg would he have been a *Wehrbär* or a *Schützenadler*? The answer was so clear it took him aback and it wasn't the *Schützenadler*.

"Don't overwhelm me with your gratitude," Hugo said.

"I- I'm sorry, sir. I'm just surprised."

"That's alright. But, please, just keep future troublemaking to a minimum. Ehrenzweig is difficult enough as it is."

"Yes, sir. There'll be no more—"

"Ah, speak of the devil," Hugo interrupted. "Reiner, do come in. The boy was just leaving."

Erich whirled around. *Oberführer* Ehrenzweig stood on the landing outside Hugo's office. He brushed past Erich, who decided it was best to get out before Hugo could change his mind about letting him stay. But as Erich carefully pulled the door shut and turned towards the stairs, the temptation to eavesdrop grew too strong. He made a few noisy steps down then crept back up and let his eyes push past the wood and stone.

"*Scharführer* Kammer tells me you intend to let the Puhl boy stay," Ehrenzweig said. "Is that true?"

"It is. Fiehler will continue with us as well."

"Excuse me," Ehrenzweig growled.

"You know as well as I how dearly we've paid for each boy here," Hugo said. "Why would you throw that away over a food fight?"

"Because someone has to clean up your messes. I warned you this would happen. If you'd listened to me it never would have gone this far. They are children. Without discipline they turn to beasts."

"And that's what you plan to write in your report?"

"That and more," Ehrenzweig said. "Left to you, this school would become a zoo. And yet for reasons I will never understand, the *Führer* has given you extraordinary latitude to run it however it pleases you. But even he must have his limits. What do you expect to happen once you've broken them?"

"Your mistake, Reiner, is to think that I have not already. How many times have you sent off your damning reports only to seethe at the silence you get in reply. You know he has what I want—this beautiful school would be impossible without him—but you've failed to understand that I have something more. I have what he *needs*."

"And what is that?" Ehrenzweig spat.

"The power to turn his lies into truths."

Before Erich could process all the treasons that were spewing from the headmaster's mouth, Hugo grabbed the hide-bound book from his desk and held it out to the *Oberführer* with both hands. There was a terrible sizzling sound and wisps of smoke threaded up from where he touched it. It was as if he'd wrapped his fingers around a pot on the stove. His doppelgänger dropped to its knees and screamed in silence as its hands bubbled and burned in place of Hugo's.

"When do you think it will be enough? When we graduate a hundred boys? Two? A thousand? You're an expert. Racial studies, right? Tell me! How many does it take to make a race into the master one?

"One day I will exceed my usefulness and I am under no illusions about what will happen that day. That's fine. I have been a chew toy to his *SS* dogs before and I will be so again. But drag me away now and what will you have left? Who will mark the boys when I'm gone? You?" With a burnt finger, Hugo tapped his forehead then cracked open the book and offered it out. "Go ahead, read it."

Scribbles of ink streaked the page, but there was no discernable order to it. The writing ran in all directions. It clashed against itself. Just looking at the words stung Erich's eyes as if he were peering into the heart of a fire. Ehrenzweig shook with anger and jabbed an accusatory finger at Hugo, but he couldn't seem to muster an answer.

"What's the matter, comrade, are you frightened?" Hugo goaded. "You should be. You have no idea what I do every day. You've never felt the lick of fire in your voice. You've never tasted your own charred tongue as it melts down your throat. Try it. Take the book if you like. The marking is easy. You stand before the offering and you read it to them. Here, I'll start for you."

The verse spat from Hugo's mouth like water from burning oil. Guttural and broken, each incomprehensible word bore into Erich until he thought his ears would burst from the inside. Still chanting, Hugo drove forward until he had pushed Ehrenzweig's back all the way up against the door.

Hugo's throat glowed amber and his jaw drooped lower and lower with every syllable. His lips curled back until they cracked and the bottom half of his face dribbled molten into his beard. He paused while his smoking flesh reconstituted itself, then breathed in and started the words anew. His doppelgänger writhed on the floor until it could take no more. It curled itself into a ball and pressed its tortured head against its knees.

Erich ran. He didn't care how much noise he made as he clattered down the stairs and raced out into the courtyard. He ran and ran until he had reached the *Wehrbären* wing and realized suddenly that he was no longer a *Wehrbär*. Erich didn't belong there anymore. He wasn't sure he belonged anywhere. Reeling, he doubled back and took refuge in the secret corridors. He pressed his back against the rough stone and tried to breathe.

Everywhere Erich saw mouths. Mouths that melted like tallow. Mouths pierced by spiny, chittering legs. Mouths of dirty children that split open and screamed from the ceiling. They swallowed him.

Though he didn't understand what Hugo had meant when he showed *Oberführer* Ehrenzweig the contents of his fire-drenched book, Erich knew that he wanted no part of it. He wished that he had never heard Hugo's infernal language or his treasonous accusations, but it was too late. Now he felt somehow involved, and worse, like he was on the wrong side. After all, it was his good fortune they had been fighting over.

When at last Erich's heart stopped slamming against his ribs, he dragged himself out of the corridors and took the longest route he knew over to the *Schützenadler* wing, which in Rouhhenberg was a very long way.

As he stepped through the front door of his friends' dormitory, he was certain that at any moment someone would jump up and accuse him of being in the wrong place. But no one did. They rose from their sofas and their chairs—something the *Wehrbär* quarters had precious few of—and greeted him with enthusiasm. He passed through the crowd, not looking anyone in the eye as he shook their hands.

"Welcome," a boy he had never met said with a firm clasp on his shoulder.

"I'm a *Schützenadler*," Erich whispered. He still couldn't decide if that was a good or a bad thing.

"We know," the other boy said. He pointed him towards one of the rooms in the back.

The door was closed and Erich stopped outside to peek within. Everyone was there. Karl, Otto and Uwe, and even Johanna, whose presence was certainly forbidden. Somehow, they had found the time to throw up a few hasty decorations. A cloth banner hung askew from one lampshade to another. The words *Happy Birthday, Eaglet* were scrawled across it. Erich had completely forgotten that it was today. He was thirteen now, though after what he'd seen, he felt far older than that.

On the table was a cake, lopsided from being smuggled in. His friends sat around it, laughing and lounging in chairs big enough to swallow them whole. They seemed happy without him.

Erich sighed, shook off his doubts, and donned a smile. As he opened the door, he pretended for their sake to be surprised.

# CHAPTER TWENTY-THREE

Though he didn't miss the dormitory toll or the endless abuses of his *Wehrbären* classmates, Erich immediately felt that something was missing from the *Schützenadler*. There was a sense of structure and purpose to the other side of the castle that he hadn't understood the value of until it was gone. Even the classes were dull in comparison. Doktor Kammer's rambling history lessons were a poor substitute for *Oberführer* Ehrenzweig's dueling and Erich quickly discovered that he didn't have Uwe's talent for transformations.

The only *Schützenadler* class that Erich truly enjoyed was the healing arts with Frau Lange. Even with a year of missed practice, it didn't take long for him to catch up. For the first time since he was a *Nassfuchs*, Erich dusted off Klaus' stethoscope. He wore it to class beneath his uniform and though he never had occasion to use it, keeping it close made him feel like he was making good on his nearly-forgotten promise to Aunt Mila.

The older boys sang endless praises for a special course Hugo taught called "Suggestion", but Erich's year were not yet invited to join them. Yet despite how often they extolled them, Otto and Uwe never let slip any details on what exactly their lessons entailed. Erich couldn't count how many times he'd heard someone threaten to use suggestion to steal away a girlfriend or make a rival embarrass themselves in front of everyone, but he'd never seen anyone actually do it. He began to wonder if they were all just bluffing.

The longer Erich spent in the *Schützenadler*, the easier it was to forget the terrible things he'd seen on the night he joined them. There were more exciting things for the boys to think about, whichever side of the castle they slept in.

Just as the tales of fighting in Africa and the skies of Britain had begun to grow stale, all attention shifted to new conquests in the east. Russia, Hitler promised, would crumble in three months. Every night, the *Schützenadler* crowded into their lounge to follow the inexorable push towards Moscow. By fall, there were more tanks surrounding Leningrad than trees and it seemed the *Führer's* prophecy of a swift victory was on the verge of coming true.

At home, new faces crowded the halls. The *Schützenadler* did not treat their new recruits with the cruelty that the *Wehrbären* had, but they still had a few initiations of their own. As the newcomers shuffled into their bedrooms for the first night, one of the older boys handed each a stuffed raccoon in place of a pillow. Compared to the dormitory toll, Erich thought this was a pretty weak attempt at humiliation, but he changed his mind one night after the pillows turned live and feral while their owners slept. For two weeks, the new boys could be easily identified by the scratches on their faces.

With the larger student body, the upperclassmen had to split their *SV* league into two divisions. Thanks to his prior experience, Doktor Kammer picked Erich to captain the lower of these, which included about half of the boys in his own year and all of the new *Schützenadler*. Every other evening, Erich held practice and did his best to teach them everything he had learned in the *Wehrbären*. It made him feel like a bit of a traitor, but spilling the other side's secrets quickly produced results. The two divisions were scored together, and by winter, the *Schützenadler* had collectively eked out a three point lead.

The one thing that did not change with Erich's transfer was the social hours with the BDM. Whenever they met, two rumors, all but confirmed by the teachers, dominated the conversation. The first rumor held that in three weeks, the school would be hosting its first holiday ball. This alone might have whipped the students into a fervor of anticipation, but the second rumor completely overshadowed it: the day after the ball, on the Winter Solstice, the *Führer* would come to Rouhhenberg.

"What do you think he'll be like?" Uwe asked.

"It's strange," Erich said. "I feel like I know him, like I've known him forever. But it really only goes one way, right? He probably doesn't even know our names."

"He might," Karl said. "There's not so many of us here in Rouhhenberg. I think it'll all be different up close. When I saw him in Nuremberg, there were thousands of other kids at the rally."

"We saw him once too," Uwe said. "Just for a moment, back in Rügen. He came to see how the resort was coming along. Otto says I'm crazy, but I still think he was looking right at me when he saluted from the car."

Otto gave him a push on the shoulder. "We were very far away. It might not even have been him."

"Of course it was him," Uwe said. "You just don't want to let on how you almost pissed yourself with excitement."

Johanna yawned and patted her mouth pointedly. "It's not like we haven't all listened to a thousand speeches already. Don't we have other things to talk about?"

"Such as?" Erich asked.

"I haven't heard one word about which of you is taking me to the ball."

Mathilde giggled and made eyes at Karl. Otto and Uwe

shrugged while Erich just blushed. As much as Erich enjoyed seeing Johanna more often, there was something about the gatherings that had made him increasingly uncomfortable as they got older. His classmates all pined for the girls of the BDM, but Erich had as of yet not managed to find that same desire within himself. He had no perverted interest in the other boys either. He just didn't understand what everyone else was talking about when they whispered to each other from their bunks about Sabine or Eva or Freida.

Even so, if the conversation ever turned to Johanna, Erich had to stifle the urge to leap up and pummel whichever boy was doing the speaking. Though realities were getting in the way, he had always felt it was inevitable that he and Johanna would one day end up together. He'd just never imagined it would have to be so soon. He wasn't ready.

"I'll take you," Karl said.

Mathilde let out a little gasp and covered her face with both hands. Behind her fingers, Erich could see her struggling not to show her disappointment. Erich turned to Johanna, certain she would now ask for his opinion on the matter.

"Excellent," she said instead. "Now that that's settled, you can all go back to talking about your first love."

Erich couldn't bring himself to move. The situation seemed far from settled. The whole exchange had happened so quickly that Karl had cheated him out of the chance to react or prepare. Erich shot a glare at him and Karl retaliated with a look of feigned confusion.

Uwe jumped in to change the subject. "Do you think the *Führer* will sit with us at dinner before the speech?"

Otto threw his arm over Uwe's shoulder. "Always the optimist," he said.

The others carried on for another half hour, going back and forth over predictions for the visit. It didn't seem to matter that they'd all had the same conversation five times before. Ordinarily it wouldn't have mattered to Erich either. But Johanna had somehow soured his taste for gossip and anticipation. As soon as the hour was up, he pulled away from the group, slipped into the secret corridors, and slumped down against the stone.

Erich kicked the opposite wall hard and the pain that shot up his leg felt like relief. He didn't understand what was wrong with him. None of the other boys had this kind of trouble. All he'd had to do was say a few words.

What right did Karl have? If it hadn't been for Erich, Karl wouldn't have made friends with Johanna at all. It wasn't Karl who'd fought a wolf for her. He hadn't shared their letters or their code. He hadn't stood up to her father. He didn't deserve her.

Erich dragged himself over to the embrasure in the wall and looked out. The forest stared back at him, bristling in the wind. He stayed there, fuming, for almost an hour before he realized that he was late for his own $SV$ practice and reluctantly left the refuge of the corridors behind.

The gym in Eckher Hall had once been a grand dining room, but the floor was completely cleared now. Doktor Kammer had helped Erich secure a variety of obstacles and props from Herr Jensson, but on many days they practiced without them, instead partnering up and dueling the way they had in the *Wehrbären*. He'd once been mystified how that could benefit them in the sport, but he understood better now how much motivation could be derived from a blend of competition and fear.

Erich had just finished dividing the twenty boys into pairs when the double doors of the hall pushed open and Karl stepped in. Though he was technically in the other division, Karl often stopped by Erich's practices and no one else paid him any mind. Now he was the last person Erich wanted to see. Karl grinned and waved from across the room.

"We have an even number," Erich said. "There's nobody for you to spar with."

"What about you?" Karl said.

That was enough to get the other boys attention and they all turned to see Erich's response.

"What about me," Erich mimed bitterly. He narrowed his eyes and they stepped into place opposite each other. "Let's have it then. Are you ready?"

Karl nodded.

As soon as Erich gave the signal to begin, the hum of patronage flared up all around him. Ordinarily he would stand back and let it buffet him as he surveyed the room, pointing out the cracks in his teammates defenses. But today he had his own partner and already a crushing pressure bore down on him.

Erich buckled under the weight, but he struck back with his own patronage and forced himself up to his feet. They pulled back and slammed into each other again and again like rams butting heads. Every time they met, Erich felt around for any weak spots where he might break through on their next collision. He found nothing. All around he could feel the other boys' defenses crumbling. Shockwaves rippled through the air as they shattered. Yet as all the other duels ended, Karl and Erich remained locked in a brutal stalemate.

As they crashed together for the dozenth time, Erich finally noticed a flaw, a tiny irregularity through which he could push more freely. They circled around to collide again and he focused everything he had onto that tiny gap. But when Erich threw his body out to strike, nothing happened. He tried again to no avail. He reached inside himself but he couldn't find what he was looking for. There was a void where his patron had been. He couldn't even sense the energy that swirled around Karl. Not until it hit him.

The blow met with no resistance. It lifted Erich up off his feet and slammed him down into the floor. Searing air tore out of his lungs and an old, familiar sensation bubbled up from his insides. He had to clap his hand over his mouth to stop himself from vomiting. Erich could almost feel the ice cold blood slithering over his shoulders. Gagging on the sour taste, he rolled over onto his back and sucked in short, panicked breaths.

Then as suddenly as it had onset, the feeling was gone. Erich's patronage rushed back in to fill the hole. He swallowed bile and did his best to stand. Karl grabbed Erich's arm and gently held him up.

"What happened?"

"I'm fine," Erich grunted. He pushed Karl away with more force than he had intended. His patronage felt too good not to use. "It was just... it was nothing. Let's go again."

Karl gave a hesitant nod. Erich hugged his chest as they moved back into position. There was a terrible pain in his ribs and he hoped that one had not broken. For the rest of the practice Karl went easy on him, but it didn't matter. Whatever had happened to Erich in that moment did not recur.

When the session was finally over, Erich quickly congratulated the other boys and then bolted off while everyone else went to shower. As he hurried down the hall, staring at his feet and ruminating on his sudden lapse, Doktor Kammer's voice called out from one of the classrooms behind him.

"Erich," he said. "In here if you don't mind."

Erich cringed and grudgingly turned back around. Inside, Mateusz the dachshund lay asleep on one of the desks.

"I saw you in the courtyard with Fraulein Engel the other day," Doktor Kammer tittered. He wiggled his fingers in excitement. "She's quite a sight. Love is in the air I think."

"It's nothing like that," Erich mumbled, looking away.

"Oh, come now, don't be shy. These are the sort of the things you need to be thinking about. It may seem far away now, but it's only a few years until you graduate. I expect there'll be a long line of potential Frau Fiehlers vying for your attention then."

Erich backed up slowly. The door looked very far away.

"Alright, alright," Doktor Kammer said. "I'll stop. Just remember that it won't seem so silly when you're older."

"Ye- yes, sir," Erich stammered.

"Anyway, that's not really what I wanted to ask you about," Kammer continued. "Frau Lange tells me you're earning top marks in her healing arts class. Is that true?"

"I hope so, sir."

"Good. I came to the right man," Doktor Kammer said. He gestured to the sleeping dachshund on the desk behind him. "It's Mateusz III. Something's happened to his leg."

"The third?" Erich said. "What happened to the second?"

Doktor Kammer gave a mournful nod. "I don't know. The same thing as his predecessor I suppose. They have the luck of kings."

Erich wondered if he should tell Doktor Kammer that Frau Murr had taken his first dog, but decided that would only make things worse. Instead, he leaned in and ran a hand down Mateusz' silky back. Several ragged gashes ran down his rear leg and his fur was caked with blackening blood. One paw was mangled and a large chunk of the pad hung off from the rest. It looked like he had tried to run through a thicket of barbed wire. Mateusz's chest slowly rose and fell, punctuated by an occasional shuddering breath. His eyes trembled behind their lids.

Doktor Kammer held his hand over his mouth and looked away. "His leg must have caught on something," he said. "Frau Murr keeps so many mouse traps about. I don't know why she can't just get a cat."

"He'll be alright," Erich said. "I promise."

After a day marked by impotence and failure, Erich was grateful for a task he could set his skills against. To his relief, the patronage poured out uninterrupted. Doktor

Kammer hovered over his shoulder as Erich set to work. He paced in circles around the desk, cane clacking against the floorboards, until it became so difficult to focus that eventually Erich had to gently ask him to sit down.

Many of his classmates considered healing and transformations to be more or less the same skill, but to Erich they couldn't have been farther apart. He didn't think he would ever be able to do a tenth of what Uwe was capable of. It was hard to turn something into a thing that it wasn't. But to mend a wound, all he had to do was to coax it into remembering what it had been before. That was simple. With a little guidance, tendons reconnected like old friends and fur resettled torn out skin. The sickly fluid hissed from Mateusz's lungs.

When Erich was finished, the dachshund let out a sputtering sigh. His newly repaired leg twitched in his sleep. As Doktor Kammer flooded him with praise, Erich saw an opportunity to sate his curiosity. He had so many questions that he couldn't make up his mind what to ask first. What had happened to his patronage? To Walther? Why could he see through the walls when no one else could? Who were the crab-mouthed men in the mines and what did any of that have to do with their bath where the blood had run cold? But in the end, what Erich wanted to understand most was the bitter argument he had overheard in the headmaster's office.

"I have a question about Hugo," he began.

Doktor Kammer squeezed Erich's shoulder. "You want to know if he's still upset with you after that mess with the *Wehrbären*."

"No, that's not really—"

"Don't worry yourself about it," Doktor Kammer said. "I'm very happy to have you in the *Schützenadler* and between you and me, I think he's thrilled with how things turned out. You have no idea how long Hugo's been waiting for a chance to do that trick with the table. It's just too bad Herr Jensson couldn't have been there to see his fireworks go off."

With that, Doktor Kammer picked up the still-sleeping Mateusz from the desk, thanked Erich one last time, and shuffled out of the classroom.

**\*\*\***

With winter came war with the United States. Yet when the news arrived, few in the castle paid it very much attention. All eyes were fixed on the east, where an act of god had stalled the Wehrmacht offensive. The early frost shielded the Soviets from their impending defeat and they hid behind it cravenly. This was not the swift victory they had been promised, but everyone Erich spoke to was confident that setback was only temporary.

In fact, the mood about the castle was as enthusiastic as it had ever been. The more enemies Germany had, the more victories could be enjoyed. But Erich found himself unable to share his classmates' zeal. He was fighting his own wars and he was losing them. The sputters in his patronage had grown more frequent. Though they never lasted long, they onset when he least expected them and he had to work hard to keep his shameful condition a secret.

Erich's other fronts were just as beleaguered. As the day of the winter ball crept closer, he resigned himself to the fact that Johanna was not going to change her mind about going with Karl. She brushed off all his not-so-subtle attempts to convince her otherwise and always managed to change the subject before he could push any further. Yet to Erich's frustration, the topic of the ball was always on her lips in other ways.

Johanna was intensely preoccupied with the question of what she would wear. Most of the other girls had already been sent something to from home, but Erich knew as well as she that Johanna's father would do no such thing.

Every time they met, she had a bitter new story about how so-and-so's wealthy mother had sent this white satin dress or those gold earrings.

Johanna despaired that she would end up going in an old potato sack, but Erich knew that would never happen. She would find something suitable even if she had to blackmail her classmates to get it. After all, she had no qualms about stealing. Though the thrill had long since worn off for Erich, Johanna still dragged him and Karl along to raid the kitchens every other week. The two of them usually only took a few treats, but Johanna always made off with whole sacks of food.

"How could you possibly eat all that?" Erich asked once on their way back.

Johanna shrugged. "I get hungry."

Erich eyed her skeptically, but she just poked him on the chest and said, "Forget that. You still haven't told me who you're bringing to the ball."

He blushed. "I... haven't asked anyone yet."

"Erich!"

Hoping to elicit some pity, he donned a plaintive frown, but Johanna ignored it. She grabbed him and pulled him in. "It's not hard. There's *way* more girls than boys. But if you ever need help practicing let me know."

Erich wriggled out of her grip. "It's not like that!"

"'Oh, Erich'," Johanna crooned, fanning herself. "'It's me, Anneliese.'"

When he didn't laugh, she punched him lightly on the arm, slung her bulging sack over her shoulder and waved goodbye. "You know where to find me."

Erich tried many times to bring himself to ask someone else, but he could never quite do it. He didn't know any of the other girls and saw no real reason why he should. He had been friends with Johanna for what seemed like forever. That was the only thing that really made sense. By the night of the dance, Erich had decided that he would go alone, if only to prove to Johanna that she was making a mistake.

But as he squeezed into his formalwear and paced back and forth between the empty bunks in the *Schützenadler* dorm, Erich began to lose his nerve. Perhaps he was the one who was making a mistake. He didn't know a single other boy who would be attending on his own and he hadn't considered how that would look to everyone else. He could already hear all the horrible things Fritz was going to say about him.

When at last the time came, everyone gathered in Rathe Hall. As the boys and girls filed in awkwardly from opposite sides, couples spotted each other from across the room and exchanged eager waves.

"All right, children, go on," Doktor Kammer squeaked.

On his signal, three of the boys bolted in the direction of their dates as though the starting pistol had just been fired on the *Siegfeld*. They made it halfway across the room before a sudden self-consciousness struck all of them at once. They slammed to a stop and glanced at each other sheepishly.

Erich rammed his hands into his trouser pockets and tried his best to act aloof while he watched everyone else pair up. After a moment he realized that he was wobbling back and forth and forced himself to stand still. Erich kicked himself for his stupid pride. How hard would it have been just to ask someone?

Johanna had not arrived yet and Karl looked almost as nervous as Erich did. Otto and Uwe, sticking close to each other, had spotted their dates and were very slowly making their way over. Neither of them seemed particularly excited.

Erich saw her before anyone else. Far away past the closed double doors, Johanna walked through a haze. She strolled up to entrance, late and unashamed. Just as Erich had predicted, she had somehow procured a dress, a flowing violet gown that was sure to clash aggressively against the demure colors that filled the room. A pearl and silver choker hugged her neck. Beyond anything in that moment, he wished he could see her the way the other boys did. Karl was lucky in more ways than one.

Johanna pushed the doors open with her shoulder. She probably wanted everyone to hear the loud creak it made. The moment he saw her, a grin exploded across Karl's face and he skipped towards the door. Johanna held out her hand, so low Erich half expected him to kneel down and kiss it. But instead he just intertwined his fingers with hers and they held their hands together for a long moment.

Suddenly, Johanna broke into a clear, bright laugh. Karl joined in, then a few others. The sound of it shattered the tension in the room and dozens of new couples embraced each other. That only made things worse for Erich. He stood by, still tottering on the balls of his feet, and felt more alone than ever.

When he didn't think he could stand there any longer, Erich ventured a few steps towards to Karl and Johanna, but he was afraid to get too close. As soon as Johanna saw him, she waved him over, scowling at his lack of a partner.

"You're hopeless," she said.

Erich shrugged and nobody knew what to say. How had he ever imagined that this could go well? "I'll just leave," he stammered.

"Alright," Karl said. He put his hand on Johanna's back and tried to turn her towards the door, but she twisted around and crooked her finger at Erich.

"Not a chance. You're coming with us."

# CHAPTER TWENTY-FOUR

The chapel was barely recognizable. All three tables had been cleared away and a massive, glimmering fir filled the center of the room. A swastika-emblazoned spearhead jabbed up from the top of the tree, nearly piercing the ceiling. The usual lights were switched off and four massive braziers hung in their place. Hot coals glowed through the slats, casting crisscrossing shadows across the floor. From the balcony, a string quartet played a slow melody.

The moment they stepped through the doors, Johanna grabbed Karl's wrist and pulled him out into the middle of the floor, leaving Erich by himself. He hoped no one was watching as he sidled over to the empty tables in the corner. He didn't mean to stare, but it felt like there was nowhere else his eyes could go but the spot where Johanna's hands met Karl's thick waist.

The only person who looked more uncomfortable than Erich was Uwe, who sat off on the opposite side with a freckled girl named Gertrude. He stared queasily out at the open floor as though no one had told him there might be dancing involved. Gertrude was trying to make conversation, but she didn't look like she was having much luck.

Otto was faring only a little better than Uwe. He'd always struck Erich as the most confident and poised boy in the school, but dancing with Freida he couldn't seem to figure out where to put down his feet. They veered a clumsy path through the other couples.

As the musicians reached the close of their piece, Freida tripped on the hem of her dress. She tumbled back into Fritz, who like a domino crashed into his partner, Sabine. The three of them lay stunned in a jumbled mess on the floor until Sabine shoved Freida off of her and dragged herself up.

Sabine—every bit a match for Fritz's personality— turned and slammed her heel down on Freida's hand, mouthing some cruel twist of words. Enraged, Otto tossed her back with his patronage, then yanked Freida up and pulled her behind him. Snarling, Fritz leapt out in front of Sabine. They circled each other like cats.

Just as the two raised their arms up, Doktor Kammer threw himself between them. He settled Otto down and then led him and Freida off the floor. After a few moments, the musicians began to play again and the rest of the children did their best to carry on as though nothing had happened. Sabine fired one last glare at Freida then pointedly wrapped her arms around Fritz.

"All alone?" came a voice from Erich's side.

He looked over to see that Gertrude had snuck up and sat right next to him.

"Just for today," Erich answered. "Aren't you supposed to be with Uwe?"

"No," Gertude said. "I think it's better this way."

Erich wasn't sure what she meant, but he didn't want to looked stupid so he just nodded knowingly.

"What happened to you?" Gertrude asked. "Too shy to ask anyone?"

"I'm not shy!" Erich snapped. "Everyone keeps saying that."

"What was it then?"

Erich looked away. "Nothing. It's like you said. It's better this way."

"Ohhh, now I get it," Gertrude said. "You wanted to bring Johanna."

Erich shook his head vigorously. "No way. We've known each other for years. She's... she's like my sister or something."

"Then why are you staring at her?" Gertrude cackled.

Erich immediately dropped his eyes to the table, mumbling a rebuttal.

After a long while where neither of them said anything, Gertrude broke spontaneously into another laugh.

"Am I just that funny?" Erich groaned.

"You're just that young."

"Young?" he protested. "How old are you then?"

"Rude!" interrupted a shout. "Don't you know you're not supposed to ask a girl her age?"

Erich snapped his eyes up. It was Fritz. He plopped down into a seat and Sabine slowly settled in at his side. Fritz lifted up his hand and Erich flinched, but it was only a pat on the shoulder.

"How's life in the *Schützenadler*?" Fritz asked. He could make the most mundane question sound like a threat.

"It's—"

Erich stopped. He couldn't find his voice. How *was* life in the *Schützenadler*? He wasn't sure he even knew. Erich couldn't think. He flashed back to all the beatings and blows. Erich tried to speak again, but all that came out was a cough.

Erich had never frozen up like this when he was in the *Wehrbären*. This side of the castle really was turning him into a weakling. Certainly his patronage had never sputtered out in the other corps. Maybe he deserved whatever cruelty Fritz had in store for him.

"Come on. Ignore him," Gertrude whispered in Erich's ear. "Let me have this dance."

She dragged him up from his seat and out onto the floor, waving an insincere goodbye to Sabine.

"I don't know how to dance," Erich whispered.

"It's easy. I'll teach y—" Gertrude broke off. She stared at something over his shoulder. "*Scheiße!*" she hissed.

Erich twisted around to look. In the shadow of the tree, Frau Murr loomed over Johanna and Karl.

"Fräulein Engel!" She grabbed Johanna's wrist, pulled her in close, then rubbed a finger down her cheek and inspected it from arm's length. "What is this filth?"

"It's nothing," Johanna said. She tried to pull away, but Frau Murr's grip wouldn't yield.

Karl took a step back, bewildered. Erich didn't understand what was wrong either. He looked to Gertrude for answers.

"She's wearing makeup," Gertrude whispered.

Frau Murr spoke loud enough for the whole room to hear. "I thought this was a school for Germans, but I must have been mistaken. I expected to see a good Aryan girl standing before me. Instead there's a painted oriental whore. A real woman doesn't need to hide behi—" Frau Murr interrupted herself with a shriek. "That necklace!" She twisted Johanna's wrist. "It looks so familiar. Where did you get it?"

"My father sent it," Johanna wheezed. Her face was scrunched up in pain, but she didn't cry out.

Frau Murr pushed her face in so close that her nose tickled Johanna's throat. Then she reared back and snarled, "Don't lie to me, you filthy thief. That's mine!" She tore the necklace away, not even caring that she broke the clasp. "That's it. I've put up with your degenerate ways for far too long. You're finished."

Dragging Johanna behind her like a sack of flour, Frau Murr beat a path through the crowd of gaping couples. Johanna flailed her legs and kicked off her shoes, but all she managed to do was tear her gown. Frau Murr hardly seemed to notice her struggling. Without stopping she rammed through the side door and out of the chapel. As it swung shut behind her, a quiet settled in. Even the musicians had stopped playing to watch.

The whole time, Karl had hardly moved. Even after Erich ran up to his side, he just stood there, stunned.

"We have to help her," Erich said.

"There's no point," Karl moaned. "If you really think about it, it's a miracle she hasn't been kicked out already."

"Fine," Erich scowled. "Do nothing then."

He hurried out of the chapel before Karl could say anything back, then ducked into the secret corridors. Erich ran as fast as the narrow passage would allow until he spotted Frau Murr through the walls.

She plowed down the hallway's long carpet, Johanna in tow. Erich couldn't figure out where they were headed. As they rounded the corner, Johanna dug her bare feet into the wall and twisted away. Frau Murr snatched at her, but she was too fast and ducked under her arm. As Johanna dashed off at full speed, Erich tore through the corridors to meet her.

But Frau Murr was faster. She bounded on stilt-like legs. Erich knew she would reach Johanna if he didn't act. Still he hesitated. He could block her path or simply trip her with his patronage, but that felt like crossing a line. He'd never thought of himself as a troublemaker, and yet he couldn't count the number of rules he'd broken since coming to Rouhhenberg. The reason for all that was obvious. It was right in front of him, arms flailing as it careened down the hall. When had he ever misbehaved without Johanna to egg him on?

Yet Erich knew what his decision would be before he even made it. He had been on this path with her for a long while and, for once, standing by to watch was not an option. He closed his eyes so he didn't have to look and thrust out, light, but firm. Frau Murr's spindly legs caught against his buffer of patronage and with a squawk she toppled over.

Johanna burst around another corner and Erich, hissing her name, slid open the passage entrance ahead of her. She charged blindly through the opening, knocking Erich off his feet. Frau Murr hurtled around the bend, shouting threats and spitting fury. Erich reached out his hand and yanked the hidden door shut with his patronage.

Johanna did not wait to see if Frau Murr had noticed. She dragged Erich to his feet and pulled him with her as she dashed off. They sped through tunnels and gaps in walls, from barracks to keep and back again, too fast and frenzied to look where they were going. Erich didn't really think Frau Murr had followed them, but it felt good to run. If they ran far enough away perhaps they might somehow wind up back in the chapel before any of this had happened.

When at last his legs felt ready to melt, Erich stumbled and slid down against the stone. Johanna collapsed at his side. Even on the other side of the walls, it was totally dark.

As he waited for his heart to slow, Erich squinted and peered out, looking for anything he could recognize beyond the passage. A pale shape was slumped against the other side of the wall. When Erich leaned in closer, it twitched and startled him. In the vague form of a person, the shape was so thin and gaunt that it made Frau Murr look plump. As Erich eyes adjusted to the dark, he could see more and more figures, surrounding them on either side, separated only by a thin layer of stone. They barely moved but to breathe.

Only then did Erich realize where they were. He had never set foot in this place and yet he had seen it a hundred times before. These were the three left turns that Erich dreaded. He was farther down them than he'd ever gone before. If he rounded one more corner, he would be there in the lair of the bone boy. It was tempting. Perhaps if he took a few more steps, he could just turn his head up, look the filthy, screaming child in the eye, and awaken to realize that everything that happened with Johanna had been a dream.

"Have you ever been here before?" Johanna whispered.

"I'm sure I have," Erich lied. "Let's just go back the way we came."

He expected her to protest and push to explore deeper, but instead she just nodded and they set off, as quiet as they could. They walked slowly, huddled close to each other. Erich kept his eyes turned down so that he didn't have to look at the ghosts that surrounded them. As they turned the last corner, Johanna grabbed his arm and yanked him aside, as though out of some danger, but when he turned to look back there was nothing.

"Sorry," she said.

"That's okay."

Soon they passed the deep corkscrew staircase of the bathhouse and Erich was able to lead them back up to a safer, more familiar part of the castle.

"I think we're in Weiss," he said. Erich pointed. "Down there is the guest bedrooms."

Johanna nodded. "Yeah. I know that part."

"Did you really steal the necklace?" Erich asked.

"Right out of her dresser," Johanna replied. "The makeup too. She owns a lot for someone who hates the stuff."

Erich glared at her. "Why did you do it?"

"It doesn't matter anymore." Johanna waited a while and then said, "I'm not going home to Father. I'd rather die."

"I know," Erich said.

She lowered herself down to sit cross-legged on the rough stone, but Erich refused to join her. He paced back and forth in the tight corridor. There had to be something he could do.

"I'm going to run," Johanna said. "Far and fast. I just need to get a few things ready."

"That's pointless. We don't even really know where we

are. There are no maps. You'd starve or get eaten by a bear or something."

Johanna shrugged.

"At least give me tonight to try to fix this," Erich said. "All we have to do is convince Frau Murr that it wasn't her necklace. Maybe yours just looked the same."

"You'd have better luck persuading the bears," Johanna said.

"Just stay here and don't let anyone see you. I think I know who can help."

***

Erich couldn't find Otto or Uwe back in the chapel. Their dates were still there, sitting together in the corner with poor Karl. He checked and checked again, then decided to try back in the dormitory. The *Schützenadler* lounge, which usually bustled with activity even late at night, was completely empty. All the lights had been switched off, and he had to pick his way through in the dark.

Erich stopped at the closed door of the room Otto and Uwe shared with Felix and tried to make out whether or not they were there. It was dark inside, but he could hear rustling noises. He knocked on the door and the sounds suddenly stopped.

"It's Erich," he said loudly. "Just Erich."

There was no response. He was about walk in anyway when the light flickered on and Otto opened the door by a crack.

"Are you alright?" Erich asked.

"We got sick," Otto said. "Must have been something in the shrimp. Come back tomorrow."

"No, no, let him in," Uwe called from inside.

Otto frowned and opened the door the rest of the way.

He really did look sick. His face was red and his uniform was half open, hanging wrinkled and askew from his shoulders. He was breathing heavily as if just coming to the door had been difficult.

"How's Johanna?" Uwe asked.

"She's fine for now. I got her away, but she'll get kicked out for sure once they find her," Erich said. "I know you're sick and all. I wouldn't ask unless—"

"We know," Uwe interrupted, sitting up in his bed. "What's your plan?"

"You both have that class with Hugo, right? Suggestion?"

"We do," Otto said suspiciously. He didn't look so flushed anymore.

"Could you... do you think you could... somehow..."

"Make Frau Murr forget?" Uwe finished for him.

Erich nodded.

"Absolutely not," Otto said. "In class, we do suggestion on rats, Erich. It's only temporary and it doesn't work on people."

"That's not true," Uwe said. His eyes flashed eagerly as he threw off the covers and jumped out of bed. He didn't seem to notice that he wasn't wearing any clothes. "I mean, he's right about the temporary part, but the rest... we've never tried it with a person. There's no reason it couldn't work."

"Temporary could be okay," Erich said. He was beginning to get excited too. "Even if she remembers after a while, she'll look like she's crazy. We just have to make her doubt herself eno—"

"No. Don't you two even start," Otto snapped. He glared at Uwe. "We're sick. *Remember?*"

"Come on," Uwe said. He grabbed Otto and shook him. "Don't you think it'll be just a little fun?"

There was a pause, then Otto breathed in deep and sighed. "Fine. Just remember that I told you both this is a terrible idea." He buttoned his uniform without looking, his eyes locked on Erich.

"We'll need her to be asleep," Uwe said. "That gives a few hours before it's safe to leave."

"Good thing," Otto said. "If we're doing this, Erich has a lot to learn."

# CHAPTER TWENTY-FIVE

Uwe let out a quiet whistle as the three of them crept into Frau Murr's room. Erich had expected that such a spartan woman's room would be as bare as Hugo's. Instead, every available surface was cluttered with Nazi bric-a-brac. There was a portrait of the *Führer* over her bed, a giant photograph of him at the Eiffel Tower on one wall, and another from the 1936 Party Congress on the opposite side.

A dozen or so other picture frames scattered the top of her dresser and nightstand. Newspapers, magazines, and postcards covered the remaining space. By one wall was a lopsided stack of what looked like every issue ever published of *NS-Frauen-Warte*. There was only one chair in the room and even it was taken up by a second full sized portrait that Frau Murr hadn't yet carved out a place for.

Erich moved carefully, afraid that if he knocked over a single item, it would trigger a chain reaction throughout the whole room. Though it was chilly inside, Frau Murr slept uncovered on the top of her bed. She lay on her back in a black nightgown, hands perfectly poised at her waist like a corpse in a viewing. Her face seemed different in the dark, more angular, but what took Erich aback was her hands. They were burned almost down to the bone. Her thin skin was leathered and red except for the few patches that swelled up into pale, smooth lumps. He could see why she always wore gloves.

The three intruders joined hands and approached. Uwe took the lead. He planted his free hand on the bed and leaned over so he could look straight into Frau Murr's closed eyes. As soon as Uwe made contact, a low murmur hummed out from her mind and ran down the chain of locked hands. According to the brief lessons they had given Erich, a waking person's thoughts are so vibrant and chaotic that making any sense of them is impossible. But asleep, there was little enough to manage.

When he was ready, Uwe signaled with a nod.

"Wake up," Otto barked.

Frau Murr's eyelids twitched and a tiny pulse of thought ran through her. All three of them at once grabbed for it and forced it down. The wayward cognition squirmed under their grip, viscous and shifting, always desperate to dart away and explode into sentience. It was like chasing an eggshell through runny yolk.

"What is your name?" Uwe asked, pronouncing every word with difficulty.

"Adolpha Murr", she said in a monotone. Something leaked out from her mind, a globule that bubbled up and slipped through Erich's grasp. She spoke again, shriller, "I was born in—"

"Quiet," Otto barked.

Erich caught hold of the leak, some childhood memory perhaps, and held it steady, but it was too late to do anything more than contain it. Like jugglers, they now had two balls in play.

"In a moment you will open your eyes, but you won't be able to see us," Uwe said.

"I can't see you," Frau Murr responded. Her eyelids pulled back, but her gaze stayed fixed on the ceiling.

"Hurry," Otto said.

"Your necklace," Uwe whispered. "The silver choker. You lost it."

"Yes, I lost it two days ago," she said.

"Johanna Engel, do you know who she is?"

"I do," Frau Murr said. Another thought snaked out. "She's a troublemaker. She sto—"

Otto wrestled it down.

"No," Uwe said. "Her father sent a necklace just like yours and you mixed them up. It was a mistake. You're very sorry."

"You're right. It wasn't her. I am sorry. It must have been someone else. Do you know who took it?"

"You lost it. Nobody stole anything," Uwe repeated.

Another globule leaked out. "No, no, that's not true. Someone stole it. Who was it?"

"It's not working," Otto hissed.

There was a foul taste on Erich's tongue like rotten blood. He swallowed and a nauseating trickle ran down his throat. *Not again,* he swore, *not now,* but it was too late. His patronage was already gone. As before, there had been no warning. It was there right up until the point when it was not. Only an empty, useless hole remained inside of him. But what happened next Erich had not experienced before. The void left by his patronage began to fill. Memories, none of them Erich's, rushed in like water to a ballast.

Bright lights and lush red fabric. A stage. Adolpha stands behind the lip of the curtain as it draws back. Across from her an open doorframe sits perpendicular to the audience. There's a man on the other side. His back is scrunched against a diagonal mirror that hides him from the crowd. To them, it's just an empty door that goes nowhere. Adolpha smiles at the man, the same as she does every night, but he doesn't smile back. His name is Ludwig.

Someone brushes past her to take the stage. Hugo. The theater falls to a hush.

"We have seen much tonight, my friends," he says. It is in English, but Erich has no trouble understanding. "Together, we have deciphered the whispers of the sphinx. We have seen death defied and hellfire quelled. We have tasted words of darkness on our tongues and felt the shiver of the unknown up our spines. But that's not what drew you here tonight. You've seen that all before. Those are old wonders from a dying age. What you came for tonight is something new. Something more than the same old tricks."

Hugo takes a few steps back and raises his finger.

"Consider this: for thousands of years the world has been shrinking. The horse. The automobile. The aeroplane. With every step the world gets a little smaller. We all come a little closer to each other. But it's not enough. Tonight, my friends, we are going to finish the job that civilization started."

Hugo throws his hands into the air and shouts, "Herr Jensson, it is time. Light the ignition!"

Adolpha has heard this same speech a hundred times before, but she still listens as though it were her first. She glances behind her as Herr Jensson slams down the massive circuit breaker. Lightning arcs above the stage. The tesla lamps have nothing to do with the trick, but the sight is still enrapturing. Bathed in their flickering, Hugo glides to the opposite side of the stage. It's a mirror image of hers: the same door, the same hidden compartment.

Adolpha steps out past the edge of the curtain, feigning nervousness and tugging on one of her long braids. She gives a shy wave to Ludwig inside the door. The audience chuckles. They think she's waving at Hugo on the other side of the stage, but she can't even see him. Ludwig doesn't wave back, but she knows Hugo does. She has to imagine the way he smiles, the way he plays up his confidence and charm.

A moment later, the man inside the door reaches out his hand. She knows Hugo has done the same. Their

timing is rehearsed to perfection. To the audience, Hugo's arm reaches seamlessly through the door on one side of the stage and out its twin far away on the other. There's a smattering of gasps, but they're not yet convinced. Adolpha turns to the crowd. It's essential that they see her face. There are a few shouts of encouragement.

Tittering, she steps forward and shakes Ludwig's hand as if it were Hugo's. Suddenly, he shifts his grip. He grabs her around the wrist. He yanks. The audience screams. He pulls her into the door and shoves her through the curtain behind the stage. On the other side, she knows Hugo has yanked her double through. They twirl around and round while Adolpha sprints the length of the stage.

It takes exactly three seconds to reach the other side. She listens for her cue in the drums, then pushes through the curtain. Her double slides back in her place. Hugo's arms are around her, but he doesn't stop spinning. Her braids fly out like swings on a carousel. She throws her arms back and he dips her. Cheers and claps. When at last he pulls her up, the audience see her face again. They are suitably amazed.

As the show ends and the crowd trickles out, Adolpha slips into the dressing room to fetch something. It's Hugo's birthday and she has a gift for him, a book. She hopes he'll read it, but knows that he probably won't. She holds it behind her back and peeks through the curtain to see if he's alone.

Hugo stands on the stage, looking out at the empty room. Just as Adolpha is about to approach, she notices that there's still one person who hasn't left her seat. At the end of the front row sits a woman. Her skin is black and she wears a tan fur coat with three long pearl necklaces. Erich recognizes her. Isabel, the woman from Hugo's photograph.

"Quite a show," she says without standing. She speaks High German and Adolpha is as shocked as Erich to hear that she has no American accent. "It's almost like the real thing."

Hugo laughs. "What do you know about the real thing?"

"Everything," Isabel says.

"You don't say," Hugo smirks. "And where did you learn this everything? In Africa?"

"Austria," she answers flatly. She toys one of her pearls.

"Ah. I meant no offense. You should come and meet our propmaster, Åke Jensson, one day. You and he are much alike." Hugo jumps down from the stage and holds out his arm. "I know a splendid place where one can get a coffee in the Turkish style. It's not far from here. Will you join me? I'd very much like to hear about this real thing of yours."

Isabel looks up at him, still not leaving her seat. "That's very forward."

"It's very good coffee," Hugo says, not dropping his arm.

After a long pause she stands up and takes it with a shrug.

"Now tell me," Hugo says. "Whereabouts in Austria was all this?"

Erich snapped his eyes open as the memory ebbed. Only a moment had passed. Otto and Uwe were staring at him in surprise and anger. He tried to pull his hand away to break the connection, but Otto had it gripped too tightly and another wave of memories crashed into him.

Adolpha sits in a restaurant in the ground floor of her hotel. She eats alone with the newspaper. She closes her eyes for a moment. When she opens them Hugo is standing above her. She no longer looks at him the way she once did.

"Nadja tells me you're headed home tomorrow," Hugo says. "Is that true?"

Adolpha nods. "I've been away a long time."

"You didn't tell me."

She shrugs. "I didn't know if you cared."

Hugo sets a book down on the table. It's the book she'd once given him, belatedly, for his birthday. After all this time, she's surprised he's kept it.

"Did you read it?" she asks.

"I did. I finally, finally did," Hugo says. "This Hitler of yours is a madman for sure." She scowls at him and he breaks out into a laugh. "Don't be upset, dear. I mean it as a compliment. No sane man has ever changed the world."

She gives a reluctant nod.

"I have something for you in return," he says. "Just in time for your trip, I suppose. I'm sorry it's so late. Go ahead, it's inside."

She slides the book over to her side of the table. The pages are slightly ajar where something has been stuffed in between. Adolpha pulls the cover back and she jolts up in her chair. There's a small booklet inside. *Deutsches Reich Reisepass,* it reads under the eagle and swastika. It's a passport.

"It has your name on it," Hugo says. "Your real name. You can go back and be just… you."

She leafs through to the second page and runs her finger over the photograph. It's more than just her name. It's her hair, her face. She wipes a tear from her cheek before it can smudge. "I don't know how to thank you."

"I'm afraid that I do," Hugo says. "A better man would have done this for you out of kindness, but the truth is I need a favor."

"It's done," she says immediately. "Whatever it is."

"Do you remember Isabel Colmán?"

"I remember her." Adolpha looks down.

"She… she has something I need," Hugo says. "She won't give it to me. I don't want to hurt her. I wish were there were some other way. But this is too important. It's what I've been searching for, what I've always been searching for. She has it and she is squandering it."

"What is it?" Adolpha asks.

"It's…" Hugo pauses for a moment. "It's a book. A manifesto. Some call it a gospel. Not unlike your Hitler's I suppose."

"And you want me to steal it?" she says.

"You must. Isabel and I have tickets to the opera tonight. Her room at the Wilshire will be empty. It's number 527." He hands her a key wrapped in a sheet of paper. "Everything you need to know is written there. Once you have the book, we'll meet at the harbor and board a ship. There'll be no record of either of us in its logs."

"Where are we going?" she asks.

"My darling, you've said it already. We're going home. We're going back to Germany."

Erich ripped his hand out from Otto's and staggered away. The memories drained and his patronage flooded back in. Otto and Uwe stared at him, surprise still fresh on their faces. He was cut off from Frau Murr's thoughts, but it was not hard to imagine what was happening inside her head. Erich had failed them. He'd failed Johanna.

"Thief," Frau Murr shrieked blindly. "That's my necklace! Who are you? Who took it?"

"It's over," Otto shouted. "We have to go. Now."

He grabbed the Uwe by the hand and rushed out the door. Erich raced to follow them. Even in the hall, they could hear Frau Murr's shouts.

"That's mine," she raged. "I trusted you!"

It was hard to say who in particular she was shouting at and she didn't chase after them. Still, they kept running until they were all the way back to the dormitory.

"I'm sorry. I don't know what happened to me," Erich said between breaths. "I just… lost everything for a second."

"It's okay. Don't worry about it," Uwe said. Otto's expression made it clear that he disagreed.

"Do you think it worked?" Erich asked.

They answered simultaneously, "no" and "maybe."

"Clearly we didn't convince her that she lost it. She's probably still screaming about the thief," Uwe said. "But I didn't hear Johanna's name in all that. My guess is that she doesn't really know who to blame anymore."

"None of that matters," Otto said. "She saw us."

"No," Uwe said. "I think that part worked. She couldn't see us. I really believe everything is going to work out."

"Well I really believe we're all going to be sent home," Otto groaned. "But we might as well get some sleep before that."

"Agreed," Uwe said. He threw one arm over Otto and swept him around in an exaggerated turn towards the door.

"Thank you," Erich called after them, but they were already gone. "For everything."

After a little searching, he found Johanna lying curled up against the wall, not far from where he had left her in the corridors. Strips of moonlight threw long shadows across her face and her dress was smeared with ancient dust. Erich shook her awake.

"You're back," Johanna whispered, bleary-eyed.

"It's all over," Erich said. "You can go back to your own bed now."

She sat up and tilted her head sideway. "What?"

He had to explain what they'd done three times before she took him seriously. Though he felt guilty for omitting the possibility that their plan might have failed, he knew it was the right thing to do. It would be better for her to be sent home than to run away.

He'd imagined that she would protest, but Johanna just got up and brushed herself off. Her shoulders hung low and she said nothing as he walked her back to the BDM quarters. The only sound was the padding of her bare feet. At the exit, she hugged him and they parted ways. Erich slid the hidden door into place behind her and dragged himself back to his room.

As he tore off his dress shirt and climbed into bed, he realized that in all the panic and chaos, he had forgotten about the *Führer's* speech the next day. He envied the other boys, all deep in their dreams of tomorrow. Even those who were stuck awake in anticipation had it better than him. All he could feel was worry.

Erich tried to remember the excitement he'd once felt, but the usual fantasies wouldn't come. He imagined the *Führer* singling him out, calling him up, and pinning a medal on his chest, but it all seemed hollow. What would any of that mean without Johanna's scowl when he showed it to her? Worse still, how could any of that ever come to pass if he lost his patronage? Why then would the *Führer* ever bother to know his name?

He would be just one of a million German boys, all the same.

# CHAPTER TWENTY-SIX

By the time Erich woke, it was almost noon. There were no classes scheduled, but for once, he wished there were. As it was, there was nothing to do until the *Führer's* speech but ruminate on the night before. It felt strange to walk out into the common room to idle greetings from the other boys. He had half expected to be treated like a fugitive.

Erich took his time heading over to the small cafeteria in Weiss Hall. He sat down at the table and wolfed down a whole salami in the time it took for Mathilde to come over with a coffee. He slurped at it greedily while he did his best to mine for gossip. But if she had any information about what had happened, she wasn't forthcoming with it.

"Do you at least know where Johanna is?" Erich pleaded with her. "She works in the kitchens, right?"

"No," Mathilde answered. "That's not where she works."

"Where then?"

"Look, if I see her, I'll tell her you're looking for her," she said, then darted off to another table before Erich could protest.

All the other girls he saw were just as reticent.

247

Eventually Erich decided he would just have to wait for the social hour in the afternoon. Johanna would show up or she would not; either way he would have his answer. Soon, Otto and Uwe joined him on the other side of the table and the three of them whiled away the hours together, nervously watching the clock and wondering if at any moment Frau Murr and *Rottenführer* Wolff would burst in to drag them away.

When it finally came time to head over, they were shocked to find Johanna already waiting for them in Rathe Hall. She sat on the floor in their usual spot, her face illuminated by a grin.

"No trouble?" Erich said. He tried his hardest to sound as if he'd never doubted the plan at all.

"You won't believe it," Johanna said. "When I woke up she was standing over my bed. I thought she was trying to stab me in my sleep, but no. The stuck-up gremlin actually apologized!"

Struggling not to laugh, Johanna leaned back and let out a high pitched coo, "'I don't know what came over me. My sister gave that necklace to me, and oh, it's just precious to me.' Then she went into this whole rant about how someone she trusted took it and how she's gonna find them and skin them alive. I do hope she blames Sabine in the end because we all know she has it coming."

Uwe prodded Otto in the rib. "I told you."

Erich gave Johanna a long look. "You should really return it. The necklace, I mean."

"Fine, fine, I will," she said. "I'll leave it in her room tonight while she's slobbering in the front row at the speech."

She beckoned to someone over Erich's shoulder. He glanced back to see Karl wobbling in the doorway. Uwe waved too and Karl reluctantly joined them on the floor.

"I'm sorry. I should have—" he began, but Johanna cut him off with a hug.

"Are you excited for tonight?" she said.

"Beyond excited," Karl exhaled, relief apparent on his face.

As the rest of them gushed about the upcoming speech, Erich stayed quiet. He still couldn't manage to summon back his enthusiasm. Erich looked Karl in the eye and tried to decide how he was supposed to feel about him. Maybe that was the problem. He'd spent all this time angry with Karl for asking Johanna to the ball because that was how one was supposed to feel. Erich hadn't really thought at all about what he actually felt. And when he did, he realized that right now he felt very little at all.

***

At dinner, the high platforms had been taken away and the four tables were all at one level. *Nassfüchsen, Wehrbären, Schützenader*, teachers, and staff all sat together, packed into one end of the chapel. On the other side eight more long tables had appeared, four for the BDM girls and another four that were crowded with *SS* men, most of whom Erich had never seen before. Out of the entire castle, the only person who seemed to be missing was Herr Jensson.

If the boys had been shoved into such close proximity any other day, fights would have broken out, but on this evening everyone's thoughts lay squarely with the *Führer*. Frau Murr muttered to herself and paced back and forth by the door. Erich had expected that she would be more excited than anyone about the speech, but instead she looked anxious. Her hand was jammed into her jacket pocket and she fiddled with something inside. Erich wondered if the suggestion had worn off yet. If he approached her, would she even see him?

"Do you really think the *Führer* is going to eat with us?" Karl whispered.

"Why else would they move the tables?" Erich said.

Uwe nodded enthusiastically, but after an hour of waiting their esteemed guest still had not arrived. Impatient and hungry, the boys whispered speculations and fidgeted in their seats.

"I heard he never keeps his schedule," Uwe said. "It throws off the assassins."

Karl nodded vigorously, but Otto didn't look convinced. "There aren't any assassins here. I don't think he's coming."

"You never know," Karl grumbled.

Uwe began to admonish Otto for his pessimism, but trailed off as the double doors of the chapel creaked open. Every head in the room whipped around. A few boys leapt to their feet and threw out their arms in salute, but it was only *Oberführer* Ehrenzweig.

"The *Führer* has been delayed," he said loudly. The disappointment took a moment to settle in. "Dinner will be served on our regular schedule. At ten thirty we will meet on the *Siegfeld* for the address."

He sat down with Herr Larat on the far end of their table. After a moment passed with no movement from anyone, he waved angrily at Frau Murr, who was still standing by the door and staring off into the distance in a stupor. She noticed him and shook herself, then scurried off to fetch the servers.

When the food finally arrived, Erich picked at his plate with disinterest, keeping one eye fixed on Frau Murr. Everyone else—Otto and Uwe among them—wolfed down their meal as though that might somehow make the wait shorter. The moment Hugo stood up to dismiss the room, everyone stampeded out of the chapel. But as soon as the *Schützenadler* group made it back to the lounge, they realized that there was still more than an hour left to wait.

The impatience was infectious and Erich found himself pacing to and fro with Karl. A frustratingly slow symphony droned out from the radio. He looked around for Otto and Uwe, but he didn't see them anywhere.

In the chattering that surrounded him, Erich could hear the same questions they had all asked and answered a hundred times before. *What will he say? How long will he be here? How much does he know about us?* And then, only in whispers, *why after all this time has there been no talk of sending us out to fight.*

After an hour that felt like four, the boys made a collective and unspoken decision that it was time. In one massive group, they poured out towards the field. But on the way through Bittrich Hall, Johanna intercepted them.

"Erich," she hissed. "You've got to come see this."

"But… the speech," he protested.

"It's more important than that."

"What could be more important than—"

Johanna grabbed Erich by the arm and yanked him away from the crowd. Karl looked back plaintively, visibly torn between his desire not to be left out again and the inexorable pull of the *Führer's* presence. The latter won out and he sprinted off to catch up with the throng of boys receding down the hall.

"I'll meet you there," Erich called after him.

Johanna tugged on Erich's arm again. They ran down the winding stairs and out onto the first floor. She dragged him into an empty classroom. Otto and Uwe were waiting, their arms crossed.

"It's bad, it's bad, it's very bad," Uwe muttered. He was staring at his feet and barely even seemed to notice Erich come in.

"What are you still doing here?" Erich said. "We'll be late."

"It's best if I just show you," Otto said. "You won't believe me otherwise."

Johanna cringed. "I'll be out here."

"Come on," Otto said.

He stepped over to the office door in the back of the classroom. With a deep breath, he opened it and led Erich inside.

Like so much in Rouhhenberg, the cramped room had been furnished but looked like it had never been used. It was dark, lit only by the dull glow of moonlight coming in from between the slats of a large window. The desk had been pushed aside and sitting in the middle of the room was Frau Murr. Her wrists and ankles were tied to the legs of a chair and a rag had been wrapped around her mouth. Her eyes were lit up with fury but her stare blazed right past Erich. She didn't even know he was there.

"What have you done?" Erich shouted once he'd recovered from the shock.

"The better question would be what have *we* done," Otto said. "And the answer... well, just ask her."

He loosened the gag around Frau Murr's mouth and she spat it out. Even as she gasped for air she began to scream. "Thief! Where is he? That liar, that cheater, that pilfering, verminous little man. I'll kill him! Where is he?" Her eyes frantically searched the room. "You, whoever you are, you'll help me right? Where is he? I need to find him."

Erich stared at her in puzzlement. She looked more desperate than angry now. "Find who?"

"The thief. That filthy Austrian who stole my necklace," Frau Murr wheezed.

"And who was that?" Otto pressed.

"I've told you people a hundred times already. Why won't you believe me?"

"It's not easy to believe. Tell us again," Otto said.

"It's Adolf Hitler," she moaned. "Adolf Hitler stole my necklace."

Erich broke into a laugh, but it immediately sputtered out as he realized that this whole situation was his fault. "She's not... she can't be serious."

"Oh, she's very serious," Otto said. "And very, very confused."

"Please, tell me where he is," Frau Murr begged. She rocked back and forth furiously. "I need to find him! Don't you know what it's like to be stolen from? That foul

cretin has it and I've got to get it back. Let me go! Wher—
"

Otto flicked his wrist in Frau Murr's direction and the gag crammed back into her mouth. Erich was still so stunned that Otto had to practically carry him out of the office.

"How?" was all he could say.

"We messed up," Otto said.

"I can see that!"

"We only finished the suggestion halfway." Uwe waved his hands wildly as he spoke. "It's like water. If you leave a gap in the middle, the mind will just fill it in. We pulled Johanna out of the story, but we didn't find anyone to replace her with."

"It doesn't make sense. Why him? She filled Johanna in with—"

"The first person she saw," Otto said.

"The first..." Erich squeezed his eyes shut and grimaced. "The pictures in her room. All those portraits."

"Exactly," Uwe said.

"We didn't know what to do," Otto said. "Johanna heard her raving about it after dinner, then Frau Murr just charged off. Who knows what she would have done if we didn't stop her. Christ, what if she'd talked to someone else instead?"

"How do we fix it?" Erich asked.

"We have to get her to sleep," Uwe said. "Then we can—"

"No more suggestion," Otto snapped. "We're done with that. Think of something else."

"You said it's temporary, right?" Erich said.

"That's true," Uwe said. "We could just wait it out!"

"How long does it take to wear off?"

Uwe dropped his eyes. "A few days," he mumbled.

"Days?" Erich sputtered. "We can't keep her here for *days*."

"Boys," Johanna interrupted. Her face was pressed into

the crack in the office door. "We have a bigger problem."

She pulled it open and pointed inside. The chair was empty. Frau Murr's ropes lay scattered on the floor, cut clean. Cool air rushed in from the open window.

"Oh god, oh god," Erich said. "She'll run and tell someone."

"I think she has something much worse than that in mind." Otto's voice was flat.

"How? What could be worse?"

"She's not thinking straight. She doesn't want to tell someone. She wants what was stolen from her. So she'll go the same place as everyone else," Uwe said. "To the *Siegfeld.*"

"You mean…" Erich trailed off.

Otto hung his head. "She's going to march up to the top the mountain and accuse the man who owns half the world of stealing a necklace."

# CHAPTER TWENTY-SEVEN

As they crested the peak, the three boys crept up to the edge of the tree line, breathless from running. Even as panicked as he was, Erich still had to stop and stare when he saw the rapt crowd and the *Führer* at the pulpit. There was nothing like it in the world. He wished he could pause everything and just take in the speech, but he knew what was at stake. Whatever it took, he had to find Frau Murr.

In the space between the *Führer's* retinue and his audience—where the three SV trenches ordinarily lay empty—was a massive pile of crisscrossing logs, each as wide as a man. Past that, the crowd divided cleanly into ranks. The teachers, staff, and *SS* stood at the front, then three columns of boys separated by their corps, and finally the huge mass of BDM girls. Erich had never seen all the girls together and he had no idea there were so many.

"There she is," Otto said, pointing.

Erich followed Otto's finger and nodded. Frau Murr stood at attention just to the side of the group of girls. She no longer seemed anxious at all. One gloved hand was stuck in her pocket, unmoving.

"We're too late," Erich moaned. "We'll never reach her without being seen."

"I... you're right," Uwe admitted, for once at a loss for ideas.

As they watched helplessly, the *Führer's* voice struck a crescendo, then suddenly dropped to a hush.

"Racial comrades," he said. "I believe we each have a power that is uniquely our own. Every one of us has a talent. We excel at that one thing more than any other. My talent is in the voice. Since I was a boy no older than you, I knew I had this ability to move my countrymen to action. With it I've done what no else believed possible. I have let loose the fighting spirit of the German people. Never before and never again will a leader inspire so much confidence in his nation."

He leaned forward into the podium and spoke as though to each one of them individually.

"I understand that you also have a talent that is just your own. Will you show it to me?"

All at once, the boys thrust their arms out in salute. The bonfire flared to life. Desperate to impress, they roared and chanted as they pushed the flames higher and higher. *Sieg Heil! Sieg Heil! Sieg Heil!* Erich could hardly see past the blaze. When the inferno reached its peak, Frau Murr charged. While everyone else was blinded by the searing light, she pulled a long, thin knife from her pocket and ran towards the impenetrable wall of the *Führer's* bodyguards.

"No!" Otto squealed. He shot out past the edge of the trees. Erich and Uwe ran behind him. Shockwaves of patronage galloped out ahead of them, but they fizzled out before they could reach her on the other side of the field. Frau Murr skirted around the bonfire and raised her knife high.

In a blink, Hugo was there. With a single flowing motion, he clapped one hand around Frau Murr's mouth. For a brief moment she shook in his grasp and then slumped down. The bonfire settled to a low burn. Though Erich had never seen it happen, Frau Murr's knife was gone, vacuumed up Hugo's sleeve. She looked as though she had simply fainted from excitement.

Panting, the three of them slipped into the rear of the distracted formation. Erich let out a quiet breath relief then stole a glance at Hugo. A shiver ran all the way through him. The headmaster's gaze was fixed on Erich. All four eyes, doppelgänger's included, bore down on him with a fury more scorching than the bonfire.

# CHAPTER TWENTY-EIGHT

Erich stood once again at the base of Hugo's tower. This time with Otto and Uwe in tow. The headmaster hadn't ordered them to come see him, but the look in his eyes had said enough. Erich was certain that this would be the end for the three of them.

As they climbed the winding outer stairs, he kept his eyes fixed upwards, unwilling to glance over his shoulder to see his friend's faces. He wasn't sure which would hurt more, Otto's furious glare or the fact that Uwe had probably already forgiven him. All this was Erich's fault, every bit of it. Because of him, they had saved Johanna only to wind up in even deeper trouble themselves.

Somehow Hugo had managed to arrive ahead of them and he was already waiting when they reached the top. He sat at his bare desk, hands resting just to the sides of the infernal book he had shown to *Oberführer* Ehrenzweig. The three of them filed in silently and stood at attention.

"Good evening, boys," Hugo said. He no longer looked so angry, but Erich still quailed when the headmaster pointed straight at him. "I thought I'd told you to stay out of trouble."

Erich could come up with no response to that.

"And you two," Hugo continued. "This wasn't what I had in mind when I encouraged you to continue your education outside of the classroom."

"We know, sir," Otto and Uwe said simultaneously.

"With that said, I must admit that some of the blame falls on me. I've known Adolpha for a very long time and I've never once seen her change her mind. So you'll understand how surprising it was when she came in last night demanding that I dismiss one of her girls and then the next morning begged for just the opposite.

"I should have put a stop to things right then, but I am, as always, impressed with the two of you and I let my curiosity get the better of me. Still, I think we can agree that this melodrama of yours has come far enough. You can imagine what could have happened to her had events unfolded less favorably."

Remorseful nods passed all around.

"This is what we are going to do. You," he pointed again at Erich. "You've been warned before. I'll do it once more now, but believe me when I say there will be no third chances. I don't want to see even a hint of mischief from you."

"Yes, sir, of course," Erich said, all in one breath.

Hugo nodded and then turned to Otto and Uwe. "As for the two of you, you will see me for tutoring every Wednesday at four o'clock. You will never again use suggestion outside of this room. Does that sound fair?"

Not once before in Erich's life had he heard an adult ask a question like that when meting out punishment. It must have surprised Otto and Uwe as well because it took them both a moment to dig an answer out of their throats.

"Very fair," they each said many more times than was necessary.

"You may go now," Hugo said.

"Ye-yes, sir," Erich stammered.

He and Otto turned to leave, but Uwe couldn't resist asking one last question.

"What will happen to Frau Murr? Will she be all right? No one... no one saw her did they?"

"No, no," Hugo said, waving his hand dismissively. "She'll be fine. *Rottenführer* Wolff is taking good care of her. The mind is a resilient thing. Once it wears off, I expect she'll remember bits and pieces, but not much more than that. If anyone asks you about her—our dear *Oberführer* most of all—she has the flu."

"Yes, sir, thank you, sir," Uwe said.

He saluted one last time to Hugo then joined the rest of them at the door. As the three lucky boys scurried down the stairs, Erich filled his lungs with a long cold breath and didn't let it out until they had reached the bottom. They vowed never again to mention what had happened and went their separate ways into the night.

**\*\*\***

That winter, a gulf opened between Erich and the others. Though they had sworn to forget it, the incident with Frau Murr hung over every interaction between the three once-conspirators. Otto was particularly cold. He rarely had more than a few words for Erich and it was hard to blame him for that. Had it not been for Hugo, Erich couldn't imagine how things could have gone any worse than they did. He wondered if there anyone else in the castle who would have responded so casually to what had happened as their headmaster had.

Thus, Erich vowed to stay away from the spotlight and out of trouble. He kept his distance from the secret corridors and even stopped accompanying Johanna on her frequent kitchen raids. A few treats no longer seemed worth breaking the rules for. Yet for reasons he couldn't fathom, she was desperate for his help breaking in. She pleaded with him for weeks before she finally gave up on persuading him. He suspected that she was just getting Karl to go in his stead, but Erich couldn't be sure.

He and Karl didn't talk much anymore either. In a span of only a few weeks something had broken between them. Yet Erich couldn't quite bring himself to do anything about it. He knew he should feel lonely or angry or resentful about the situation, but he didn't. There was something he liked about the isolation. Since the end of their *Nassfuchs* year, it had been one crisis after another—none of which had truly been his fault. Erich needed distance and time to think.

Too many things had been left unattended for too long. Their ruinous attempt at suggestion had been the final straw and Erich finally accepted what he'd refused to admit before: he was losing his patronage. The nauseating moments when his power would desert him came more and more frequently. And even when he could coax his patronage into flowing, it left in sputters and weak bursts.

It wasn't just Erich either. His old bathing partner Fritz suffered from the same. Neither of them had ever admitted anything to the other, but the truth came out in subtler ways. Patronage was king in Rouhhenberg and without it Fritz's standing in the *Wehrbären* was visibly diminished. Eckhard and Fester no longer followed in his footsteps and even his old standby Anton had taken up with a new crowd. Worst of all for Fritz, he had lost his *SV* captaincy—an indignity Erich had so far avoided—and therefore had to play. He did his best to hide the moments of weakness on the *Siegfeld*, but once Erich started watching for them, it was easy to spot the lapses.

Erich's own struggles came in his coursework. He was determined not to let his inadequacy show, but that was no longer easy. He had to be clever and efficient with his technique, compensating for the fact that every day his peers grew stronger and he weaker. It was painfully unfair that he suffered while all his friends remained so strong and carefree.

Desperate to hold onto what little patronage he had left, Erich spent endless hours practicing and even more time than that searching for a way to recover what he had lost. Before long, he was ready to do just about anything to get his patronage back. If he could only figure out how.

For a long time, Erich had preferred to dismiss his descent into the mines with Fritz as no more than a nightmare, but that was too much of a luxury now. Whenever he closed his eyes he could see his patron's crab-mouthed servants looming over him. Too often he woke in the night, still feeling briny fingers prying apart his jaw or something sharp and wriggling forcing its way down his throat.

*What you have will not last long unpaid,* the creatures had warned him, but Erich didn't understand how he was expected to repay a debt if nobody would tell him what he owed. On the first night they went down to the bathhouse, Hugo had promised them that they owed nothing, but at least in Erich and Fritz's case that seemed to be far from true.

The more he thought about it, the more convinced Erich became that it all came back to the one terrible moment in the bathhouse when the blood had run cold. He could still remember the stench of it, the way it congealed as it slithered down his back, and the coppery bile that had filled his mouth in Larat's class. Whatever rite they had been doing must have gone wrong, leaving Erich and Fritz one night short.

Walther too had suffered from a cold bath. Erich shuddered whenever he thought of what might be happening to him down in those mines. But something about that didn't make sense. Why had they been let free while Walther never returned?

It all came down to the bathhouse. If so, maybe a dose of pig's blood really was all his patron needed. Uwe had once brought a whole hog back from the dead. With practice, Erich might be able to do the same. But that didn't seem right. If any old pig would do, then why had everything gone awry in the first place?

He was certain Frau Murr would know. Whatever mistakes had led to cold blood for Erich, Fritz, and poor Walther, she had tried to cover them up more than once. But Erich's one opportunity to root around in her mind had long since passed. He had no intention of trying that again and the few scattered recollections he had gleaned from her were useless.

There was, however, one place Erich had yet to look. Even in his desperation, the thought of it still made him shiver. He'd never understood why his dreams of bone boy on the ceiling frightened him so much, but that didn't change the fact that they did. He knew in his gut that whatever lay at the end of those three left turns would make him regret ever finding it.

Yet as the snows thawed, Erich's desperation overtook fear and he wondered if it was worth waiting any longer. If he was going to take that path eventually, why not now? Why not get it over with? It was time. He would let his patron's leash tug him wherever it lead and live thereafter with the consequences.

# CHAPTER TWENTY-NINE

Erich pulled away the false back of the broom closet in Bittrich Hall. He used his hands, unwilling to waste any precious patronage. It felt right somehow to enter the corridors the same way he had done for the first time almost three years ago. Once inside, he knew the turns by heart.

The first corridor was the longest of the three. Defying perspective, it almost seemed to grow as it stretched into the distance. But at the corner, Erich spotted something on the floor that he had never seen in his dreams. He crouched down to get a closer look.

It appeared at first like a metal jaw, but it was actually two mouse traps bound together by a rag. Scraps of wire had been filed into barbed teeth and wrapped around the spring bars. Erich jostled the contraption and its hungry mouth snapped shut. There was old blood on the floor, dried and nearly black. This must have been how Mateusz III tore his leg. Maybe it felled the dachshund's predecessors as well.

The splotches of blood continued down the hallway and swerved left at the corner. There the stone floor began to slant down and widen. Erich followed the trail, though he didn't have to guess that it would take him left. The only time he'd ever been this far was the night of the ball, when he and Johanna found themselves here by accident. Even then, Erich had managed to get her turned around before they could go any further.

Just before the third turn, Erich stopped and took in a long breath. His arms tingled. It felt like all the blood in his veins had pooled at his fingertips. Erich gave a moment's thought to turning back and then, closing his eyes, he took a step around the corner.

In his dreams, the final corridor had always been a wide dead end, empty but for the scattered bones on the floor and the boy on the ceiling. But now when Erich opened his eyes, a huge swastika-emblazoned curtain blocked the path. It looked exactly like one of the red banners that ordinarily draped from the sides of the high tables in the chapel. Whatever he was looking for was on the other side. Erich inched closer. He couldn't bring himself to let his eyes pierce through it.

Dread weighed him down, but as he advanced Erich could feel something else. It started as just a tickle on his neck but grew stronger with every step. The hairs on his arms pricked up and soon his whole body hummed. It was the same feeling he got every night that he descended the bathhouse steps as a *Nassfuchs*. It was patronage, raw and untapped. With every step, it was returning to him. It was coming home to where it belonged. Erich ran his fingers over the back of his neck and traced the semicircle mark. It resonated in answer. Even before he reached the curtain, he drew it back without touching the cloth.

From the other side, the bone boy lunged. This was no nightmare. He was as real as the dull dagger he clutched in his little hands. He stabbed it down as he hurled himself forward. Had Erich opened the curtain by hand, the wild swing would probably have met its mark, but instead the boy's slash caught nothing but air.

He leapt again, but Erich was ready. He could feel the

patronage surging within him. At the slightest provocation, it rushed forth, slamming into the boy from both sides. He froze mid lunge. For the first time in a long while, Erich felt in control. This really was the creature from his dreams, but in daylight, the demon who had haunted him for so long was nothing but a scrawny child.

Erich laughed. He couldn't stop laughing. This was what he'd been afraid of? This fragile thing? Effortlessly, he lifted his attacker up until the boy's pedaling feet dangled in the air. Erich had never once been able to silence the terrible shrieking in his dreams, but now it was easy to glue those lips shut. He looked pathetic. There were no bones at all. His stolen *SS* shirt dangled over his flailing legs like a dress. Even suspended as he was, the boy's whole body quivered with anger.

Erich twisted the boy's tiny wrist until he dropped the dagger. He tossed him up and his back smacked against the ceiling. It was as easy as lifting a balloon. In two steps, Erich was under him. In the dream, he'd always had to look up and meet that fiery gaze. But this was not a dream anymore. All he had to do was turn his neck down and it was like the boy wasn't even there.

"Erich, no!"

At the sound of Johanna's voice, Erich jerked back. His concentration snapped and the boy dropped from the ceiling. He smacked against the stone at Erich's feet. Johanna sprinted towards them, jettisoning a laden sack from her shoulder as she ran. She shoved Erich away and then hurled herself down to the bone boy's side. He didn't seem to want anything to do with her. He scrambled away and jumped up to his feet, snatching up his dagger and thrusting it out. His arm vacillated between the two of them, unable to decide whom to point the blade at.

Johanna glared at Erich. "You shouldn't have come here."

"Shouldn't have come wh— do you *know* him?" Erich shouted back.

"Yes," she huffed, then threw her arms around the boy, oblivious to the dagger he was brandishing. "His name's Heinrich." She gently pried the hilt from his hands. "Heinrich, this is Erich. You don't need to be afraid of him."

"Get away!" Erich yelped. "He tried to kill me. He's dangerous"

"*I'm* dangerous?" Heinrich said. He wriggled out of Johanna's grasp and pressed himself against the wall, clutching his bruised ribs and glaring at Erich. He was probably trying to figure out how best to get the dagger back.

Johanna sighed loudly and pointed a finger at Heinrich. "You stay here," she commanded.

"I never do anything else," he grumbled.

"I know, I know," she said, then dragged Erich around the corner, ignoring his protests.

"Are you sure it's safe to leave him alone?" Erich said once they stopped. "Where did he come from? Who is he? Is he a spy? Is he a Jew?"

"He's just a boy," Johanna said.

"That's not an answer."

She gave an exasperated groan. "He's not a Jew. And he's definitely not a spy."

"What is he then?"

"He's a communist. Or, I mean, his father was one."

"Then he *is* a Jew! And a spy! Both!" Erich hissed. "How did he get here? Where did he come from? We have to tell— He could be—" He twirled around in his haste to get away, but Johanna grabbed his wrist. Her nails dug into Erich's skin as he tried to wrest himself away, but she wouldn't let go.

"You can't!" Johanna's voice rose to a shrill pitch. "He didn't come from anywhere. He's been here. He's been here as long as you have. A little longer, really. You... you don't understand. I told you he's not a Jew, but... but the others, the ones that come now. They are. There are hundr—"

"Others!" Erich twirled around frantically. "Hiding? In the walls?"

"No, no, it's not like that at all," Johanna said. She grabbed Erich by the shoulders and made him look at her. "They're not hiding, they're... prisoners. And Heinrich, he's escaped. Look," her voice cracked and she pulled back her hand to cover her mouth. "When I told you I work in the kitchens... I-I lied. I haven't worked there in a long time."

"You're not making any sense," Erich said. "Where then? And what does that have to do with him?"

"I work in the same place as all the other girls that Frau Murr doesn't like," Johanna said. "I work in the bathhouse."

# CHAPTER THIRTY

Erich ran until he couldn't run anymore, until his legs melted and the insides of his stomach splattered across the dusty stone. He continued to heave and retch long after there was nothing left within him. His whole body ached from the effort, but he felt like if he pushed hard enough he might expunge all the things Johanna had told him about what was inside the bathhouse. Only when he could no longer muster the strength to wring his guts out any further did he lie back against the wall.

Afraid to face his own imagination, Erich kept his eyes open and unblinking even as they dried up and stung. But that did nothing to stop his mind from flooding with pictures of what Johanna had described. Meathooks and ankles split open, rusty pipes stained red, bubbling skin and ironbound flames.

He should have known. For years he had heard whispers about costs and debts and oaths. Nothing comes for free, least of all a thing as rare and remarkable as patronage. And yet for all that talk, he'd never imagined that the price could be so high. For every night that Erich and Fritz had drenched themselves in the promise of a great tomorrow, someone else's future had been cut short.

It couldn't possibly be worth it. And yet, he didn't want to imagine what his life would be like if he had not come to Rouhhenberg. What kind of nothing would he be now if he had stayed in Messerich and grown up like everyone else?

An hour passed before Johanna finally found him. She slid in beside Erich and wrapped her arms around him, ignoring the vomit that soaked into the hem of her skirt.

"Hugo," Erich croaked. "He's a monster."

"Yes," Johanna whispered. "But he's not the only one. Heinrich's mother, she said—"

"It doesn't matter what she said," Erich snapped. "She's a liar."

Johanna squeezed him tighter. "Okay. Alright."

Neither spoke for a long while, but eventually the silence became too much and Erich had to say something just to get rid of the rattling in his head. "Is it every day? Do you have to... to go there every day?"

"Not me, not every day," Johanna said slowly. "But someone. There's always someone working." She buried her face in his shoulder. "You went down there every night too. Did you really not know?"

"Of course not," Erich said.

"With your father and everything. Couldn't you tell the difference? I mean, you lived right above a butc—"

"No!" Erich shook his head violently. "I didn't. I didn't know."

"I'm sorry, then," Johanna said.

"For what?"

"For telling you. I think it might be better not to know."

"Maybe," Erich said. "It's too late now." He slumped down further against the wall and rubbed his eyes. "What happened to his mother?"

"She left," Johanna whispered. "A while after they escaped she just... left."

"She left him all alone? That's horrible."

"It's not like that," Johanna said. "You weren't there. I-I think she did it for him. From the start she was sick, really sick, and she told me she wanted to stay behind in the bathhouse. But we couldn't make him come without her. So I found a way to get them both out. They were staying in the tunnels, you know, the ones by the kitchen. But it was bad. I couldn't get food—that was before you and Karl. She could hardly move at all. Heinrich kept catching rats and god knows what else, but even for just him it would have barely been enough."

"You're saying she was trying to save him?"

"Yeah," Johanna said. "That's what I want to believe." She waited a minute and then finally said, "I think he still eats them, the rats. He doesn't take help easily. He wants to do everything on his own." Johanna wiped her nose and took in a raspy breath. "I don't think he even likes me."

She was crying. Erich badly wished he could do the same, but his eyes were filled with sand. "I'm sure Heinrich likes you," he said. "Everyone likes you. You're a nice person. The nicest. You know that, right?"

Johanna shook her head and didn't reply. At last, she got up, held out her arm, and helped Erich to his feet.

"Would you like to meet him?" she asked. "Properly this time."

After everything Johanna had told him, Heinrich was the last person Erich wanted to see. But he didn't feel like he had a choice and—though a part of him loathed himself for it—he already missed the swell of patronage he felt in the boy's presence.

"Do you really trust him?" Erich asked.

"Why would he hurt us?" she said. "Nobody else is going to help him."

When they arrived at Heinrich's makeshift home, the curtain was already drawn back. Erich had been so intent on the boy before that he hadn't paid any attention to his surroundings. He'd expected to see the filthy, bone-littered warren he'd stood in so many times in his sleep. Instead, the dead-end cubby was tidier than Erich's own bedroom.

There was a stack of books in one corner and a jug of water in the other. Plastered to the back wall was a torn-off magazine cover featuring Shirley Temple from *Der Kleinste Rebell.* Erich assumed that was Johanna's handiwork. Heinrich himself lay on his back on a rectangle of folded blankets on the floor. Ignoring his two visitors, he was reading a book that he held up with both arms over his head like it were a roof.

Johanna indicated with her eyes that Erich should go over and re-introduce himself. Grudgingly, he took a few steps out past the threshold of the curtain. But when Heinrich took one hand off his book and pushed his long hair out of his eyes, Erich stopped dead. On the center of the boy's forehead was a marking of sorts. It was a half ellipse, impossibly black and identical one that adorned Erich and Fritz's necks. Erich had always thought of it as a hill of some kind, but seeing it on Heinrich's brow he realized he had been wrong. It was an eye.

All at once Erich understood. It was not just anyone that Johanna had rescued. This boy was Erich's. By all rights, Heinrich should have long since been dead. His warm blood should have drained down from the very top of the bathhouse to where Erich and Fritz waited in its depths. Instead it had been someone else, a substitute, a cold, failed stopgap who would take Heinrich's place while Frau Murr and *Rottenführer* Wolff scoured the castle for their two escapees. The crab-mouthed man's words repeated in his head over and over. *Did you suppose that one offering could simply be exchanged for another? That you could come before a god only to haggle like a beggar at market?*

"What did Heinrich's mother have on her forehead?" Erich asked, certain he already knew the answer.

"It looked like a spiral," Johanna said.

Erich cringed. That was Walther's mark. Erich wasn't sure whether Heinrich's mother had died or escaped, but it didn't seem to matter. By the time they descended into the mountain, she was already long gone. Erich and Fritz had been given a second chance—and the eyes with which to find it—but Walther, with his quarry out of reach, had no such luck. The mines had swallowed him whole.

With a painful swallow, Erich forced himself to sit down at Heinrich's side. This close to the boy, his patronage flared up so furiously he could hardly keep it from bursting out of him.

Heinrich sniffed loudly, but didn't look away from his book. "You stink," he said.

Erich glanced down at his vomit-stained shirt and shrugged.

"What are you reading?" he asked. Erich could see the cover perfectly well—*In Desert and Wilderness* by Sienkiewicz—but he didn't know what else to say.

"Why do you care?" Heinrich said, his voice utterly flat.

"I care because…" Erich dragged out the words, unable to find a good answer.

Heinrich snorted. "That's what I thought."

"I care because we're stuck together," Erich said. He finally hit on the right words. "We're stuck together in more ways than one. I don't know if I like you or not and you definitely don't like me. But that doesn't matter right now. I think you have something I need and, well, I'm sure there are things I can get that you need as well."

"Like what?"

"I don't know," Erich said. "You've got to want something."

"It's not something you have."

"Then it won't hurt to tell me," Erich said. "Come on, what would you like?"

Heinrich slammed his book shut and turned to look Erich in the eye. "Fine. Here's what I would like. I want to go somewhere so far away that I never have to think of—or smell—you, your stupid girlfriend, or anyone else."

"She's not—" Erich began, but he cut himself off with a sigh. "I don't know how to give you that, you're right. I hardly know where we are right now let alone where you could go. But I could bring you some new books. That would be sort of the same thing." Erich glanced back and saw Johanna nodding her approval. He wondered if she realized what kind of beast she had just let into the sheep-pen. "Good then," Erich said, still without any answer from Heinrich. "I'll bring you something from the library next time."

"There's a next time?" Heinrich said. He rolled over and mumbled into his bedsheets, "Fun."

✳✳✳

Erich didn't think anything could possibly be the same after that. Yet on the other side of the walls, nothing had changed. As he floated amidst his naive classmates, Erich would begin to forget the things Johanna had told him. There was something numbing about the way he could wrap himself up in ordinary life and the inconsequential troubles of other people.

On most nights, Erich and Karl would stay up late in the *Schützenadler* common room, whispering to each other until long after midnight. Karl could fret for hours over the way Johanna rarely spoke to him anymore or how Mathilde, who he had taken a liking to, was spending so much time with Felix. Erich didn't mind. It was an easy way to stave off sleep. The bone boy, having now intruded into Erich's waking life, vanished from his dreams. But the nightmares that replaced him were far worse. Every morning, Erich would wake up coughing on smoke that wasn't in his lungs and wiping illusory blood off his palms.

But for all the horror, there was one good thing to come of Erich's discovery. He had his patronage again. For the first time in a long while, he felt like he belonged in Rouhhenberg. He could throw away the tricks and distractions he had hidden behind in class. And no longer fed by impotence, the bitterness that had crept into all of Erich's relationships ebbed.

Even so, the threat of losing it hung over him. Erich understood now that every scrap of power he had hinged on the whims of a patron who was leading him somewhere. He had felt the stick. Now he was gobbling on the carrot. But what would happen when he finished it? To maintain his patronage, Erich had to visit Heinrich's cubby every day and soak in the boy's presence. It was a constant reminder of the precariousness of his situation.

Erich never felt welcome on the other side of Heinrich's red swastika curtain, but after a while the two learned to tolerate each other. Every time he visited, Erich would bring a book or a treat from the kitchen, set it down in the center of the room, and then sit up against the wall. No matter how tempting it was, Heinrich's pride never let him move to claim the prize while Erich was there. But as soon as he left and turned the corner, Erich would look back through the wall and watch Heinrich scurry over to take whatever had been left for him.

When Johanna found out that that Erich had been visiting often, she was so overjoyed that she kissed him on the lips, which made him more uncomfortable than anything else. He refrained from telling her the reason why he had been seeing Heinrich so often, but he suspected that she already had some notion. But regardless of his intentions, Erich could tell Johanna was relieved to have someone she could share her secret with.

He couldn't imagine how she had borne everything alone for so long. As much as he tried to focus on the parts of his life that had gotten better, all his attempts to stave off the horror of what she had told him came to nothing. Whenever Erich was at his most masochistic, he would consider paying a visit to the bathhouse and looking, really looking, through the walls. But he never once managed to work up the courage. As much as he wished it were a lie, Erich had no doubt that everything Johanna had told him was true. He didn't need to see it to be sure.

All this pain and misery had sprung from the mind of one man. Hugo, who had seemed so wise and powerful at first, was nothing but a fraud and a murderer. He had no real power to call his own. He was a con man who had honed his charms on the crowds in his theater before unleashing them on a long sequence of unwitting victims: Frau Murr, Isabel, whoever she was, and then, impossibly, the *Führer* himself. At the very end of this chain of deceptions was Erich. He had never done anything wrong and yet now he found himself with blood on his hands.

He knew that if he could somehow get the right message to Berlin, this whole terrible mess would be sorted out. But he couldn't figure out how to send it or even what it should say. Every letter that left the castle was picked apart and scrutinized. If *Oberführer* Ehrenzweig hadn't been able to break through Hugo's deceptions, then how could Erich stand a chance alone?

He tried many times to enlist Johanna's help—there was no one better than her at this sort of scheme—but she rejected the idea outright. She agreed that their headmaster was a monster, but based only on gossip and prejudice she had decided that what was happening in Rouhhenberg came all the way from the top. To her, the *Führer* was not Hugo's unwitting victim but his master. In Johanna's mind, Hitler had taken on a comical level of villainy, presiding over a vast network of evil so insidious and entrenched that it could put the international Jew to shame.

In the end, they spent more time arguing than they did plotting.

"Gertrude says there'll be a new group of *Nassfüchen* here tonight. Bigger than any of the other years," Johanna said glumly.

"Bigger?" Erich moaned. "What can we do?"

"I don't know," Johanna said.

"If we could just—"

"Don't start with the letter thing again," she snapped. "You'll get Heinrich caught."

"I'm just trying to help. If we can convince him what Hugo's done, the *Führer* will do something about it. I promise."

"How can you possibly believe that?" Johanna shouted. "These people come here by the hundreds! And I'm not talking about the *Nassfüchsen*. Who do you think sends them?"

"Hugo!" Erich said again. "Who else?"

"You just don't get it. This isn't about him. It's not about Rouhhenberg. It's not about your stupid patrons or your little magical world or anything else like that. It's bigger than that. You should hear what they say, Erich. The places they've been before this. It would—"

"They're lying!" Erich interrupted. It took everything he had not to lift Johanna up and shake her. "These people can't be trusted. They're not like Heinrich. They're not like us. They're Jews and criminals and worse. They hate Germans. They hate us and they're lying to you and you're falling for it."

"I don't know what else I can tell you," Johanna said. "They're not."

"What if I prove it to you?" Erich said. "I'll go up to his tower. I'll make him confess. You'll see."

Johanna shook her head. "You don't know what you're doing."

She tried to put a hand on Erich's shoulder, but he threw her back. "Don't touch me!"

Before Johanna could protest and further, Erich sprinted off through the corridors, trying desperately to hold onto his fury. He couldn't lose his nerve.

Erich made it all the way to the closed door outside the top of the headmaster's tower before the anger drained away and the fear set in. He hovered his hand over the big brass knocker, unable to push himself any further.

Erich could already see the headmaster on the inside where he sat at his desk and calmly leafed through papers. His doppelgänger crouched next to him, pointlessly miming his movement with its ruined hands. Erich shivered in the cold wind and pulled his hand away from the door to hug his chest. He was just about to turn around and slink back the way he'd come when he heard a voice from inside, louder than it should have been.

"Do come in, Erich," Hugo said.

Erich shuddered. He almost made a run for it, but it was too late for that. He could no longer fathom how he had thought coming here would be a good idea.

As he pushed open the door and walked in, Erich scrambled to think of some excuse or an alternate explanation for his visit. Instead, the words he no longer meant to say tumbled out anyway.

"I have a question, sir," he said, far more politely than he had originally intended. "It's about the baths we took when we were *Nassfüchsen.*"

"Speak."

"The blood… it isn't pig, is it?"

Hugo fixed Erich with a long dispassionate stare. "Who gave you that idea?"

Erich didn't answer.

Hugo thumbed his chin for a moment and then finally said, "It's not pig."

"Then what is it?" Erich said, punctuating each word.

"I see," Hugo said. "That's why you're here. You want me to say it. Then you can act surprised, get mad, and call me a devil." He shrugged. "Fine. I'll say it just how you want me to. Outside of the kitchen larders there are no pigs in Rouhhenberg. The blood you've taken is human, though your *Führer* might attach a prefix to that word."

There was not even a hint of remorse in Hugo's eyes, but Erich couldn't hold back the anger that burned in his own.

Hugo caught his glare and held it. "Don't pass judgement on your elders, boy," he snarled. "To be honest, I'm surprised you're so shaken. I'd have thought all that would have been drilled out of you by now. Have not been paying attention in class?" Hugo seethed with sarcasm and contempt. "The blood of the animal. The blood of the Jew. Do you not trust Germany's savior when he says they are one and the same?"

"Don't pretend he has anything to do with this," Erich shouted, surprising himself. "Getting rid of the Jews was one thing. That was— that was— justice. This is murder!"

"And where do you think he get rid of them *to?* England? Madagascar?" Hugo's mouth split into a grin so wide it threatened to crack his lips. "Zion?"

Erich crossed his arms. "Poland," he mumbled. "To work."

Hugo loosed a long, shrill laugh. His doppelgänger flapped its mouth along with his. Its few remaining teeth clattered against each other.

"I was wrong; you have been listening," Hugo gloated. "And where was your sanctimony then? When you learned that a million slaves fill your belly with food, you sat and smiled and did nothing. Yet now you come here and judge *me.*

"I am not the villain you wish I were. Did you know that less than a year ago, fifteen of Himmler's top cronies sat in a room and decided how best to exterminate every single Jew in Europe?"

"That's not true!" Erich snapped.

"I was surprised too," Hugo said, raising both his arms. "When I started this endeavor, I thought Hitler would be just the kind of tyrant who could feed my efforts. Such people never have any shortage of dissidents to put to death. But I never imagined that one day it would be bakers and farmers and shopkeepers who would climb my bathhouse steps.

"Trust me when I say that our Rouhhenberg is a drop

of blood in your precious *Führer's* bucket. Everything that happens here would have happened just the same somewhere else. I have taken advantage of an opportunity. That's all. From one side of the continent to the other there are men who do the same thing as me for worse reasons. The chemical barons and the gun moguls and the census takers. They line their pockets selling means of killing to a man who will never have enough of them.

"I have such a means as well. And I don't do it for money. It is not a pretty task, but I don't care what happens to me or my soul in the end. I don't care how stained or broken I become. This place is the only thing I've ever wanted. This future. This world we are creating, a world where before our pointless, wretched lives come to an end, each person has a chance to see one truly extraordinary thing.

"One day this so-called Third Reich will crumble under the weight of its *Führer's* thousand lies. And on that day, because of me, a single good thing will have come of all this: there will be magic in the world again."

Erich stumbled back. He fished for words, but he had none. Already, Hugo had gone back to his papers as though their conversation were over.

"Hate me if you must," Hugo said without looking up. "Curse me and praise Hitler in a one breath if you can stomach the hypocrisy. But, please, do it somewhere else because I cannot."

# CHAPTER THIRTY-ONE

Erich kept his head down as he took his seat at the table, afraid to look up to the balcony where Hugo doubtlessly sneered down at him. Karl elbowed Erich and pointed over to the low table where the crop of new *Nassfüchsen* were sitting.

"They'll outnumber us soon," he said gleefully.

Erich sunk down lower in his chair. Johanna had been right. There were almost a hundred of the newcomers. He tried not to contemplate the cold mathematics that implied. Instead, he focused on the new faces among the *Schützenadler*. They had only just escaped the mines yet their smiles were bright and honest and their cheeks glowed with a sense of purpose that Erich could only vaguely recall.

He stared at his plate while Hugo stepped up to the podium.

"Good evening, my darlings," the headmaster said. "It is a momentous night for many of you. Some have just begun your journey. Others are emerging from its end. Every year, I tell our arriving *Nassfüchsen* that they need do nothing to claim the gift we offer here. I tell them I will bear any weight that might fall on them.

"But tonight I have been reminded that there is one request I must make of you all. Do not squander this patronage. For all good things come at a cost, even if we are not always the ones who pay it."

Even though his words were blatantly aimed at Erich, Hugo never even glanced in the direction of the *Schützenadler* table. Seething, Erich couldn't decide whether to be angry or sad or guilty. He fixed his eyes on the grain of the tree trunk table and fumed.

Nothing Hugo had said in his office could possibly be true. As if whisking a card up his sleeve, Hugo had tried to shift the blame elsewhere. In his mind, everyone was responsible except for himself. The headmaster was a liar by trade and though his tricks might work on everyone else, Erich refused to be fooled. One day—he wasn't sure how—Erich would find a way to expose him to the world.

"With that said, I do have one announcement to make," Hugo continued. "As you may recall, my suggestion course for advanced students was canceled last year due to logistical challenges. Tonight, I am pleased to announce its replacement." The silence in the already silent chapel somehow deepened. Everyone was leaned forward in anticipation, as though this trivial piece of news were the most important thing in the world. Erich felt like the only boy at the table not slavering over Hugo's every word. "Beginning tomorrow, Herr Larat will teach a new class on the subject of security. I think you will all find it a worthy challenge."

"What do you think that means? Security?" Uwe whispered as Hugo sat back down.

"Sounds like the *Schützenadler* word for fighting," Otto said.

"Yes, very funny," Uwe said. "I have to say I still miss suggestion, but I suppose we'll always have our private lessons with Hugo." He tapped his finger on the table in front of Erich. "You should see if he'll take you in."

"I'd rather die," Erich said under his breath. But he

must have spoken too loudly, because Uwe recoiled and Otto flashed him a glare. "Sorry, I don't mean that," Erich backpedaled. He fished for a way he could explain his misgivings without saying too much. "It's just I don't think we can trust him. He's always fighting with *Oberführer* Ehrenzweig and you know he rep—"

"That's just politics," Otto interrupted. "Everyone wants to be in charge."

"Hugo's the best thing about this place," Uwe said. He crossed his arms defensively. "Sometimes it feels like he's the only one of the teachers who really gets Otto and me."

"Just keep one eye open," Erich said. "Alright?"

### ***

When dinner was over, Erich found himself in the secret corridors without even thinking about it. His feet followed the three turns they had long since memorized. The wide, red curtain to Heinrich's cubby was pulled back and the boy himself was nestled into the corner. An open book lay on the floor next to him, but he wasn't reading it. His eyes stared off into a distance that wasn't there.

Erich set two wrapped pieces of chocolate down at Heinrich's side and then crawled into the opposite corner. He pulled his knees close and hugged them. Neither said anything for a long time, then Heinrich flipped the book beside him shut, startling Erich.

"What do you think happens to him?" he said.

"Who?"

"Him," Heinrich said again. He tapped the cover of his book. "Captain Nemo. Do you think he survives after the end?"

"There's a sequel," Erich said. "I haven't read it, but they must have it at the library. I could get it for you."

Heinrich shook his head. "That's not what I meant.

What do *you* think happens to him?"

Erich paused a while to think. He could hardly recall the book. "Well," he said. "At the end, they're sucked into that big maelstrom, yet somehow the professor survives, what's his name…"

"Aronnax."

"Right, him. He makes it out in a tiny boat. If that's true, then a submarine should have had no trouble. But…" Erich suddenly reconsidered his answer as he remembered more. "I guess that doesn't seem very much like the captain, does it? Why would he want to escape? He's done with the surface. So maybe he does go down there." Erich looked over at Heinrich, which was something he normally tried to avoid doing. "I'd like to think that at the bottom of all that water he finds what he's looking for. Whatever it is. Maybe down there he can get away and, I don't know, forgive?"

"I think you're right about the first part," Heinrich said, glumly. "He could get out if he wanted to. And I think you're right that he wouldn't. I think he would turn off the engines and let it all drag him down. You're wrong about the why though. Someone like you couldn't understand." Heinrich met Erich's stare. The boy's face somehow managed to be utterly blank yet furious at the same time. Even the eye on his forehead smoldered. "Nemo's not looking for anything down there. You don't find something good at the bottom of a place like that. It's just better than all his other options."

As if struck, Erich pushed himself back into the corner. He wasn't even sure what Heinrich had meant, but something about it had cut. He could feel the tears welling in his eyes and he pressed his face into the wall so Heinrich wouldn't see. Cold air shook in his lungs and his chest felt like it would cave in. Erich curled up tighter, his dribbling nose scraped across the stone.

Mercifully, Henrich left him alone after that. He didn't seem to care enough for that. Erich cried until his eyes burned and his breaths came aching and dry. When he couldn't do that any longer, he slipped onto his side and, utterly spent, fell asleep.

When Erich woke, there was a blanket covering him but Heinrich was not around. Dim blue light fell in from the embrasure on the wall. Erich pushed himself up. His whole body ached, but there was a sort of relief in the pain. After a whole night here, he brimmed with patronage and yet at the same time could already feel it dripping away. He was a bucket with a hole in the bottom.

Erich had just enough time to make it back to the *Schützenadler* wing, get dressed, and meet up with Karl before they had to head out to their new class with Herr Larat. He didn't speak much on the way and just let Karl chatter in his ear. They hadn't had a lesson with Larat since their *Nassfuchs* days and neither of them knew what to expect. The fact that Erich didn't care did nothing to stop Karl from laying out a dozen different theories as to what "security" might be like.

Already, there was a line in the hallway outside the classroom. Everyone was as curious and eager as Karl, but the door was shut and nobody was brave enough to be the first to go in.

Karl turned up his nose in disgust. "It stinks like a farm."

"Just like home," Erich grumbled, but he didn't really resent it. He couldn't remember the last time he'd taken in the scent of hay and dung and grass. It reminded him of a time when his shoulders had not been hunched.

The door opened suddenly and Herr Larat popped out. "What are you boys waiting for?" he cried. "In, in!"

The procession of boys tumbled into the classroom and as soon as Erich crossed the threshold, the source of the smell was immediately apparent. Stacks upon stacks of rattling cages covered the teacher's desk. The menagerie spilled out from there and overflowed across the floor.

Badgers, rabbits, lizards, parrots, snakes, and even a

baby fox all jostled in their wire enclosures. Legs thumped and bars jangled as the multitude of animals called to one another in echoed squawks and barks. Scraps of hay littered every surface. Herr Larat had to yell just to be heard over the din.

"Get to your seats," he said. "We've a lot to cover and very little time."

"What are the animals for, sir?" Karl asked.

Herr Larat silenced him with a look. "Come to the front when I call your name," he said. Then he picked up a clipboard from on top of one of the cages and beckoned over Felix, who jumped up with a big grin on his face, delighted to be called first.

Felix stroked his chin for a second and then pointed towards a brilliant blue macaw, but Herr Larat swatted his finger down and shoved a hamster cage into his arms.

"Keep that one away from the snakes," he said, then shooed Felix off before calling the next name.

When Karl came up, he held out his arms eagerly and Herr Larat handed him one of the few glass cages. Erich couldn't see anything in it other than a decomposing log. Karl pressed his face into the glass, searching, then suddenly recoiled, almost dropping it. A huge, flat insect had scurried up out of the log and planted itself on the side of the glass. Karl held the cage out as far away from him as possible, twisting his face in disgust as the rest of the students cackled.

"What is it?" he moaned.

"The Madagascar hissing cockroach." Herr Larat spoke as though this was something he encountered every day. "That's a luckier draw than you know. One day after we've blown each other all to bits, the roaches will be the only thing left on this earth. Just don't lose her about the castle."

Larat called Erich last, and by then there was only one animal left.

"For Fiehler, the wood turtle," he said. "You'll be

grateful for that shell before the year is over."

Erich took the cage mutely and returned to his seat. While everyone else tittered over their new pets, he stared blankly at opposite wall. Herr Larat raised his arms in a vain attempt to get the attention of a classroom that was far too busy playing to notice him. He cleared his throat loudly, but the chatter didn't stop. Herr Larat sighed heavily and walked over to where Felix sat on Erich's left.

"What are you going to name him?" he said, pointing to the hamster.

"Dirk, I think," Felix said. "It's a handsome name, right?"

"Very," Larat replied.

He lifted up the latch and reached his hand into the cage then ran two fingers up the hamster's back. It recoiled and scurried away, but Herr Larat was faster. His hand shot out and coiled around the critter's puffy face. He twisted his grip as its tiny, panicked feet scrabbled against the hay. The color drained from Felix's face as if he were the one suffocating.

"Quiet everyone, please," Felix squealed. "Please!"

One by one, heads turned and the chatter fell away, but Herr Larat kept his fingers locked around the hamster's snout. His grip twisted so tight that Erich half expected its brains to suddenly burst from between his fingers like jelly. After an uncomfortably long time, the hamster's little legs stopped moving and its body slumped down. Herr Larat pulled his hand away and let its crushed head drop. Felix's whimpering was the only sound in the room.

"You," Herr Larat said. "You've failed my class. Out."

Felix pulled back in surprise, pointing to himself as if there were anyone else their teacher might be speaking to.

"Swiftly, please," Herr Larat said. "The rest of us have a lesson to get to."

Felix frantically gathered up his belongings, holding one hand over his face to hide tears. He ran towards the door, then suddenly turned back and grabbed the dead hamster's cage to take with him as he left. There were a few muffled sniggers, but most of the students were too frightened to laugh. The *Schützenadler* had forgotten what it meant to be disciplined. Herr Larat returned to the front and scowled.

"Let me explain how this will go. The subject of our lessons is security. That is to say the art of keeping someone or something safe. You will mark your calendars for the day of our final, December 10th, 1943. On that day, if your new friend's tiny heart is still beating, you pass. If at any point the creature should die, then you are out and you will spend the remainder of the year assisting my Physics lessons with the *Nassfüchsen*.

"There are no exceptions. You may fail on the first day, as we've seen, or on the last. Assume the worst and you will succeed. I don't recommend the other outcome." Herr Larat smiled widely at the class. "Are there any questions?"

*** 

As the boys went about the rest of their day, the brew of terror that Herr Larat had concocted slowly wore off and the excitement of their new companions took over. Much to *Oberführer* Ehrenzweig's frustration, the *Schützenadler* carried their new pets with them to the remainder of their classes, doting on them whenever the teachers turned away. Doktor Kammer had the opposite reaction. He spent almost half his class going down the rows and examining each pet in turn.

"What are you going to name him?" Doktor Kammer asked as he reached Erich.

"I don't know," Erich said flatly. Recalling what had happened to Felix, he pulled the turtle's cage closer to him and then without even thinking gave an answer. "Arden."

"He's in good hands," Doktor Kammer said with an

affirming nod. He moved down the row and ran his index finger over the glass of Karl's cage. "What do we have here, Auch?"

"Mathilde," Karl blurted out, but Kammer had already moved on.

Erich arched his brow. "You're naming a cockroach after Mathilde?"

"I guess I didn't really think about it that way," he said sheepishly.

After dinner, Erich finally let the turtle out of his cage. He desperately needed something to take his mind off of Hugo and their new class had come at just right time. Determined to finally distract himself, Erich ruffled the covers of his bed up into tiny mountains, then let the turtle slowly traverse them with stubby, brown legs. As he watched, his eyes got lost in the thin ridges that spiraled over Arden's slate shell like a fingerprint.

Karl soon stopped by, though he declined to take Mathilde out of her glass enclosure. Otto and Uwe arrived too, carrying leftovers from the meal. Erich wished he'd thought of that.

"I'm not even sure what turtles eat," he said.

"Damned if I know," Otto shrugged.

"Let's find out," Uwe said and began to set up a miniature banquet on Erich's bed.

In the older boy's session, Uwe had gotten a white dove, which he'd already taught to perch on his shoulder. Otto carried a squirrel that ran up and down his arms and over his shoulders before eventually settling into a perch atop his head.

"How did you get them trained already?" Karl asked.

"Wouldn't you like to find out," Uwe said with a wink at Erich.

"I'm going to leave you all to it," Otto said. "I'll be back in a little while. From what I hear, I think Felix could use someone to talk to right now."

Uwe got up to follow him, but Otto shook his head.

Uwe frowned then turned back to watch Arden. The turtle didn't seem interested in any of the things they had brought, ignoring the sausage, potatoes, green beans, and rice. He did eventually take a nibble at a piece of lettuce. But when Karl set Mathilde's cage down on the bed, he dropped the greens, pushed his neck out as far as it would go, and eagerly pressed his face into the glass.

"We know what he eats now," Erich said.

Karl snatched up the cage and cradled it in his arms. "Not happening. She's all mine."

Uwe winked. "When are you planning to tell Johanna?"

Karl blushed and mumbled something incomprehensible.

"It was just a joke," Uwe laughed.

Erich's smile faded. Uwe had reminded him of Johanna and that had reminded him of Heinrich and that reminded him of Hugo. Every time he tried to pull away and pretend to be ignorant like his friends, something would break through. The headmaster's smirking face seemed to loom everywhere.

Erich wished he could just forget. He wished he could shed his guilt and his doubts and leave it all for Johanna to figure out. Everyone had been better off when she had kept her secrets to herself. But Erich knew that even if it were possible give it all back, he wouldn't be able to do it. No matter how far away he ran, he would always feel the tug of his patronage pulling him back.

# CHAPTER THIRTY-TWO

Every day, Herr Larat subjected their pets to some new and inventive torture. And every night Erich spent hours in Heinrich's cubby, stitching up Arden's wounds and weaving new protections into his shell. The others were not as good at the healing arts as he was, so Erich took the role of doctor, hanging his long-forgotten stethoscope around his neck and making rounds in the *Schützenadler* common room. He learned something from every cut, scratch, bruise, and burn. Piece by piece, Arden was broken down and put back together, tougher than he'd been before.

Though the boys had to fight viciously for their pet's survival, everyone was grateful for the uplift in mood the animals brought. All throughout winter, the news from the east worsened. After more than a year, Erich had almost forgotten that they had once expected victory in Russia to come after mere months. With the casualties mounting at Stalingrad, the question that dominated all conversation was why the *Führer* had not yet called on the Rouhhenberg boys to fight. Bitter brawls broke out in the halls as the death notices poured in and the students turned their anger and frustration on one another.

Sometimes when Erich was feeling particularly dispirited, he would let Johanna talk him into coming with her to one of the unused rooms that had a radio. While he soundproofed the doors and windows, she would try to coax the set into picking up longwave signals from the BBC. This would tell what Johanna promised was the "real story". But even when she attached a long aluminum wire to the antenna, they got little more than static.

"I don't think it's possible," Erich said after their third session.

"Of course it's possible." Johanna pointed to the bright orange card that was attached to the cable. "It says so right there on the tag."

Erich pulled the cord towards him and inspected the label. "All it says is that we could go to prison for doing this," he grumbled.

"Exactly," Johanna said. "They wouldn't need to say that if it wasn't possible."

"I don't see—"

Johanna shushed him. "Listen!"

The radio belched out a loud sputter as she adjusted the knob, but in between the bursts of static he could make out a few words.

*... last winter ... mutinous ... strike ... senselessly ...*

"It's no good," Erich said, secretly a little relieved it wasn't working. "It's got to be a thousand kilometers to London."

"It'll work. The signal's best at night," Johanna insisted. She twisted the knob by another hair, squeezed her hand tight around the makeshift antenna, then closed her eyes as if in prayer. Whatever god of treason she had invoked must have heard her pleas because, shockingly, the words began to overpower the static.

*... end is near, not yours, not Ger ... the so-called destruction of Germany is as empty ... nonexistent ... as the victory of Hitler ... the end of the ... robber, murderer ... liar state ... National Socialism ... end comes for its ... disgraceful philosophy ... trash*

*which have sprung from it ... accounts will be settled, devastatingly settled, with its bigwigs, its leaders and ... servants and beneficiaries ... generals .... and Gestapo hyenas ... shield bearers .... pseudo-philosophers who licked its boots ... Germany will be cleansed of ... ever had anything to do ... the filth of Hitlerism ...*

"I've heard enough," Erich said.

*... control ... ideas which connect man with God ...*

"But it's just starting to—"

Erich pulled the radio's plug from its socket and Johanna's face dropped.

"This was a bad idea," he said. "I'm sorry."

He tried not to look her in the eye as he hurried out of the room.

***

It began to feel like everything in the castle existed only to remind Erich of something he would rather forget. There was hardly anywhere he could go to get away. And so he found himself more and more fleeing up the mountain. There, he sought refuge in the workshop and home of Herr Jensson, *SV* mastermind and Hugo's old propmaster. Erich had passed off his *SV* captaincy at the beginning of the year—but a simple idea kept coming back to him whenever the painful thoughts intruded. He wanted to make a bookshelf for Heinrich.

To Erich's delight, Herr Jensson was kind enough to lend his assistance and the use of his workshop without asking too many questions. The bookshelf needed to come apart and reassemble easily enough that it could be smuggled piece by piece into the cubby. This was far more complicated than any such project Erich had worked on before, but Herr Jensson was a patient tutor and within a few weeks they were able to put together something he could be proud of.

When the shelf was finally delivered, Heinrich didn't betray a hint of joy or gratitude, but Erich nonetheless felt so good about it that he immediately dove into a second woodworking project. He pushed everything else away and drowned himself in the smell of sawdust and the mind-numbing noise of Herr Jensson's endless machining.

Herr Jensson was something of a loner. He never came down for dinner, though Erich supposed that his black skin would have been made it inappropriate for him to sit with the Aryan teachers and staff. Johanna said the girls hated delivering him supplies so much that they drew straws every week for who would do it.

The only other students who Erich ever saw visiting him were Otto and Uwe. And in all his time in the workshop, he never saw another adult. Even Hugo stayed away, which made it an even better place to escape to. As such, it came as a surprise when one evening Erich arrived to find Herr Jensson deep in conversation with Herr Larat.

Pausing outside the workshop in the back of the SV hangar, Erich peered at them through the wall, but decided not to interrupt. They were hunched over a table strewn with papers and spoke intently in low voices about whatever lay before them.

Even after Erich gave in to his curiosity and used patronage to draw out their voices, he could still barely understand what they were saying. Every third word was scientific jargon and the things that he could piece together made no sense. Erich wasn't sure if he should be excited or worried to see the two best minds in Rouhhenberg colluding, but he was undeniably curious.

Yet after a half hour they still showed no sign of breaking up their meeting or revealing its purpose. Erich shrugged and decided he would have to keep an eye on Herr Larat going forward. It was just the kind of distraction he was always looking out for now. Alas, there was very little to see. Even after a few weeks of intermittently trailing Herr Larat via the secret corridors,

Erich didn't spot anything suspicious. He did catch him meeting with Herr Jensson a few more times, but their topic of conversation remained as impenetrable as it had been before.

Erich had just about given up when at the end of one security lesson Herr Larat asked Erich to stay a moment after class. Arden had just spent a minute in a tank of boiling water and Erich was very proud that he had survived.

"That was impressive, Fiehler," Herr Larat said. "I'd never have predicted it after your first year but you've been a very consistent student in Security. And don't think I haven't heard about you playing doctor."

"Thank you, sir," Erich said.

"I'd like to see you push yourself further." Herr Larat picked up a small glass globe from his desk. It was hollow and a little marble sat within. The continents of the world were etched in white on the outside. Larat turned it in his hand, letting the marble roll back and forth. "If you can remove this marble without breaking the glass, bring it back to me and I'll have a very worthwhile proposition for you."

"Is that even possible?"

"Do let me know," Herr Larat replied as he walked out of the classroom.

For weeks, Erich tried everything he could think of to solve the puzzle, yet it constantly thwarted him. He yanked and pulled and twisted on the marble, shattering the glass more times than he could keep track of. He melted a hole in the side, though he knew that wouldn't count. Once, he spun the globe around until the marble within flew so fast he could hardly see it. He hoped that if it achieved enough velocity it might simply skip to the other side. That seemed promising until he lost his grip. The marble crashed through the glass like a bullet and permanently lodged itself in the wall next to his bed.

Every day after class, Herr Larat would hand him a new

globe without a word, never asking whether or not Erich had broken the last one because he always had. They didn't look cheap, but seemed to possess a bottomless supply of them.

If Larat had invented this puzzle to distract Erich from his secret meetings, then it was working. Soon, the globe was the only thing Erich could ever think about. He put even his new woodworking project on hold, though he still sometimes went to Herr Jensson's workshop to practice. There and Heinrich's cubby were the only places he could really concentrate.

The students had a voracious appetite for $SV$ obstacles and so Herr Jensson was always working on new ones when Erich visited. But whatever row he was brewing up now must have been an incredible undertaking, because he was always working on the same thing.

It didn't look like much, just a door that went nowhere, but all around its frame was intricate machinery. Whatever it was meant to do must have required incredible precision. Herr Jensson would make hundreds of tiny parts, but only a few would pass muster and make it into the finished product. He kept the doorway hidden under a black tarp, which didn't do anything to stop Erich from peering through. Yet even when he snuck in one night and examined the machine up close, Erich couldn't work out what the doorway was meant to do.

Eventually, frustration with Herr Larat's unyielding puzzle overcame Erich's determination to do it on his own and he decided to consult Uwe, who always seemed to have a knack for this sort of thing. He found him in the *Schützenadler* lounge, sitting at one of the small tables and folding paper birds. Otto sat opposite him, watching Uwe's hands crease and turn.

"Do you think it's possible for something to pass through walls?" Erich asked, pulling up a chair. "Without breaking through them, that is."

"That's why they make doors," Otto replied.

Uwe smiled and pondered the question for a moment. He plucked idly at the corner of his paper. "It's a very interesting question. I'm sure it's possible. Everything's possible. But that seems like a lot of effort when you could just go around."

"What if there is no way around?" Erich pressed.

"Then you make one."

Uwe looked down at his half-finished creation and tucked in a few edges before folding it back on itself. When he was done, the red paper lay flat in a square. A gold sheet poked out from the middle. Uwe pulled gently on one side and it split open, gilt wings thrusting out as its body aligned itself and took shape.

Uwe set the bird aside casually, took out a fresh sheet, folded it diagonally down the middle, then separated it again. There was something in the motion that stood out to Erich. The corners of the page were far apart at the start, then came together so close that they were almost the same point.

"I think... that's right," Erich said under his breath.

He scurried back into his bedroom, dove under the covers, and produced a little light that hovered above his head. It felt silly, like he were a child reading in secret, but he wanted to shut everything else out. Determined that it would be the last one he ever needed, Erich held Herr Larat's globe in his palm and set to work.

As with the folding paper, there were two points on the sphere, one inside, the other out. He had been trying for months to move the marble from one to the other by passing through the glass wall, but that was entirely wrong.

If you unfurl a globe, it becomes a map, a flat sheet that Erich could fold any way he wanted. He tried to think back to his lessons. *History is not the same thing as the past*, Doktor Kammer had said once. *It gives us an imperfect view. The story is up to the teller and you'd be surprised how much it changes. Consider the difference between a map and a globe. A globe is as accurate as it is impractical; maps are easier. And yet they are so malleable. With the right projection what's large can be made small. Two countries can be neighbors in one and on opposite sides of the earth in another.*

Perhaps it was the same for this globe. If Erich could just come up with a projection, his two points could come together. He began to twist and fold the space, randomly at first, then with increasing precision. The marble had to move by less than a centimeter, but it still took all night to find the right pattern.

Light flooded through the window and Erich could hear the other boys waking up and getting ready, but he refused to let his eyes stray from the globe. With one final fold, the marble move into an uncertain state, simultaneously inside and outside the globe. From there it was easy. All it took was a little nudge and the world made up its mind. The marble popped out into Erich's hand.

Energized despite not having slept, he leapt up from his bed, hurled himself into a uniform, and sprinted off to find Herr Larat before their class started. But he was too late. Though there were still twenty minutes before they were scheduled to begin, a long line of fidgeting students had already assembled outside the room. He found Karl at the back, holding Mathilde the cockroach cupped in his hand. No longer squeamish at all, Karl raised her up to his ear and slowly stroked her mottled, hissing back.

"Why's everyone here so early?" Erich asked.

"Let me think," Karl said. "Could it be because our final is today?"

"Oh." The exhaustion Erich had staved off the entire night hit him all at once.

"Do you even have Arden with you?" Karl said. When Erich didn't respond, Karl shook him gently on the shoulder, "Are you feeling alright?"

"Yeah, I'm fine," Erich mumbled. He twisted away. "I'll just… uh, I'll go get him."

By the time he had fetched the turtle and made it all the way back, class had already begun. All the desks had been cleared away and the students stood in a long line with their backs to the wall. Less than half of their original number remained. A long, squat wooden platform sat a few paces ahead of them and they had each set their animals down on it. Everyone was doing their best to keep the creatures still, but nobody had had much spare time for training and the unruly pets wandered. At the front of the line, Herr Larat paced back and forth, a pistol in one hand.

"You're late, Fiehler," he sneered. He pointed with the gun to an empty spot at the front of the line. "Why don't you go first."

Erich rubbed his eyes and suppressed a yawn as he walked over and set Arden down on the platform then walked away. He felt vaguely as though he just stepped in front of a firing squad, but the alarm he knew he should be feeling was hard to muster. Nothing seemed entirely real, as if the globe puzzle had been his true final and all this was just for show.

"The exam is simple," Herr Larat said. "One bullet is all that remains between each of you and passing marks in my class."

Herr Larat took a menacing step towards Arden. Erich had no idea how to stop a bullet, but he was still too foggy-headed to be afraid. Even as Herr Larat pointed his pistol towards Arden and moved his finger over the trigger, Erich felt nothing.

"Are you ready, Fiehler?" Herr Larat said.

Erich nodded slowly. "Yes, s——"

The blaring shot cut him off. It jolted him from his stupor. He stared over at Arden in horror. None of the uncountable protections he had woven into the turtle's shell had done anything to stay the bullet. It had pierced straight through and blood welled up in the crater it left behind. Arden's stubby legs gave out. Even as Erich scurried over to repair the wound, he knew it was too late. The turtle's right lung was shredded. Arden let out a final, wet breath and went cold.

With little more than a shrug, Herr Larat moved down the line. The other animals, spooked by the gunshot, had erupted into cacophony of shrieks, caws, barks and whimpers. Their owners tried to calm them as best they could, but all of them had to be held down by patronage so they didn't run from the executioner. Herr Larat's face didn't move as he went from boy to boy, most of whom struggled to cover up tears even before he reached them. He would ask once if they were ready, then regardless of the answer, fire and proceed down the line. No one's attempts to save their pet succeeded and Herr Larat paused the massacre only to reload.

By the time he reached Karl at the very end of the line, the room was awash with blood and tears. Some of the animals had died right away, but others still held on to a few remaining breaths. There was no hope for any of them. Erich watched Richard put his marmoset out of its misery with a snap of the neck. Several others followed his example, but some still egged their pets on, hoping that even a fading heartbeat might earn them a passing score.

Erich said his goodbyes to Arden and then turned to watch the last exam. Mathilde whipped her antennae back and forth frantically and her tiny legs scrabbled in all directions, but Karl held her vertically in the air above the block. A terrible sound screamed out from her shell as she struggled to get away. Herr Larat closed one eye and took aim. Perhaps, Erich wondered, Mathilde would be just be small enough for their teacher to miss.

"Keep her steady," Herr Larat snapped.

Strangely, Karl was the only boy in the room who didn't look sad, scared, or angry. "Yes, sir," he said.

There was a loud hiss of air as Karl spoke, but Erich wasn't sure where it had come from. It didn't sound anything like the hisses Mathilde made.

Herr Larat hovered his finger over the trigger, then pulled back suddenly. He cracked a tiny smile as he examined the weapon.

"You emptied the air from the barrel," he said. "That's very clever. No oxygen, no fire. Just like I taught you."

"Thank you, sir," Karl said.

Herr Larat lowered his pistol back into place. He fired. The shot sounded dull in Erich's already ringing ears. Karl's attempts had amounted to no more than anyone else's. There was nothing left of Mathilde but a splatter on the wood. Karl's mouth hung open and he wore the same expression of shock as all the other boys in the room.

"When we're done here, I suggest you head over to the library," Herr Larat said. "Look up the components of gunpowder. You might find that information illuminating."

He calmly holstered his pistol and surveyed the room.

"What was the point of all that?" Karl moaned.

"Let me be frank with you for a moment, everyone," Herr Larat said. "I don't like you. Not a single one of you. You are sloppy, arrogant children who have been given much and earned little. You live in this castle surrounded by masters of their craft, men who have spent their whole lives perfecting an art a thousand times difficult than anything you've ever done. And yet you strut around as though this place is all yours.

"Our beloved Germany had been driven to the brink and for what? A generation of hotheads and arrogant fools? What good is a grand future if there's no one left to inherit it but you imbecilic sycophants?" Herr Larat waved his pistol about menacingly as he spoke and Erich half expected it to go off at any moment. "You want to know what the point is, Karl Auch? I'll tell you. The point is that for all your pretensions to power, when someone holds up a gun you get out of the way like everyone else." He left one furious glare behind and then stormed out of the room, yelling, "I'll see you all here next year."

Suddenly, Erich remembered the puzzle and, without thinking, ran after him. "Herr Larat, wait!" he shouted.

"What is it, Fiehler?" Herr Larat barked.

Erich pulled the globe and marble out of his pocket, suddenly feeling very foolish for having picked this time to announce his success. "I- I did it. I solved it."

Herr Larat's harsh expression fell away. "Come with me." He grabbed Erich and led him down into one of the never-used classrooms in the basement. He carefully looked both ways down the hallway before shutting the door.

"I wasn't lying when I said I don't like you. But," Herr Larat held up one finger, "as much as it pains me, you boys have something that I do not."

"Patronage," Erich whispered.

"Correct," Herr Larat said. "I need your help with an undertaking. It's dangerous and Hugo would not approve, but you'll learn things you could never even imagine on your own. Are you interested?"

No secret had ever brought good things to Erich, but he had never been skilled at saying no and he was still curious to find out what Larat and Jensson had been talking about. The opportunity to disobey Hugo was just a bonus.

"What do I need to do?" Erich asked.

"You'll have to get a lot better first. Solving that globe is just the beginning," Herr Larat said. "I'm setting up a space in the *SV* warehouse where we can start lessons in the new year." He flicked his eyes to the door. "I want you to understand that what we are going to do must be kept between the two of us. If we succeed, history will remember us as heroes. If we fail, no one will ever know what we attempted. Do you agree?"

"Yes, sir. But I still don't understand. What will we be doing?"

"Fiehler." Herr Larat put one hand on Erich's shoulder and looked him in the eye. "You and I are going to win the war."

# CHAPTER THIRTY-THREE

Erich looked towards the start of 1944 with a mixture of excitement and dread. He was desperate to learn more about Herr Larat's plans, but with all that had happened, it was hard to be optimistic. He was certain that whatever his teacher had planned, it would—like everything else—end poorly.

The only person Erich told about his deal with Herr Larat was Johanna, and he regretted it immediately. She was, in a way, not on their side and it still made Erich uncomfortable to remember the treacherous words he had watched her slurp up from her illicit radio. *The end is near. Accounts will be settled.*

But ultimately it seemed Erich had little to worry about. Other schemes occupied Johanna's mind, much smaller in scope than Herr Larat's. Again and again, she promised Erich that she would find a way to get Heinrich out of Rouhhenberg. Yet in all that there were few concrete ideas. Even when she did put one forth it was always too preposterous to be taken seriously.

For the most part Erich humored this endless plotting. It seemed to relieve Johanna's conscience. And his too, in fact. Her ideas were so unlikely to come to fruition that

Erich could feel like he were helping without any real risk that Heinrich would escape and take his patronage with him.

But while Johanna focused entirely on freeing Heinrich, Erich had his eyes on the real problem, on Hugo. In a world that was so hard to make sense of, here was a single constant, a man of absolute and unquestionable evil. And yet Erich had no idea what he could do to stop him. Perhaps the answer would lie with Herr Larat. If the *Führer* could defeat his enemies abroad, would he finally be able to confront these traitors at home?

And so, though he was eager to act, there was nothing for Erich to do but wait. While the radio blared about shortages and sacrifice, the sleepy life about their castle continued unsullied by want. Even the annual solstice feast was placid and there was no special guest in attendance. Given what had happened the previous year, Erich was at peace with that.

In place of the usual festivities, Johanna decided to plot a Christmas celebration of her own. It would be just the three of them, herself, Erich, and Heinrich. Erich chided her that if Jews didn't celebrate Christmas then communists probably didn't either, but she insisted that that was nonsense. Heinrich objected to it no more or less than he did to anything they asked him to do.

At the beginning of the break, Johanna left a pair of boots under the embrasure on Heinrich's wall and slowly filled their toes with treats. A few days later, she brought in a potted seed and convinced Erich to try to make it grow. It wasn't too different from healing a wound and with a little effort he was able to coax out a small but not insignificant tree.

On Christmas morning, Erich passed Heinrich his gift, a collection of front stories by Werner Beumelburg. Heinrich kept one eye closed while he peeled back the newspaper wrapping as though it the package were a book-shaped explosive. But when he finally extracted the present, Heinrich quietly leafed through the pages with a hint of a smile on his lips.

"Thanks, I guess," he mumbled. Johanna shot Heinrich an expectant look and he shrunk down a little. "Oh, this is for you," he said and pulled a small, badly wrapped parcel out from between his pile of blankets. He handed it to Erich.

From the handwriting on the tag, it was obvious that the present was really from Johanna, but Erich thanked him and opened it anyway. Inside was a bright red kerchief with torn edges along one side. After staring at it for a moment, he recognized the color and glanced back to see the spot on the corner of Heinrich's curtain from which it had been cut.

"Are you sure you didn't need that?" Erich joked.

Heinrich shrugged and burrowed down beneath his blankets until neither of them could see him any longer.

**\*\*\***

When at last the new year came, Erich climbed up to the peak and waited at the entrance of the *SV* hangar. He was certain their meeting would actually take place in the side room of Herr Jensson's workshop where the strange doorway was kept, but he didn't want to arouse any suspicions.

Herr Larat arrived wordlessly and ushered him through just as he'd expected. To Erich's disappointment, the doorway was still covered in its black tarp and Herr Larat ignored it completely. He led Erich over to a small table with two chairs in the corner of the room.

"What's under that?" Erich asked, pointing hopefully at the tarp.

"That," Herr Larat said as he took a seat, "is for later."

Erich sighed and sat down opposite him.

"Have you been practicing with the globe I gave you?" Larat asked.

"No, sir," Erich said. He had thought he was past that.

Herr Larat let out a bark of frustration and muttered something under his breath. He pulled one of the globes out of his pocket and set it on the table. "Fine then. Let's see how much time we need to make up for."

Over the weeks, they went through the process of transporting the marble so many times that Erich began to miss the days when he got to smash the glass. Every repetition went the same. He would project the marble out, then back in, then out and in again. Whenever Erich's form was anything less than perfect, Herr Larat would snatch up Erich's hands and twist them into a painful configuration to demonstrate how it should have gone.

And yet, the longer this went on the more Erich realized how little Herr Larat was helping. He didn't know anything. He was ordinary. He had no patronage at all. Like Hugo, like Doktor Kammer, like all the adults in Rouhhenberg, he was nothing but an illusionist. Skilled, but powerless. Any progress that Erich was making, he was making on his own.

Between lessons, Erich carried the globe with him everywhere. He would hold it under his desk during class, endlessly transporting the marble back and forth from one side of the glass to the other. It wasn't long before he could move the whole thing between his two shirt pockets with a twist of his fingers.

As Erich buried himself in months of practice, Johanna's plans for Heinrich grew worryingly specific. She hoarded food and scoured every map she could find to figure out what direction she would need to travel. Erich gently reminded her that there was nowhere to run, that Germany's reach extended from one end of Europe to the other, but that did not dissuade her.

Her obsession recalled the days when her coded letters to Messerich were filled up with silly plans to break free from her father's grasp. It was not lost on Erich that after a long stretch of such talk, she had suddenly just done it. He still didn't know how she had schemed her way to Rouhhenberg and it wouldn't do for the same to happen now.

Erich sympathized with Johanna's goals, but the closer she got to achieving them the more he understood that he didn't want things to change. Was it really so bad for Heinrich right now? He was safe, after all. Here he had food and books and friends. As lone fugitives in the mountains, he and Johanna wouldn't get far.

The last snow melted into spring before Herr Larat finally threw off the tarp that covered Herr Jensson's magnum opus. Overnight, a thick cannister and crank had been added to the side of the doorway. Within its steel body, the addition teemed with miniscule gears, wires, prongs, and glass tubes. It looked so intricate and fragile that a few errant grains of sand would be enough to gum up the works. No wonder Herr Jensson had been toiling over it for so long.

"What... is it?" Erich asked. He didn't have to fake the wonderment in his voice.

"It's exactly what it looks like." Herr Larat ran his hand along the frame. "It's a doorway. A perfect replica of the one in my laboratory in Berlin."

"But what does it do?"

Herr Larat turned his palm up and Erich's marble globe appeared from nowhere into his hand. Erich reached down and patted his pocket. It was empty.

"Think of it like the puzzle," Herr Larat said. He tossed the globe to Erich, who barely caught it. "The inside of the globe is Rouhhenberg; the outside is Berlin. Once we're done, you'll be able to pass right through the doorway here and come out there. Five hundred kilometers in a single step."

Herr Larat sat down at their tiny practice table and motioned to the empty seat on the other side.

"Erich, what you hear on the radio is not always true. There is no offensive in the east anymore. For three years, our soldiers have frozen and died in the winters only so that their brothers can slog through endless mud in the spring and summer. Now, all that sacrifice is about to come to nothing. The Wehrmacht is broken. The only options left to them are retreat or death. In a few months the Bolsheviks will be at our doorstep." He pointed to Herr Jensson's contraption. "Think what this doorway could mean for us. We are not losing to Russia's men. We are losing to Russia itself. It doesn't have to be like that. Imagine it. An army that can cross continents in the blink of an eye. A newly minted panzer division appearing out of nowhere in Red Square. Ten thousand Waffen-*SS* on the streets of London."

"Why keep it a secret then?" Erich asked.

Herr Larat frowned. "Have you ever wondered why Hugo has not sent a single one of you to join the war?"

This had long been a topic of discussion among the boys, but Erich didn't believe any of the more popular theories. He knew the answer already. Hugo would not send them to fight because he didn't care if Germany won or lost. Their headmaster had done the math and, one way or the other, he would come out on top.

"It's the same reason you've never been expelled. Hugo sees you boys as a father would his children," Herr Larat said. "You are precious to him. No matter how bad it gets, he'll never send you into harm's way. And let me be clear, Erich. This doorway is not a toy. What I am asking of you will be as dangerous as any battlefield." Herr Larat locked eyes with him. "Five years ago you swore an oath, so help you god, to give your life for the *Führer*. My question to you today is this: did you mean it?"

It was hard for Erich to even recall the time when he had said those words, when the worst things he had to be afraid of were the tools that hung from his *Fähnleinführer's* belt. *I swear to devote all my energy and all my strength to the savior of our country, Adolf Hitler.* Erich hadn't done a very good job of that since. And how could he have?

Everyone had a different idea about how that oath could be fulfilled. Hugo said to do nothing. Johanna wanted him to denounce it. And now, Herr Larat had come to him with this. But Larat's idea was not like the others. It had no ambiguities to contend with. No Heinrich, no bathhouse, no victims, and no monster but the hordes in the east. There was the enemy and here in Erich's hands the means to defeat them.

"I meant it," Erich said.

Herr Larat nodded. "So we begin."

Herr Larat got up with barely word and went off to fetch the doorway's architect.

"Good evening, Erich," Herr Jensson said as he came in. He inclined his head towards the doorway. "What do you think?"

"It's... amazing," Erich said. "If it works."

Herr Jensson smiled. "That part is up to you."

He grabbed the door's crank with both hands and started to turn. There were so many gears that their individual whirrings blended together into a low continuous hum. Erich stepped up and pressed his hand to the door. Staring at the unvarnished wood in front of him, he tried to look past it to see the table full of tools on the other side, but there was nothing there. The moment Herr Jensson had fired up the device, the space past the door had gone black. When he walked around to the other side it was the same in reverse.

"Whatever you do," Herr Larat said. "Don't open that door until you've finished. There's no telling what could happen. We could all be sucked in or worse."

Erich nodded.

"Now, whenever you are ready."

Though Erich's task theoretically resembled what he'd done with the globe puzzle, this was infinitely harder. It had taken him months to figure out how to bring together two points on the opposite sides of a thin piece of glass. Now they were separated by mountains and forests and plains.

Herr Larat paced back and forth, dishing out sharp critique as they worked through exercise after exercise, but Erich soon learned to ignore his endless remonstrances. They no longer contained any worthwhile advice. This was, after all, new ground to tread for the both of them. Progress was slow and by the end of each night of lessons, Erich could barely drag himself back down the mountain and into his bed.

The moment he told Johanna what the doorway was for, she insisted on seeing it for herself. They crept into the workshop at night and she peeked under the tarp. But before she could get a good look, Erich realized that she might want to sabotage it. He pretended that he saw Herr Jensson coming and they had to run. After that, she asked him about his progress every single day, but there was rarely any change.

Whenever he could, Erich would stop by Heinrich's cubby before his lessons to ensure that he would have the patronage he needed to work on the doorway. Alas, Heinrich was not always there. By spring, he was absent so much of the time that Erich began to wonder if he were deliberately hiding whenever he expected a visit. It became a sort of unacknowledged game, as Erich tried to mix up his timing to catch Heinrich unawares.

"Where have you been?" Erich asked once, as he spotted Heinrich returning.

"Places," Heinrich said. He plopped down on top of his bedsheets. "Why do you care?"

"It's not safe for you out there. The others, they're not like Johanna and I. They won't be nice to you if they see you."

Heinrich snorted. "And you two are?"

"Don't be ungrateful," Erich snapped. He wanted to get up and give Heinrich a good thwack across the head, but he knew that he would get told on if he did. "Johanna is very nice to you. Sometimes maybe nicer than she should be. Think where you'd be without her. Did anyone come to bring you books in the bathhouse?"

"No," Heinrich said. He covered his head with his blankets and Erich felt a pang of guilt for being so harsh on him.

"I'm sorry," Erich said. "I just... I just want you to stay here where it's safer."

Heinrich said nothing. Erich wanted to leave him alone, but there were still a few minutes before he had to head up to meet Herr Larat and he couldn't waste the opportunity to soak up a little more patronage.

"How did you end up in there anyway?" Erich asked. "Your father must have made a big mistake to get your whole family in trouble. What did he do?"

"He played the piano," Heinrich said.

"That's not what I meant."

"Then I don't know."

"He must be out there looking for you," Erich said.

"Probably not," Heinrich mumbled.

"You're a very pessimistic person, you know," Erich snapped. "Think about it. If he was never here, then he must be somewhere else. Somewhere safer."

Heinrich poked up from under his blankets long enough to flash Erich a disdainful look.

"You really believe it, don't you?" Erich shook his head. "What Johanna says, that the *Führer* knew what would happen and he sent you here just to kill you."

Heinrich didn't respond and after a while Erich got up and dusted off his uniform.

"I have to go," he said. "But you're wrong and you'll understand that one day. Once the war is over—and that'll be sooner than you think—the *Führer* will come looking for his missing prisoners, the ones who were supposed to be put to work towards our victory. And there'll be a reckoning then. I promise."

Erich wasn't sure he could promise anything all, but it felt good to say. Hearing the words leave his own mouth, they seemed more real. He turned as he passed under the curtain.

"So stay put. It won't do anyone any good if you're caught before we find a way to get you out."

***

"We'll get it tonight," Herr Larat said, the same as he always did.

"Yes, sir," Erich replied out of instinct.

He clasped the doorknob and started to map out the projections he would need to make. Compared to the globe, the path from Rouhhenberg to Berlin was longer and the pattern of folds and twists more devilish. But here the thousand, byzantine mechanisms that surrounded the frame proved invaluable. Like a curved glass, they amplified each fold Erich made. If he bridged the distance in miniature, the door would handle the rest. It was not so different from the old puzzle after all. He wondered how Jensson and Larat had ever managed to build such a thing without patronage. Who had taught them?

The closer he came to the other side, the more the blackness inside the frame faded. Erich had seen a blurry glimpse of Larat's far-off laboratory several times before, but every time he would make a wrong move before the picture could become clear. All it took was one mistake to send him tumbling back to the beginning.

Tonight, frustrated by what Heinrich had said, Erich was determined to succeed, and after three false starts, it appeared that he might. As Erich put into place what he hoped would be the penultimate fold, the darkness within the frame thinned. The other side emerged like a coastline from the fog.

Herr Larat's laboratory was nothing like the workshop Erich was standing in. A clutter of expensive-looking equipment covered row after row of desks. Radios and speakers vibrated while attendants flipped switches and twisted knobs. Spinning steel cylinders sat in towering racks, endlessly cycling through strips of translucent tape.

Bits and pieces of the scene blurred and crystallized in front of him as Erich teetered on the threshold. He knew he only had to make one more fold to close the distance, but curiosity made him hesitate.

A woman stepped into view. She wore a brown army jacket and skirt that was too blurry to identify. She carried a steaming cup, which she immediately set down on one of the attendant's desks. Straining her eyes, the woman took a few steps forward and looked Erich right in the eye. He pulled in a little closer and the image sharpened.

Then he recognized her. She wore no pearls or grand furs, but she was unmistakable. She was the same woman from the photograph on Hugo's desk, briefly glimpsed in Frau Murr's memories. Isabel, from whom Hugo had stolen his infernal book.

But Erich didn't care about any of that. It was her uniform that he couldn't stop staring at. It was her uniform that made his blood freeze and his breath catch in his lungs. The eagle badge on her hat. The twin pins on the tips of her lapels. It was, like the uniforms of everyone else in the so-called laboratory, American.

Herr Larat's doorway did not lead to some research center in Berlin. It went straight into the stronghold of the enemy. He had promised that together they would end the war, but he'd never said for whom. His invention didn't prophesize panzers in Red Square but American G.I.'s in the Reich Chancellery.

No wonder he'd warned Erich not to open the door before it was done. Blind, Erich would never have known that he was one fold away from ending everything. Only the eyes of his patron had saved him.

He had to break away. He had to warn someone. But as Erich loosened his hand on the doorknob, a voice shot through him.

"Wait!" It was coming from the other side. From Isabel. "You've seen it, haven't you? You know what Hugo has done."

Erich gave a fraction of a nod.

"Then you will let me through."

"I can't," Erich said wordlessly. He knew he should cut it all off and walk away, but curiosity gnawed at him. This woman had helped that monster become all but immortal. Why? Had he fooled her like he had everyone else? "You worked with Hugo before. Why should I let you through just so you can do it all again."

The question took Isabel aback and there was a lengthy pause before she answered. Or maybe it was only a second; over all this distance, it was hard for Erich to tell.

"You're right. I did help him. And that was a terrible mistake. The same terrible mistake you are about it make. Believe me, if you close this door tonight you will regret it forever. Let me fix this. Let me face him."

"I'm sorry," Erich said. "I-I- can't. I won't."

He lifted his hand up from the knob and darkness rushed in to fill the frame. Isabel was gone. Mumbling, "I have to go," Erich rushed out of the workshop with his eyes on his feet.

"What happened, Fiehler?" Herr Larat yelled after him. "Are you tired or just weak?"

Erich ignored him. He needed to tell someone about what he had seen. Johanna came to mind at once, but he knew it was well past time for that. This was bigger than either of them and for once he could not pretend that Johanna's dissidence would be harmless.

Doktor Kammer would know what to do. Erich ran to his office, but the light was out on the other side. He banged furiously on the door in the vain hope that he would somehow materialize.

When that failed, Erich scribbled a hasty explanation onto a note and slid it under the door. He started down the hall to try *Oberführer* Ehrenzweig next, but as he turned the corner, he ran headlong into Johanna.

"We need to talk," she said. Johanna glanced back over her shoulder then whispered, "I had an idea."

"It's really not a good time," Erich said, but she grabbed him by the arm before he could protest further and dragged him into an empty classroom.

"You told me Herr Jensson's doorway is like a... a bridge to another place," Johanna said. "Step through here, come out in Berlin."

"Yes, but it doesn't—"

"What if it could be pointed somewhere else? Somewhere Heinrich might be safe."

"That's what I've been trying to say," Erich cringed. "It already is."

# CHAPTER THIRTY-FOUR

The moment the words left his mouth, Erich knew there would be no turning back. Telling Johanna where the doorway led was a terrible idea in a long string of terrible ideas, but when had he ever been able to keep something secret from her?

"We can shut it the moment he's through," Johanna reassured him as they hurried towards Heinrich's cubby. "Then you can smash the thing, or tell someone, anything you want."

"This is a bad idea. What if I can't figure out how to close it?" Erich said.

"You will," she said. "I know it."

Heinrich's red swastika curtain was drawn shut across the corridor. Johanna pulled it back by the corner and tiptoed over to where Heinrich slept. She knelt down and shook him awake.

"It's time. Get your things. We're taking you out of here."

"Very," Erich added.

Heinrich rubbed his eyes and nodded along as Johanna explained everything. Surprisingly unfazed by her story, he padded over to the bookshelf Erich had made and pulled out his copy of *Twenty Thousand Leagues Under the Sea*. He withdrew a sealed envelope from between its pages then let the book fall out of his hands.

Curious, she and Erich both peered over Heinrich's shoulder. On the front of the envelope was scribbled *For After*.

"What is that?" Johanna asked. "I've never seen it before."

"That's because it's none of your business," Heinrich snapped. "It's from *Mutti*."

"Alright, alright," Johanna said. Heinrich pushed past her and walked straight through the curtain. "You don't want to take anything else with you?"

Heinrich glared at her incredulously. "Like *what?*"

"Nevermind that," Erich said. "We need to leave."

Though he was eager to put the whole affair behind him, Erich made sure they took the slowest and safest route out of the castle. They waited to leave the secret corridors until the last possible moment and he didn't allow even a dim light on the climb up the mountain. Only once they were safely inside did he permit Johanna to turn on her flashlight.

As the three of them crept over the long, multivariate shadows of the obstacles that lined the aisles, a sense of melancholy settled over Erich. He felt like this were goodbye to Rouhhenberg, as if he were the one leaving and not Heinrich. The looming shapes flooded him with memories of the old game: Otto and Uwe's dog posts; Fritz's smashed door; Karl's shattered pane of glass. He missed it, the simplicity of *SV*, the flag at the end of the lane that told him whether or not he'd won.

"Why did you build all these?" Heinrich said.

"I didn't," Erich replied. "Herr Jensson did."

"Then why did *he* build them?"

"I don't know. It's just a game."

"But wh—"

"Shh," Johanna hissed. "Quietly now. We're almost

there."

Once inside the workshop, Erich brightened his light and pulled the black tarp off the doorway. Johanna grabbed Heinrich by the hand and led him over to the crank. It took a surprising amount of force to move it—Herr Jensson had made it look trivial—but together they managed to get the gears turning.

As the mechanisms slipped into their familiar hum, Erich decided to test his suspicions. He put his hand around the knob, squeezed it tight, closed his eyes, and pulled the door open. There was nothing, no screaming void on the other side, just an empty blackness. Herr Larat's warning had been as empty as his promises.

Now that he had succeeded once, Erich assumed it would be easier to make the connection to the other side, but he had trouble focusing. He missed Herr Jensson's steady hands. Heinrich and Johanna's uneven cranking made Erich feel like he were trying to draw a map during an earthquake. After several abortive attempts, he could see that they, like him, were beginning to lose steam.

Erich suggested a break and Johanna reluctantly agreed. She sat down on the floor and waved over Heinrich, but he wouldn't come. He paced to and fro, clutching his mother's letter tight to his chest.

"I'm sorry I haven't gotten it yet," Erich said.

Johanna smiled faintly. "It's not your fault."

After a while, she rummaged around in her jacket pocket and produced two thick oat cookies. Johanna got up to give one to Heinrich and then broke the other in half to share with Erich. She barely nibbled on it.

"If anything happens..." Johanna said. She trailed off and wiped her eyes on her sleeve. She couldn't manage to look at Heinrich, so she stared at Erich instead. "I guess if there's no time for goodbyes I just wanted to say... thanks and... I'm sorry."

Heinrich rolled his eyes at her. "Is it time yet?" he grumbled.

"I think it is," Johanna said. She put her uneaten cookie back in her pocket, then got up and dusted off her skirt before grabbing the crank with both hands.

Erich reached out towards the door and pushed leisurely through the first folds. He had done these so many times he hardly had to think about them. But as he went through the same tired motions, a thought struck him. He had an advantage now that he'd never had before. Standing right in front of him, furiously helping Johanna to crank was the very wellspring of Erich's patronage. He didn't have to conserve his energy then scurry off to Heinrich's cubby to recharge. The boy was mere steps away, just waiting to be drawn on.

As he pulled from Heinrich—tentatively at first—it shocked Erich how different the task became. Where before he had relied on tricks and careful navigation to bridge the distance. Now he could push through with force alone, twisting and creasing great waves of space down onto each other. What would once have taken an hour, he accomplished in a few short minutes. But just before Erich would have crashed through to the other side, he stopped.

"I'm not sure about this," he whispered, almost to himself. "What if she comes through? What if they all come through?"

"That won't happen," Johanna said.

"But—" Erich began. He silenced himself.

He knew what he had wanted to say. And he knew what Johanna would say in response and how he would react to that and on and on until at last they reached some resolution that would resolve nothing. Maybe she was right—about Heinrich at least; he deserved to live free— but that did nothing to change the fact that Erich didn't want her to be. He couldn't bear it.

Sending the boy through would solve everyone's problems but Erich's. How could that be fair? If he opened this door—even if all they did was shove Heinrich over and then close it—that would be the end. Whatever debt Erich owed his patrons would remain forever unfulfilled. Continents and oceans would stand between him and the patronage that he had been promised.

The gift from below the mountain no longer felt at all like something that had been bestowed on him. Rather it seemed as if it had grown from within. He couldn't remember what it was like before he had it. Integral and identifying, his patronage had swelled until it could no longer be separated from his person. There was no Erich Fiehler without it. To lose it would be to die.

Why was it only he who had to make this choice? The skin of every boy in Rouhhenberg was soaked and stained in blood. Yet it was Erich, only Erich, who had to peer through this blackened doorway and decide whether or not to let go of everything he had.

Erich deserved his patronage as much or as little as any of the others. More, even. He had to carry the truth on his shoulders while they pranced around the castle, free and unburdened. How could it be fair to punish only him? And what really was his crime? *You need do nothing*, Hugo had promised and nothing was exactly what Erich had done. He had never touched those people in the bathhouse. In all his life he'd never hurt anyone. He was as much a victim of Hugo's madness as Heinrich.

It was no more Erich who had killed those people than it had been him—or Johanna for that matter!—who left poor Arden Moritz bloodied and broken on that farmhouse floor. It was the Engels and the Hugos of the world who were responsible. They were the engineers of this cruelty. Let them be the ones to suffer. Let them pay the price, not Erich.

In fact, of the three people in the room, it was Johanna who had the most blood on her hands. Was it not she who had climbed up the bathhouse steps every night while Erich had only ever gone down? For years she had toiled as a bloody cog in Hugo's machine while all he had ever

done was turn his neck down and wait. Erich had never
wheeled a corpse into the fire. He had never told a
doomed man that everything would be all right.

He turned to look at her, to tell her this, and then he
stopped. In an instant, Erich realized what should have
been obvious to him the whole night. The truth was right
there in her eyes. When Johanna had said her goodbyes
and thank yous earlier, she hadn't been speaking to
Heinrich. She was saying goodbye to Erich.

She was not helping Heinrich escape out of some
righteous beneficence. Her motivations were just as selfish
as Erich's. She wanted a way out for herself. After all the
years they had been friends, she intended to abandon him
with barely a word, to turn coat and run while he remained
here, alone and forever impotent.

*Never*, Erich swore to himself.

The thousand intricate projections inside the doorway
had been painstaking to set up, yet they were trivial to tear
down. Erich raged at them. He clawed and smashed and
ripped until all his careful work lay in tatters. He wished
there had been more just so that he could break them.
Erich glared at Johanna and a hundred furious words
jockeyed to form a shout, but before they could burst out,
he heard a call from outside the workshop.

"Erich, are you there?"

Erich's anger dissipated in an instant. His stomach
plummeted.

"It's Kammer," he hissed. "I left him a note. I... I
forgot."

"Idiot!" Johanna snapped. She snatched Heinrich's
hand and tugged on him, but he wouldn't let go of the
crank. "We need to hide. Look over there." She pointed
towards a half-finished $SV$ row in the corner, a closet with
doors on either side. When Heinrich still wouldn't budge,
she grabbed him by the waist and dragged him over to the
hiding place.

Erich took one last glance back through Herr Jensson's

doorway and stopped dead. The blackness inside the frame was still there. More than that, it was thinning. All on its own, the crank turned and turned. Standing in that fading blackness was Isabel. She grew closer, her arm outstretched. Perhaps she had always been doing half the work, guiding Erich along, but now she did it alone. Piece by piece, she was reassembling Erich's handiwork.

Johanna waved frantically at Erich from the closet where she and Heinrich had hid, but Erich couldn't bring himself to move.

"He's coming!" she hissed.

When Erich still didn't move, she slammed the slatted door shut. Doktor Kammer spun around the corner and his eyes flew wide as he took in what was happening.

"What have you done?" he shouted, jabbing his cane at Erich.

"I- I-" Erich stammered, still stunned. "I have to close it."

He shut his eyes and inhaled, then turned to the doorway and hurled every scrap of patronage he had through the gap. All the projections that Erich had thought he'd torn down had sprung back into shape, stronger than ever. Every time he tried to tug at them he felt Isabel reciprocate from the opposite side. She was strong and it was all Erich could do to hold her back.

"Fiehler!" a voice yelled. It wasn't Doktor Kammer's. "Step away from the doorway."

Erich lost his concentration and twirled around. Herr Larat stood just outside. He moved into the room, his pistol pointed straight at Doktor Kammer.

"You know how this ends," Herr Larat said. "We've played it out already. Let her through or it's a bullet for the *Scharführer*."

"Go ahead then!" Doktor Kammer squeaked. "Shoot me. I'm right here."

Erich could feel Isabel gaining ground with every second his attention was diverted, but he couldn't look away.

"Erich, don't stop," Doktor Kammer said. "End this."

"Why should he?" Herr Larat said. "Fiehler, I didn't send you here tonight. You came on your own. You figured out where this doorway leads and yet here you are all the same. You must have wanted it open. Why? You're a curious boy. You've seen something in this castle, haven't you? You know what happens in that bathhouse tower and there's no going back from that."

"Yes, but I—"

"It doesn't matter why you came," Doktor Kammer said. "The only thing that matters is the choice you are making right now. And I understand why it might give you pause, Erich, I do. I have felt everything you are feeling. At times I think this place is a miracle. And at others I wonder if we live over the mouth of hell. But opening this doorway will solve nothing.

"What do you think will happen once it's done? Once they've widened it? When they crash through with their tanks and their planes and their hordes of men? What will you do when the bombs fall on Messerich and your Aunt's home is a smoking pile of rubble? They will leave us nothing in defeat and you will have no one to blame but yourself."

"I never lied to you, Erich," Herr Larat pleaded. "I told you this doorway would win the war and that is truer now than it has ever been. I am not talking about a victory for Hitler but for Germany. We are dying in the east; we are dying at home; we are dying for no reason at all but to quench the bloodthirst of a—"

As Herr Larat spoke, Doktor Kammer had crept closer. He swept out at Herr Larat's pistol with his cane, but he was still too far away. Herr Larat fired. He struck Kammer in the shoulder. He shot again and the bullet split through Kammer's throat.

Erich screamed.

He lashed out and slammed Herr Larat back. The gun

discharged again as he flew. Herr Larat's body cracked against the wall, but Erich didn't let him to fall. Patronage crushed against him until his eyes might pop. Without letting go, Erich whipped around to face the doorway.

Isabel was almost through. Already her arm had crossed the frame into the Rouhhenberg side. Veins bulged on the back of her hand as her fingers slowly constricted. Erich tried to throw her back, but he might as well have been trying to move the mountain they stood on.

Erich could still feel Heinrich. His little hands clutched at the slats of the closet where he and Johanna hid. Yet no matter how much Erich drew from him, there always seemed to be more. He dug deeper, sucking up patronage like poison from a wound and spitting it out through the doorway. The more he pulled from Heinrich, the faster it came. He smelled blood in the air. Painstakingly, the projections inside the doorway began to retreat. One at a time he forced them down. The frame darkened.

Erich glanced back towards the hangar. Reinforcements were on the way. Hugo and *Oberführer* Ehrenzweig. Frau Murr and *Rottenführer* Wolff. There was one last fold to undo and then it would all be over. Isabel would not come through. He let Herr Larat drop from where he still hung, then pushed a last burst of patronage through the doorway. As the others rushed into the workshop, the crank on the door slowed to a stop and the blackness inside the frame vanished. Isabel's arm, cleaved from her body on the other side, fell to the floor, seeping blood.

Erich felt his knees give, but Wolff's tattooed arm was around him before he could fall. He held Erich up as Ehrenzweig stepped past Herr Larat on the floor and came over to look Erich in the eye.

"What happened here?" he said, pronouncing each word slowly.

Erich pulled in a long breath and then, with as much caution as he could manage, explained what Herr Larat had intended. He left out anything to do with Heinrich and Johanna. Though Larat pulled himself up to sit against the wall, he said nothing the whole time, not even when Erich lied and said that they had just been having a lesson.

At last, when the story was almost done, Erich flitted his eyes over to Hugo. He sneered at Erich from above. Even his doppelgänger wore a smirk. None of this would have happened had it not been for him. Without Hugo, Doktor Kammer would still be alive. Heinrich would be at home with his mother. Johanna would never have come to Rouhhenberg. Perhaps the world would even be at peace.

Erich wished he could throw Hugo up against the wall as easily as he had Herr Larat. But what good would that do? It would hurt the wretched creature behind him while the headmaster himself escaped unscathed. To really get his revenge, Erich would have to find something that Hugo valued more than his life. As he stared into the headmaster's cold, slate eyes, he realized that he knew exactly what that was. Hugo had told him. The thing he cared about most was Rouhhenberg, and Erich knew exactly what to say to take it away from him.

"The whole plan... it was Hugo's idea. The two of them have been working together from the start. Hugo showed him how to build the doorway and he said... he said... he said that the *Führer* is a liar and that accounts will be settled and that Germany is bound to crumble."

There was a glimmer in Ehrenzweig's eye as he turned to Herr Larat. "Is that true?"

Herr Larat smiled as wide as Erich had ever seen him smile.

"Down to the last word."

# CHAPTER THIRTY-FIVE

"The boy is obviously a liar," Hugo said. He laughed and his doppelgänger kicked up its ruined head to join him. "His story is ridiculous. Did you know that he once tried to—"

*Oberführer* Ehrenzweig reared back and snorted like a bull. "I'm done listening to you speak," he said and then smashed his fist into Hugo's jaw. Swung out, Hugo tripped over himself and sprawled out on all fours.

"I'd almost given up, you know?" Ehrenzweig said. He drew his pistol. "When it comes this, I thought I'd have to settle for dreams and fantasies."

He pressed the muzzle of his P38 against Hugo's ear and discharged all eight rounds into the side of the headmaster's face. Erich flinched with every shot, but Frau Murr and *Rottenführer* Wolff hardly moved. As the echoes of the final shot died away, Herr Larat, unperturbed by the possibility that he might be next, broke into a laugh that shook his whole broken body.

The ringing in Erich's ears drowned out everything long after the gunshots had faded, but somehow—only in his head perhaps—the wet see-saw rasping of Hugo's breath came through perfectly clear. He shuddered with every rise and fall of his chest as he tried to suck in air only to gag on blood and dislodged teeth. Erich would have felt bad for him if he hadn't deserved it so much. Hugo's doppelgänger squirmed and writhed on the floor, but the headmaster himself lay still on his back. His eyes stared straight up, unfocused. He waited for his pulped face to heal.

"Do you know how many letters I've sent to Berlin?" Ehrenzweig said. "I don't. It's too many to count. In every one I lay out your failings page by page. That's a list that never gets any smaller. For anyone else, a tenth of that would be enough. Hell, in Nuremberg I used to arrest people for greeting each other with *Guten Tag*. But somehow you're special. In all these years, the only response I've ever gotten is 'wait'."

Hugo turned his head and spat a plume of darkened blood across the floor. Ehrenzweig crouched down and gripped him by the jaw.

"Look at me," he growled. "That's over now. I won't need pages for this next report. It'll fit in a quick telex. And I have a feeling that once the *Führer* reads it, you'll be able to hear the reply from one end of the earth to the other."

Hugo wriggled out of Ehrenzweig's grip and rolled onto his side.

"Ad- Adolpha. Help me," he wheezed at Frau Murr. He took a painful looking swallow. "You remember what it was like before me, don't you?"

Frau Murr crossed her arms over her chest. "I can't help you this time," she said.

Rage threatened to tear Hugo's already shattered face apart. "You were nothing," he screamed at her. "And that's what you'll be again. They'll sniff you out before you can blink."

Wolff took two loping steps forward and silenced Hugo with the heel of his boot. Ehrenzweig stood up and spat on the floor.

"Did you have to do that?" he said.

Wolff shrugged.

When Ehrenzweig turned around, he looked surprised to see Erich still standing there. But after a second, he recovered and threw on a warm smile.

"Come on," he said. "I'll walk you out."

With a hand on his shoulder, Ehrenzweig shepherded Erich through the door and out into the darkened aisles of the warehouse.

"You did me a favor today, you know," he said once they were alone. "But I do have to ask: did you make that whole story up?"

Erich took a hard swallow and didn't answer. He decided that anything he could say would only make it worse.

"I figured," Ehrenzweig said. "There were two traitors in that room but Hugo wasn't one of them. He's something worse than that, if you can believe it."

Erich's gaze darted over at the $SV$ rows on either side. The temptation to run almost overwhelmed him. It would be easy to sprint away, to hide in the labyrinth of iron that surrounded them. But where would he go then?

Ehrenzweig didn't stop walking or even look over at him. Unsure what to do, Erich followed mutely until they emerged from the warehouse. A car waited just outside.

"It's funny," Ehrenzweig said as he pulled open the rear door. "The thing I always hated most about Hugo was the way he coddled you students. He'd let you all get away with anything. Tardiness. Disorder. Sedition. Perversion. It was disgusting." Ehrenzweig shoved Erich into the backseat. "But even in the end, he wins, because here I am about to let you off with barely a warning. You're my star witness, after all."

Ehrenzweig slammed the car door shut. It began to pull away.

"*Heil Hitler*, Erich Fiehler," he called out. "And if you take one lesson from tonight, let it be this: mind the company you keep."

**\*\*\***

It was more than an hour before Erich arrived back at the *Schützenadler* dormitory, ready to drop to the floor and fall asleep in his clothes. The whole winding way down the mountain, the driver had gone so slowly that it felt like they weren't moving at all. It would have been faster if he had just gone on foot, but Erich had been too lost in worry to care or wonder why. The torturous silence of the back seat left nothing to distract him from himself.

He should have been consumed by *Oberführer* Ehrenzweig's warning, but instead he found himself thinking about Johanna. He hoped she was all right, but even more than that, Erich dreaded seeing her again. He knew she would hate him for what he'd done. Yet why should she? Erich had made the choice that was best for everyone.

If Johanna were truly worried about Heinrich, she would have done the same. It was Hugo's madness that the boy had fled from in the first place. Now that was at an end. The bathhouse would be shuttered and no more lives would be lost. She had to realize how much of a sacrifice that was. There would be no more *Nassfüchsen*. The school was as good as dead.

But for all Johanna's posturing, she didn't care about any of that. Like every other time in her life, all she really wanted was to run away. First she had fled from her father to come here. Now she intended to desert Erich and go to America. Erich wondered if she would ever be satisfied.

When he finally made it back, the *Schützenadler* lounge had long since gone dark. But light still seeped out from under one of the doors—Otto and Uwe's. Past the thick walls, Felix and the rest of Otto and Uwe's roommates sat up on their beds and traded whispers. Erich's tired body begged him to ignore whatever was happening, but he knew that his curiosity would never allow him to sleep. The long night wasn't over yet.

Dragging his feet behind him, Erich stumbled across the lounge and knocked on Otto and Uwe's door. The whispering inside instantly cut off and all the boys jerked up, alert. They glanced back and forth at each other, wordlessly bickering over who would have to answer the knock.

"It's me, Erich."

"Oh," Felix said.

Relief swept over his face and he got up to crack the door.

"I saw the lights were on," Erich whispered. "What happened?"

Felix pulled Erich in.

"They just came in while we were all sleeping and yanked them both out of bed. Didn't even let them get dressed."

"Who's *they*?" Erich said.

"Frau Murr and *Rottenführer* Wolff," one of the boys whispered.

"Otto and Uwe," another said at the same time.

"She said they were going to be expelled," Felix said.

"In the middle of the night?" Erich asked. "For what?"

Felix shrugged.

Otto and Uwe had long been Hugo's favorites, but Erich hadn't considered the precarious position that might put them in now that he was deposed. Still, as stern as *Oberführer* Ehrenzweig was, he had never seemed unnecessarily vindictive. Otto and Uwe were as loyal to the *Führer* as anyone.

"Do you know something?" Felix asked.

"I'm not sure," Erich said. "Maybe. Just... just go back to sleep. I'm sure it'll all make sense in the morning."

He backed out and shut the door more loudly than he

had intended. As he scurried away from the dormitory and into the secret corridors, Erich's heart thumped too fast for the rest of his tired body to keep pace with. He scanned through the walls for any sign of Otto and Uwe.

They were not hard to find. Just past the *Nassfuchs* wing, eight figures crowded together in the hallway. Otto and Uwe shuffled side by side while Frau Murr led the way, flanked by two *SS* men. Whenever the boys lagged too far behind, she would snap her fingers at *Rottenführer* Wolff and he would give them a push from the rear.

The procession turned sharply and spilled outside into the courtyard, where Erich could not follow. He watched through the stone as they marched across the grass, their destination growing more obvious with every step. Otto and Uwe must have known it too. The closer they grew to the bathhouse, the more sluggishly they moved. But they were not permitted to stop. The mouth of the ironclad spire was opened wide, ready to breathe them in. At the landing of the bathhouse's spiral staircase, Otto and Uwe paused, unsure which way to go.

"Up or down?" Erich whispered to himself.

Wolff answered Erich's question with a shove. Uwe stumbled to the right, catching himself on the rising steps. Up was not good. Otto helped Uwe to his feet and hand-in-hand they began to climb. Erich waited until the last man had disappeared into the bathhouse and then— ignoring his own misgivings—set out to follow them. Once he was sure it was safe, he slipped into the bathhouse and snuck up two flights before stopping to peer through the ceiling to where the slow procession still wound its way around the tower. From his perspective they hardly looked like people at. The only things Erich could see were boots and swinging arms.

As they reached a landing, Otto dug his heels into the ground and stopped.

"I demand to see Hugo," he said quietly. When it didn't look like anyone had heard him, he repeated himself, louder this time. Uwe leaned over to whisper in his ear, but Otto pushed him away. "If we're going to be expelled, I want to see the headmaster first."

Frau Murr stopped and turned around. "I'm sorry, dears. Hugo is gone."

"Gone?" Uwe said. His voice quavered. "What do you mean? Gone where?"

"He's dead. Or as good as," Frau Murr said.

Uwe shook his head furiously. "I don't believe that."

Frau Murr dropped down a few steps and reached out her hand. Otto moved to block her, but all she did was rest her palm on Uwe's cheek.

"I know. I can't blame you for loving him," she said. "He has a way with misfits like us. It's easy to fall for. He loves us when no else does. No, because no one else does. Because we're so starved for affection that we'll take it from anyone." She gave a slight nod to Wolff. "If you'd lived a little longer you'd have seen that for yourselves."

Wolff grabbed Otto by the shoulders and shoved him onto his knees. With his tattooed arm, he reached for the gun at his belt.

Erich shivered and hugged himself. He felt like his chest were packed with ice. He wished he hadn't come. He didn't want to watch this, but nor could he bring himself to try to stop it. He wondered what Johanna would do if she were in his place. Would she rush up the steps? Would she charge in to save them? Of course not, he decided. The two of them had been in this exact situation before in Messerich. They had hid in that wardrobe together, and like him, the only thing she had done was watch.

Wolff's hand twitched as he drew his gun. "*Scheiße!*" he hissed, dropping the pistol. He clasped his wrist, but that didn't stop another spasm from rocking the whole thickness of his arm.

"What's wrong with you?" Frau Murr snapped. She realized what was happening at the same time as Erich did and screamed, "Now. Do it now!"

But it was far too late. When Wolff's arm shook again, it wasn't the muscle or bone that shifted. It was the ink. The long, green serpent that ran from Wolff's shoulder down to his wrist had moved. This was Uwe's doing. No one could do transformations like him and Erich could have recognized his skillful handiwork anywhere. Flesh rippled and swelled. Scales pushed up through taut skin that stretched until it could stretch no longer. With a crack and a hiss, the snake tore itself out from his flesh.

Fangs bared, it shot out and wrapped its pointed snout around the nearest neck it could find. The *SS* man at Wolff's side stiffened and fell as the serpent bore into him. Wolff howled and staggered back, unable to tear his eyes away from the hollowed out flap of skin that had once been his muscled arm.

Otto leapt at the opening. He lashed out and Frau Murr, lifted up on a swell of patronage, hurtled to the side and cracked against the curving wall. She landed on the steps and slid down. All at once, the three remaining men shut their gaping mouths and aimed their pistols. One shrieked and his wrist cracked back until the bone protruded like a spearpoint, but the other managed a shot. He struck Otto in the arm, twisting him around. As Otto dropped, he tossed his shooter up to break against the ceiling.

Hands shaking, the last remaining man took aim at Uwe's serpent and opened fire on the ever-shifting thing. It coiled up and then rocketed its body out. Fangs buried themselves in the man's chest. The snake tore away and slithered down the steps towards Wolff.

Wolff crawled backwards with his one good hand, leaking a wet, dark trail across the stone with what remained of the other. Uwe left his creation to finish the job and spun around to take care of Otto, who had pulled himself over to the wall and was staring blankly at his red stained sleeve.

Neither of them noticed as Frau Murr lifted up from

where she lay, but Erich did. Her arm thrust out with a gun he hadn't realized she even had. Erich felt like he should call out in warning, but he didn't. The air didn't want to leave his chest.

Frau Murr hesitated. It was long enough for Otto to see and limply raise his finger. Uwe whipped his head around. Frau Murr fired. But when the flash subsided, nothing had changed. For a moment, Erich thought she had missed. Then he spotted the bullet. Flattened by an impact with nothing at all, it floated centimeters from Otto's forehead. It shouldn't have been possible. This was what every boy in Herr Larat's class had tried and failed to do.

But there was no time for any of them to take in the accomplishment. Frau Murr fired again. The bullet stopped. She fired again. And again and again until Uwe could no longer keep up. Erich looked away. He lowered his neck. It ached from watching from below and a surge of relief arced down his spine.

Erich didn't crane back up until long after the shots had stopped echoing around the stairwell. Frau Murr still clicked uselessly at the trigger. Wolff had stopped crawling away. He sagged, barely conscious. The snake that had once been his arm fared no better. Already its lower half had reverted back into an ooze of flesh, ink, and shards of bone. It dragged its body down the steps, slowly sinking deeper into its own inchoate sludge.

Bleeding himself, Uwe knelt down and kissed Otto on the forehead. When he pulled back up, Erich thought he would turn around and lash out at Frau Murr. Instead he did nothing. He sat down next to Otto, closed his eyes, and lay still.

But Uwe had one more thing left in him. Erich could smell it even before he saw it. Water. It filled the air with a pungent brine. Rolling down from the upper floors, the wave wrapped around the staircase like it were filling a conch. Uwe did not move as it roared towards them, rising in a great crest that loomed over Frau Murr. She clutched at her pistol, maniacally trying to fire as though she might somehow shoot her way through a tsunami. As it slammed over her, Erich jolted to his senses.

He ran, jumping down the steps two at a time, not looking back until he had reached the bottom and hurled himself out into the night. He tripped and fell, tumbling across the wet grass and onto his back. Erich's chest shook as he gulped for air. He stared straight up into the sky, but all he could see was the bathhouse looming over him. Water spilled out from the doorway and seeped into the ground. It soaked Erich's back, but by the time he got up it had all drained away. The only thing left on the steps was glistening stone and eight dripping bodies.

The sea had come to Rouhhenberg.

# CHAPTER THIRTY-SIX

Erich stepped up onto the crowded train platform and groped around for somewhere to stand. Everywhere clusters of boys had formed, but he didn't feel like he belonged to any of them. Even for June the weather was hot, yet Erich had worn his thick jacket anyway. He had itched and sweated for the whole drive down the mountain, but still refused to take it off. A farewell like today's was supposed to be wintery. It was an affair for fur coats and steaming breath. Instead, two hundred Rouhhenberg boys would go off to war under a bright and furious sun.

Not Erich. In a few minutes, the train would come to carry away three quarters of his classmates and leave him behind. The castle's hallways already felt terribly empty without Doktor Kammer or Otto and Uwe. Tomorrow they would be as barren as they were the day Erich had arrived. But they wouldn't be the same.

In the month since Hugo's ouster, *Oberführer* Ehrenzweig had wasted no time remaking Rouhhenberg as he had always wanted it to be. He had immediately summoned up three officers from Berlin, *Untersturmführer* Eichel, Dunst, and Dürr, to assist with character interviews and the necessary rites that would induct the boys into the *SS*. There was no such thing as a *Wehrbären* or *Schützenadler* anymore; whether here or at the front, they were all just *SS-Schütze* now.

Among the thousand questions about his parents, home, and school life, the trio of *SS* inquisitors had asked Erich to name the three of his classmates who were least dedicated to *Führer* and *Volk*. It felt terribly morbid, but the safest answer Erich could think of was to accuse Otto and Uwe, then claim that he didn't know of anyone else. That seemed to placate the *Untersturmführer*, but he knew that many of his peers would have answered differently. The night after the interviews, he tried not to dwell on the many faces that were missing from the table, repeating to himself what was becoming a refrain: *nothing Ehrenzweig could do would make him worse than Hugo.*

On the other side of the train platform, Erich finally spotted Karl, Felix, Richard, and Bardulf huddled in a circle, but he couldn't bring himself to go join them. They were leaving and he was staying here. He wondered if he never went over there, would Karl come to say goodbye or would he just get on the train without another word?

Standing by himself, Erich wished he could melt down and slip between the wooden planks at his feet. The eager voices that chattered all around him were driving him mad and he couldn't wait for the train to come drown them out with its horn and clatter.

Off to the side, the BDM girls had assembled into neat ranks. At their vanguard, Frau Murr leaned against a pair of crutches. Her whole leg was bound in a splint. Erich had not expected her to survive the night she had brought Otto and Uwe to the bathhouse, but clearly he had underestimated her resilience. The official story was that she had fallen down the stairs, which, admittedly, was true.

Johanna stood not far from Frau Murr's side. She looked desperate to run over and bid farewell to Karl, but she was not allowed to leave the BDM ranks. The girls were there to wave at the train, not to say goodbye. Erich averted his eyes before Johanna could catch him looking. She had hardly spoken to him since the morning after Heinrich's failed escape when he had told her what had happened at the bathhouse the night before.

"The other boys have been talking. They say Otto and Uwe were..." Erich had trailed off, unwilling to go further.

"*Warme Brüder*," Johanna finished for him.

"Do you really think that's true?"

"Of course I think it's true," she scoffed. "Did you ever not?"

"No!" Erich said. "I mean— I didn't— they were close but I didn't think— that's, it's not natural."

"Name one thing in this place that is," Johanna said. "They're dead, idiot. They're seventeen years old and they're dead. *That's* not natural."

Erich hardly heard her. He was still thinking about what she'd said. It was almost a relief to hear Johanna confirm the rumors. She always knew the truth about things like that. Here was an explanation, something Hugo's crimes had come with precious few of. If Otto and Uwe really were homosexuals, Erich could understand why *Oberführer* Ehrenzweig might be troubled by having them at the school. Their punishment had been harsh, horrible, but at least there was *some* reason.

"Are you even listening to me?" Johanna snapped.

When Erich didn't respond, she rammed her fist into his stomach. Erich squealed and doubled over. He was soft. It had been a long time since his *Wehrbär* days.

Johanna kept going. "Do you want to know what else isn't natural? What you're doing to Heinrich. Don't think I don't know. You should have seen him last night. He was bleeding, Erich. He didn't have any cuts or scratches or anything. It was just coming out of his pores. Like sweat."

"That's not my fault!" Erich protested. "If you hadn't made me open that door I never would have had to use him to close it. Besides, I didn't do this to him. I didn't put that mark on his forehead. That was Hugo. Now Hugo's gone. That's one thing I did do and you and Heinrich should be thanking me for it."

"You're not even listening to yourself anymore," Johanna said. "You've got so obsessed with Hugo you can't tell that he's not the one hurting Heinrich anymore. It's you, Erich. It's you now, and I don't know how to make you stop."

Whether she knew how to or not, Johanna did try. From then on, whenever she saw Erich was coming to visit Heinrich, she would block the corridor and beg him to stay away. Erich hated that. He hated the way it made him feel when he then shoved her aside. It wasn't at all fair. He didn't have a choice about whether or not to visit Heinrich. That decision had been made for him years ago. By Hugo. Erich could no more keep himself away than Johanna could stop him. Still, as he sat in his corner and soaked, the thing he hated most was himself.

With every day that had passed, Erich had grown less and less certain that he had done the right thing on the mountaintop. He had assumed that the end of Hugo would mean the end of death and suffering in Rouhhenberg, but everywhere there were signs that this was not true. Despite all the fighting that had taken place on the bathhouse steps, the myriad smokestacks that wrapped the tower did not stop their blackened spewing for even one day. And every night, just as before, the huge *Nassfuchs* class gathered to march down into the bathhouse.

Erich did not envy those boys. When he spoke to them in groups, they would assert that everything was still normal, but that was an obvious lie. The infirmary brimmed with poor, retching children and the few *Nassfüchsen* that Erich spoke to alone told him familiar stories of cold and sickening blood. Whatever *Oberführer* Ehrenzweig was doing, it wasn't working.

Erich didn't understand. Ehrenzweig had despised

Hugo. His crimes should have been the first thing the new headmaster put a stop to. Instead, it was the one part of Hugo's Rouhhenberg that he had allowed to continue. The fact that it was producing no patronage at all somehow made the whole thing worse.

Though it sickened him to think about it, Erich finally understood what Hugo had meant that night in his office. *Everything that happens here would have happened just the same somewhere else.* Maybe he had been right. Maybe Rouhhenberg truly was an expression on evil not the cause of it. That was more or less what Johanna had been saying all along. That Hugo was not the real problem. That he was just a leech sucking on the hind leg of a greater beast, of Hitler. Erich had never wanted to believe her, but it was harder now than ever before to find an alternative explanation.

Mercifully, a voice interrupted. "*Schütze* Fiehler!"

Erich looked up and Karl's wide, grinning face filled his view, a reddening island in a sea of field grey.

"Were you planning on sneaking off without saying goodbye?" Karl asked. "That would be even worse than when you turned sixteen without telling us."

"N-no," Erich mumbled. He glanced down at his feet. "I was just about to come and say—"

Karl slapped Erich on the shoulder. "Hey! It was just a joke."

"Yeah."

"So you're staying then," Karl chugged along. "Those three either really liked you or really hated you." He clapped his hands together excitedly. "Oh, I forgot!" Erich couldn't tell if Karl's ruddy mood was genuine or forced. "We've been taking bets," Karl said. "Where do you think they'll send us, east or west? Killing Amis or Bolsheviks?"

"They wouldn't tell you?"

"No." Karl wiggled his eyebrows. "It's a surprise."

"I see. It'll be west then," Erich answered. He wanted to add, *it's already lost in the east,* but thought better of it.

Most of the boys in Rouhhenberg—Karl included—had dismissed the American landing the week prior with derision, but Erich had a squirming feeling in his gut that with or without Herr Jensson's doorway, Doktor Kammer's last words were about to come true. *They will leave us nothing in defeat.*

"Americans it'll be!" Karl shouted.

The blaring horn of the approaching train drowned out anything else he had to say. Erich stayed quiet while the boys cheered its arrival.

"Take care of Johanna, will you?" Karl said once the noise had settled.

Erich nodded, not certain that would be possible or necessary.

"And... I don't know how you managed to piss her off, but you should think about fixing it if you don't want to spend the rest of your time here alone."

"It's not that simple," Erich said.

"Who cares? I bet she doesn't. Will you think about it at least?"

"Fine," Erich groaned.

"Good," Karl said. "I should get going then. There's a train waiting to take me to... god knows where. Hell maybe."

"We've taken that train already," Erich said under his breath.

"Huh?"

"Nothing."

"Alright then," Karl laughed. "*Heil Hitler*, my friend."

It took Erich a while to think of what to say in response. "Stay alive!" he eventually blurted out, but Karl was already gone.

The train spat out a thick glob of smoke and the wheels churned into motion. It rattled off down the tracks, growing smaller and smaller until all that was left of it was a dark stain across the sky. By the time it dissipated, all the other boys had gone and Erich was alone.

He didn't need his jacket anymore, so he finally took it off and sat down on the planks to watch the little black cars carry the remaining few up the mountain. He imagined that if he stayed on the platform long enough another train would arrive. It would chug to a stop and out would come a fresh crop of nervous boys with callouses on their necks. Erich could hide among them. He could start over, make new friends, and discover the castle like it were his first time, unburdened and unashamed.

After a while, a train did pass. But it did not stop and the only trace it left behind was a rush of hot wind. Erich's stomach knotted with hunger and he had sweat so much that his newly issued *SS* uniform was soaked. It was time to go. Erich took one last look down the tracks and then began the trek up, wondering at what precise moment everything had gone wrong.

# CHAPTER THIRTY-SIX

Erich stepped up onto the crowded train platform and groped around for somewhere to stand. Everywhere clusters of boys had formed, but he didn't feel like he belonged to any of them. Even for June the weather was hot, yet Erich had worn his thick jacket anyway. He had itched and sweated for the whole drive down the mountain, but still refused to take it off. A farewell like today's was supposed to be wintery. It was an affair for fur coats and steaming breath. Instead, two hundred Rouhhenberg boys would go off to war under a bright and furious sun.

Not Erich. In a few minutes, the train would come to carry away three quarters of his classmates and leave him behind. The castle's hallways already felt terribly empty without Doktor Kammer or Otto and Uwe. Tomorrow they would be as barren as they were the day Erich had arrived. But they wouldn't be the same.

In the month since Hugo's ouster, *Oberführer* Ehrenzweig had wasted no time remaking Rouhhenberg as he had always wanted it to be. He had immediately summoned up three officers from Berlin, *Untersturmführer* Eichel, Dunst, and Dürr, to assist with character interviews and the necessary rites that would induct the boys into the

*SS.* There was no such thing as a *Wehrbären* or *Schützenadler* anymore; whether here or at the front, they were all just *SS-Schütze* now.

Among the thousand questions about his parents, home, and school life, the trio of *SS* inquisitors had asked Erich to name the three of his classmates who were least dedicated to *Führer* and *Volk*. It felt terribly morbid, but the safest answer Erich could think of was to accuse Otto and Uwe, then claim that he didn't know of anyone else. That seemed to placate the *Untersturmführer*, but he knew that many of his peers would have answered differently. The night after the interviews, he tried not to dwell on the many faces that were missing from the table, repeating to himself what was becoming a refrain: *nothing Ehrenzweig could do would make him worse than Hugo.*

On the other side of the train platform, Erich finally spotted Karl, Felix, Richard, and Bardulf huddled in a circle, but he couldn't bring himself to go join them. They were leaving and he was staying here. He wondered if he never went over there, would Karl come to say goodbye or would he just get on the train without another word?

Standing by himself, Erich wished he could melt down and slip between the wooden planks at his feet. The eager voices that chattered all around him were driving him mad and he couldn't wait for the train to come drown them out with its horn and clatter.

Off to the side, the BDM girls had assembled into neat ranks. At their vanguard, Frau Murr leaned against a pair of crutches. Her whole leg was bound in a splint. Erich had not expected her to survive the night she had brought Otto and Uwe to the bathhouse, but clearly he had underestimated her resilience. The official story was that she had fallen down the stairs, which, admittedly, was true.

Johanna stood not far from Frau Murr's side. She looked desperate to run over and bid farewell to Karl, but she was not allowed to leave the BDM ranks. The girls were there to wave at the train, not to say goodbye. Erich averted his eyes before Johanna could catch him looking. She had hardly spoken to him since the morning after Heinrich's failed escape when he had told her what had happened at the bathhouse the night before.

"The other boys have been talking. They say Otto and Uwe were..." Erich had trailed off, unwilling to go further.

"*Warme Brüder*," Johanna finished for him.

"Do you really think that's true?"

"Of course I think it's true," she scoffed. "Did you ever not?"

"No!" Erich said. "I mean— I didn't— they were close but I didn't think— that's, it's not natural."

"Name one thing in this place that is," Johanna said. "They're dead, idiot. They're seventeen years old and they're dead. *That's* not natural."

Erich hardly heard her. He was still thinking about what she'd said. It was almost a relief to hear Johanna confirm the rumors. She always knew the truth about things like that. Here was an explanation, something Hugo's crimes had come with precious few of. If Otto and Uwe really were homosexuals, Erich could understand why *Oberführer* Ehrenzweig might be troubled by having them at the school. Their punishment had been harsh, horrible, but at least there was *some* reason.

"Are you even listening to me?" Johanna snapped.

When Erich didn't respond, she rammed her fist into his stomach. Erich squealed and doubled over. He was soft. It had been a long time since his *Wehrbär* days.

Johanna kept going. "Do you want to know what else isn't natural? What you're doing to Heinrich. Don't think I don't know. You should have seen him last night. He was bleeding, Erich. He didn't have any cuts or scratches or anything. It was just coming out of his pores. Like sweat."

"That's not my fault!" Erich protested. "If you hadn't made me open that door I never would have had to use him to close it. Besides, I didn't do this to him. I didn't put that mark on his forehead. That was Hugo. Now Hugo's gone. That's one thing I did do and you and Heinrich should be thanking me for it."

"You're not even listening to yourself anymore," Johanna said. "You've got so obsessed with Hugo you can't tell that he's not the one hurting Heinrich anymore. It's you, Erich. It's you now, and I don't know how to make you stop."

Whether she knew how to or not, Johanna did try. From then on, whenever she saw Erich was coming to visit Heinrich, she would block the corridor and beg him to stay away. Erich hated that. He hated the way it made him feel when he then shoved her aside. It wasn't at all fair. He didn't have a choice about whether or not to visit Heinrich. That decision had been made for him years ago. By Hugo. Erich could no more keep himself away than Johanna could stop him. Still, as he sat in his corner and soaked, the thing he hated most was himself.

With every day that had passed, Erich had grown less and less certain that he had done the right thing on the mountaintop. He had assumed that the end of Hugo would mean the end of death and suffering in Rouhhenberg, but everywhere there were signs that this was not true. Despite all the fighting that had taken place on the bathhouse steps, the myriad smokestacks that wrapped the tower did not stop their blackened spewing for even one day. And every night, just as before, the huge *Nassfuchs* class gathered to march down into the bathhouse.

Erich did not envy those boys. When he spoke to them in groups, they would assert that everything was still normal, but that was an obvious lie. The infirmary brimmed with poor, retching children and the few *Nassfüchsen* that Erich spoke to alone told him familiar stories of cold and sickening blood. Whatever *Oberführer* Ehrenzweig was doing, it wasn't working.

Erich didn't understand. Ehrenzweig had despised Hugo. His crimes should have been the first thing the new headmaster put a stop to. Instead, it was the one part of Hugo's Rouhhenberg that he had allowed to continue. The fact that it was producing no patronage at all somehow made the whole thing worse.

Though it sickened him to think about it, Erich finally understood what Hugo had meant that night in his office. *Everything that happens here would have happened just the same somewhere else.* Maybe he had been right. Maybe Rouhhenberg truly was an expression on evil not the cause of it. That was more or less what Johanna had been saying all along. That Hugo was not the real problem. That he was just a leech sucking on the hind leg of a greater beast, of Hitler. Erich had never wanted to believe her, but it was harder now than ever before to find an alternative explanation.

Mercifully, a voice interrupted. "*Schütze* Fiehler!"

Erich looked up and Karl's wide, grinning face filled his view, a reddening island in a sea of field grey.

"Were you planning on sneaking off without saying goodbye?" Karl asked. "That would be even worse than when you turned sixteen without telling us."

"N-no," Erich mumbled. He glanced down at his feet. "I was just about to come and say—"

Karl slapped Erich on the shoulder. "Hey! It was just a joke."

"Yeah."

"So you're staying then," Karl chugged along. "Those three either really liked you or really hated you." He clapped his hands together excitedly. "Oh, I forgot!" Erich couldn't tell if Karl's ruddy mood was genuine or forced. "We've been taking bets," Karl said. "Where do you think they'll send us, east or west? Killing Amis or Bolsheviks?"

"They wouldn't tell you?"

"No." Karl wiggled his eyebrows. "It's a surprise."

"I see. It'll be west then," Erich answered. He wanted to add, *it's already lost in the east*, but thought better of it. Most of the boys in Rouhhenberg—Karl included—had dismissed the American landing the week prior with derision, but Erich had a squirming feeling in his gut that with or without Herr Jensson's doorway, Doktor Kammer's last words were about to come true. *They will leave us nothing in defeat.*

"Americans it'll be!" Karl shouted.

The blaring horn of the approaching train drowned out anything else he had to say. Erich stayed quiet while the boys cheered its arrival.

"Take care of Johanna, will you?" Karl said once the noise had settled.

Erich nodded, not certain that would be possible or necessary.

"And… I don't know how you managed to piss her off, but you should think about fixing it if you don't want to spend the rest of your time here alone."

"It's not that simple," Erich said.

"Who cares? I bet she doesn't. Will you think about it at least?"

"Fine," Erich groaned.

"Good," Karl said. "I should get going then. There's a train waiting to take me to… god knows where. Hell maybe."

"We've taken that train already," Erich said under his breath.

"Huh?"

"Nothing."

"Alright then," Karl laughed. "*Heil Hitler*, my friend."

It took Erich a while to think of what to say in response. "Stay alive!" he eventually blurted out, but Karl was already gone.

The train spat out a thick glob of smoke and the wheels churned into motion. It rattled off down the tracks, growing smaller and smaller until all that was left of it was a dark stain across the sky. By the time it dissipated, all the other boys had gone and Erich was alone.

He didn't need his jacket anymore, so he finally took it

off and sat down on the planks to watch the little black cars carry the remaining few up the mountain. He imagined that if he stayed on the platform long enough another train would arrive. It would chug to a stop and out would come a fresh crop of nervous boys with callouses on their necks. Erich could hide among them. He could start over, make new friends, and discover the castle like it were his first time, unburdened and unashamed.

After a while, a train did pass. But it did not stop and the only trace it left behind was a rush of hot wind. Erich's stomach knotted with hunger and he had sweat so much that his newly issued *SS* uniform was soaked. It was time to go. Erich took one last look down the tracks and then began the trek up, wondering at what precise moment everything had gone wrong.

# CHAPTER THIRTY-SEVEN

The emptiness closed in around him and Erich couldn't breathe. Twisted statues warped and the floor's red and gold carpeting enveloped his vision as if it were the sky. Erich doubled over. He gripped his knees and sucked in breath after breath. The air stank of blood and brine. He wanted to run away and hide, but the secret corridors that had become his second home could offer no refuge. They belonged to Heinrich now.

Erich could not bear to look up. One moment he had been walking down the hall and the next it had overwhelmed him. The void of it was too much to handle. Doktor Kammer was gone, Otto and Uwe were dead, and now even Karl had left. When was the last time the castle had been so silent? Erich remembered that Uwe had once said something about "the privilege of watching Rouhhenberg fill up." He'd never said anything about watching it empty.

Erich tried to push himself up from the wall—he had to; he was late and *Untersturmführer* Dürr would be furious with him—but he couldn't keep his balance. He lurched forward and almost tripped. Maybe it wouldn't matter if he was late. What punishment was there left for him? A beating? Demotion? Expulsion? A bullet to the head like Otto? Erich didn't care. He slipped down and buried his face in the grey folds of his trousers.

But something wasn't right. He pulled his head back. His uniform was crisp. He had just trekked up from the train station; it should have been wrinkled and sweat-stained. Maybe that had been yesterday? Or the day before? He couldn't be sure. Erich looked up and peered at the clock hanging in the room on the other side of the wall. It was quarter past one in the afternoon. That was too early. That wasn't right. No. Or yes. It had been at least two days, he decided. He had just finished class. *Oberführer* Ehrenzweig had lectured for hours, but Erich couldn't remember a single thing he had said.

"You look terrible, Fiehler."

Erich slowly peeled his head up to see who had spoken. He shuddered to see that it was Fritz. He had to draw on all the strength he had not to burst into tears at the sight of him. Why, out of everyone, had they chosen the worst other boy to remain?

"Go ahead," Erich moaned, ready for whatever tortures Fritz had in mind.

Fritz held out his hand. "Have you eaten?"

It had to be a trap. If he took that hand, he would find himself slammed into the ceiling floating upside down on a surge of patronage. But then Erich remembered that Fritz had barely any of that left. He probably couldn't even muster the patronage to lift a balloon. Like Erich, he was defective. That must be why they were here.

"I... haven't," Erich mumbled.

"Come on then," Fritz said. "We'll miss lunch if we don't get there soon."

Erich ignored Fritz's hand and scrambled up on his own.

"We're just about the only two left," Fritz said as he set down the hall.

Erich scurried after him. "What?"

"In our year. We're the only boys left." He thwacked Erich on the back of the head. "What's gotten into you, Fiehler? You're acting even dimmer than usual."

"I- I'm not sure," Erich stammered.

"I get it," Fritz said. "You're wishing you'd gotten on that train the other day."

Erich didn't have the energy to disagree. "Yeah, that's it," he said.

Fritz laughed half-heartedly. "I do too a little. But I'm not stupid. It doesn't make a difference if they headed east or west. They're all dead either way."

"You shouldn't say things like that," Erich mumbled.

"Why? Are you gonna run off and tell the *Untersturmführer*?"

"No."

"I'm just being realistic," Fritz said. "The war's almost lost. Even on the news they can hardly find a way not to say it. They're not fooling anyone with this *strategic withdrawal* business. I'm telling you, you and I need to start practicing our English."

"You're insane," Erich said. "Even if all that's true, *Oberführer* Ehrenzweig won't just open the gates and let us out to make smalltalk with the enemy. He's too stubborn for that."

Fritz laughed. "You'd be surprised..." they turned the corner and stumbled into a gaggle of *Nassfüchsen*. Immediately Fritz affected a giant grin. "You'd be surprised how fast they'll turn and run with Rouhhenberg boys on the front line. I guarantee it. The advance will break before the year is out. It'll be no time at all before even the *stubborn ones* are ready to surrender."

"I think you're underestimating him— I mean, the stubborn ones," Erich said.

"We'll see, won't we?"

They followed the *Nassfüchsen* into the lunchroom in Weiss hall, where two dozen boys congregated around the radio set, shoveling down meatballs and boiled potatoes.

Erich and Fritz slid in at the end of the table just in time for the news. Erich felt better once he had swallowed a mouthful. The setup reminded Erich of the days when they had been underclassmen themselves. It was hard to believe it had been almost five years since he had sat on the cold floor of the *Nassfuchs* lounge, fresh from the baths, and let himself fill up with all the hope, pride, and belonging that could squeeze through the grille of a radio.

Now there was nothing but ill-disguised bad news and rallying cries that could no longer inspire him. The broadcaster spouted at length about the vengeful hail of rockets that the *Führer* had unleashed on England, but Erich heard nothing about movement in the west. He assumed the worst. Someone prodded Erich on the shoulder and he flinched, but it was only Fritz.

"Pass the salt, will you?" he said.

"Oh, yeah, sure," Erich mumbled.

In his head, Erich still imagined Fritz as the smug bully who had tried to steal his stethoscope on their first day, but that was not the boy who sat next to him. Fritz's hair was tangled mess that flared out in all directions and the dark bags under his eyes blended seamlessly into bruises that ran from his right cheek down to his jaw. Patronage was everything in Rouhhenberg and with no access to Heinrich, Fritz must have become little more than a punching bag. Maybe that's why he'd turned so pessimistic.

"I want to show you something," Erich said.

Fritz cocked his head. "Huh?"

"It's not far. Come on."

"But I'm still eating," Fritz whined. "And they're just about to start the music."

"It'll be worth it," Erich said. "I promise."

They abandoned their half-filled plates and headed outside into the courtyard. In the early days, Erich had found his way through the secret corridors with the landmarks he could see on the other side of the walls. But now he needed to do the opposite. From the outside, he scanned the maze of narrow passageways that lived between the walls until he found Heinrich's three left turns. Still voicing his complaints, Fritz followed sluggishly as Erich traced the way past the bathhouse and over towards a little garden that was tucked away on the far side of Bittrich Hall.

"This is a nice spot, isn't it?" Erich said. He gestured to a stone bench. "Sit down."

Fritz moaned. "Please tell me we didn't just miss half of lunch so we could go flower picking."

"I told you to sit," Erich snapped.

He intended just to nudge him, but Erich lost control of his patronage and instead slammed Fritz down against the bench.

"Oww," Fritz squealed.

Erich pushed harder, but there was no resistance from Fritz. Fritz had learned his own helplessness well. Even so, Erich couldn't stop. His heart thrummed and blood tingled at his fingertips. He remembered the shame of all the beatings in the *Wehrbären*, of hanging from the tapestry in Rathe Hall or grappling with Anton for his stethoscope. He'd only intended to provoke Fritz into reaching for his patronage, but it felt too good not to keep going. Fury fed into power and back again. The stone bench under Fritz groaned and threatened to crack.

"Stop!" Fritz yelled. "I'm sorry, I'm sorry. I shouldn't have—"

Erich sealed his mouth shut. Fritz's lips ballooned but none of his squawking escaped from between them. He thrashed and flailed until he fell off the bench and rolled onto the ground, but Erich didn't relent. Fritz sank into the grass. He squeezed his eyes shut as the dirt began to seep over his face. His squirming only dug him deeper, until at last, with the mulch tightening around him like quicksand, Fritz broke.

He reached for the last meager thread of patronage that

remained to him and hurled it at Erich. Shock rippled over Fritz's face as the blow, though easily deflected, did not fizzle out. It must have felt incredible. For the first time in more than a year, Fritz would have had no upsurge of nausea or weakness in his limbs. Here, separated from Heinrich by little more than a wall and a short distance, he could access what had long since abandoned him.

Erich let up for a moment and allowed Fritz through just enough to feel his heels slip back through the dirt, but that turned out not to be necessary. The second blow lifted Erich up off his feet and tossed him onto the grass. Cackling with delight, Fritz tore himself up from the ground, spitting patronage and dirt in all directions.

Erich laughed with him. They grappled and tugged and rolled about until neither of them had any strength left to stand and they collapsed, spent, onto a heap of uprooted flowers.

**\*\*\***

The curtain rings slid back with a shrill rattling. Erich cringed at the noise. He wished he could be silent. In fact, he had tried not to come at all. But even after all the roughhousing with Fritz, Erich had not been able to sleep. He was exhausted in a way that no amount of rest could fix. He needed patronage—raw and up close.

As he had lay in bed, fighting over whether or not to come, Erich had promised himself that Heinrich would be asleep, Johanna would be gone, and he would be able to slip in and out without anyone knowing he was there. But even before he pulled back the curtain, Erich could see that he would not be that lucky. Heinrich was awake. He knew the curtain's sound so well by now that the moment he heard it, Heinrich slithered back against the wall and pulled his filthy blankets up over his head. Erich wondered how long it had been since Johanna had replaced the boy's linens. He promised himself to bring fresh ones next time.

For once, Erich wished his eyes would leave the world opaque. He knew he shouldn't look through the covers that Heinrich had thrown over his swollen face, but the sight drew him in. Heinrich shut his eyes and tugged his knees in closer to him. Dark red blotches mottled his skin, permanent since the night he had almost escaped. In the weeks that followed, Erich had made a hundred attempts to remove the blemishes. But eventually he conceded that it was impossible. It was a closed system. The patronage Erich needed to heal Heinrich's wounds would first have to be sucked from him.

Erich slumped into his usual spot in the corner and stared at his feet. He breathed in and let the warm, soft sensation flood from the back of his neck down to his toes. A nauseating, mineral smell hung over the cubby. The mist was almost thick enough to see. Erich chewed on his lip until his own blood spurted into his mouth. He swallowed and let it mask the smell and taste of Heinrich's.

"She's going to kill you, you know," Heinrich whispered.

Erich clenched his jaw. This was not a good time for Heinrich to make him angry.

"Who, Johanna?" he snapped.

"No," Heinrich said, his voice flat. "You know who I mean."

Erich shivered. He wished he could curl up like Heinrich, but that would make him look weak.

"I'm not afraid of a one-armed woman," he said. "Not any more than I'm afraid of you."

Heinrich did not respond, leaving Erich nothing but his own anxiety and frustration to stew on. He was so tired. He finally felt ready to sleep, but he feared that if he did he would wake up with a knife in his belly. The narrow walls of the cubby mocked him. Every time he visited they felt a little tighter. It was as if some cruel god were pushing his side of the room and Heinrich's a few centimeters closer whenever Erich wasn't looking.

Erich pressed his cheek against the rough stone and peered up. The magazine cover that Johanna had put on the wall grinned down at him. In the dark, he could barely make out the figure on its cover, but his imagination filled in the forms. Shirley Temple's teeth hung over her lips like fangs. Her red cheeks were pulled up as if by strings into a tortured smile. Her eyes radiated scorn and superiority. She leered at him with the same haughty look that Johanna had given him from atop her bicycle on the day they first met.

Erich hated that. For years she had flashed him that same arrogant and sanctimonious glare, always paired with some terrible accusation that couldn't possibly be true. She barely ever had evidence of anything and yet it was obvious now that so much of what she'd said over the years was true. It made Erich want to scream.

She had been right about Hugo. The choking darkness that spewed from the castle's highest tower had not come from him. Nor had it come from under the mountain. The sickness was, as Johanna had always said, passed down from the top. From Hitler. Rouhhenberg was just one of the hydra's thousandfold heads, perhaps not even the most important or vicious one. And when Erich had cut down Hugo, *Oberführer* Ehrenzweig had risen to replace him. Johanna was right about Erich too. He was not blameless. He had been made part of this place in a way that he would never escape.

Without getting up, Erich tore the smirking poster from the wall and shredded it into a hundred tiny pieces in the air. The scraps rained down like confetti. He pulled down Heinrich's bookshelf and it crashed against the stone. Erich's shoddy craftsmanship splintered apart. Pages fluttered as the books tumbled out and spilled over the stone. All Heinrich could do was burrow deeper under his blankets and wait out the storm.

Erich stayed in the corner even after he had soaked up

all the patronage he could contain. He didn't want to linger but nor did he really want to drag himself up and leave. When he had no other choice, Erich shuffled home and slammed his face into his pillow. His teeth struck something hard. He stifled a shout and then, jaw aching, peeled himself up to sit on the edge of the bed.

Erich's old stethoscope lay on the pillow. He didn't need to wonder who had put it there. It was the same place Johanna had always left her secret notes. *You broke your promise*, the stethoscope screamed in Aunt Mila's voice. Furious, Erich snatched up the stethoscope and crushed the prongs together so hard he could feel the metal scrape against his finger bones. A scorching pain shot up his wrist like fire in his blood. He dropped the stethoscope with a yelp and it splatted against the floor, half molten. The cord's leather sheath smoked and burned until there was nothing left but a puddle of brass.

His hands empty, Erich's anger flared out as quickly as it had come. He glanced around, certain he had woken someone, but the room was quiet. Unable to hold himself upright for another minute, Erich fell back onto the bed and within seconds was asleep. He dreamed of black fingers around his neck and a long arm that ended in nothing.

# CHAPTER THIRTY-EIGHT

To Erich, no day seemed all that different from another anymore. The sense of purpose that once permeated the castle had disappeared along with its architect. Even the adults seemed lost. Erich could almost feel sorry for *Oberführer* Ehrenzweig. He had waited so long for the chance to rebuild Rouhhenberg in the image of Hitler rather than Hugo that there was no longer anything left to work with. The castle was gutted and the *Führer's* grand dream for Germany looked farther away than it ever had.

In September, the *Nassfüchsen*—the biggest group of them that Rouhhenberg had ever seen—headed down into the mountain. None of them returned. Erich thought for certain that would mean the end for the bathhouse, but the very next day a new class of *Nassfüchsen* arrived by train, this time only seven in number. Erich couldn't decide if the smaller enrollment was deliberate or if the *Führer* had simply sent over the last eligible boys left in Germany.

Every night, the radio blared out announcements mandating that all remaining men, ages sixteen to sixty, report to training for the *Volkssturm* militia, a furious people's uprising that vowed to hold fast at all costs should the enemy breach Germany's borders. Erich thought at first that the directive might apply to him and Fritz, but he never heard a word about it from the three *Obersturmführers*. Perhaps they weren't wanted. That was why he was still here, after all. There was no one left in Rouhhenberg but the rejects. There were the children and the invalids; the traitors; the prisoners and the guards. In a way, Erich was all of these things at once.

That winter, good news came at last. The whole castle swelled on the reports of a devastating Wehrmacht offensive through the Ardennes. But two weeks later, the broadcasters were still rehashing the same events. According to Fritz, this meant the push had stalled out. Fritz always seemed to know just a little more than the official story and Erich suspected that his sources were not all strictly legal.

The lack of information grew so maddening that Erich was himself tempted to surreptitiously tune into the longwave BBC, but the thought of it reminded him too much of Johanna. These days, he avoided anything that would do that.

Erich was no longer sure what to think about Hitler, but he knew for certain that he didn't want the enemy to win. And with the official radio's help, Erich tried to stay optimistic. Germany was poised to win the war, they radio promised again and again. The enemy advance had slowed. Their supply lines were subtly flawed and ready to break. Their specific movements were deemed so trivial they hardly deserved mention. Instead there were stories to tell. Ordinary Germans were swaddling grenades with their bodies and braving enemy fire to deliver the payloads of their *Panzerfäuste*.

Yet whenever Erich began to lull himself into believing, Fritz would laugh and pull out his map.

"Last night, the woman who burned down her own house after filling it up with GIs. Where was that?"

"Outside Frankfurt, I think," Erich said.

"Right, Riedstadt." Fritz circled it with his pencil.

"What about the night before?"

"There was a bombing. The Luftwaffe took out an airfield in Orléans."

"Of course they did," Fritz said. "What else do remember?"

"There was a bit about how the enemy uses armored divisions with no ammunition to frighten Germans into surrendering, but I don't think they named any places."

"Not true," Fritz said. "They said the *Panzerfaust* is so simple to use that a group of *Volksschule* teachers were able to hold off a Russian armored advance for two days. A group of *Volksschule* teachers in—"

"Schwedt," Erich blurted out.

"Exactly." Fritz circled there too. "Two weeks ago we were turning the Russians back in Poland. Now they're getting blown up by German schoolteachers. And in the west we said Reinstadt, right? Two weeks ago it was Koblenz. It goes on and on."

"Maybe it'll turn around," Erich said. "What about Karl and the others? They have to count for something."

"Karl is dead, idiot," Fritz gloated. "Don't you remember what happened to that cockroach he liked so much?"

"Mathilde."

"It's an insect. No one cares what its name was. The point is it's a splatter of bug guts now. Karl couldn't stop a bullet from a pistol and he certainly can't stop a shell from a tank. Those boys aren't going to save us. The V-2s aren't going to save us. The war's over. We lost. That's not worth worrying about anymore. The question you and I need to answer—the reason I'm keeping this map—is who is going to reach Rouhhenberg first?"

Erich remembered what Heinrich had promised him about Isabel. *She's going to kill you, you know?*

"I hope it's the Russians," he said.

Fritz laughed for a long time. "No, I don't think you do."

\*\*\*

The first morning in May, Erich stumbled out into the lounge and found that the radio was gone.

"It's done then," Fritz whispered in his ear.

"What do we do?" Erich asked.

"We wait."

The three *Obersturmführer* were gone—fled, Fritz claimed—but Ehrenzweig remained. He acted as though nothing had changed and dismissed any questions from the students, sending them off to class as usual. For a week, they subsisted on rumors until at last the *Oberführer* called an assembly in the chapel.

The high tables were cleared away and two lines of *SS* enlisted men stood where they had been. The boys gathered in ranks and stared up at the empty podium on the balcony. They had to wait several anxious minutes before Ehrenzweig appeared in the doorway. He walked all the way to the edge where the balcony dropped off without a railing, then paused a long while before speaking.

"Comrades, I have grave news tonight," Ehrenzweig said. "Seven days ago, in a fierce battle on the steps of the Reich Chancellery, the *Führer* was mortally wounded. They say that he fought until there was no breath left in his body, but knowing him as we do, I imagine it was a little longer even than that."

Ehrenzweig never raised his voice, but it may as well have been a bullhorn over the deathly silence that gripped the chapel.

"He loved us, all of us in this chamber and beyond. I have no doubt that we will carry the lack of him with us for the rest of our lives. But, please, never let that sadness overwhelm the joy you have in your memories. Never forget how lucky you are. You lived in his time. No German born hereafter will be able to say that.

"So many of you are too young to remember life

before the *Führer*, but I do. There was no justice then. Like fools, we had settled for slavery. We imagined that the chains on our wrists were iron. Hitler showed us the truth. He showed us that Germany's shackles were nothing but words scribbled on paper, and with will alone, he smashed them.

"He severed the thousandfold tentacles of international Jewry, and by doing so, he proved that those who live only to oppress and control are not invincible. *They can be punished.* And for that, Adolf Hitler made an enemy of the entire world.

"They came for him. They all came for him. They descended on Germany with fire and steel and most of all lucre. They thought we were weak. They assumed we would succumb to treachery as we had before. But no. For five years, seven months, and twenty-nine days, the *Führer* held fast. He was a bulwark against the evils that arrayed against us. But now that bulwark is broken. We are alone.

"I must admit that it took this terrible event for me to finally understand the greatest gift the *Führer* gave to us. Time and time again, he gave us the strength and conviction to hope. No matter what, he held to the unwavering certainty that tomorrow would be better than today. Now, for the first time in more than twenty years, I no longer believe that is true. I can... I can no longer see any path to victory."

Over the course of his speech, Ehrenzweig's shoulders had sunk. He cast his eyes down until his face was all but hidden in his silver hair. For a painful minute he said nothing. Finally, he lifted himself back up to continue.

"There has been a surrender at the highest level," he said. "The war, for us, is over. May Germany one day again find peace." Ehrenzweig shut his eyes. He looked as though he could not believe what he was saying. "For we here, I have likewise made an arrangement. In five days time we will open the doors of this chapel. When that moment comes, I expect each and every one of you to—"

The sound of Ehrenzweig's voice cut off. His mouth continued to open and close but no words escaped. He cleared his throat and begin again. The result was the same. Erich glanced to his left and right, wondering if one of the other boys had done it, but everyone else was flashing each other the same confused looks. Ehrenzweig stomped his foot and jabbed one finger at the assembled crowd, screaming mutely. When nothing changed, he drew his pistol and fired five times into the air, but even that could not crack the silence.

The *SS* men on the sides of the hall hesitated to break their ranks, unsure whom to blame for the disruption. Before they could make up their minds, a loud creak broke the quiet. The chapel doors were opening. Even Ehrenzweig paused his ranting to stare as they slowly pushed apart. A boy stood in the gap, a *Nassfuchs* by his age. Erich thought he might be one of those who hadn't returned from the mines in the fall, but his soaked and tattered uniform was the pale brown of the *Jungvolk* not the *SS* field grey they wore now. Water dribbled from his fingertips.

"That's not possible," Fritz whispered in Erich's ear.

"What do you mean, who is it?"

"Don't you recognize him?" Fritz said. "It's your old friend. It's Walther."

Erich was ashamed to realize that he couldn't summon up exactly what Walther had looked like. He remembered the glasses and the pouch he'd always worn at his waist, but the face behind them was murky. It seemed like those days had been so long ago. If Fritz was right and this newcomer really was Walther, then he hadn't aged at all. He was as young as he had been the day he had gone down into the mines.

"Are you certain?" Erich asked.

"Absolutely," Fritz said.

The longer he stared, the more Erich had to agree. It was Walther, or at least it wore his face. He wondered if everything about him was the same. Had he carried back the enthusiasm and hopefulness that he and Erich had once shared? Did his life begin and end with the Hitler Youth and its glowing promise for fatherland and future? Did he know nothing of wars and blood and guilt? Erich knew he should be worried about what Walther's return could mean, but all he could feel was an envy so corrosive he thought it would hollow out his chest.

None of the other boys looked like they recognized him. That struck Erich as odd until he remembered that he and Fritz were the only ones old enough to have known Walther. Perhaps Ehrenzweig recognized him as well, but that did not stop him from resuming his mute shrieking. He gestured angrily at the those who had stopped to size up the intruder, but there was nothing they could do.

Before most could even move, Walther had raised both arms and, all at once, lifted the thirty-odd *SS* men into the air. Their limbs contorted as they rose, but never quite enough to break. A collective gasp went up from the *Nassfüchsen*, who had never seen anything like it. For that matter, neither had Erich.

Walther dropped his arms, but the men did not fall. They hung in the air like puppets on tangled strings. He stared at Ehrenzweig and spoke in a slow radiating voice that didn't sound like anything Erich remembered of him.

"You are a coward," Walther said.

Ehrenzweig aimed his pistol at the boy and fired three noiseless shots. Walther didn't move at all as they cracked against the stone around him.

*"Do as cowards do."*

Patronage laced Walther's every word and with it came a suggestion stronger than anything Erich had learned from Otto and Uwe. Though the brunt of it struck Ehrenzweig, Erich had to hold his own arm down to keep it from rising. His lips parted without having been told to.

The aura of silence around the balcony broke and everyone could hear Ehrenzweig whimper as his trembling hand inched towards his face. Erich wished he could look away from the sight of the P38's thin muzzle sliding into Ehrenzweig's mouth, but his neck wouldn't turn. He pulled the trigger, yet there was no shot. The gun was empty.

Walther's face crinkled in a flash of petulance and for a moment Erich was reminded that he really was just a child. Then the look was gone. Steely faced again, Walther shrugged and sent a spasm through Ehrenzweig. It ran up his spine and culminated in a gruesome snap of his neck. He crumpled into a twitching pile at the lip of the balcony.

Only then did Walther let go of the men hanging in the air. They dropped and the room fell quiet. There was nothing but the shuffling sound of entangled soldiers separating themselves from each other. They rose, eyeing Walther warily, but no one seemed willing to challenge him.

"Is the *Führer* a liar?" Walther said.

No one responded.

He asked again, "Is the *Führer* a liar?"

"No," came a voice from the back of the room. Frau Murr pushed through the crowd of boys with her crutches and stepped out closer to Walther than anyone else would dare.

"He has never lied," she said.

"Is the *Führer* a liar?" Walther repeated. He spoke without impatience, prepared to ask as many times as it took to get a reply from the whole room.

"No," Frau Murr replied for the second time. But now she was not alone. Erich could hardly believe it, but Fritz had joined her. When had he become a patriot again?

Walther asked once more, "Is the *Führer* a liar?"

Fritz jabbed an elbow into Erich's ribs.

"No," Erich blurted out.

It didn't matter. The reply had come so thunderously that no one would have been able to tell that Erich hadn't spoken.

"Why then would you disbelieve him?" Walther said. "This traitor says that Berlin is fallen and that Hitler is dead. But that is impossible. Why? Because we know that the *Führer* does not lie. Because if the *Führer* has said that this Reich will last for a thousand years then it will last for a thousand years. If he has said that Germany will win the war, then for him we will win the war.

"I don't care who is coming or in what numbers. It does not matter. We are Germans. We have tried surrender before and the taste was not to our liking!"

The triple *Sieg Heil* that roared out from the crowd had not been heard so loudly in the chapel for years. In it, Erich could almost hear the voices of boys long gone. Karl and Otto and Uwe, but also someone else, a proud boy from Messerich who Erich had thought dead.

When at last the cry dwindled away, Walther bowed his head. Barely audibly at first, he began to sing. Frau Murr joined her voice to his and soon the whole hall rang with the old anthem.

*The rotten bones are trembling,*
*Of the world before the war.*
*Their lies we've smashed,*
*We are victors heretofore.*

*If when all is over,*
*Naught but ruin remain,*
*Ha! The devil may care,*
*We'll build it up again.*

*Let the old wag their fingers,*
*Let them rage, scream, and crack.*
*Though all the world may fight us,*
*Nothing shall hold us back.*

*They won't understand our song,*
*They see only slavery, only war.*

CAMERON LORIS

*While they bicker, we flourish,*
*Let the flag of freedom soar!*

*We march unending onwards,*
*Though all may sink and drown.*
*Freedom began in Germany,*
*And tomorrow the world surrounds.*

# CHAPTER THIRTY-NINE

Once again, Rouhhenberg transformed itself. Everyone who remained, whether young or old, boy or girl, now worked and slept in a short stretch of the castle between the chapel, kitchens, bathhouse, and *Nassfuchs* wing. All else was walled off and day by day they filled the hallways up with countless blockades and traps mined from the Herr Jensson's warehouse. The frenzy of preparations left Erich little time to reflect on what was happening around him. He didn't even realize that he'd turned seventeen until the day after his birthday, but he didn't mind any of that. The worst moments for him were always the ones when he stopped moving long enough to think.

With no authority holding them there, Erich half expected Fritz to bolt. But he remained. Like Erich, he was bound and chained to Heinrich now. Outwardly, Fritz spoke with a blazing conviction to Walther's new order, but when they were alone he changed. He wanted only to maximize his odds for survival, and as before he worked fiendishly to predict the enemy's arrival.

Five days after *Oberführer* Ehrenzweig's announcement, the first trucks—American, to Fritz's relief—appeared in the distance. Some of the boys wanted to rush out immediately to face them, but Walther refused to let anyone past the main gates of the castle. A tent city sprang up around the train station, but it took days of waiting before a lookout spotted the first vehicle winding its way up the muddy road from the base of the mountain. According to him, the small truck had stopped long before reaching the castle's gates and let out a single passenger, a dark-skinned woman who was now making the rest of the journey on foot.

"Whoever she is she doesn't look like she's armed," the lookout said to a small gathering in the chapel. "She probably wants to negotiate."

Erich shuddered. He was more afraid of Isabel than the whole army that had assembled below. The urge to run and hide was almost irrepressible, but he doubted that even the deepest corner of the castle would provide him any sanctuary.

"I know this woman," Walther said. "Don't be fooled by anything she says. She is a savage at heart. You say she is unarmed, but like us she is a weapon herself. She hasn't come to negotiate. She is here to destroy us and she will not be satisfied until our home is rubble, our *Führer* is disgraced, and our patrons are forgotten."

"What can we do?" one of the *Nassfüchsen* asked.

"You don't have to do anything," Walther said. "I am warning you because she is dangerous not because you should be afraid of her. Let her in. Let her come to us. She will say what she's here to say and then I will send her down into the mountain in chains."

In the first few days after Walther's return, his voice had inspired a rapturous awe in the boys, but now they were beginning to inure to it. They clutched timidly at weapons raided from the arsenal, but none of them were really trained to use them. Most were in the awkward span where Erich wasn't sure if they would be better off defending themselves with a gun or with patronage. The adults held themselves with more confidence, but even they must have been starting to wonder what they had been thinking when they allowed this child prophet to become their leader.

For all his power and bluster, Walther had not proven to be particularly effective in his role as surrogate *Führer*. He gave few specific orders and those that he did were vague and contradictory. In only a few days, any discipline *Oberführer* Ehrenzweig had created disintegrated into a state of near anarchy. Even now, with an invader about to pass through the gates, there were boys working in far off parts of the castle who were probably unaware of what was happening.

Erich wished there were something for him to do other than wait. His stomach knotted and he started to think it might be better for Isabel to just arrive now and finish him off. To distract himself, Erich debated the question of whether Johanna would finally forgive him if he died today. He had settled on *no* when a one-armed figure appeared on the chapel steps.

Isabel's face was blank as she approached, seemingly unafraid of the armed assembly that awaited her. But contrary to what the lookout had said, she was not alone. Another woman walked with her, dressed in an identical brown skirt, jacket, and cap. Without Isabel's missing arm the two would have been almost impossible to tell apart.

But as the pair grew closer, Erich realized that he had misunderstood. Though she didn't have the horrific injuries or shambling gait, the emptiness in the one-armed woman's eyes was unmistakable. That was not Isabel. It was her doppelgänger.

As they passed through the chapel doors, Isabel spotted Frau Murr and opened her arms wide.

"Adolpha," she beamed. "It's been too long!"

A murmur of surprise passed through the crowd of boys who were hearing this foreign woman speak in unaccented German for the first time. Isabel took a few steps closer and then jumped back as Frau Murr spat at her.

"Fine, no hug then," Isabel said. "Tell me, dear, who's in charge here?"

The ranks parted to let Walther through. "That would be Adolf Hitler," he said. "But you may speak to me in his absence."

Isabel had to choke back a laugh. "I'm not sure which is more desperate. To be led by a dead man or a child."

For a moment, Isabel's eyes caught Erich's. *I remember you,* he heard her say, though her lips had not moved. *What's happened to the boy you tried to bring me?*

"He's safe," Erich said under his breath.

*So says the wolf of the lamb in his belly.*

Erich looked away and down at his feet.

"Enough with the secrets and whispering," Walther snapped. Could he hear them? "Why are you here?"

"The boys down there are rather afraid of you, I think. They've heard stories; maybe they've met a few friends of yours."

Erich perked up. Perhaps Karl could be alive after all.

"So they sent me to find out if you're ready to surrender," Isabel continued. "But that's not why I'm here."

"Why then?"

Isabel crossed her arms and her doppelgänger tried to do the same. Somehow its face was even more unsettling than Hugo's, which had always been so ruined that it didn't resemble that of a real person's.

"Your old headmaster took something from me. A book; you'd know it if you'd seen it," she said. "I want it back."

"Then I haven't seen it," Walther said.

"You're lying. *Where is it?*"

Erich's boots scraped back a step against the stone, buffeted by the patronage that seethed in Isabel's voice. He had to clench his jaw to stop himself from blurting out every scrap of information he had about Hugo's book. But

Walther did not move. He taunted her with his eyes.

"It's like I told you," he said. "I don't know what you're talking about."

Isabel nodded and for a while neither of them spoke. Perhaps they were talking to each other in a way no else could hear or maybe they were just each waiting to see who would move first. Erich didn't know whose side he should be on. He was terrified of Isabel, but was Walther any better?

Everything Erich had done since Johanna told him about the bathhouse had felt like a choice between two evils. He was tired of fighting himself over which was the lesser. Maybe Fritz had the right idea. Once Fritz had been a fanatic, the *Wehrbär* bully who couldn't tolerate the fact that Erich had *Schützenadler* friends, but that boy was long gone, lost along with his patronage. The only thing that mattered to Fritz von Keppler now was Fritz von Keppler. Erich could already see the gears spinning in his head as he furiously recalculated which outcome he stood to gain the most from.

From now on, Erich promised, he would look out for himself. And so, as the swells of patronage roared up around Walther and Isabel, he did the same thing as everyone else. He took two steps back.

# CHAPTER FORTY

To a fresh *Nassfuchs* who had come hoping for
fireworks, it must have looked like nothing was happening.
Isabel and Walther stood at odds, their gazes fixed and
their bodies unmoving. But to Erich and the older boys,
the room was awash in activity. A hundred swirling arcs of
patronage devoured the air. They smashed up against each
other, dissipated, and then reformed stronger than before.

At first it seemed totally unlike the tug-of-war dueling
that *Oberführer* Ehrenzweig had taught them, but the longer
Erich watched the more he recognized the ebb and flow of
it. This was the same game, but instead of fighting over
one rope, they had a hundred in play. Even with Heinrich
at his side, Erich doubted he would stand a chance against
either of them.

Without warning, the innumerable skirmishes that
clouded the air dissipated and regrouped into two
enormous slabs on opposite sides of the chapel. They
reared back and rushed at each other, shattering as they
met. Patronage shrieked out in all directions, knocking
unprepared onlookers off their feet. For a single second
everything lay calm and then all the energy that had been
released was slurped back up into the center of the hall.

High windows shattered in a multicolored spray. The double doors buckled as though struck by a battering ram.

Glass and dust and shards of wood swirled around Walter and Isabel in thick, screaming clouds, but neither of them moved within. They thrust and riposted unperturbed by the raging storm that enveloped them. Debris, kicked out of orbit at odd angles, peppered the crowd. Those with patronage threw up hurried defenses against the shrapnel while those without scrambled for cover. After taking care of himself, Erich was tempted to widen his reach to protect the others, but he held back, reminding himself how he'd promised to be more like Fritz. He needed that patronage. Who knew when he would get another chance to sit with Heinrich?

At last, the whirling clouds unraveled, tossing splinters out to clatter against the stone. Everywhere, grown men and children alike had thrown themselves behind the wavering protections of the few thirteen or fourteen year olds who hadn't been sent to the front. The others, those who had been too proud or stupid to take shelter, suffered for it. Wood and bright glass stuck from their skin like quills. On the opposite side of the chapel, one *SS* man—barely older than Erich—clung to his throat, trying vainly to stopper the flow of blood from where a sky-blue dagger had lodged itself in his neck. A few of the boys ran over to help him, but it was probably too late.

Walther and Isabel kept their footing, if just barely. The furious wind had smoothed the stone beneath their feet into a shallow crater and left them with a few jutting quills of their own. Breathing heavily, neither looked ready to strike again. Isabel had it worse off, yet while Walther's injuries showed no sign of abating, she stood taller and taller. The shards that had struck her pushed themselves from her body and left nothing but clean skin behind.

To anyone else it would have looked like she escaped the encounter unscathed, but Erich could see that wasn't true. Like a whipping boy, her doppelgänger had paid the price. With every splinter that ejected from Isabel's body, it began to look more and more like Hugo's. Flesh hung from its wounds in ragged chunks and its legs could barely hold its own weight.

Walther reached with shaking hands for the two long slivers of glass that jutted from his shoulder and forearm. But Isabel would not allow it. As Walther wrapped his fingers around the amber shard in his shoulder, the glass began to wriggle. Fleshy yet still translucent, the sliver fattened as it writhed, slowly widening into something thick and larval.

Walther squeezed the crystal worm tighter, but it slithered out of his grasp, burrowing its body deeper into his shoulder. Blood spurted into its glassy stomach like ink into water. Aghast, he could do little but watch as the second piece of glass began to change.

Without hesitating for another moment, he pushed himself up onto his toes, arched his feet, and whipped himself around in a circle. He held his wounded arm out as straight as he could manage. It blurred like a top. His movements were so balletic and effeminate that they provoked sniggering from Erich and Fritz, but that scorn evaporated when Walther completed another revolution and a whirlwind of fire shot up all around him. Isabel's glass leeches shimmered and blackened in the flames. Their pincer teeth loosened and dislodged until the creatures were flung off to shatter against the floor.

Walther did not stop spinning. The inferno that roared around him intensified until it was all Erich could see. Waves of heat buffeted his face and he had to cover his eyes to shield the glare. A fiery jet whipped off Walther's whirling body and spat at Isabel, but she flicked it away. He twirled to a stop and slammed his foot into the stone. The blaze erupted so high it licked at the ceiling. Choking smoke poured out over Isabel. She held her arms in front of her face and dug in her feet.

Walther let his hands fall and the firestorm slammed

down onto Isabel. It broke against her crossed arms, but even as they crashed against the stone, the flames did not abate. They swirled around her, flitting lustily through the cracks in her patronage. Isabel dropped to one knee. Her doppelgänger opened its mouth wide as its flesh ignited and began to melt, but whatever sound it might have made was drowned out by a shrieking rush of wind. The banners that draped the chapel's upper walls flapped up and thrashed in the gale.

A sharp pain lanced through Erich's ears and the roaring of the fire gave way to utter silence. In a panic, he gasped for air but there was none. Walther's flames sputtered and spat, crying out for oxygen. A moment later they were gone. The air swept back into the chapel and Erich filled himself up with it over and over again. He'd never imagined how grateful he could be for a few breaths. He stretched his jaw and let his ears pop.

Dizzied and bleeding, Walther looked ready to drop.

"You can always surrender, you know," Isabel said.

"No," Walther said. "There are—" his voice cracked. He inhaled deeply and tried again. "There are two possibilities. Either we are good Germans or we are bad Germans."

Erich recognized the words. He had heard them a hundred times before on the radio. The closer the end had come, the more frequently they had been repeated.

"If we are good Germans all is well," Walther continued, speaking more to himself than to anyone else. "If we are bad Germans then there are two possibilities. Either we believe in victory or we do not believe in victory. If we believe in victory, all is well; if we do not believe in victory then there are two possibilities."

Ever since Walther had returned, Erich been trying to work out if this boy was really his old friend or if they had all been fooled by some imposter wearing his skin. Erich still didn't know the answer, but there was no longer any doubt that some part of the Walther he had known lived on. Who else would pause in the middle of losing a fight to recite this long and convoluted proof?

"If we do not believe in victory, then either we hang ourselves or we do not hang ourselves. If we hang ourselves, all is well. If we do not hang ourselves then there are two possibilities."

"Enough of that," Isabel said.

She lashed out, knocking Walther to his knees. He hit back weakly, still refusing to let himself be interrupted.

"Either we give up the fight or we do not give up the fight. If we do not give up the fight, all is well. If we give up the fight then there are two possibilities."

Walther forced himself up, but immediately his strength failed him and Isabel slammed him back down again.

"If we give up the fight, then either the Anglo-Americans shoot us in the neck or the Red criminals deport us to a damnable wasteland. If we are shot, all is well. If they deport us then there are two possibilities.

"Either we die in the march or we do not die in the march. If we die in the march, we deserve it. If we do not die in the march, then there are two possibilities.

"Either we die slow as slaves or we die quickly for their amusement. Both possibilities end in death. Therefo—"

"It's over," Isabel snapped.

"No," Walther hissed. He rose again and struck out with more force and fury than Erich thought he had left. "Therefore," he squeaked. "There are not two possibilities. There is only one. We must win the war! We must win the war!"

Isabel stepped to the side. She dropped her defenses and let Walther's desperate thrust slam past her. As he threw himself forward, her patronage cracked out like a whip in the opposite direction. Walther's body twisted one way and his neck the other. His recitation cut off into a snap and a gargle. He sagged, lifeless, onto his knees.

Isabel curled up her nose in disgust. Erich couldn't tell

if she had meant to strike Walther as hard as she had, but either way she did not linger long over his corpse. Before most of the boys around her had even absorbed what had happened, she swiveled around to face them. Her eyes fixed immediately on Erich and drilled in.

"I don't want any more lies," she said. "Where is the book?"

Erich tripped backwards towards the door, but his legs seized up and he couldn't move.

"You, Vinzent's boy," Isabel said. "Tell me! Where is it?"

"I- I don't know," Erich stammered. "I mean, Hugo had it. In his office. I..."

The words dried up in Erich's throat. He could no longer pay attention to what Isabel was saying. Instead he was transfixed by what was going on over her shoulder. Walther was on his feet again.

"Behind you," Erich croaked.

She dropped him in an instant and spun around. Walther's neck was still twisted the wrong way. To face her he had to stand backwards. He coughed and a stream of water poured out over his lips. It splashed across the spiral mark on the rear of his neck. He reached behind him and wiped his chin.

Walther threw his head back—or was it forward—unhinged his mouth, and loosed a long, gargling screech. His cheeks began to stretch. They pulled wider and wider until they threatened to rip in two. A globular bulge slithered up his neck like the Adam's apple he didn't have yet.

As soon as he saw it, Erich understood what would come next, but nothing could prepare him to watch it happen. The crustacean legs tore up from the deepest part of Walther's throat, eightfold and mottled. Their sharpened, chitinous points punctured the taut skin of his cheeks and then bent inwards, chittering as they felt out the limits of their new host's jaw.

Whatever remained of Walther Tuerk was gone. For the first time since she had arrived, Isabel looked afraid.

"Wh- W- Whhyyyy," Walther croaked. It took a moment for the thing in his mouth to adjust itself to his vocals. His chin flapped up and down far more than any human's would, but soon the squelching noises gave way to words. "Why did yhqu do it? Yhqu abandoned them. They gave yhqu everything and yhqu sqhuandered it. Yhqu locked away the gohquel. Yhqu qharved them. The patrons still sqhumber because of you."

"You're right," Isabel pleaded. "I tried to do all those things. But what does it matter anymore? I failed. I trusted the wrong man and he stole back your precious gospel." Her face set and her voice rose. "Now you've got the blood you wanted. Rivers of it. So where are your gods?

"You've branded and you've bleeded and you've sang, but not one patron has awoken. The only apocalypse I've seen is the one I had to travel through to get here, the one men made without your help. These past months I've seen more doom in the eyes of soldiers, captives, and slaves than any god, old or new, has ever wrought.

"Don't you get it? You've given us the fading dregs of their power in exchange for blood that does nothing. Your gods don't want to wake up. There is nothing locking them in their palaces of dark water; they sleep by choice. They sleep because it is easier to dream than it would be to watch the cruelties of their own creations unfold. No ritual will ever change that."

"Yqhu don't qhnow that!" Walther screamed. He pointed straight at Erich and Fritz. "How then do you explain their *eyes*."

Isabel's defiance was draining. She looked so scared. Almost at a whisper, she said, "how much more useless blood do you need before you'll understand?"

Walther's mouth-legs whipped themselves into a frenzy and he wailed, "Mooorrrreee!"

He stumbled backwards towards Isabel with his arms

stretched out behind him. His fingers clutched at the air, wrapping around her throat from afar. Isabel recoiled, but hers was not the neck Walther had in his grasp. Her doppelgänger lifted up off the floor. Its feet twitched in the air and the veins in its neck strained.

While it rose, Isabel fell. She crumbled onto hands and knees. Her eyes bulged red and glistened wet. Her fingers scratched at the floor uselessly. Walther's loose jaw swung open and closed with a guttural chortling. His laughter turned infectious and soon the whole chapel rang with it.

At first, Erich joined in out of reflex—it was what everyone else was doing, after all—but as he watched Isabel's fingernails scrape over the wind-smoothed stone something else overtook him. It *was* funny. Here she lay, as arrogant as she was ancient, now undone and prostrated by scrawny eleven-year-old with his head sewn on backwards. How furious that must make her.

Even so, she was no more willing to surrender than Walther had been. Though her lips went purple and her whole body shook, Isabel would not stop scratching at the floor.

"Is she trying to make herself a hole?" Fritz sneered. "Dig faster, mutt, dig!"

Suddenly Erich was no longer laughing. He could see what she was doing and it wasn't digging. She was projecting—just as Herr Larat had taught Erich, just like the globe. With every curl of her fingers, Isabel cinched tighter the space between her and Walther. She kneaded and twisted. And when at last she was finished, she dragged herself one step forward.

For an instant she was in two places at once. Then Erich blinked and the Isabel on her knees was gone and there was only the one who stood directly behind Walther. She grabbed him by the shoulder, buried her hand in his mouth, and tore the crab-thing from his throat. Its shell cracked in her grip and pus sprayed out. Walther wobbled on his feet and his torn jaw swung back and forth. His knees buckled and he fell.

Isabel tossed the creature's carcass aside and drew in a whistling breath. She wiped her eyes with the back of her sleeve and then turned once more to Erich. But before she could rasp out any words, a thunderous blast from outside tore through the chapel. Mortar fire. Every head in the room swiveled towards the sound and for a silent, interminable second, nothing happened.

The far wall above the chapel doors exploded inwards. Chunks of stone shattered into a spray of rubble. Boys and men too close to the middle scattered like ants, but the avalanche buried them all the same. Choking dust flooded the air. Fritz was shouting something, but Erich couldn't hear anything other than the echoes of the blast. Fritz shook him by both shoulders then gave up and sprinted off. For some reason only then did Erich realize that he didn't need to hear to understand what Fritz had been yelling. It should have been obvious.

"Run!"

# CHAPTER FORTY-ONE

Erich could barely see Fritz through the fumes, but he kept behind him as best he could. Together, they crashed through the side door of the chapel and out into the old *Nassfuchs* wing. Another blast tore out behind them, shaking the ground. Dust clouded everything, but Erich could see flashes of gunfire ahead. He grabbed Fritz's arm and dragged him back, shouting, "Other way!"

As they reversed and fled, Erich glanced over his shoulder to see an American infantryman push around the corner and raise his rifle. Before he could fire, three *Nassfüchsen* burst from the chapel just ahead of him. Covered in dirt and blood, they looked as shocked to see him as he was to see them.

"Hurry," Fritz screamed.

Erich jerked back. He was lagging and had to sprint to catch up. Gunshots cracked and Erich could feel an onrush of patronage behind, but he couldn't afford to slow down to see what had happened. Fritz turned sharply left and they spilled outside. They ran across the grass then back into Weiss and up the stairs to where the covered bridge led over to Bittrich Hall.

As they charged across, Erich's ankle snagged on

something. He kept running, only noticing a second later the crossbow bolt that had whizzed dangerously close to his brow. He shoved Fritz down before another tore through the air.

They were well outside the safe part of the castle now and Erich feared that all the traps the boys had laid would do more to slow him and Fritz down than they would to waylay their pursuers. Still, there were few options but to press on.

"Where are we going?" Erich yelled.

"Anywhere!" Fritz said.

They tiptoed across the remainder of the bridge, but immediately ran headlong into a slipshod barricade that forced them to turn downstairs again.

"I- I know a place we can hide," Erich said. He grabbed Fritz's arm as they tumbled out onto the second floor landing. "Here. Come on!"

Erich poked his head around the corner. As far as he could tell, the hallway was clear. A few steps away was the closet where he had first met Johanna. He yanked the door open and charged in, shoving brooms and mops aside. The hidden panel at the rear of the closet slid away before him, but when Erich looked back, Fritz was still standing outside the door. A queasy grimace cut across his face.

Fritz shook his head. "I can't."

Erich had seen that look on him before. It was the one Fritz had worn on the day they had been lowered together down into the tight confines of the mines.

"There's no way anything in here is worse than what's out there," Erich said. He ducked through the secret door and waved at Fritz to join him.

"I really can't," Fritz said. "You go ahead. I'll find somewhere else."

"I get it. It's scary. It's cramped. But that's the point. There's nowhere better to hide."

"No, no," Fritz moaned.

Erich decided to take a gamble that he and his old

bathing partner were alike in more ways than one.

"You might never have been inside," Erich said. "But you've seen into here before, haven't you? Through the walls. It's like Walther said. You have the same eyes as I do," Fritz swallowed loudly and nodded. Erich kept going, "There's a turn, a left turn. Then another. And another after that. You want to look but you're afraid of what you'll see."

"Yes," Fritz whispered.

"I was afraid too. Not of the tight space but, even so, I was having nightmares about it every time I closed my eyes. And then finally it got so bad I just decided to go there, to face what I was afraid of and..." Erich wanted to say that everything had been better from then on, but he couldn't bring himself to lie so badly. "And I... I didn't have to be scared after that."

"Fine," Fritz said. "I- I'll try it."

He cringed, squeezed his eyelids together, and then stumbled as quickly as he could through the closet and into the narrow passage. Erich slammed both doors shut and waited for Fritz to adjust to the space around him. Unfortunately, that didn't seem to be working. Fritz looked worse even than he had been in the mine. He refused to open his eyes and he couldn't manage to pause between breaths.

Erich squeezed his shoulder. "Slow down. It's not so bad, right?"

"For you," Fritz wheezed. He immediately yanked himself away from Erich, but at least now his eyes were open. "I'd always wondered how you got in here."

"You never tried?" Erich asked.

"God no," Fritz shuddered. "Why would I ever want to?"

"I'll show you why," Erich said.

He set off without looking back, hoping that Fritz would prefer to follow than be left alone. Indeed, the moment Erich went around the corner, Fritz called out,

"Wait!" and scrambled to catch up to him. From then on, he kept pace dutifully, pressing against the side walls with both hands while he walked as if he were trying to shove them apart.

Erich could hear the muffled sounds of fighting from outside, but the artillery fire had stopped and to his relief he never once heard the roaring of airplanes from above. With any luck, it would all be over soon.

As they neared their destination, the corridors widened and Fritz's condition improved a little. Soon Erich almost wished he would go back to being frightened. The way he perked up as they drew closer was all too familiar to Erich. There was a hunger in his gaze and by time they reached the final left turn it had all but eradicated the fear.

Heinrich's curtain was drawn shut, but Erich slid it back before they even reached the corner. At the screeching sound, Heinrich jumped up from where he sat on his bed of blankets. Erich could see the disappointment on his face that it was not Johanna who had come.

"*Hallo*, Heinrich," Erich said. It felt a little transgressive to ignore the mandatory Nazi greeting, but that didn't seem relevant anymore. "This is Fritz. He's a friend."

"Not mine," Heinrich said under his breath.

"What was that?"

"Nothing," Heinrich mumbled.

"It didn't sound like nothing," Erich snapped, eager to prove to Fritz that he was in charge. "It's rude to pass judgement on someone before you've even met them."

Fritz, however, didn't look offended. He had no interest in what Heinrich had to say. He had never been this close to the boy, and the sensation of it must have overwhelmed him. With a pleasured gargle, Fritz pushed past Erich, almost tripping in his haste to come closer.

"Get him away!" Heinrich wailed. He pressed his back into the wall.

Fritz turned to Erich. He didn't blink as thick tears flooded his eyes. "Look at it! Isn't it beautiful?"

Behind him, Heinrich squeezed tighter up against the wall. He was no longer moving of his own volition. His back scraped against the stone and he slid upwards until he stopped halfway up the wall.

"I understand now!" Fritz cried. "I understand why our patrons, or their servants, or whoever it is that this power comes from have been punishing us."

"Put him down," Erich said. "You're not to hurt him."

"No, no, no, you've got it all wrong. That's exactly what we're supposed to do. Come on, look at it, look at its mark." Fritz jabbed his finger at his own forehead then the back of his neck. "This is why we're here. It's why we're still breathing while Walther is dead with that thing in his mouth. We should have been lost down there in the mines, but we weren't. They sent us back and they did it for a reason."

Fritz jammed his hand out and Heinrich crunched against the masonry. His already mottled skin flushed purple. Heinrich tried to scream, but the pressure on his chest was so great that the only sound he could make was a raw wheeze like a punctured balloon.

"You've been trying to have it both ways," Fritz said. "You want to be special, but you don't want to accept what that means about everyone else."

"Put Heinrich down," Erich demanded. "Or I— I'll—"

Fritz's eyes flashed and Erich felt something slam into his stomach, buckling him over. Fritz struck again and Erich twisted around. He crashed against the curtain and his limbs entangled with the red fabric, dragging it down to a slant. Erich drew everything he could out of Heinrich and spat it at Fritz, but even that wasn't enough to break through and reach him.

"Stop!" Erich yelled. "He's..." The word *mine* died on his lips. "He's not yours."

"You're right," Fritz said. "He's not mine. He's ours. And we can either take what's been given to us or go back to being nothing."

Behind him, Heinrich continued to scrape upwards. His back crammed into the rounded corner and Fritz began to drag him, lighter than air, across the arch of the ceiling. Heinrich's arms swung out below him like the chains of a chandelier. The closer Fritz drew Heinrich to himself, the less Erich could do to stop him. Erich's meager patronage scratched uselessly at a wall of stone. Heinrich slid into place directly above Fritz and with a shredding sound the blood began to flow.

After so long, Erich had almost forgotten what the baths had felt like, but the moment the smell reached him, all he could do was remember. It dribbled, just out of reach, promising purpose, belonging, power, and most of all permanency. In this blood was a future. It was the trumpets and the drums and the joined song of a thousand boys just like him. It was the voice that called down from above to say, *you are my favorite; you are my chosen.* It was a paradox—specialness and community at the same time.

And why shouldn't Erich have a little? It wasn't his fault that it flowed. He could do no more to stop it than he had done to cause it.

Fritz didn't bother to hold him back anymore. Dragging the curtain behind his feet, Erich shoved himself up against Fritz's chest. As the thin trickle splattered against his head, the breath caught in his lungs. Warm and viscous, Heinrich's blood curled its way through his hair. Erich buried his face in Fritz's shoulder and bit down on the fabric of his collar. With necks turned, they rocked back and forth, dragging the stream across them in alternation.

Erich. Fritz. Erich. Fritz. Erich.

Lost in the blood throes, Erich didn't even hear the gunshot. As Fritz collapsed beneath him, he still did nothing. Only when the patronage that held Heinrich aloft faded and he dropped from the ceiling did Erich lift his eyes to see Johanna at the end of the hall. Shaking, she clung to an American pistol with two hands.

"Tell me why I shouldn't kill you too?" she said.

Erich peered down through blurring eyes at the scrawny, punctured boy at his feet. "I don't know."

"That's not enough!"

Erich didn't understand why he needed this thing so desperately. Why even now, as he took in everything he and Fritz had done, he could already feel himself coaxing errant drops of blood to creep across the stones and slither up his leg.

"It wasn't me," he sobbed. "It's not my fault. Please. It was Fritz, just Fritz. He made me do it."

"That's not what I saw," Johanna said.

"Then you saw wrong!" Erich screamed. "You have to believe me. They put something in me. Hugo did. Or, or Hitler. You've always said it was him, right?" Erich tried to wipe his eyes, but all he could do was spread around the blood and tears. "They gave me this thing, this beautiful thing. They told me it was mine. They told me I deserved it. *And then someone took it away!*" Shrill and deafening, those last words tore themselves from Erich's throat and left him breathless. *And then they took it away,* they echoed silently. Sweat shook from his hair. He could no longer voice more than a moan, "Do you know what that feels like? Do you? To have something like that and lose it? It hurts so much. I can't—"

Johanna's eyes bulged. "Heinrich, no!"

Something pricked at the back of Erich's leg. It barely stung at first, but when he twisted around to look, the movement sent a vicious pain tearing through his calf. The hilt of a dagger protruded from just above Erich's right ankle. The blade seared hot enough to boil blood. Erich's leg could no longer support his weight and he slipped down onto one knee. He stared disbelieving at the old blade with a growing certainty that it was his own. *Blood and Honor.* Heinrich grabbed hold with his tiny fingers and yanked the blade out. For an instant there was nothing in Erich's world but wet suction and fire.

Enraged, he lashed out with what should have been a bone-shattering wave of patronage, but Heinrich did not move at all. Bile sputtered up from Erich's stomach and into his mouth. He coughed and the acrid spittle that streaked his chin was tinged with blood. He scrambled for the patronage that ordinarily flowed so freely from Heinrich to him, but it would not come. The dagger swept down again and plunged into Erich's back. This time, there was no jolt of agony, only a spreading numbness. It was as if this were all happening to someone else.

Erich crashed onto his side. Johanna dropped her gun and ran towards them. Erich thought she was coming to help, but she stepped right over him and out of view. He tried to turn his neck and follow her, but it wouldn't move.

Erich couldn't be sure for how long he lay on the floor. Johanna and Heinrich whispered to each other behind him, but Erich couldn't work out what they were saying. Soon even that faded away. The silence took on a sound of its own. It buzzed and gnawed and clawed at his brain, underscored by a terrible drumbeat. A strange, rhythmic clicking grew louder and louder as it approached. Only once the sound reached him did Erich realize that it was nothing but boot heels against stone. He half opened his eyes.

"Out of the way, girl!" a voice barked. Isabel's.

Carrying a briefcase, she swept right past where Erich lay and was gone. There was no sign of her doppelgänger, but that wasn't surprising. The walls were opaque now. His patron's eyes had left him. Everything of his patron had left him.

Erich wished he could turn back to see what was happening, but all he could look at was the tangled curtain and the long narrow hall ahead. He wondered how many times Heinrich had watched that same hallway, waiting in nervous anticipation for the moment when Erich would round the corner. Maybe that was why the curtain had always been shut when he arrived. It was better not to know.

What seemed like only moments after Isabel arrived, Heinrich was on his feet again. He stepped right over Erich, then stopped to look back. Beneath the shred of his oversized shirt, the cuts that Fritz had inflicted were gone. Even his mottled skin had cleared.

Heinrich glared down at Erich. There was something infuriating about the way he towered over him. Just to see up to Heinrich's face, Erich had to tilt his neck as far as he could get to turn. How could they all just stand there and watch while Erich bled out onto the floor?

Isabel stepped gingerly across the broken curtain and took Heinrich by the hand. She had to tug on his arm to get him to stop looking at Erich and turn around. When they reached the corner, Heinrich twisted away and took a last glance back. His eyes were as dead as Isabel's doppelgänger's had been.

"Wait," Johanna shouted. She almost tripped over Erich's body as she ran after them. "Let me come with you."

"I'm afraid that's not possible," Isabel said.

"Please," Johanna begged. "Heinrich, you'd like it if I came along. I- I was always nice to you, right?"

"It's time to go," Isabel said.

She pulled on Heinrich's hand, but he refused to move.

"Remember that time. Christmas with—" Johanna's voice cracked. Apparently, she couldn't even speak Erich's name anymore. "I mean, Christmas when we filled up our boots with treats. Or, or that time I swapped some cigarettes for that book you like so much. Or after stupid Baldur von Schirach was here, when we ate so many leftovers from the feast that we got sick. Or that night when your mother gave us dancing lessons even though she could barely stand up."

"I remember those things. I do," Heinrich said quietly. "I also remember when you told me this place was just for a while. That was five years ago. I remember the night you woke me up and said we were getting out. But from then on, I mostly just remember wiping the blood off my skin." He looked down at his feet and mumbled, "And, out of all that, the thing I remember most is the time when you told me I didn't need to be afraid of him."

"Heinrich," Johanna rasped. "I'm sorry."

"Goodbye, Johanna," he said.

Isabel tugged on Heinrich's hand and this time he didn't resist. A second later they were gone. Erich and Johanna were alone. She fell down and wailed as if there were some sound she desperately needed to drown out. Erich was grateful to avoid the silence too. He wished he could cry out with her, but he wasn't sure his lungs could hold onto enough air for a scream. Little by little, he dragged his body against the wall, but he couldn't find the strength to sit up. Johanna finally fell quiet.

"Help me," Erich moaned.

Johanna glanced up, surprised to hear his voice. She wiped her eyes.

"Help me," he repeated.

"I tried," Johanna said. "I tried for a long time."

She slumped down and lay on her back next to him, staring up at the cracks in the arched ceiling like they were stars.

Erich wished he could feel angry at her. He wished he could dump all his rage and guilt and shame into an earsplitting tirade that would make her understand everything he felt and everything he had or hadn't done. But he couldn't turn that into words. It all seethed inside him, unable to manifest as anything but self-loathing. Erich wondered if Johanna were feeling the same thing. She looked like it. Maybe they were both dying in different ways.

"I'm sorry you couldn't go with them," Erich said. "One of us should have gotten what we wanted in all this."

Johanna inhaled and for a long while refused to let it go. "No," she finally said. "We got just what we deserve.

Heinrich's right. I thought I was helping him. All I did was build him a new cage."

"That's not true," Erich said. He coughed, hard enough to shake his chest and scorch his throat. Pressing his cheek into the cold stone, he let the bloody spittle dribble out of his mouth so that he didn't have to swallow it.

"It is true," Johanna said. "Do you remember what you said to me on the night you found us here? I do. I told you that Heinrich didn't like me and you said, 'Of course he does. You're a nice person. Everyone likes you.'"

"Because you are," Erich croaked.

"Maybe I am. But what good does that do? Look at Otto and Uwe. They were nice people. They loved each other. They loved you and me and Karl and the Fatherland and the *Führer* and their mothers. They even loved those stupid pets. It didn't make a difference. They were monsters just like you and me."

Erich shut his eyes, too tired to hold them open. "I don't understand. Are we—" Erich coughed. It felt like sandpaper against his lungs. "Are we talking about the same Otto and Uwe you once punched me in the stomach for insulting?"

"Yeah, I guess we are," Johanna said with a weak laugh. "It's something I never told you. Honestly, I think I tried to forget it ever happened."

"What... what did they do?"

"In a way, nothing. They did nothing," Johanna said. "It's... I saw them once while I was working. In the bathhouse. They were always Hugo's favorites, you know, and he was giving them a tour. *A tour.* This is the place I'd had nightmares about for years and he was showing it to them like it were a chocolate factory.

"Uwe couldn't stop smiling. He's so curious all the time. He was asking these questions. 'Why do the subjects need to be marked? What would happen if we let the baths run longer than a year? Do you think we could concentrate the blood with a centrifuge? Would that let us use more than one subject per bath?'

"I didn't believe it. I looked over at Otto. I was certain he would say something. Usually he keeps Uwe from going too far. But no. All he did was nod along. 'Interesting.' 'Good idea.' 'I hadn't thought of that.' It was like they were totally different people. And at the time, that's what I told myself. I just acted like it wasn't them. It was two people I'd never met."

"I always thought I was the only boy who knew," Erich said.

"I doubt that. We all knew."

"I wonder what they would have done if Heinrich had been theirs instead of mine."

"They would have turned him in," Johanna answered immediately. "That's the part I didn't understand before. The Otto and Uwe I saw then weren't different people at all. They were acting exactly like themselves. They were acting the way nice people act. They smiled and laughed and asked questions. All the same things they would've done in the chocolate factory."

Johanna stood up and went back behind Erich. When she returned and sat down, there was a book in her lap. It was Heinrich's favorite, *Twenty Thousand Leagues Under the Sea*. Johanna leafed through until she found what she was looking for between the pages.

"What's that?" Erich asked.

"It's Heinrich's letter," she said. "He forgot to take it with him."

"The one from his mother?"

Johanna nodded and showed him the envelope. *For After*, it read.

"After. That's now, isn't it? Are you going to read it?"

Johanna slammed the book shut.

"Never," she said. "It's not ours."

# THE END